THE UNSEEN

A SUFI MYSTERY

LAURY SILVERS

Published by Laury Silvers

The Fell Types are digitally reproduced by Igino Marini. www.iginomarini.com

Map of Iraq, Leiden codex Or. 3101, used with the kind permission of Leiden University, and the assistance of Karen Pinto.

ISBN: 978-1-7775313-4-8

❀ Created with Vellum

For all my Shia friends and family

"Loving one another is half of wisdom"
Sayyidina Ali ibn Abi Talib

ACKNOWLEDGEMENTS

My partner, Michael, carefully edited, debated story points, reminded me of my characters' motivations, and pointed out gaps. He works with me on all the fight scenes and explains how the characters would feel in a fight, their strategy, physicality, and mindset. As always, I relied on him every step of the way. He is my partner in crime.

I want to thank Adam Gaiser, scholar and archer, who suggested the victim die by an arrow shot and made up PowerPoints explaining all the parts of a bow, an arrow, how they arc, how they land (and why, still weird to me, the arrows shot in this book would land straight on, not at an angle). All the cool archery stuff comes from him.

Some of the academic and primary sources I relied on for the writing of this book are mentioned on my website. Here, I would like to thank those who were generous in sending me published and unpublished works that helped me build this world and/or answered my questions when I got stuck or confused. My sincerest thanks go to Aun Hasan Ali, Ahab Bdaiwi, Nassima Neggaz, Raha Rafii, Rana Makati, Stephennie Mulder, Rachel Schine, Kristina Richardson, Eric Hanne, Danielle Widemann, Matthew Pierce, Karen Pinto, Farhad

Dokhani, Nicholas C. McLeod, Nebil Husayn, Ash Geissinger, Alan Godlas, Khalil Andani, Mahdi Tourage, Kecia Ali, Joumana Medlej, Ali Olami, Hasib Noor, and everyone on the "Shi'i Studies: Medieval and Modern" Facebook page. Sincere thanks to Cyrus Zargar, who pushed the Qarmatis on me as a story angle. You were right. Finally, in the scholarly category, my thanks go to several historical podcasts, most especially "Abbasid History," "New Books in Islamic Studies," and "Ajam Media Collective." At times, I have to choose one scholarly interpretation over another and go with the one that creates the most narrative tension.

So many people guided me on all the little things that are very big things once they hit the page. Murat Coskun helped me understand what Junayd would tell and hold back from a student. Alan Godlas was always available for any question on early Sufism. Sara Abdel-Latif helped me understand Shatha's role in this novel. Saud Bashar Abdulmunem answered all my questions about Baghdadi dialect and cultural matters. Nadeem Ahmed of Eran and Turan, a living cultural history group, gave me advice on clothes and material culture. Sarah Shah, Zainab Naqvi, Farhad Dokhani, Aslisho Qurboniev, Zishan Syed, Rodnesha Jackson, Shannon Chakraborty, Imran Khan, and all those others who answered questions and talked me through questions that led to changes in plot and representation. Everyone on Facebook who discussed how Sunni and Shia Muslims might approach the trolly problem, including Mahdi Tourage, Peter Grey, Saadia Yacoob, and Greg Recco. Peter Grey for the Khidr intervention that led to important changes in the narrative. Vernon Schubel for his nudges regarding al-Hallaj. Everyone on Facebook and Twitter who piped up to answer quick questions or offer references. More than a few asked me not to share their names. Unfortunately, some names I have forgotten. These thanks are for you.

Special love to John Austin Yoshino and Jibril Stevenson, my writing buddies. John, especially, met with me every other week to talk about our writing projects through the thick of the pandemic. He was a sanity lifeline. Jackie Stansbury and Brenda Scott patiently read a messy draft and helped me understand what readers unfamiliar with Islam would need explained and suggested two important structural changes. They demanded the defined terms in the note on history. Amina Wadud for always being willing to read my books, offer guidance, and cheer me on. Simon Wood who taught me how to write a thriller mystery. Karen Heenan gave the book a thorough edit with her keen eye and made much needed style suggestions. And, as always, Shaheen Ali, who gives all my novels one last read before they get sent off. Any typos or other errors are because I fiddled with the text after I got it back from these two exacting women.

And to my support team! All the Muslim creatives on Facebook and Twitter who have built up a beautiful community in which we hold each other through our struggles and hold up each other's successes, especially Nakia Jackson, Layla Abdullah-Poulos, and Ausma Zehanat Khan who have been very generous with their time. Thanks to Kathleen Self, always. My fellow historical fiction support squad, Marian Thorpe, Karen Heenan, and Bryn Hammond. Everyone at Twitter #HFChitChat, especially Janna G. Noelle, for making me feel like I belong.

My love to my family, Michael, Kaya and Ryan, Mishi and Ben, Eleonore, Tracey, Nancey, Catherine, and Candace and all the Quinseys for their support. And shout out to Mom. I know you read all the drafts of this book in the Good Place. Thanks to all my neighbours, Bev and the Irish especially, for cheering me on, especially through the pandemic as we connected over fences, and Billie Girl, as always, for being the very best dog. And sincere gratitude goes to my teacher, Murat Coskun, for his guidance, and our community for their constant support and companionship.

A NOTE ON HISTORY

Unlike the first two novels in the Quartet, the story of *The Unseen* takes place on a larger historical field. Some readers may find the following introduction helpful. There is also a glossary at the end of the book.

The novel is set in Baghdad, 295H/908CE, about 150 years into the dynasty of the Abbasid Caliphate. There are two major groups of Muslims, **Shia** and **Sunni**. The roots of the division go back to several causes, but for the novel it is enough to know about the dispute over the succession to the Prophet Muhammad:

Shia hold that **Ali**, then after his death, his sons, **Hasan** and **Husayn**, by Ali's wife and the prophet's daughter, **Fatima**, were the rightful leaders of the community after Muhammad died. Most Shia believe that leadership of the caliphate is hereditary through the Prophet's line. Their name comes from "Shiat Ali," or "the Party of Ali," those who sided with Ali after Muhammad passed.

Sunnis hold that after Muhammad died, the leader should come from the foremost companions, but Muawiya instituted the first hereditary caliphate, the Umayyads. Sunnis were not named "Sunni" in early Islam, but I use the term to help unfamiliar readers more readily grasp the basic tensions. There were a range of attitudes towards the Shia among the Sunni, from brotherly companionship and sympathy to outright hatred. Their name comes from "the folk of the Sunna (the way of the Prophet and his companions)."

In the troubles of succession, Ali was eventually chosen as the fourth caliph, but was soon assassinated. Hasan, Ali's son, followed him as caliph, but Muawiya challenged his appointment. Hasan agreed to cede by treaty if Muawiya would name no successor. Muawiya betrayed the treaty. His son, **Yazid**, became caliph, beginning a hereditary caliphate, the Umayyads.

Shia and many others wanted Husayn to lead instead of Yazid. The caliph Yazid demanded that Husayn pledge allegiance. Husayn refused. When the people of Kufa, Iraq, asked Husayn for help against Yazid, he went with a band of loyal warriors and his family, descendants of the Prophet. They were stopped by Yazid's army at Karbala. Vastly outnumbered, Husayn and many others were slaughtered. Their heroism and that of the survivors, like Fatima and Ali's daughter, **Zaynab**, continues to inspire Shia and Sunni ethics to this day, while Yazid's name, for many, has become synonymous with despotism.

In the tenth century, most Shia held out hope that Prophet's family line would regain political leadership. These spiritual and, in some cases, hopeful political leaders are called **Imams** (with a capital "I" in the novel). Disagreement over which descendants qualified as Imam led to different claimants to rightful leadership, and, so, different Shia communities.

Although there were a number of Shia communities in the tenth century, most of which no longer exist, in this novel you will meet four: **Imamis, Fatihis, Ismailis, and Qarmatis.**

A Note on History

Imamis were followers of the Twelfth Imam, the son of the Eleventh Imam. They are now known as Twelvers and are the most numerous Shia today. But at the time the novel is set, they had been weakened and were under threat of disappearing entirely.

Fatihis are those who follow the doctrine of the early al-Fathiyya who held that a brother can inherit the imamate rather than a son. The group I name "Fatihi" were historically called "Jafaris," but to distinguish them from other Jafaris and, importantly, Imam Jafar as-Sadiq, I gave them the name of the doctrine they follow. They were one of four communities who believed that the Eleventh Imam had no son, so the imamate went to his brother, Jafar, and then to Jafar's son. While Jafar is seen as a positive figure by Twelvers now, that was not the case in the past. He was known as "Jafar the Liar," and is called by that name in the novel.

Ismailis are followers of an earlier division and while we meet only one Ismaili character in the novel, the Ismaili Imam at the time looms large as a figure who could bring down the Abbasid caliphate. And they will ultimately take control over North Africa and some of what we now call Saudi Arabia, becoming the famed Fatimid Caliphate.

Qarmatis are a controversial community that broke with the Ismailis. At the time of the novel, the Qarmatis had successfully captured Bahrain and the roads to Mecca. Early in their formation, they proposed a non-hierarchal society. They believed that Islamic Law had been suspended as the Mahdi had arrived. Eventually, they would take Mecca itself. Like the Ismailis, they loomed as a serious threat to the caliphate.

The threat to the Abbasid government by the Shia that I describe in the novel was not unfounded. In 909 CE, just one year after the timeline of the novel, the Ismailis will have their first victory in North Africa, with Baghdad as their ultimate goal. Twenty-five years later, the Buyids subdued the Abbasids in Baghdad, taking much of Iran and Iraq. These caliphates would usher in what is called "The Shia Century."

Other important players are the **Mahdi**, **Viziers**, the **Twelfth Imam** (the leader of the Imamis), and the **Agents**.

The Mahdi is a messianic figure. Many religious communities have pinned their hopes on a pure figure who will lead them out of their suffering into a land of peace and justice, either in their own day and age or in end times. In Muslim societies, it was not uncommon for different people to claim to be a mahdi-like figure or call themselves Mahdi.

Viziers are chancellors to the caliph, who acts as a king. A few powerful viziers were Imami and tried to protect their Imams and their community from the Abbasid caliphs, who saw them as serious challengers to their rule. Historically, a number of Imami leaders were held under house arrest, possibly even assassinated, by the caliphate. In this book, you will read about Ibn Furat, one of the Banu Furat (the "Sons" of Furat).

The Twelfth Imam was only seen by those in his closest circle and the agent who carried messages between him and the Imami community. At the time the book is set, many Imami followers understood that he must remain hidden to protect himself, but others began to doubt that he lived at all. These Imamis left to follow other Imams or even became Sunni.

If readers are interested in knowing more details about this difficult period, *The Occultation of The Twelfth Imam* by Jassim M. Hussein is helpful. Also on the reasons for the occultation, see *The Sun Behind the Clouds* by Muhammad Baqir Majlisi. Both are available online for free on al-islam.org.

HISTORY AND FICTION

While the background, some storylines, and even some dialogue are adapted from historical and literary accounts of Abbasid Baghdad and its inhabitants, this is a work of fiction. The book takes up some uncomfortable realities of life at that time. Social norms such as slavery, racism, shadism, gender divisions, marriage, drinking habits, mosque attendance, and class divisions are all grounded in historical sources.

My novels do not assume to speak for or about the Iraqi people nor the nation of Iraq. They are an exploration of a shared Abbasid past and ultimately how that past is remembered in the Muslim present.

Please turn to the work of Iraqi writers such as those found in Hassan Blasim's Iraq + 100 collections, Shakir Mustafa's anthology, or Baghdad Noir collections of short stories, and the works of Shahad Al Rawi, Sinan Antoon, Dunya Mikhail, Leilah Nadir, and Ahmed Saadawi. Also see the online journal, "Arab Lit Quarterly."

Historical resources are on my website: www.llsilvers.com or my Facebook page https://www.facebook.com/laurylsilvers. Follow me on Twitter @waraqamusa and Instagram @laurylsilvers.

Allah
The Unseen
The Merciful The Compassionate
The Holy The Peace The Guardian of Faith The Protector The Firm
The Compeller The Dominating The Creator The Crusher The
Praiseworthy The Forgiver The Evolver The Bestower The Provider
The Dishonouring The Knower The Constrictor The Expander The
Abaser The King The Forbearing The Exalter The Honouring The
Hearing The Seeing The Everlasting Refuge The Opener The Subtle
The Aware The Great The One The Trustee The Grateful The Most
High The Most Great The Preserver The Wise The Restorer The
Embracing The Glorious The Resurrector The Light The Responsive
The Patient The Nourisher The One Who Forms The Revered The
Generous The Watchful The Strong The Mighty The Friend The
Reckoner The Accounter The Originator The Able The Unique The
Life Giver The Slayer The Alive The Equitable The Finder The Noble
The Avenger The Powerful The Expediter The Delayer The Most
Exalted The First The Last The Manifest The Loving The Governor
The Accepter The Pardoner The Clement The Gatherer The
Distresser The Possessor of the Sovereignty The Lord of Majesty and
Bounty The Self-Subsisting The Sufficient The Enricher The
Withholder The Incomparable The Everlasting The Open-Handed
The Right Guide The Supreme Inheritor The Wise The Good The
Truth The Judge The Just The Witness The All Forgiving

DAY ONE

Baghdad 295H/908CE

1

Ammar at-Tabbani squatted beside the body, reading the language of its wounds. The young man was splayed out on the side of the road. Yellow earth dusted his clothes and stuck to his skin. His mouth was slack, the last breath he could not pull to survive stamped on his face. One arrow pierced his eye. Blood soaked through the sleeves of his robe, but the fabric was whole. The investigator for Grave Crimes pulled back the robe and felt the wounds through the cloth of his qamis. There were cuts in the victim's arms. Another arrow had pierced the waterskin still in his hand. A narrow trail of water had seeped out of the skin leading away from the body.

The message was clear. *Abbas.*

The victim was killed in the exact manner of Abbas ibn Ali, martyred at the Battle of Karbala over two hundred years ago. It could only signal a coming attack on the Shia community.

Ammar's leather cuirass grew tight across his chest, sweat pricking at him and raising a sour stink.

When Tein gets here, he'll call it a coincidence. Ammar started a silent argument with his partner and old friend from their days fighting on the frontier. *But these wounds are no coincidence.* He stood and tugged at his cuirass to get a decent breath, and looked past the crowd pressing against the watchmen. *Where is he?*

For how many months had he been watching his step with Tein? Their friendship had never fully recovered after their last big case. He had become wary of commanding Tein and, in response, Tein had stepped into the breach. Their sergeant, Ibn Marwan, even treated Tein at times as if he were the lead investigator for the Karkh office of the Grave Crimes Section.

But Ammar would not budge on this. Tein was going to have to accept that these wounds meant there was an explicit grudge against Shia being acted out. He complained Ammar read everything through the tragedy at Karbala and it clouded his judgment. But it was not because of Karbala that he misread that last case. Walla, it was Karbala and its lessons that pulled him back from the edge.

He took a kerchief from his sleeve and wiped his face and the back of his neck. The victim was from Buratha, but he did not recall his name, only that his parents clung to the Fatihis. His mother had pointed them out in the Buratha market place one day and complained that anyone should doubt the existence of their Imam, the Twelfth Imam, Muhammad ibn al-Hasan. She asked who could follow another? Yet this family attached themselves to the Fatihis, accepting Jafar the Liar as the twelfth in line, and now his son, instead of the rightful inheritors of the Prophet's legacy.

His mother grieved over how many doubted the Twelfth Imam's existence, abandoning him for other claimants to the imamate or leaving the Shia fold altogether. There were unassailable men who had testified that they met the Twelfth Imam when he was a child. But that certainty had dissolved into doubt over the years when there were no more attested sightings and he failed to show himself publicly. Where once the Imamis had dominated Baghdad, now their numbers were dwindling.

All the same, her complaints in the marketplace that day were not about the victim's family, but rather his own father. Not a day went by when he did not taunt her with his rejection of the Imam to whom she was devoted. The young man and his family had become convenient objects for the frustration a good wife should not articulate, even to her son.

Ammar scanned the horizon through the rising dust to determine where the archer would have taken his shot. A close shot was not likely given the depth of the arrow in the eye. The way the body fell, there were only two trajectories. Either from on top of an estate wall bordering the road or from the Cemetery of the Martyrs. No one saw the shooter. Was it possible for a man to have stood atop an estate wall, draw his bow, and shoot without being seen? Ammar's bet was that it came from the direction of the cemetery, most likely the tomb of the Seventh Imam, Musa al-Kazim. Looking past its thick clay walls to the small, domed tomb, he feared what might be coming.

Who would dare kill from that holy place except someone with no respect for the Prophet's family? Who could have shot with such precision to mimic Abbas' wounds? And the cuts in his arms? They also echoed those suffered by Abbas. If not intended, then they were looking at arrows gone astray after a sword or knife fight. It was possible the man had fought with his shirt off, then dressed himself if the wounds were not too deep. Or perhaps they were old wounds that opened. But his gut and his eyes told him this was purposeful.

"You!" Ammar called out to a watchman. "Go to the tomb and examine the grounds, look for a weapon, any sign of the killer."

The watchman went into the crowd and tried to get past a large woman wanting a better view, sending her into the arms of the man behind her. He yelled at the watchman. "Your mother should have left you to die when the devil pulled you from her belly!" Others joined in, their curses drowning out the gossip and prayers of those around them.

Sighing at their curses, Ammar studied the faces in the crowd for likely suspects. But there was no one with a telltale furtive, smug, or fearful expression. Only the usual curiosity or horror at the body and disgust with the police.

An old woman in a threadbare black wrap covering all but one browned and wrinkled eye peered at him. The squint, the intensity of the gaze, there was no mistaking the hatred. And she was not alone.

A man further away, covered in mud stains from brick-making, pulled back his head, made an unmistakable sound and lobbed his phlegmy spit in Ammar's direction.

Ammar expected their distrust, but it ate away at him all the same. There wasn't a cursed thing to do to change their minds. In name, the police were an independent arm of the military, funded by the taxes of the people of Baghdad, but in practice they were brutal and corrupt, and most often the caliphate's tool.

Grave Crimes was no different from other police sections. At one point he would have said that there were good men, but then, knowing the depths into which he himself had fallen, he understood. There could be no goodness when the system itself was corrupt. He turned away from the old woman, ashamed, and squatted down beside the body again. Touching the empty waterskin, he asked himself, *Whose side am I on?*

A watchman ran up. "Ghazi, sir, I have a witness!" He pointed toward a young scholar standing nearby wearing an unadorned linen robe and turban wrapped in the manner of the Imami Shia. The man was sweating in the sun and worrying his prayer beads.

Tein hailed Ammar from a distance.

Ammar waved over Tein, then told the watchman, "Bring the witness here and wait with him."

Men parted for Tein as he walked past, while one of them yelled "Zanji" at his back. Ammar watched as Tein ignored what the fool took for slander. To be accused of being among the enslaved black men who rose up and nearly brought down the Abbasid caliphate? "Zanji" was no insult, but a name Tein embraced with pride.

But Tein was the sort of man who drew attention, anyway. He took after his Nubian mother's famed beauty, but was taller and more muscular than most men, and walked with a commanding gait despite an old battle injury. Men bridled at him or respected him, while women stole glances at him.

He was also late. Frustration broke through Ammar's voice as he approached. "There you are."

"I came as soon as I got the message. I'd been going door to door on the old woman's case."

"Did you find her nephew?"

"He's in a cell."

"Did Ben Hadad take down his confession?"

"Was there time for that?" Tein snapped. "A watchman found me and told me to come immediately."

Ammar bit back his reply, saying only, "Of course," then turned back to the body to indicate Tein should come with him, but he had already walked over.

"No one likely in the crowd?"

"I may have missed the killer while examining the body."

"I told you. I came as soon as the watchman reached me."

Ammar said, "It wasn't a reproach, only a statement of fact."

"Do you have the name of the victim?"

"The watchmen asked, but no one is offering. My mother pointed him out to me once. He has family in Buratha. I'll ask her." He crossed his arms. "What do you think?"

Tein examined the way the body had fallen, the depth and angle of the arrow in the victim's eye, then followed the likely arc. "I'd say it came from the area around Musa al-Kazim's tomb."

"Why not up close?"

Tein bent over and turned the man's head to the side, exposing his intact skull. He saw what Ammar had already noted. The arrow had gone deep through the eye socket, but had not penetrated the back of his skull. "As I said, the tomb."

"I sent watchmen for evidence."

Tein looked toward the graveyard. There were several small, domed tombs dotting the expansive grounds surrounded by gravestones. "Maybe the shooter was too low with the first shot, hit the bag, then went too high with the second."

Ammar hesitated a moment, bracing himself. "We should consider that the killer intended those shots to hit the eye and the waterskin."

"Where is the evidence for that?"

"Did you notice the blood on the arms?"

Tein did not answer. He took his dagger from its sheath and bent down to cut open the sleeve of the man's robe, then the qamis underneath, and examined the wounds. "Fresh cuts from a sword. Maybe a dagger if the killer knew how to do more than stab with one." He squinted in the morning light. "Was he fighting with someone in his sirwal, thought the fight was over, dressed, walked away, and then was shot?"

"In the heat of the fight he might, if the right muscles weren't cut."

"Someone would have noticed that fight, at least."

"The watchmen canvassed the area, but we only have one witness so far." Ammar gestured towards the scholar waiting for them. "Any other witnesses might not have waited around to talk to us. But people lie."

"Did you question the witness?"

"Not yet."

As the two approached the scholar, Ammar bowed his head and placed his hand on his heart. "Assalamu alaykum. I'm afraid the watchman who brought you here did not give me your name."

He expected the scholar to complain about being left to stand in the sun, but he replied graciously, "Wa alaykum assalam. Irfan ibn Ali al-Qummi. At your service."

"What were you doing here?"

"Whenever I am worried about some matter, I come to sit with the Imam and God makes my situation easy."

"There may have been a sword fight near the tomb and the killer shot the victim as he left. Did you see or hear anything?"

Surprised by the suggestion, he replied, "If there had been a fight, a crowd would have gathered." He gestured to the people. "This is a busy street. There would have been yelling. I assure you, there was no fight."

"And the shooter?"

"I heard the thump of the arrows being released."

That was that. The killer had taken his shot from the tomb.

Irfan ibn Ali continued, "If I had seen the servant of Yazid who martyred this young man, I would have taken hold of him myself."

Ammar held his breath in anticipation. *Let Tein get it from him.*

"Servant of Yazid?" Tein asked. "Martyred? Do you know the killer?"

The scholar looked between the two detectives as if the question were some sort of trick. "Forgive me. You must have noticed. I can see the blood on his arms from here. His eye. The waterskin."

"Tell us." Ammar encouraged him.

Irfan ibn Ali addressed Tein. "His wounds are those of Abbas. May God be well-pleased with him."

"Which Abbas?" Tein blurted out, then blinked with impatience.

He remembered the story, after all. On the days and nights they spent waiting for battle as young ghazis fighting along the frontier, Ammar had recounted the stories of the bravery and sacrifice of the family of the Prophet and the warriors who stood by them at Karbala. He only hoped Tein would let the scholar speak and prove the point for him.

The scholar's eyes filled with tears, his back softening with sorrow for the pierced body. "Abbas ibn Ali ibn Abi Talib, the half-brother of Imam Husayn." Then he pulled his shoulders back and faced Tein. "Abbas was the standard bearer of obedience to the Imamate. He was martyred at Karbala when he offered to carry water for the children from the river. In the tent of the women and children, he found the little ones crying out in thirst, rubbing waterskins against their bellies in desperation. Poor little Sukayna, first among them, begged her uncle Abbas to get them water. His heart broken by the sight of them and Sukayna's plea, he picked up a skin and, with Imam Husayn's permission, entered the battlefield. But Yazid's army held the river. So extraordinary was his bravery that Abbas faced thousands of men crossing the battlefield to reach the river with nothing but a sword."

Tein tried to interrupt, "Yes, I..."

Ammar reached over and put his hand on Tein's arm, asking him to wait. Almost imperceptibly, Tein pulled his arm back.

"Abbas made it to the river and filled the skin, but had to fight his way back to the children. One soldier raised his sword against him, cutting his right arm such that he could no longer hold his sword. Undaunted, he bent over and took up his sword with the other against the enemies of God and the Prophet's family, but another soldier swung against him, cutting his left arm. His arms now useless and his sword lost to him, he kneeled to the ground and bit the waterskin with his teeth to carry it back to the children, but as he stood, the arrows came flying. One pierced the waterskin, draining it of water, and another his eye, ending his life and abandoning the children to their burning thirst."

Fighting back tears, knowing the story and what had not been said, Ammar let out a rough breath to loosen the lump in his throat. "Thank you. We understand."

Tein replied to Irfan ibn Ali with a tone of respect. "I appreciate the connection you are making. We will consider it. May we speak to you again if necessary?"

"Of course. I teach out of my home in Dar as-Silsila. Ask for me by name, someone will direct you." The scholar bowed his head and stepped back, turning towards the tomb.

Tein's face was impassive, but Ammar had no trouble understanding the silence of his features. There was a subtle expression of resignation Tein wore when he knew he was about to hear something that would anger or disappoint him. Ammar kept his thoughts to himself.

A watchman pushed through the crowd, holding a bow. Ammar looked at it eagerly and held out his hand. It was an impressive hunting bow, sound, the finest craftsmanship. But also beautiful. The bowyer had painted the grip well beyond the arrow pass to resemble snake skin in a kind of blue that changed colour as the bow was moved in the light.

Tein's face lit up with obvious interest as Ammar turned it in his hand. "We can trace that fine piece of work."

Ammar smiled. "We can, indeed."

Tein asked the watchman, "No sheath?"

The watchman shook his head. "There were large boot prints over the bare footprints and sandal marks. The soles were in good condition."

"Well done. What's your name?"

"Shabib ibn Yusuf," he replied, standing at attention, then gestured toward something in the distance. "The donkey cart is here for the body."

Ammar handed the bow to Tein. "Let's take him to the hospital to get the arrowhead out. That's no bow for battle. It's going to be a hunting arrowhead, but we need to confirm. Good boots, a bow like this. Killer is not a poor man, unless he stole the bow and boots. One of us needs to double-check the tomb area."

"I'll check the tomb and take the body to the hospital," Tein offered with a kind of studied casualness that Ammar knew masked his eagerness to go see Saliha. "Which corpse washer in Buratha?"

"There's one next to the mosque. Take him there. The family can't object," Ammar replied. "I'll inform them of his death. There's nothing more to get here."

"Nothing here? After that story?" Tein did not hide a challenging tone. "You don't have an opinion on it?"

Ammar wagered. "The interviews will tell us if there's a connection."

The worry was still there, but Tein's face softened. "See you back at the office after you talk to the family?"

"I'll be there." Ammar waved the driver to bring the donkey and its cart forward. The crowd parted, then closed in behind them.

2

As the police investigator scanned the crowd, Utbah ibn Harb ducked behind a large, sweating man wearing a red turban wound comically wide. For the barest moment, as if his world had not just turned against him and he were not hiding from the police, he laughed at the man, enjoying the thought that if not for the man's girth, the turban might have toppled him over. But his arrows, shot in a moment of unthinking panic, as if Bishr were a doe in the field, had ended his own life as surely as they had taken the life of his friend.

Bishr, what were you thinking?

Utbah rubbed his hand flat against his robe, his palm burning where he had held the bow and in horror had thrown it aside behind the tomb. The bow was a masterwork, a showpiece, and might be traced, but there was no going back and finding it before the watchmen did. An echo of his dead father's voice mocked him. *Useless, as always.* Looking toward the tomb, he prayed under his breath, "Let it be stolen."

A sharp exhalation of relief escaped him. That was the way out. He would claim a boy had stolen it off his horse as he travelled through the streets of Baghdad. God knows even the widest thoroughfares were thick with thieves ready to cut a purse and run. A bow in its sheath tied to his saddle? It was reasonable. *Further, if the police find me*, he reassured himself, *a message from my uncle sent to the vizier will handle it. Surely, I am safe.* But he was not at all sure and prayed again, *Lead the police astray.*

Utbah recognized the investigator and hoped he had not seen him the night Ammar at-Tabbani came to get his elderly father home from a street-side tavern. Utbah and his men had been visiting the taverns, working to cultivate doubt about the existence of the Twelfth Imam. The old man was an easy target, always complaining about having to pay the tithe to support an Imam no one had seen for decades.

The investigator's father was an absurd, small man who ridiculed his wife's devotion to the memory of Husayn's sacrifice in one breath and his son's betrayal of Husayn's courage in the next. "My son!" the old man would exclaim. "My son, the police investigator, is no better than a thug serving a caliph who would kill every one of us Shia, just like Yazid's men slaughtered Husayn's army at Karbala!"

If his own father were still alive, Utbah would have sat the two old men down for a drink. *Imagine them going at it.* Ammar at-Tabbani's father would curse Yazid and the succeeding Umayyad caliphs who stole the leadership of the Muslim people from the Prophet Muhammad's family line. His own father would raise his glass to Yazid, then curse Ali, the Prophet's cousin and son-in-law, and Ali's sons, Hasan and Husayn, the Prophet's own grandsons.

In his mind, the two old men's slurring curses would turn into drunken, ineffectual swings. Utbah imagined pulling his father up off the ground, his turban lost, vomit on his lips and staining his robe, and explaining to the man who had given him nothing but unimaginable wealth that he, Utbah ibn Harb, would do what he never could. Complete the work of Yazid and destroy the Shia once and for all.

He taunted his father's memory. *Who is useless now?*

But the memory of his father answered him back, *If only the dupe, Bishr, had not betrayed you.*

Utbah stiffened at the imagined rebuke. He had gained Bishr's trust, manipulating him through the girl, Aisha, and used the fool to work his way into Shia society in Karkh and Buratha, where he had become a student of their factions. Each community followed a different Imam protesting that only theirs was the true guide of the Shia people and calling the other Imams liars and traitors to the memory of the Prophet, Fatima, Ali, Hasan and Husayn. Utbah planned to exploit these divisions, one by one, until the Shia people were nothing but a memory mourned by no one.

He would begin with the weakened Imamis, the followers of the Twelfth Imam, who, confused by his failure to show himself, doubted his very existence. Their only connection to the Twelfth Imam was through his agents, especially their leader entrusted with their tithe, meeting the Imam in person, and communicating his guidance to the Imami community. The key to destroying the Imamis, Utbah had decided, would be to instil doubt about the agents. He would start with the lost men who drank in the taverns at night. A word here and there. These men would then complain at home, seeding doubt. Their women would whisper it in secret amongst themselves. They would do his work for him, chipping away at the faith of the Imamis from the inside.

Utbah eagerly pledged himself to the Imam of the Fatihis. Poor Bishr thought he had converted him. After that, it was easy to convince Bishr and his friends to rob the agent of the Twelfth Imam of the tithe and give the money back to the Imamis. Money in hand, Bishr and his friends, sincere followers to a man, would earn the people's trust and convince them once and for all that their Twelfth Imam was a phantom and his agents nothing but thieves and liars. They would call the grateful to follow their own Imam. Utbah shook his head at their innocence. After he had used them to ruin the Imamis, he would turn against the Fatihi Imam, then destroy each Shia community in Baghdad in turn. He planned to go to his father's grave and gloat before pissing on the now sunken spot where the earth was slowly swallowing his soul into hell.

The detective's father had been among the first they turned. Drunk at Old Malik's tavern one night, he accepted cup after cup of wine and listened as Utbah complained about having to pay a tithe to men he did not know for an Imam he could not see.

Before Abu Ammar could agree, his drunk hands gripping the table edge, another old man stood and spoke. Swaying with drink but faithful still, this one tucked his thumbs into the sash at his waist, his turban awry, and spat on Utbah, saying, "You're no better than those nawasib scum! You're no Shia to me!"

Utbah restrained a smile. It was true. He would do anything to destroy the Shia and took on the slanderous accusation with pride.

The faithful man stumbled into the night and Abu Ammar took up Utbah's complaint with his own, mentioning how his "fine" sons paid the tithe in his stead to appease their mother's piety. He had no intention of parting with his hard-earned money to anyone, he declared. Utbah agreed, pretending to be drunk, his thick tongue slurring, "Curse these agents who empty the pockets of us poor souls!"

As the investigator came to pull his father out of the tavern that night, Utbah stepped into the shadows. The old drunk struggled against his son to free his arm and cursed him for his kindness.

Old Malik confided as the two left. "Watch out. The Twelfth Imam's agents are working with the caliph's viziers to protect their Imam and keep the peace. The police will do the viziers' bidding. You expose yourself to that old man, he'll let it out to that police son of his when he's drunk. Then you'll find yourself in manacles and left to rot in the jails built into the walls of the Round City."

"You think I don't know that the Imami viziers sucking on the caliph's tit want us all strung up?"

"You'd suck from that tit yourself if you had the chance."

"If I did," he snapped, "it would only be to cut it off."

At the memory of Old Malik's warning, Utbah straightened up, angry, and peered over the shoulder of the man in the wide red turban, not realizing he was sending jagged breaths down the man's neck.

The man jerked around. "Off, you!"

Utbah's hand easily slipped to his dagger, at first in fear that the man would expose him, but as the man's face tightened with terror, he found he was grasping the dagger with an erotic pleasure he did not understand. The man, eyes on the dagger, stepped to the side until a woman was between them, then scurried away, leaving Utbah in a confused state of alarm and satisfaction. He turned back and stared openly at Bishr's body, the life he had taken, and wondered at the power God had put in his hands.

He watched the investigator turn over the waterskin pierced with his arrow. Utbah could not remember when his aim had last gone astray. Riding a galloping horse, he could shoot open the latch on a bird cage tied to a high pole, releasing the birds into flight. For an arrow aimed at Bishr's chest to hit his waterskin? Then the second landing higher than expected, piercing his eye? And the blood seeping through the sleeves of his robe? There had been no sword fight between them. The blood had appeared the moment his arrows found their mark. The arrow shots, then the wounds on his arms. Exactly like those that killed Husayn's comrade, Abbas, at Karbala.

There was no other explanation for it; it was a clear sign from God that Bishr was no better than the slaughtered Abbas. He spat at his father's memory. *God chose this for me. Bishr's betrayal was God's plan to hold me up as the new Yazid. God thought nothing of you. Me! Never you!*

"Utbah!" Bishr had gripped his arm that morning outside the tomb of Imam Musa al-Kazim, saying in a frenzy, "The Twelfth Imam came to me in a dream. Abbas was dead in his arms. He was with Lady Fatima. She held a tablet in her arms. The names of the twelve Imams were written on it. His name was there! Muhammad ibn al-Hasan is the Twelfth Imam. The righteous Imam!" Utbah tried to pull away from him. "The Imam we sided with is false, don't you see?" Bishr dug his fingers even deeper, the horror of unanswerable guilt mottling his face. "The Twelfth Imam told me never to doubt his existence. He is al-Muntazar. He is the one we have been waiting for. Our Mahdi! He warned us to return the tithe. Hell will be our reward for this robbery!"

At first, Utbah tried to convince Bishr that it was not a vision, but merely a dream borne of weak conviction. Prying Bishr's hand from his arm to hold it in his own, he reasoned, "It is not possible to have a visionary dream of a man who does not exist."

"He exists!" Bishr's eyes were wild. "I must tell everyone! I'll preach it in the streets!" Raising a finger to the heavens, he declared, "My life for his! The Twelfth Imam is the inheritor of the line of the Prophet, alayhi salam, the progeny of our first Imam, Ali, the Lion and Lady Fatima, and their son, our third Imam, Husayn, Lord of the Martyrs!"

"This is madness!"

As Bishr ran from the tomb area, an animalistic fear mixed with desire gripped Utbah, and he lost all sense of himself. His first arrow leapt onto the bow's notch without his awareness and let loose, striking the waterskin. Bishr turned to face him, holding out the skin in horror, and in that moment, the second arrow found its mark.

Now, observing Bishr's slain body from within the crowd, Utbah felt again the strange mixture of satisfaction and fear surge through him. The dream was visionary, but did not mean what Bishr thought. The dream only foretold his own death. *Bishr is Abbas, dead in his imam's arms. I am Yazid. God directed my arrows and killed him before he betrayed me.* Then he said aloud without realizing it, his hands out in supplication, "Never despair of God's mercy."

The voices of those around him rose in a sigh to his supplication, "Amin." Utbah moved back further into the crowd, rubbing his burning palm against his robe.

3
_____

A drop of rain fell through a crack in the roof onto Zaytuna's cheek. She brushed it off and rolled to the other side of the narrow room. The mud and straw jammed into the reed roof should still be solid there. Another drop hit, this time on her shoulder. It was fat with water and soaked through her qamis.

Scolding herself for not patching the roof when she should have, she sat up and felt for the threadbare blanket folded at her feet in the pitch black of night, but it wasn't there. Her hand patted around the box holding her spare clothes and precious things. The blanket wasn't there, either. She found the edge of the box and opened it, feeling inside. Not there. As she shut the box, another drop fell, then another, until the rain started coming heavily.

Crawling over to the door, she stuck her hand out into the darkness and felt for Tein. Maybe he had come in the night and taken her blanket to sleep outside her door. He wasn't there, either. The rain was hitting thickly, turning the dirt courtyard into mud and spattering her hand. Pulling her hand back inside, she wiped it on the reed mat beneath her. But there was no point; the rain was soaking right through the roof and the mat was sopping. She grabbed her fishskin prayer mat and lay it over her box and her mother's drum to protect them. Sitting beside them, she shivered despite the sweltering heat. A chunk of mud and reed from the roof thudded beside her, then again across the room, then another, and another hit her shoulder. She lay over the box and drum as the mud hit her back.

There wasn't a sound from Qambar, Yulduz, or Saliha. Their rooms must be safe. She squatted and picked up the drum and box, making sure the mat covered them, and carried them to the door, each step a sickening squish underfoot. Pushing the thin curtain open, she ducked out the door screaming, "Saliha! Yulduz! Qambar!" But there was nothing.

In the pitch dark and driving rain, she made the few steps across the small courtyard that would put her at the door to Yulduz and Qambar's room. But there was no door, no wall. One unseeing step at a time, she crept forward yelling through the thundering sheets, "Yulduz!"

She shifted the box and drum to her hip so she could hold them more easily with one arm, then waved her hand, palm out, searching for the wall. Nothing. Saliha's room was to the left. She turned, knowing exactly where it should be, but there, too, was nothing.

The rain was streaming down her face, making it hard to breathe. Coughing and spitting, she put down the drum and the box and bent her head over. The pressure of the rain became too much, and she knelt in the mud, laying over the box and drum to protect them. The mud sucked at her knees and the box tipped to one side. The mud pulled at it, then the drum, too. Zaytuna grasped at them frantically, her fingers slipping as the few things she had left from her mother disappeared under the earth. She rolled onto her side and stood up unsteadily, screaming as the mud grasped at her feet. Her mouth gaped, but there was no sound.

Watery light dawned, and she found herself alone on a muddy plain that reached out to the horizon. A wave higher and broader than the walls of the Round City was coming at her. She turned to run, but the wave was before her. Turning again, the wave was there. The wave encircled her, growing taller and more fierce, engulfing overhead as it crept closer. Dropping onto her knees and elbows, she wrapped her hands over her head to brace for its crash, but none came. Instead, the thick drumming of rain subsided, and she was surrounded by terrifying silence.

Taking a shallow, trembling breath, she unclenched her fingers and placed her hands on the ground to push herself up, expecting them to sink into mud. The ground was cold and firm instead, smooth as a stone. Afraid of what she would see, she kept her eyes shut as she stood. But the warmth of the rising sun radiated within her until her muscles relaxed, strand by strand, each falling into rest until she wanted nothing more than to lie down again, now to sleep. She opened her eyes instead. Glittering drops of watery light flitted around her like butterflies under an oceanic dome of swirling crystalline and foaming waves.

"I am dreaming," she said aloud.

The dome fell away.

In the distance, an army of men, women, and children marched forward, the sun rising behind them, silhouetting each in perfect detail. They came at her with such speed, swords at the ready, bows in hand, that for a moment she nearly turned to run.

She said again, "I am dreaming," and waited for them.

The army made no sound as it arrived, streaming behind one man. He was an Arab in a black turban, his black wrap draped loosely over his head and one side thrown over his shoulder. He was neither tall nor short. His forehead was broad, his eyes an even deeper brown than his skin, and his beard thick, black coils. He cradled a dead man in his arms.

An extraordinary woman walked to one side of him, dressed in shining robes with a wrap sewn from ribbons of multi-hued light drawn around her. She carried a tablet in her arms.

Another man, tall and broad, his face obscured, walked behind them carrying a leather butter sack filled with coins clinking in the silence. She felt drawn to him, as if he had an answer to an unknown question.

As the procession drew near, she saw that the cradled body had been shot with an arrow through his eye and that wounds on his arms had seeped blood through the sleeves of his qamis and robe. A waterskin with an arrow through it rested against his chest.

The beauty of the man leading them was incomparable. The light of justice shone on his face. She desired him and looked down at her own body, shocked, the feeling exacting an unforgivable betrayal.

He lay the corpse before her. "Do you know who I am?"

She dropped to her knees, then down to the ground, placing her cheek on the cool, hard earth. "The lady beside you is Sayyida Fatima, the beloved daughter of our prophet, Muhammad, peace and blessings on him and his family, and you arrive to us through her, by honoured lineage. You are the Mahdi. He who will come to us at the beginning of the end of time to set right all that has been wronged."

"The world is ending," he said. "Are you coming?"

Bowing her head, she whispered the truth, "I cannot."

He laughed lightly. "You do not know what is required."

"Will you tell me?"

"Stand."

She stood. His mouth parted in a smile. His white teeth gleamed opalescent. His eyes softened her. Wanting him engulfed her, and her face burned with it. She lowered her gaze.

"Behind you."

She stepped back rather than turning and trod on the foot of the one behind her. Lifting her foot in surprise, she nearly fell. The person put a hand on her back to steady her, and she wheeled around to hit whomever would touch her without asking. But it was Mustafa. What she felt for the Mahdi was now for Mustafa. Desire thrummed through her until every cell in her body was alive, pulsating, and moved toward its end. Her eyes fluttered in confusion. Moaning, she fell into Mustafa's arms.

Mustafa held her as she fell, bringing her carefully to the ground, and said to her softly, "My love."

Nausea smothered her spent desire. Trying to free herself from him, she pushed against his chest with one hand. "I can't."

At the first touch of resistance, he let her go. Mustafa asked the Mahdi, "What do I do?"

"Be gentle with her. The world is ending. Now, wake up."

Sunlight shot through the cracks in the roof of Zaytuna's room. Her body trembled from the dream in a way she did not recognize, and she did not like it. A surge of panic immobilized her. The world was ending. Mustafa. As if held down by unseen hands, she watched dust motes move along gentle currents through shafts of light, while inwardly she desperately searched for some place to put down what she had experienced in her dream. But the dust motes called her to recognize them, to leave her frantic sense-making and remember.

Something within her heard them and pulled her away from her search and there she was, a child again. She, Tein, Mustafa, and the other children were sitting with Uncle Abu Bakr al-Wasiti. Late afternoon light came through a window and caught every speck of dust in its arms, holding them aloft in a gentle breeze.

He asked, "Are you afraid of how the wind sets dust into motion?"

They objected in their childish voices, "Of course not."

One finger up, he said, "Do not be afraid of God's will. All the worlds are nothing other than dust motes like this."

Even though she had protested that she understood along with the other children, she had been afraid of God's will then, as she was still. What had God done to her? He left her bereft of a mother, knowing the brutality of men, and given no reason to love. She explained to Mustafa once that she trusted God, trusted that He had created a stone of a world for poor souls to hone themselves on.

She was incapable of trusting any man well enough to love him-- and she could only think in euphemisms or she would become sick with the horror of it--to love him in that way. Saliha teased her relentlessly, but her fear of men, *in that way*, had broken her and she had never, up to this moment, ever, felt such a thing. But then grief overlaid the bitterness inside her. The one man who loved her and who she might have loved fully was out of her reach.

This was God's will.

"Mustafa," she moaned in sorrow. "I have lost you."

The panic and loss gripped her in broken-boned pain. Her lower back tightened into a brittle knot. She rolled over onto her side and sat, gasping from pain and eyeing her box and drum to make sure her mother's precious things were still there. Reaching out for her water jug and cup, simply to touch what Mustafa had made for her when he had still wanted her, her hand hit the jug awkwardly and she nearly knocked it over. As she jumped to keep it from falling, the muscles in her back and hips spasmed again. "God help me."

"She's awake." Yulduz's voice carried in from the courtyard.

"Is she sick, sleeping so late?" Saliha asked.

"Check on her."

Saliha poked through the curtain, saw her distress, and rushed in. Crouching beside her, she demanded, "What's happened?"

"Bad dream," she replied, shivering.

"That's all?"

"My back, I did something."

"You slept so late. We were worried."

"True enough. When do I sleep?" Zaytuna managed a small cough of a laugh that sent fractured pain through her chest.

"Were you praying all night?"

She deflected. "Not to make me sleep like this."

"Will you be all right?" Saliha stood.

"I need to loosen my back."

"Yulduz is outside. I have to leave for work."

"I heard her."

Yulduz yelled in her Turkmen-accented Arabic, rounding every vowel beyond recognition, and clipping her consonants like a Baghdadi street urchin, "Come out 'ere and let me feed you!"

Saliha called back. "Her back is twisted up."

"Send 'er here. I'll pull it out."

Saliha lifted her eyebrows, questioning.

"I'll let the old bird pull on me. I need it." Zaytuna took Saliha's offered hand and stood up well enough, but pain shot down her back through her leg and she buckled. Saliha tucked her arm around her and guided her out into the courtyard.

Yulduz's eyes widened. She waved them over.

The sun stung Zaytuna's eyes, yet she looked up, expecting to see the glittering dome of water overhead. There was nothing but a sky faded blue from the mounting heat. Prickling numbness climbed up her legs, working its way to her heart such that she thought she might stop breathing, and her eyesight faded around the edges. Holding tight onto Saliha, she lowered herself down.

Saliha stood before Zaytuna braiding her hair over her shoulder, then brushed it back behind her. She tied a white kerchief over her head, the braid free on her back, then lay her voluminous blue and white wrap over that, draping it with a flick of her wrists so it covered her curves, uncontained by her qamis and sirwal. For the first time in all the years Zaytuna had known her, she wondered at Saliha's voluptuous beauty, wanting to be such a woman. No, she wanted it for Mustafa, wondering if he would want her, wait for her, if she were more like Saliha, instead of tall, bony, and long-faced like a horse.

Yulduz moved to get behind her. "Now let's get you bent over, slowly. Put your arms out in front of you."

Zaytuna did as she was told, tucking her legs beneath her, bending until she folded over her thighs, her cheek on the rough courtyard floor, her arms outstretched before her. The grit rubbed against her cheek and called her back to when she bowed in humility before Lady Fatima and the Mahdi. *Is the world truly ending?* All this, Yulduz's hands on her. Her friends. Her family. Would the Mahdi draw us all into the battle against evil? Who would die? Who would live for the days of peace that followed until the angel Israfil blew his horn, transforming the earth into the plain of judgement? *God help us.* She wept openly.

"I've got you." Yulduz moved her fingers along Zaytuna's spine. The sturdy old woman hit a tender spot, and Zaytuna whimpered. A sob released from deep within her and a fresh fear rose. *What is my role in the battle to come?*

Keeping the fingers of one hand wide and firm on her back to calm her, with the other, Yulduz pressed gently where it hurt, saying. "At least you've got some meat on you now or there'd be nothing to rub to get the knot out." With the old Turkmen woman's touch, the pain receded, but the horror of the dream remained.

"Your face!" Saliha said, standing over her. "What was it, a bad dream?"

"I don't want to talk about it." Where could she begin? What could she say? She did not want them to know any of it.

"Was there sex in it?" Saliha teased.

Zaytuna's face grew hot.

"I knew it!" She laughed.

Yulduz broke in before Saliha could dig further. "Stop it! Dreams come from either God or Satan, and we should spit three times over our left shoulder and ask God to protect us if we have a bad one. If it put you in such a state, then you need to spit as soon as you can manage it."

Saliha snorted. "Tell us, first. Then spit."

Yulduz ran her hands firmly along either side of Zaytuna's spine until she exhaled deeply. "There you go, girl. Nearly there."

"Come on." Saliha tapped Zaytuna's leg with her foot.

The dream laid out its parts before her in perfect clarity, nothing lost to her but its meaning. She wanted her friends to tell her the world was not ending, and that she was not bereft of Mustafa. Her cheek still on the ground, she said, "Help me up."

Yulduz and Saliha supported her as she pushed up with her hands to seated, her legs still tucked beneath her. She stretched to one side lightly, then the other, still tight with pain, but the worst of it was over. The two helped her move back until she was resting with her back against the warm mud bricks. Yulduz sat beside her, nearly shoulder to shoulder.

"I have to leave." Saliha insisted. "Come on, tell me."

"It was soaking rain here." She felt the fear again. "All of you were gone. After, the rain turned into a wave."

"A wave?" Yulduz asked.

"It was a dream. A wave surrounded me, like a dome."

"And?" Saliha prompted.

She was not sure if she wanted to say more.

"Oh, please!" Saliha complained.

Yulduz patted her leg, prodding her to continue.

"Fine." She collected her thoughts, considering how much to say. "A man approached carrying a body in his arms who had been shot like Abbas at Karbala."

"Abbas?" Yulduz asked.

"Did you not grow up with these stories of Karbala? Did Qambar not tell you?" Saliha teased, "What kind of Shia is he?"

Yulduz started in, "Now, you...," and mistakenly pushed Zaytuna's shoulder with her own, jarring her.

Zaytuna moaned, taking the push as a signal from God to keep silent and refused to say more.

"Oh, girl, sorry!" Yulduz leaned over, trying to steady her.

"The two of you!" Zaytuna scolded. "That's it, that was the dream."

"I suppose that's not so bad a dream, girl, but spit just in case."

"You can tell us the rest later. See you tonight. Layla will have moved in by then. We should have something special for her to eat as a welcome."

Her back spasmed at the reminder that she would be stuck caring for Layla now, as if she did not have enough. "The world is ending," she mumbled, then reproached herself for belittling the dream with such a petty thought about the girl.

"What?" Saliha asked.

"Nothing. It hurts."

Saliha left, giving Yulduz a look that told her to take care of Zaytuna.

Yulduz got to her knees. "Come on now, turn toward me so I can rub that back again."

Her firm hands took hold of the pain once again, working Zaytuna's back in silence while all the old objections to Layla rushed through her mind. The girl shouldn't be living with them. None of them could care for her. How long would it be before she was back at Maryam's door, begging for her old job back so she could enjoy the comforts of a good room in a grand house, food fine enough for her master, and a housekeeper who loved her like a mother?

"Be good to that girl."

Zaytuna found her breath as Yulduz pressed into a tight spot again, and the pain eased. "Why wouldn't I be good to her?"

"No one's asking you to be a mother to'er," Yulduz said in her ear, "but she'll be family to us now."

"She doesn't need a mother. I didn't have a mother at her age."

Her hand on Zaytuna's shoulder, Yulduz said, "You and Tein had Mustafa's mother after your own mother died. Don't act like you're a hard woman. That girl's still a child, no more than ten years old."

"What do the poor know of childhood?"

"They should. Don't you deny'er what little she can get."

Not having the wherewithal to object, she patted Yulduz on the hand and moved back to sit against the wall, saying, and meaning every word, "May God reward you. My back is better."

Yulduz sat down next to her. "Maybe Layla will keep you out of trouble."

"What trouble?" Then, understanding what she meant, she closed her eyes for a moment in frustration.

"Umm Parvaiz is still angry."

"She *told me* she suspected her husband had another wife."

"The woman was complaining, for sisterly sympathy, not asking you to investigate it. Now she knows he has another family and she didn't want to know."

"That is not how it happened. She asked me."

"Well, she's angry about it now."

"Let her be angry with her husband."

Yulduz sighed and changed the subject. "That housekeeper sending things?"

"Yes, Maryam's sending a bed, everything Layla needs."

"Will Maryam take'er back if this doesn't work out?"

"No." Zaytuna shook her head. "We're all she has now."

"Hired someone else so fast?"

"Of course, this is Baghdad. There's always a child needing work."

"Well, can she visit Maryam for a good meal now and again?"

"I'm sure." Irritation gave voice to her fears. "But what will we do if Saliha leaves us and there's no more money for meat in our stew? How will we feed her? The money we make washing clothes doesn't go far."

"Why would Saliha leave us?" Yulduz scoffed.

Zaytuna opened her eyes wide. "Tein? If they marry? They won't live here with us. They'll have to find a place between her work at the hospital and the Grave Crimes offices at the Round City."

"You are worrying about things that will never come to pass. Saliha's declared she won't marry and he's declared he won't have'er if she won't."

"Yet they are with each other every chance they get." Zaytuna's stomach was empty and burned. "You think that's not leading somewhere? They love each other. You know that."

"You see Saliha agreeing to marry him?"

She grabbed hold of those few words like the rope of God. It was true. Love or no love, Saliha would not marry any man. Her last husband, a brutal man, had died in a fire and she walked away a widow, freed. The knot of burning fear in her stomach released. She repeated Yulduz's words, "And Tein won't be with her if she won't."

Yulduz patted her on the arm. "So don't worry." She brushed the dirt off the knees of her sirwal, adding, "But I don't know why you don't want to gain a sister, even if she has to move away."

Zaytuna stared, and Yulduz clacked her mouth shut in protest.

The sound of something being dragged came through the narrow passageway that led to the alley. It had to be Layla. Yulduz rolled on her side, then to her knees to get up to meet the girl. Zaytuna stayed put.

Layla came through backwards, her bottom sticking out as she pulled a sack that was too heavy for her, putting her weight into it. She glanced over her shoulder at them, grinning. "Aunties!"

Yulduz approached quickly, her multitude of small braids flying this way and that under her embroidered Turkmen cap. "Did you drag that thing all the way yourself?"

"Auntie Maryam paid for a donkey cart, but they only go to the square."

"Let me help you with that. Zaytuna's hurt her back." She sucked her teeth at Zaytuna. "That's why she's not getting up."

Layla dropped the bag and ran to her, taking up her hand, kissing it and not letting go. "Auntie, can I help?"

"I'm better now." But she found herself strangely reluctant to let go of the girl's hand and only did so in order to stand. The pain had eased, but the fear of the Mahdi standing before her made her tremble, but then the trembling turned into desire. She muttered, "God protect me."

"Is it that bad, Auntie?"

"I'm fine, really." She took the girl's hand again and swung it lightly, mustering a welcoming face. "You're here."

"Alhamdulillah, Auntie." Layla blushed, grinning such that even her back teeth showed, then let go of Zaytuna's hand and ran back to her sack. Yulduz was pulling at it, but Layla waved her off.

Zaytuna stood back, hands on her hips, and watched as Layla dragged the sack to the room left empty by Umm Farhad.

"Girl," Yulduz said, "where's your mattress?"

"I've got four blankets. Auntie Maryam insisted on a mattress, but I'll be comfortable enough. If Auntie Zaytuna can sleep on the floor, so can I."

"Well, she sleeps well enough," Yulduz chuckled. "She slept right through the morning prayer today!"

"I should have prayed it immediately, not let you rub me like that."

"And how're you supposed to bend and bow in that pain?"

She needed to make up her prayer, but she wanted nothing more than to walk out of the passageway and go to Auntie Hakima with the dream. Not YingYue, despite being instructed to see her first. She could tell the mystic prodigy about the Mahdi and the signs of the Last Day, but how could she sit before YingYue and recount a dream in which she lay in such a state in the arms of Mustafa, the man YingYue loved and would marry any day now? She waited at the edges of a thought, then grabbed it. Perhaps this dream came just in time to stop the marriage from going ahead altogether?

4

Tein leaned against the wall of the men's surgery in the Barmakid hospital, watching a doctor examine the victim's skull. The doctor seemed far too young, but this was not complicated, and Tein was just grateful it was not Judah. He was not sure that he could control his fists if he had to hear one word of Judah's vengeful jealousy over Saliha. After trying to tug the arrow out and failing, the doctor said eagerly, "I'll need to cut out part of his skull to get the arrowhead for you."

He was uneasy with his macabre interest, but agreed.

As familiar as Tein was with killing from his days on the battlefield on the edges of the empire, he turned away when the saw came out. Finally, the arrowhead clinked in the copper basin. When he looked again, the doctor had cut open the victim's face, flaying back the skin and had removed half of his skull. The piece of skull was set aside in another basin with part of his brain, revealing a gaping emptiness in the victim's head. The bloody surgical tools were in yet another basin to be sterilized before being used again. Seeing the victim harmed further made Tein wish he were the kind to say a prayer. The doctor took the basin with the arrowhead to the sink on the far wall to wash.

"Do you need the shaft?"

"Better hold that for me, too."

Drying both as he returned to Tein, he held up the arrowhead before placing it in his hand. "It was lodged in the back of his skull."

Tein turned it over. An exquisite bow and a hunting arrowhead. Their murderer was a wealthy person who hunted for sport. Now why would a wealthy person kill in such a public place and in such a way?

The doctor examined the wounds on the victim's arms.

"Are they fresh or old?"

"I need to wash the blood away to know," the doctor replied.

He brought over a jug of water and a basin with a fresh cloth and washed the now dried blood from the wounds and examined them. "Fresh cuts from a sword or dagger and shot by an arrow." He quipped, "Another day in Baghdad."

Tein did not laugh. This elite physician who was never touched by the everyday violence of the city had no right to joke. "His sleeves were intact," he said. "Could he have had his clothes off and put them back on after being attacked?"

"Look here." He pointed to the location of the cuts. "The muscles needed to move his arms were not injured. He would have been in extraordinary pain, but it is possible. You must know from your days on the battlefield, injured men find the spirit to keep fighting."

Tein nodded, wondering again how no one had seen the fight.

"But," the doctor added, "it could have happened a day or two ago. Tissue does not show the signs of stitching for two, three days, or even more. The wounds could have stopped bleeding and opened when he fell."

Tein picked up the dead man's robe and qamis and examined them. "These blood stains are recent, nothing dried or blackened."

"As I said, day-old wounds opened again." The doctor shrugged. "Do we need to release the body immediately," he asked, "or can I call in a few of my colleagues? As long as the skull is open, I mean."

Tein wanted to find Saliha, but wasn't sure if he should leave the body. Giving into desire, he answered, "I may have a bit of time here yet, but I need to take the body to the corpse washer. You'll put him back together," he said, pointing to the piece of skull and brain, "and bind his head before I take him."

"Of course." He left the room.

Tein followed him out and turned to the left in the hallway, walking to the rear of the building to the women's corpse washing room. The door was shut, but there was movement inside. He waited a moment, placing his hand flat against the wooden door as if he could feel her within, and silently begged her to come out. Then he pulled his hand away, backing up, so no one could hold any suspicion against Saliha. Suspicion would reward him with a hearty slap on the back while she would be ruined. Leaving, he passed the pharmacy and peered inside. Stopping in to greet Ibn Ali wouldn't be a problem. Maybe by then Saliha would come out, and he would get to see her after all.

Ibn Ali did not look up to acknowledge his presence, but continued pouring a cloudy liquid from a long-necked flask through a funnel into a beaker of darker liquid simmering over a small table-top brazier. Even at work, the pharmacist dressed elegantly, and Tein admired him. The deep blue of his turban set off the blackness of his skin and matched his blue and red patterned robe cinched with a tooled leather belt.

Tein waited for him to finish, examining the wall of ceramic and glass jars holding the herbs and minerals that Ibn Ali compounded to treat the hospital's sick. Local pharmacists and herbalists had similar walls, but here Ibn Ali worked with the hospital's doctors to better understand disease and create new medicines to treat them.

When the pharmacist put the flask down, Tein greeted him, "Assalamu alaykum, ya Ibn Ali."

"Wa alaykum assalam!" He rolled down his narrow sleeves, happy to see him. "I hope you are here on a case and not your own health."

"Alhamdulillah." He gestured toward the surgery down the passageway. "The poor man on the table down there is not."

"Can they save him?"

"He was dead at the scene from his injuries. Shot in the eye. I only brought him here to have a doctor dig out the arrowhead for us. Maybe it will help us trace the killer."

"Dead from a shot in his eye? Not simply blinded?"

Tein shifted his weight back and forth on his feet. "All I can say is that the arrow entered the eye and became lodged in his skull. He died from it. The doctor had to remove part of the skull, his eye, and the brain to retrieve the arrowhead."

"Was all that necessary? Removing the maxilla would have been sufficient. Did he ask to allow others to see the body? They rarely have the opportunity to examine the brain."

"Yes, I gave him permission."

"Without the family's approval?"

"I have rights over the body until we release it to the family." He sounded defensive and regretted it. "They will not be doing more than observing what the first doctor did to remove the arrowhead."

Ibn Ali bowed his head with respect for Tein's authority, making him feel even more foolish. "Of course." Then Ibn Ali conceded, "We must have these opportunities to learn. Typically, families are not eager to allow us to perform autopsies on their loved ones."

Tension hung in the room and Tein did not know how to remedy it, making him want to turn around and open the door to the corpse washer's room for Saliha no matter the risk. Instead, he stood awkwardly, shifting on his feet again, and hedged. "God willing, all to the good." He tried to change the subject, "How is your family?"

"Alhamdulillah. And your sister?"

"Alhamdulillah."

"My wife asks after her. Bring her to our home soon."

Tein was stuck not knowing if the invitation was a formality or meant sincerely and gave the only possible answer. "Inshallah, if God wills."

Ibn Ali smiled, but something was still wrong. Then with his hand over his heart he said, "I am sorry to say I must get back to work."

"I should as well."

As he left, Ibn Ali called out, almost as an afterthought, "We have not seen you at Baraqan's paper shop."

Relief washed over Tein. Ibn Ali had not shut him out. He answered less formally than he usually spoke with him. "I've been busy. I'll try to come by tomorrow."

"Glad to hear it."

Out in the passageway, he glanced back at the door to the corpse washer's room, but it was still shut. He turned toward the long inner courtyard and saw her walking with her back to him, nearly to the wide entry leading to the street.

There was no calling her name, so he hurried to catch up with her, making his way around the bitter orange and lemon trees to the front entrance. The heat and light in the street hit him after the cool and breezy shade of the hospital. He stopped for a moment, squinting in the light, looking for her, then turned left around the corner toward the marketplace. And there she was. Her blue and white wrap flitting in the breeze behind her, the curve of an ankle showing itself with each step. Chasing after her, he forgot the old pain in his thigh. Finally, he was close enough to speak. "Saliha."

She turned, welcoming him with her laughing eyes, calling him to her with his name. "Tein."

"Come with me," he said and walked toward the shady passageway they both knew led to a narrow alley lined with ruined squatters' houses. She checked to see if anyone was watching, then followed him.

He stopped in the arched doorway they thought of as their own and waited for her to decide how close she would come to him. She teased him, playing with her wrap, opening it slightly here, tugging it against her there. There was pain and joy with each of her steps until she was in his arms, her thighs pressed against his, her face upturned for a kiss. He brushed his lips against hers, teasing her in return, as he knew she liked, so she had to reach up to pull him against her.

She backed away before there would be no stopping them, but his hand paused on her back longer than it should. She looked up at him as if to say, "No," so he slid his hands to her hips, giving her the distance she wanted. Raising her hand to his face, she traced her finger across his high cheekbone, down his wide nose to his full lips, then tugged on the scruff of beard on his square chin, saying in a voice still husky from their embrace, "Here on a case?"

The question did not sound as if it needed an answer, but he gave her one to keep from sliding his hands around to her backside and bringing her closer. "I had to bring a body into the hospital."

"Tell me," she demanded.

"You want the details?"

"I suspect it will make this easier." She raised one eyebrow.

"There was an arrow stuck in a man's head. We needed the doctor to remove it." Then he remembered and ran cold with reproach. "I have to take the body to the corpse washers. I left the man there. So I could find you."

She stood aside, adjusting her wrap. "Go back. I can't stay. Shatha will expect me soon from the market."

Torn, he tried to pull her back. "I have time. The man isn't leaving there on his own accord."

"What would your sister, the Lady Zaytuna, 'She of All Just Things', say to that joke?"

"That I'd put another weight on the scales damning me to hell." His face fell when he remembered criticizing the doctor for joking. Then worse, he thought of what Ibn Ali would say if he knew he had left the man's body unsupervised, especially after insisting on his responsibility over it.

"Are you worried about what Zaytuna will think?"

He did not know how to explain, so he made himself smile and brushed his thumb across her soft cheek. "It's nothing."

"Don't give me that," she said, pushing his arm and letting her hand linger a moment too long. "If it's not Zaytuna, then it's Ammar. What did he do now?"

Relieved at her misunderstanding, if only to change the direction of the conversation, he told her, "I'm worried he might go with another otherworldly motive for this killing."

"Uff, not again."

"Let's see where it goes."

"You'd better watch him," she scolded. "After what happened last time."

"I've been watching him." He stared down the alley, annoyed by her telling him to do what he cursed-well was already doing.

She reached up and turned his face back to her, then stood on her toes, hand still on his cheek. "What's down the alley?"

He softened with her touch. "You want all my attention, do you?"

Peering at him from underneath her eyelashes, she nodded slowly.

"Then how would I have time to watch Ammar?"

She prodded. "What's Ammar thinking? Jinn?"

"It's Karbala again."

"To listen to Ammar, you'd think that Karbala held the key to understanding every human instinct."

Stopping himself from saying, "To be fair...," he answered instead, "It's not that. The man was shot in the exact way that an important companion of Husayn was killed at Karbala. It seemed staged."

Her back straightened, and she pulled away from him with interest.

"To me," he continued, "they were an impossible pair of shots for it to be purposeful. It must be a coincidence."

"Maybe not?"

Shaking his head, he replied, "I don't understand."

"Maybe not a coincidence. Zaytuna was just telling me she had a dream about Husayn's companion, Abbas. A man came to her carrying a dead body, killed as Abbas was killed. Was he killed like Abbas?"

Tein grew hot and wanted to push her off of him and get some room.

Noticing the change, she stepped back, unhappy. "What's wrong?"

"It's not you. Now it's the two of them I have to worry about. Zaytuna meddling in this case and Ammar having me follow up imaginary leads until we end up..."

She finished his sentence, "...arresting and convicting the wrong person."

"That's right." He set his jaw.

"But Zaytuna's dream. It can't be a coincidence."

"Correlation is not causation."

Pushing against him again, her eyes narrowed. "Fancy words!"

"Just because two things seem associated doesn't mean there is a single cause that connects them."

"Something you learned sitting with Ibn Ali?" She eyed him skeptically.

He couldn't tell from her tone if it was an accusation or a question. "We talk about philosophy. I'm learning from the men there. What's wrong with that?"

Saliha soothed him, taking a bit of his robe in both hands to draw herself in. "No, I like it." She shrugged one shoulder. "So, in other words, you think Zay's dream and the murder are a coincidence."

It was a jab, and a good one. He took it, letting out a laugh that shook them both. They gazed at other with an intensity of desire and affection, a feeling of such simple goodness he almost forgot they would never be husband and wife.

"Come and see me tonight," she whispered, coming in close again, their thighs touching, again.

"Are we to be married?" he asked, hoping it sounded playful.

She backed away in one quick step, her arms across her chest. "Enough of this, Tein. I won't marry. I can wait until the end of days, if that is what it takes. Holding out isn't going to make me let you have a say over me."

The sudden distance was a slap. A moan rose up within him, but he choked it off, forcing himself to say instead, "I can't be with you and risk your reputation."

Turning her face from him, she objected. "How many times! My reputation is mine to lose, not yours. And I am through saying this, I don't need your protection."

The pain of distance turned to frustration, as it always did in these fights with her, and he bit his tongue to keep from saying what he had said too many times before, that her free spirit was exactly why she needed his protection. She did not want to admit what this world would do to her.

She grunted. "I know what that silence means."

"Be happy I'm not saying it, then."

"Listen, you." She pointed at him. "You came to me that first time. You came back to me after we'd agreed this would never work. You. Not me."

"I came to apologize. I came to explain."

She offered up a jaded expression he knew too well at this point.

"I shouldn't have. I shouldn't have let you. I betrayed myself."

"I have to get back to work," she said in a flat tone and started down the passageway, then stopped and turned to face him. "I love you, but I'm done. Come to me on my own terms. No more 'protecting my reputation' by meeting me in alleys and dark corners."

He felt punched in the gut at the lie she so easily put to his motivations. Every muscle tumbled down in the loss of her, the weight of his guilt and fear keeping him from rushing to her to promise her whatever she wanted. She did not wait for an answer.

No longer young enough to think punching a brick wall would help anything, he hit back at himself. *What kind of man are you? Leave her alone so you won't hurt her and betray yourself again.*

Straightening his back against the wall, he made his way out onto the hot street again. He forced himself not to glance in the direction of the marketplace, hoping to glimpse her, and walked directly back to the hospital.

A donkey cart was waiting outside the hospital entrance. The driver leaned against the cart, chewing on a miswak while the donkey snorted and twitched its tail to slap the flies off of its hide. "You!" Tein called out, "I'm going to have a body to bring to Buratha in a few minutes. Are you interested?"

"What if I don't get a fare back? You'll have to pay me for both ways."

"I'll pay both ways if you wait to take me back, but I'm heading all the way to the Round City on my return."

The driver grinned at the price of the trip. "Done."

Tein hurried through the entrance hall and by the time he was halfway around the courtyard, he was in full stride out of worry that Ibn Ali would see him and question where he had been. He stared straight ahead as he walked past the pharmacy. Opening the surgery door, he saw two doctors leaning over the body. There was an additional piece of the man's skull cut out, and more skin beside it, in a basin on the small table next to the surgery bench. He said in a low growl to keep from taking hold of the men and throwing them across the room, "Hands off him, now."

The two straightened at his voice, almost knocking each other over. One was the young doctor who had pulled the arrow out for him. Of course, the other was Judah. His high arched eyebrows and long nose made it seem like he looked down at everyone, even a dead man. It was the kind of face some women found noble. He never understood how Saliha found him attractive, so unlike himself in every way, from his pallid skin to his slim stature to his officious nature.

"Are you behind this?" Tein made it sound like an accusation.

Judah straightened his robe. "Is this body under your watch?"

Knowing what he was implying, Tein did not give him the satisfaction of replying defensively. He pointed to the other doctor. "Put him back together and bandage his head so I can take him to the corpse washer's. Now."

The young doctor bumped into the small table that held the skull and scalp of the dead man, rattling it. He steadied the table, then rushed to get the bandages.

Judah observed the other doctor's fumbling and shook his head, then turned his attention to Tein. "Did you leave your watch to catch our beautiful corpse washer in a private moment? Is that why the body was unattended and left for our study? I should speak to Shatha about her behaviour, most unbecoming a sacred profession."

"The garbage that falls out of your mouth when you open it," Tein said as he loosened his body, his sandalled feet holding ground, feeling the relaxed joy of the instant before he threw a punch at someone who deserved it. Judah did not register it, not knowing how men who love to fight hold themselves before the moment comes. Instead, the ass stood before him, triumphant, while Tein was ready to punch the smirk off of his face.

A sudden feeling took hold of him. Someone was coming up behind him. *Saliha.* He turned, ready to get her out of the room so she would not get hurt, but there was no one there. Swinging back to face Judah, the moment was lost. Judah had taken a few steps back to let the young doctor put the man back together and wrap his head and was now out of reach, leaning against the back wall, smiling. "You will need orderlies to carry the body out. I am assuming you have a donkey cart waiting?"

As Judah walked around him to the door, Tein took hold of his arm. Judah glanced at the great hand encircling his forearm, then up at Tein, unimpressed.

Replying to his unspoken question, Tein hissed, "I haven't killed a man in a very long time, but I will do you with pleasure if you harm Saliha."

"I suppose you think I should fear you."

"You don't need to fear me, you only need to understand me."

"I understand you are putting a good woman at risk with your selfish behaviour. Take your hand off me now or I will share your threats with the director of the hospital, Dr. ar-Razi, who will no doubt make certain recommendations to the staffing of our corpse washers as well as speak to your superiors."

Tein let go of his arm slowly. "I don't need to be police to find you."

A shiver of awareness, then fear, crossed Judah's face for a moment. Tein was satisfied.

5

Ammar opened the front courtyard gate at his family's home in Buratha. His father had built the house and grounds on the city's edge so that his mother could gaze at the plains of Karbala. It was some seventy-thousand cubits in the distance, but to her, close enough to touch its hallowed ground. The front courtyard was well-tended. Gourd and melon vines twined themselves round on old, sturdy trellises built back when his father had cared about his home and family and had not yet retired to sit drunk in taverns, relying on his sons to care for their mother. Garlic, onion, and leek greens grew high next to mounds of thyme and mint. The goats were beyond the back wall of the home in the open plains. His brother's son Hasan would be walking beside them with a stick twice his size. He had done the same when he was that age, watching soldiers marching along the great road connecting Baghdad to Kufa and wishing for a way out.

"Ummi!" He called for his mother as he opened the door. There was no answer from within. Instead, he heard her footsteps coming around the side of the house. She had tied her hair up in a kerchief and rolled up her sleeves. Her old wrap was around her waist like an apron. She was cooking.

Her arms open, she met him halfway and embraced him. "Habibi, habibi, alhamdulillah, come and eat with us."

"I should go in and greet my father."

"He's asleep right now." She patted his arm. "Leave him."

She pulled him around to the back courtyard. The tannur oven was hot, but the stew had yet to be prepared, let alone cook on the hot coals. The small wooden table positioned next to a bench was still piled with greens. There was a bowl with a cloth over it to keep the flies off of what would surely be meat marinating in spices and, knowing his father's tastes, sour goat's milk. She crossed to the oven and took up a long branch, curved and black on one end, the same one she had always used, and tapped a round loaf of hot bread, sending it out of the oven onto her cloth-covered hand. Setting the loaf aside, she returned to him. "Sit with me, habibi. The food won't take long."

"I can't. I'm in Buratha on a case. I only came to ask you a question."

"How can that be? How can you visit your mother only to ask a question?" She took him by the hand, pulling at him until he sat down beside her, then left to go into the pantry shed to pour him a cup of cool water. He stood to stop her. These were the parts they played. He must try. She must succeed. The day she could not care for him, his mother said, would be the day she returned to God. The thought of her death, even for a moment, pained him such that he was impatient for her return. Soon she was there, cup of water in hand with a sprig of mint, pinched from the garden. He took the cup with one hand and held her hand to his lips with the other. "May God reward you for your kindness with a long, healthy life."

She pulled her hand away and sat down. "Amin, but God has already rewarded me with the gift of such a son." Patting him, she asked, "Now, when will God reward me with a daughter and grandchildren?" She held her hands out in supplication, praying, "God! Bring this boy a woman he will love and who will love him, be good to him, and give us many beautiful grandchildren." She snuck a glance at him, and finished, "Perhaps a girl like Nasifa."

Ammar knew what that meant. He was going to be forced to eat another uncomfortable lunch with another girl and her family. Nasifa. The name didn't register, but then he did not know most of the girls his mother had arranged for him to meet. And they were girls. He had no interest in these girls schooled in duty alone. But even if she found him a woman, it would never work.

If his mother found him the right woman, and if this wife were to live with him in his room near the Round City, she would be alone most of the time given his irregular hours. If she lived with his parents, she would be as good as alone, because he would still have to spend most of his nights in that room to be near work. There would be no traveling from Buratha to the Round City every day unless he took skiffs along the canals and the Tigris that he could not afford. He made less now than when he was a foot soldier in the infantry along the frontier. The thought of it all made him angry. Truly, she would be a daughter for his mother because she would never see him enough to be a wife for him.

Protesting, he always reminded her that his brother, Muhsin, and his wife, Tahirah, lived next door. They had given her two grandchildren already, and a third was on the way. What more did she need? "*Your* children," she would answer, "and *your* wife to become *my* daughter." Other days, like today, he simply answered "Amin" to her prayer while silently reminding God of his own needs.

"Habibi," she said touching his cheek, "I know that face."

"I'm fine." He shook off the thought. "It's this case. I need your help."

She sat down beside him, taking his hand, and sighed as she gazed out toward Karbala.

"A year ago or more, we were walking into the market and you called my attention to a family who follow Jafar the Liar's son instead of the Imam. Do you know where they live?"

Her face changed, taking on a hard edge, but nothing anyone other than her children would notice. "What do you want with those Fatihis?"

"Their son has been killed. I recognized him. I need to tell them."

Shocked by the news, she said, "We belong to God and we must return to Him. May God forgive the boy." But then she put down her compassion and rushed to blame. "It is his parents' fault, raising him to follow a false Imam." She took a breath, and another. She was reconsidering her ill feelings, both felt and stated, and took her time. Offering what she could at the moment, she prayed, "May God guide them to the truth."

"Do you know their names?"

But then she wept, having come around to her good heart as he knew she would. "What if it had been you, my love? May God protect all parents from what they must be feeling." She paused, taking the rag she had tucked into her apron-wrap to wipe her eyes. "God give them ease. The father's name is Abu Bishr Dalal ibn Hasan. I saw them on Miller's Road once. Perhaps the boy is Bishr. They may have another son."

"Miller's Road," he repeated. "You don't gossip, Mother, but have you heard anything that might help me solve this case?"

"We don't know their people. They don't know ours." Her voice caught. "How did he die?"

Ammar hesitated to tell her, but went ahead. "He was shot twice, one arrow in the eye, the other his waterskin."

Her back stiffened, and she gripped his hand. "Were his arms cut?"

"Yes."

"Ya Rabb! What does it mean to be killed like Abbas?" Fear and confusion crept into her voice. "Was it a warning from God? If he was killed, martyred like Abbas, what does it mean?"

"Nothing like that," he said, to reassure her as much as himself. "I think it was probably intentional, but not a message from God, a message from a person. But I won't know until I find out who and why he was killed."

"I'm worried," she said, then took a breath as if to say more.

He did not answer, but waited for her to speak, turning her hand over in his. These hands had fed him, cared for him, and never once shown him harm. The last thing he wanted was for her to worry.

"Perhaps it is a message that we Shia are going to be under attack," she said. "We are already under so much pressure. The people will fight. The caliph's men will fight back. Whoever did this will escape while we suffer."

"I don't think it means that. Please don't worry." But he was afraid that was exactly what it meant.

"At least we Shia will fight together for our lives." She sighed, and continued haltingly, "If only the Imam would show himself. Why does he remain in hiding? Everyone would see the light of Prophet, the blessed family, in his eyes." Her voice was tinged with confusion and guilt for saying it. "Who would dare commit any crime if they could see his face!"

"I understand." He squeezed her hand. "But it's not safe. How many of our Imams did the caliphs hold captive? How many of them did they poison? If Imam Muhammad Hasan had not disappeared as a child, he would not have survived."

"But the Imam is no threat! We only want his guidance. To see his face," she pleaded with him, as if he could change things.

"These caliphs have never trusted our Imams in the past. Why would they trust him?" He tensed with frustration. "Even with Shia viziers in power, there is no trust. The Imam's agents are so careful that only the most senior one among them knows where he lives. They even hide the tithe and letters to be picked up and delivered in secret so no one can follow and give away his whereabouts. The caliph's spies are everywhere."

"I do not doubt him. I only long for him, habibi."

"Of course, Mother." He raised the back of her hand to his lips and then to his forehead. "You are devoted, an honourable woman."

"There are so few of us now." She drew her hand back and glanced quickly at the house, where his father lay sleeping the day away. "So many have abandoned the Twelfth Imam for these false Imams or the path of the Imamate all together."

"You have his guidance, you carry it with you always. Mother, I'll solve this case. Nothing will happen to you."

"Or to all of us? Do nothing that would hurt us, habibi. The caliph will find any excuse."

"I'll be careful." But in any investigation, no matter who was guilty or why, secrets and weaknesses were inevitably exposed, destroying families, sometimes whole communities. Finding out who killed this young man and why might put them all in the caliph's line of sight.

"It's better to let it go." She gripped his arm.

"I'll be careful," he repeated.

Her voice became desperate. "You do not want the ire of God, the Prophet, and his blessed family on you for this? For what? To know who killed a man?" She stood, letting go of him. "The boy is dead. What good will it do to know who did it and why?"

"But if I cover it up, it will be worse. The Shia of Baghdad and Buratha will soon hear how he was killed. It has to come out, if it hasn't already. Which one of us would not see it as an attack on us as a community and want it avenged?"

She replied in a voice he was unused to, "Ask yourself whose side you are on, this caliphate you work for, or ours?"

Hearing his own question from his mother's lips stung, but gave him his answer. The only way out of this, for his people, for Baghdad, was to solve the crime. There was still a way to do what was right on this job and this case proved it. He stood. "Mother?"

"Yes, habibi?"

"I'll keep you safe. I promise. But I can't stay. I have to tell his parents."

"Of course. I'll see you and my sweet Bilal on Friday." Her voice held none of the hope or tenderness in her voice that too often accompanied a hint of marriage. "I'll have something special for you. It will be a surprise."

That could only mean that this Nasifa and her family would be at lunch this Friday. He placed his hand on his heart and left her standing in her outdoor kitchen, chopping herbs for the pot and fearing for their future.

Out the gate, Ammar turned toward the centre of Buratha. He

knew Miller's Road cut through the centre of the city, leading out to grain mills beyond the marketplace, but he was not familiar with the streets in those neighbourhoods any longer. He had known every bit of this town as a boy. Built up by the merchant classes at its centre and edged by small herders and farmers like his parents, he had run through these streets and alleys every chance he got, looking for trouble, adventure, anything other than tending goats. But a lot had changed. New alleys had taken shape as the poor crowded in, building one-room houses out of sun-dried brick that leaned on others for support, just like in the poorest sections of Karkh.

At Miller's Road, he asked a group of men carrying sacks on their backs where he could find the victim's father. All but one man walked on without a word. The remaining man considered whether he should answer, then pointed to an alley not far off, saying to keep going until he saw a blue wooden door on the corner, and turn there.

The alley was so narrow that Ammar's broad shoulders nearly touched each side. Oncoming passersby took one look at his police turban and stood their ground. Not one of them let him pass. His first impulse was to put his hand on the hilt of his sword, but a wave of exhaustion rolled through him, taking the impulse in its wake, and he flattened himself against the wall. One after another sniggered or made comments under their breath as they passed him. Then he could not find the cursed blue-doored house on a corner.

A large man came around from another alley ahead of him. Ammar sighed aloud in frustration. One of them would have to go back and tuck into an alcove; he turned around to go, then heard the booming voice of the man. "Police! Come ahead, I'll back up."

He saluted the offer.

"I spend all day backing up around corners here!"

As he approached, he said, "You are kind to do so. Sir, where does Abu Bishr Dalal ibn Hasan live?"

His smile fell. "God have mercy on Bishr's soul. We belong to God and are returning to Him. Are you going there because of his death?"

The victim was Bishr, and word of the murder was already out. He would need to get ahead of the news before people started coming up with ideas about who had done it themselves and how they would get their revenge. He would not be informing the family, but maybe he would get the answers he needed. "I am. I am the investigating detective. Grave Crimes."

"Let me take you there, it's behind you. You've passed it."

Ammar grunted and shook his head.

"Been wandering in this warren long?"

"Yes." Ammar moved past the corner so the man could get into the alley and lead him. He turned down an even narrower alley to another corner, and there was the blue door. The labourer had given him the right directions after all, with just a few details to lead him astray. Two houses further down and they were there.

Three young men and a boy stood outside the home, one weeping. Ammar thanked the man, who bowed his head and left. The four stared at him, recognizing him as police, but none stepped forward to greet him. Instead, they moved to block the door to the family home; the boy posturing like a little man.

"Baghdad Police. I'm here to find out who killed Bishr."

The young men reconsidered after a moment and stood aside, pulling the boy with them. He approached the door. They had woven reeds together and tied them off so that it was as stiff as wood. Still better than cloth, which was more typical, but it would still offer little protection from wintry winds. He wondered about the house with the solid wood blue door and the jealousy it must inspire.

Soft wailing came from within. He called out, "Assalamu alaykum, I am Ammar at-Tabbani from Baghdad Grave Crimes Section. I am here about your son. May God have mercy on his soul."

A boy with eyes swollen from weeping opened the door and stepped into the alley, forcing Ammar back.

"May God forgive me for intruding," he said to the boy. "I am the detective investigating Bishr's death. Is Abu Bishr here?"

The boy stared at Ammar and called out, "Baba!" Ammar looked past him into the room. The father came out into the alley with him. Grief had torn up Abu Bishr's sun-ravaged face so that Ammar could not tell if the man would fall into his arms or strike him.

A young scholar followed the father out, one hand on his shoulder. The scholar was physically imposing, having the neck and shoulders of a wrestler, not to mention the swollen ears, and a flattened nose from one too many blows to the face. A wrestler and brawler turned scholar, trying to lift himself up with a foppishly trimmed beard and fine clothes. Nothing like the father's over-mended robe and frayed qamis and sirwal. Strange, too, was that he wore the turban of an Imami scholar, not a follower of Jafar the Liar, like the family. The man was out of place.

Both waited for Ammar to speak.

"May God have mercy on your son's soul," Ammar said. "I am the investigating detective. I am sorry to intrude, but I have a few questions."

The father opened his mouth to speak, but the scholar cut him off. "The family is grieving, sir. Can we not leave this to another time?"

"I only have a few questions. It's important that we investigate the crime immediately. Waiting might mean we never find the killer."

Abu Bishr whispered, "Ask."

The scholar squeezed the father's shoulder. "I am here."

The familiar gesture bothered Ammar. It made no sense that an Imami scholar would have such a sense of propriety over a family of Fatihis. He asked the scholar, "How do you know the family?"

"I grew up here, in the home with the blue door. You may have noticed it. This man is as good as my father. Bishr's mother is as good as my mother. Bishr is," he hesitated, "was, God have mercy on his soul, as good as my brother. I came to them as soon as the news reached me."

He guessed that explained the scholar's presence, but he did not like it. Ammar addressed the father. "Your son was killed near the Cemetery of the Martyrs. Why he was there?"

The father took a breath and was about to speak when the scholar interrupted again. "He would go to share his troubles with Imam Musa, alayhi as-salam. We would go together sometimes."

That propriety over the family again. "I appreciate you wanting to help, but I need to hear from his father."

The scholar's back stiffened visibly. "The man is grieving."

"Yes." Ammar kept his eyes on the father and put his hand over his heart in a gesture of conciliation. "I am sorry, but I need to ask. What might have been bothering your son? Why he might have gone to the Imam's grave?"

Abu Bishr wiped his face and said, his voice gaining sudden clarity, "There was a girl he wanted to marry, but their family denied him." He paused. "We denied him, too."

Ammar jumped at the possibility the murder may have been a private matter, easily solved and saving them from the violence that could follow. "Did her family threaten your son? I assume no one had introduced them properly or there'd have been no opportunity to object."

"She was the sister of one of his friends. Went everywhere with her brother. Had we known, we would have tried to stop them. We told him we'd never accept her as soon as we found out. So did they. Her parents are Hanbalis, her father one of Barbahari's men."

His chest tightened, but he did not react at the mention of the name Barbahari, an extremist Hanbali who took it upon himself to police the morals of the people of Baghdad, and who was no friend to the Shia. This might be it. "What was a Hanbali boy of that sort doing with Shia friends?"

The father's grief quickly turned to anger. "The father killed him!"

"Did he threaten your son?" Ammar asked evenly.

"He came here once with his people." Abu Bishr replied, still hot. "Told Bishr to leave the girl alone. We told them we'd never let our son marry one of their girls. Barbahari's men aren't like our neighbours. These are good people. We may disagree. We may fight. But we are still neighbours. These Hanbalis, no one is good enough for them, no one is Muslim but them. I told him what I thought of them. They left, satisfied."

"Do you think the two continued to see each other?"

"Bishr told me the brother came by once more without his sister and said he'd not come back. That was that." He sounded sure of it.

But the scholar discreetly shook his head over the father's shoulder.

Ammar nodded slightly, indicating he had seen, wondering what sort of game he was playing, protecting the father and now secretly disagreeing. But more than that, he wondered at a Hanbali son continuing to see his Shia friends, despite his family's disapproval, and thought the girl had not given up either.

Barbahari's crew had a cruel imagination when they sought justice. It would not be beyond them to kill Bishr like Abbas. In fact, such an elaborate gesture would be exactly like them. He burned at what they had done in the past, and his own unwitting complicity in it. His sword hand twitched at the thought that some of the same men might be responsible here and he would be able to set things right, finally.

"I know you," the father said. "Ghazi Ammar at-Tabbani?"

"Yes."

"You do your family proud. You fought on the frontier."

"Thank you, sir."

The man's voice turned bitter out of nowhere. "But now you serve the caliph, oppressing your own people?"

Bitterness toward Barbahari's men was still in his throat and he retorted without thinking, "Am I oppressing you by finding the killer of your son?" Hearing himself, he gasped, took a step back, and put his head down in apology for his inability to control his response.

"We'll see," Abu Bishr replied.

Ammar did not reply. The man was owed the last word. Then he asked the scholar, "Did you know any of his other friends?"

The scholar's neck flushed red. "No."

Ammar pressed, "You said, Bishr was like a brother to you."

"Well," he stammered, "I mean to say, well, there was a time where I saw him with a group of young men and tried to call him over, but he waved me off."

"What about the name of the girl? Her family?"

The father muttered, "Aisha, if you can believe it."

The girl was named after Muhammad's youngest wife, who was willing to do anything to stop Imam Ali from becoming caliph after the Prophet died, including calling men to kill and be killed in battle for her cause. "And the father?"

The scholar stepped in, "Abu az-Zubayr Umar ibn Abdulghani."

Ammar held back a laugh. As if "Aisha" were not bad enough. Umar? The father was named after the caliph, whose actions, as far as his people were concerned, led to the death of Lady Fatima, the Prophet's daughter and Ali's wife. And az-Zubayr? His son was named after a man who fought at Aisha's prodding at that bloody battle. He asked, "So is az-Zubayr the name of Bishr's friend?"

"No, that's the younger brother. Bishr's friend is named Talha."

"The entire family is named after those who fought Ali at the Battle of the Camel!"

"A marriage would be quite impossible," the scholar added.

Ammar eyed him suspiciously. "You know a lot about his friends for someone who was waved off."

Taking hold of his robe, the scholar tucked his head back in offence. "I am only repeating what the family has told me!"

"Where's my son's body?" The father broke through in the same tone he had used when accusing Ammar of betraying the Shia community.

"He is on his way to the corpse washers next to the mosque. You should have him by midday." Then to the scholar, "We may need to speak to you again. I didn't catch your name."

"Aqil ibn Akib ibn Sadruddin ibn al-Hasan ibn al-Habib al-Burathi. While my family's home was just there," he said, gesturing pretentiously toward the blue door as he reported his lineage, "my wife, children, and I needed more space and have moved. You can most easily find me in Dar as-Silsila studying among the theologians there. It is becoming a veritable little Qum, a bastion for us Imami scholars."

6

Zaytuna barely greeted Ziri as he answered the door, pushing past him straight into the courtyard at her Uncle Junayd's. Her only thought was to find Auntie Hakima and tell the old woman about her dream. She stopped short only when those seated in clusters nearby turned to stare at her rushed entrance. Pulling her wrap over her face, she bowed her head in apology and retraced her steps into the main reception hall. She wanted to crawl into the space beneath the stairs where seekers had been sitting in contemplation since Abu al-Qasim al-Junayd opened the doors of his home to the mystics of Baghdad. No one was there, but she could not enter without permission. As a child, she was free to hide in it and even pretend to sit in prayerful remembrance, but not now. And certainly not to escape the embarrassment of letting her fear drive her so rudely through the door and into the courtyard. She stood for a moment, trying to collect herself.

When she approached the courtyard again, no one glanced in her direction, as she knew they would not, preserving her from further embarrassment. Those chatting or waiting to see the great mystic and teacher, Junayd, had gathered in small circles in the shade under the balcony or along the wall where the sun had not yet hit. It was still early, but the heat was already upon them. Junayd sat on sheepskins against the wall. As always, he dressed simply; his turban was never too long or grandly wound, and he was giving all his attention to those before him. He was a slight man, unlike Uncle Nuri, who towered over everyone but their mother, and then Tein and Zaytuna when they grew up. But Junayd held the room. He was a man of great beauty and majesty. She turned from him to search for her Uncle Nuri, despite it being several months since his passing, and endured a pang of loss at not being able to rely on his tender care anymore.

Auntie Hakima was not in her regular place near the kitchen at the rear of the courtyard, either. The sun was shining there, though. Perhaps she was inside where it was cooler. Zaytuna retreated into the main reception area again, this time hoping to find her teacher in the small side rooms where women could perform their ablutions out of sight of the men. As she came around the corner, though, no one was sitting at the bench where women waited their turn. She stuck her head into the ablution room and there was YingYue, on her knees, back to her, cleaning the basin set into the brick-lined floor. Zaytuna stopped short with a quick intake of breath, and backed away, step-by-step in silence, not breathing easily again until she was in the courtyard. She had to find Auntie Hakima before YingYue came out.

Auntie Hakima, where are you?

She did not know when she was a child that these people who took them in as family were the greatest mystics of Baghdad. All the children in the community played among them, learned to read and write from them, and were guided by them. But the care and stability they gave to her and her brother, Tein, was not a thing either of them could measure.

Their mother's ecstasy was a wild, uncontrollable thing. Wherever the ecstasy overwhelmed her, that was where she shared her teaching with strangers. In the streets or the graveyards, Zaytuna would hold on tight and hide her face against her mother's belly, while her mother, in God's grasp, would let go of her in the sea of people, lifting her arms to the heavens and reciting her poetry of dissolution in God's love. Tein, just a boy, would circle the crowd, always watching for anyone who might harm them out of fear of her power or a crushing desire to know God for themselves.

Their mother's love for them was fierce, but it was the kind of love borne from loving what God loved for her, not what she loved for herself. And so, the mystics of Baghdad had become her family. Mustafa's mother, another mother to her. Uncle Nuri, a father. And Auntie Hakima. How many times had she retreated into the old woman's arms? But now she was nowhere to be found.

Abdulghafur came in through the rear courtyard door near the kitchen, and, catching sight of her, bowed deeply, his hand over his heart. Any other day, she would have beamed at the young man, so happy in his place, but today she was grim. Such an innocent face. *If this end is coming, what will happen to him? What will happen to us all?* She steeled herself. The Mahdi had come for her. She would be strong. She would fight. Maybe she should talk to her uncle, since her aunt was not here. Then she doubted herself. He would only tell her to go to YingYue. She took several aimless steps and checked to see if YingYue had come out yet and considered leaving instead.

Zaytuna had come to accept that despite her youth, YingYue was the spiritual prodigy all had claimed her to be. Her father had left their family behind in Taraz to find his young daughter a teacher, first traveling to Marw where Abu Bakr al-Wasiti taught her until he had taken her as far as he could, then he directed her to his own teacher, Junayd, in Baghdad. Soon, Junayd had put her in charge of the novice women, including Zaytuna. Despite a harsh regimen of fasting and praying since childhood, Zaytuna had not entered onto the Sufi path until four months ago. At twenty-eight, she was ten years older than YingYue, but younger than her on the path by as many years, if not more. Worse, YingYue was not only spiritually accomplished but also beautiful and gracious. Now she had Mustafa's love.

There were good days and bad days since Zaytuna had entered the path, but it was as if the whole of it for the first couple of months was struggling with her jealousy and resentment toward YingYue.

The feelings came and went until she thought she had got them behind her, until they would sneak up on her again.

One day she had come up behind Mustafa and YingYue walking alone together in the street, discreetly leaning into each other, their fingers just touching. Grief pulled her by the gut into a nearby doorway where her open sobs called an old woman she did not even know to come and embrace her. It was a day of heartrending clarity. She would never be Mustafa's wife. The old woman held her until she found her ground again. She let go of him, this time, she thought, for good. But with last night's dream, that firm ground had turned into mud, sucking her down to her knees.

Maybe Ziri would know how she could find Auntie Hakima. If the old woman was gone, she would leave. Returning to the main reception hall, she found Ziri standing by his post near the door, ready to open it at the first knock. Hand over her heart, she apologized for her earlier behaviour. "Forgive me for rushing by you before. I was upset."

"I didn't notice, sister," he responded. "What can I do for you?"

"I need to speak to Auntie Hakima. Have you seen her?"

"She's gone to see her sister in Basra."

"Oh." Her muscles twisted in pain and the tingling in her legs returned. Instead of going to the door and out into the street, she returned to the courtyard. Guiding herself along the wall with one hand as her eyesight narrowed in panic, she found a free spot in the sun. She lowered herself carefully, restraining a moan as she watched her uncle speaking with seekers across the courtyard, and silently begged him to help her. Her wrap fell over her face, and she hid behind it, trying to breathe through the terror of the world's end and the misery of losing Mustafa, again.

The numbness in her legs had only receded when she saw the shadow of a man through her wrap. "Assalamu alaykum."

Reluctantly, she pulled her wrap away from her eyes. A young man with skin as rough and brown as his woollen robe and scrap of turban on his head stood before her. He had kohled his dark eyes. They glistened with such beauty and kindness that she wanted to reach out and take his hand. Instead, she touched her own burning cheek.

He turned away, saying in a hush, "Shaykh Junayd asked for you."

Zaytuna pulled her wrap over her face again, pleading with herself. *What is happening to me?* Wanting to run for the door, she forced herself to stay put. Breathing through the panic, she could not find the rhythm, leaving her panting and dizzy. Then the calming waters reached her, softening the edges of her fear, and she heard a voice within herself whisper, *There is no god but God.* She stretched towards the voice until she echoed it and her breath paced the words and the meaning loosened the knots of her body and soul and freed her. She rolled to her side to get up, putting a hand on the wall, worried that she would hurt her back again as she stood.

"Zaytuna, sister, are you in pain?" Abu Muhammad al-Juwayri was before her, holding out his hand.

"No!" She jerked back, fearing what would happen if he touched her.

He watched her with concern and stood to the side in case she needed help. How many times had he previously had to comfort her in states like this in order to bring her back to some decorum? She did not know how to tell him she did not trust her own body. He turned to lead, and she followed him, keeping a few steps behind, protecting herself from the possibility that her body might want him, too.

Her uncle, and now guide, Shaykh Abu al-Qasim al-Junayd, watched her approach with loving eyes. But the others whom she saw had been waiting before were still there. Because she could not control her emotions, these people whom she did not even recognize, some not even Baghdadis who had likely traveled great distances to sit with him, were being made to wait. She put her hand over her heart to beg their forgiveness, but they did not see her.

Abu Muhammad sat down beside Junayd. She made herself kneel without visible emotion before her shaykh until she realized she would have to take his hand and became afraid at what she might feel, even for him. Lowering her gaze, just in case, she took his hand

and brought it to her lips to kiss. As was the custom, he pulled it away before she could do so. But instead of desire, the touch of his hand sent the calm of divine waters through her. The sheepskin and reed mat underneath her softened to hold her, and what was left of the pain in her back and hips washed away.

"Assalamu alaykum, my daughter," he said softly. "You've had a dream."

She lowered her eyes to the sheepskin, as she always did in these moments, observing the curl of the worn and packed wool from so many seated there every day before him.

"When my companions have such a dream, I am informed."

She looked up. He knew. Her back and hips spasmed.

But then he said, "Tell me." His voice was even, not betraying anything. Perhaps he did not know what had happened, only that there had been a dream?

She replied haltingly at first, "There was rain, a storm, the roof came in, then waves overtook me." Her breath quickened with fear. "There was so much rain that I thought I would drown from it. The rain stopped and waves came. They were higher than the walls of the Round City."

"Did you check the condition of your roof? Did it rain last night?"

His joke broke the tension, and the calming waters reached her again.

"Were the waves coming from one direction or did they surround you?"

"They surrounded me, then the waves came together in a dome overhead, instead of crashing and drowning me."

"Yes?"

"Drops of water, like glittering light, fell from the dome, and it disappeared. I saw an army coming towards me as the sun rose on the horizon." She paused, wondering if he would believe the rest. "A man and a woman were leading an army. They were Lady Fatima and the Mahdi. Fatima carried a tablet in her arms, but I couldn't read what was on it. The Mahdi told me that the world was ending. He held a dead man in his arms. The man was injured as Abbas was at Karbala."

"Is that all?" He said it as if he had heard a dream warning of the coming of the end of the world a thousand times before.

"A man carried coins in a leather sack used to churn butter."

"Anything else?"

She pulled back, unwilling to tell him the rest, and lied, "No."

"What do you want to know about the dream?"

"Is the world ending, shaykh?" Her voice trembled.

"What does it mean for the world to end?" he asked, holding her attention with his eyes and words as if he held her in his arms like a child. "Where were you before creation on the Day of the Covenant when God held the future children of Adam in His hands, the blessed in His right, and the wretched in His left, and asked, 'Am I not your Lord?' Where were you before God placed you in your mother's womb? What world was your mother's womb to you? Where are you when you fall into ecstasy and this world falls away? Where are you when you return? There is always one world ending and another beginning."

She did not understand. *The world is ending, but existence is one world ending after another, so there is nothing to fear?* But these worlds were not the same, and she blurted out, "Being born does not require you to lose everyone you love on the battlefield of good and evil."

He raised his eyebrows. "Has that been your experience?"

The question silenced her. She had been born onto such a battlefield.

"Daughter," he said, his voice softening, "the world is always ending. In my lifetime and the lifetime of my father, so many men have claimed to be the Mahdi, each one declaring the end. Only God knows when the Mahdi will be born or his identity. This dream is about you. Your world is ending," he gestured to the courtyard and to all that lay beyond it, "not ours."

Sinking in shame, she wished she could pull the sheepskin over her head and scolded herself. *See how you drove yourself into a panic!*

When he spoke again, his words arrived in that uncanny tonal frequency that pulled her attention to him and away from her swirling thoughts. "Look at me."

She raised her head unwillingly.

"There are three stages to the path so that you may live in a new world. In that new world, God will be present to you so that you will know the truth of the verse from the Qur'an, *Wherever you turn, there is the face of God.*"

She nodded slowly, captured by his voice, but not comprehending, and prayed that some part of her soul would understand.

"On the first stage on the path you recognize that you have been following your own desires, making gods of your sadness, anger, and desire and following them wherever they lead. When you see it and answer the call, it is the ending of one world."

"That is when I came to you."

"Yes, you became a companion on our path. This world of the soul that takes itself to task. It is the beginning of the end of your old world in which followed your capricious soul without question. The soul who loved its pain more than God. It never wanted what was best for you. To bring it under control, I asked you to do the opposite of what it demands. This is the world through which you have been journeying so far and which you will carry with you as you enter the boundaries of each world ahead. No matter how far we journey, we always need to watch our lower soul."

"Even you?"

"All of us."

"I've been following your instruction, but trying and too often failing."

"You will always fail. Each failure shows you where attention should be given to your lower soul. As long as you keep taking your lower soul to task, you are always coming closer to the next world. And you have."

"Alhamdulillah," she whispered, allowing herself to feel some hope.

"You are approaching the second stage of the path. This is the world of dreams and inspiration. Here you will let go of the pleasure you have taken in giving up the impulses of the lower soul."

Pleasure? She forgot herself and sat up at the thought of it, her back complaining along with her. The second stage of the path had been nothing but a struggle. She had taken no pleasure in it. "I don't understand," she protested. "It has been hard." Stumbling, she wanted to take the words back lest he think it had been too hard and she was not worthy and would give up on her. "I mean, I can do it. But there's been no pleasure in it."

"Zaytuna, stop now and listen." He did not raise his voice, but she felt the sting of the slap he meant it to be. "You had such a dream, yet you indulge in these moods? If you wish to be worthy of it, stop."

She shut her mouth, wanting to say more, and made herself listen.

"Pleasure, even ecstasy, arises from giving up your lowest desires and worshipping God. As you free yourself from the old world, you feel the release into the new. But you also have been struggling by dint of your own will."

"But what else could I do?"

"That was appropriate in the beginning. But as you take yourself to task, you begin to worship God by God's will alone. As a result, you taste knowledge of the unseen. Dreams, such as this one, become more common. You will sense that which is not sensible. You may sense the truth when someone lies to you. You may know if someone you love is safe or in danger."

"But, Shaykh, even at this second stage, I, I fell into ecstasy. That can't be from my will." She stammered, thinking of moments in which she was lost to herself, and she found herself speaking in a voice about God unfamiliar to her. "I don't remember myself in it."

"One is given tastes of the various stages before having earned them. God may even give them to you to draw you onto the path or to encourage you in the beginning. There is always a kind of madness of love at the start. Sometimes these early experiences bring the risk of losing one's way, though." He added, his tone shifting as a warning, "People have misunderstood and believed that sanctity has been conferred upon them before they have even submitted to God."

Her head dropped, knowing she had secretly wondered if these moments meant she had a touch of her mother's sanctity and she felt closer to her through them than she had even as a child, when she was alive.

"But there is another matter, Zaytuna, my daughter." He leaned forward. "You have been worshipping God to come nearer to your mother."

She said what her mother would want her to say, but it felt like too much to ask of her. "I must come for God's sake alone."

"There is a further risk, Zaytuna. As these experiences become more common, you will not always know the source of what you are sensing. It may be from God, the angels, your own soul's hidden desires, or even the devil. As you progress on the path, the danger increases. Even if what you are sensing, or what you have dreamed, comes from God or the angels, you may misread it and lead yourself astray. Even if you do not misread it, there are those who remain in this stage, enjoying its experiences, and give up seeking God for God's sake. If you want to find the firm ground of this second stage that allows you to approach the third, do not fall into this trap."

Fear for herself replaced the relief of knowing that the world around her was not ending. Her own world was ending. The fear that she would not find the courage to fight for the Mahdi if called, was nothing in the face of being called to be a warrior on the battlefield of her own soul. Failure spread out before her. She took a deep breath and shook it off, telling herself, *Stop. You can do this. You've made it this far.*

Junayd, her uncle, her guide, gave her an encouraging smile. "My daughter, let me tell you about the fourth stage."

"Please, Uncle...I mean, Shaykh."

"The fourth stage of the path is the beginning of the end of the multitudes of worlds of consciousness you have experienced. As you lose yourself in ecstasy, little by little, giving over your will for God's will, God has victory upon victory over you. Only then you may enter the stages of victory, in which you, as a world, end, and your soul comes to be at peace with God."

As she listened to the promise of that world, he raised his head, noticing someone walking into the courtyard. She followed his gaze and saw YingYue. Her hand was over her heart, her head gracefully bowed in greeting to him.

Everything the shaykh had said to her fell away as she watched the young Chinese woman approach. Zaytuna sighed in frustration, losing her determination not to be swayed by her emotions.

YingYue was petite and softly featured, where Zaytuna was tall and all hard angles. YingYue had braided her long dark brown hair into a multitude of thin strands tied off with coloured yarn, covered only by an embroidered Turkmen cap and the drape of her wrap. Zaytuna had wound up her straight black hair, with its one matted strand, through which she threaded one of her mother's beads, into a faded red scarf that reminded her of her mother. YingYue's wrap was made of delicate cotton, rich in patterns of flowers she had never seen before, in different shades of pale pink and green on a cream background, each colour setting off the pink of her round cheeks. Even Zaytuna's good wrap was worn, the plain stripes faded to nothing and the embroidered edge frayed.

Of course, she thought, her heart sinking with the bare truth of it. *Of course Mustafa loves her.*

As her sorrow took hold of her, she forgot everything Junayd had just said to her, and told herself that the dream was visionary, as he said, but that its meaning was to taunt her with the truth. She still loved Mustafa and could be a wife to him. But also that it would be impossible. *Your world is ending.*

Junayd turned to Zaytuna. "YingYue is here. You can ask her for clarification."

She balked inwardly.

"Tell her, so she can explain what I said," he insisted. "Especially, ask about the risks of this stage on the path, misreading the signs, so that you are better able to judge your experiences as they arise."

As she reached out to kiss his hand goodbye, he stopped her.

"Zaytuna, dreams like the one you had may have a part about which you may be embarrassed. You may experience divine ecstasy in such dreams. But the body interprets divine ecstasy in the only language it knows. There is no reason to be ashamed if it did, and forgive me for mentioning it, if it did not. But if it did, do not think more of it."

She let go of his hand abruptly and stood. That was that. What she had experienced with Mustafa in the dream meant nothing. Something she felt she could never know with a man was only her body's capacity for the language of God's love. It pulled her heart in two directions. Relief at his words, as if a tree had spread its leaves over her, cooling her as she lay underneath it. She was still herself. But as she lay under that tree, it was as if its roots came up and wound around her neck, choking her. She was still herself. Unwanted, incapable, unloved. Her eyes pricked with tears as she fell back into her reliable state of sorrow, her back and hips screaming in pain.

Junayd waved over YingYue, who came up behind her and, seeing she needed help, put her hand on her elbow. It somehow felt fitting, and Zaytuna allowed it. She said, choking out the words, "Uncle said I must tell you about my dream."

YingYue tucked her hand through Zaytuna's arm. "Tell me your dream and tell me what he said."

She would, but not everything.

As they walked to find a shady spot to talk, YingYue leaned into her, whispering, "My father has given Mustafa and I permission to marry. It took Shaykh Abu al-Qasim so long to convince him. But we can complete our marriage contract." She pressed her hand against Zaytuna's arm. "I did not want you to hear it from anyone else first."

DAY TWO

7

For once, Tein was in the office before Ammar and he lay down on one of the long low couches that edged the room. Drifting in and out of a half-sleep, he thought he heard light footsteps behind him, but his body was too heavy to turn. Warmth enveloped him, and he felt, more than heard, a voice humming in his ear. "You'll marry her, yet. Do not despair, my son."

Recognizing the voice, he sat up with a start. "Uncle Nuri?"

Ammar leaned in the doorway, facing the centre of the Round City, watching passersby come and go from the police and military offices or further on, from the city's mosque and gardens. "No, it's me. Late night?"

Tein swung his legs around and rubbed his eyes. "Dream. It's nothing." It was not nothing. Longing for his uncle clung to him, but it was laid over with gratitude that he could still pull the old man's voice from deep within himself to say what he needed to hear. Standing, he went to the corner of the room, where they kept their water jug. It was empty. "I'll go fill this." He checked the light outside. "What time is it?"

"Mid-morning. Leave the jug. We're heading out."

"That late? Where were you?"

"I had to go find Ubaydallah."

"Ibn Marwan okayed you looking into Barbahari again?"

"If Ubaydallah informs on Barbahari and his men for the offices of Public Good, why can't he share what he's got with us?"

"Can't let him go? Or is this related to a case?"

"I saw our victim's family yesterday. The victim's name is Bishr. It seems he was secretly involved with the daughter of one of Barbahari's men and finally went to the father."

"Now he's dead."

"Barbahari's men are obsessed enough to stage a killing with a message telling Shia men not to mess with their women. Our people killed Abbas, we'll kill you, too."

With this explanation, Tein had to admit the possibility that the placement of the shots might not be a coincidence, but intended by a human being, and was relieved. The case was turning down a road that no longer seemed like Ammar would force supernatural interpretations on natural events and raise old tensions between them. "What did Ubaydallah say?"

"That the girl's father is a brutal man. They suspect he organized several raids on neighbourhoods north of here. He and his men have kicked down gates, beaten up guards, smashed wine jars in the estates, even dragged men and women into the street. They almost killed an old man for adultery and flogged his wife in front of him saying she was his mistress."

"Who is handling those cases?"

"Public Good. They're rounding up who they can. But it's never anyone important. Ubaydallah told me that Barbahari recruits poor young men who don't want to work. He throws them some money and gives them a way to prove themselves in the world. The recruits do the work and the recruits are the ones arrested and the recruits are the ones who suffer while their bosses go untouched."

"We were the same," Tein said bitterly. "Killing for the empire to feed the caliph's greed." He slapped his thigh, running his hand along the length of it, and stood. "Our shooter doesn't fit that profile. That bow."

"A rich layabout, tired of his family's wealth and corrupt ways, might. He's become a true believer?"

Tein nodded, but was not sure he agreed.

An errand boy appeared. "Ibn Marwan wants you. Now."

Without moving from the doorway, Ammar grabbed the boy by his short robe. "No 'assalamu alaykum'? No respect?"

The boy held firm, smirking as he said, "Assalamu alaykum."

Ammar let go of him, and he sauntered away.

Tein remarked, "Come on, you were like that. You had no respect for anyone and would back down from nothing."

"Never." Ammar cracked, as he pushed off the doorway and gestured for Tein to follow him down the arcade.

They passed by several open doors until they reached Ibn Marwan's outer office. Tein turned his hand up at Nuruddin, gesturing, "What is it?" But the office assistant gave nothing away and waved them past into Ibn Marwan's office, garnering the ire of those already waiting.

The sergeant sat stiffly on a low couch, frowning. His desk, always in front of him, was moved to one side. Ammar gave Tein a look, telling him to watch himself, irritating him as if he did not know how to read their sergeant or hold himself.

But Ibn Marwan had always controlled his temper, no matter what went wrong. Their sergeant was a master at juggling bureaucratic demands on the office. The man had backed them even when viziers got involved, demanding a case go a different way than the facts required. He had protected Ammar when he did not deserve protecting. Tein hated himself more and more on this job, but if he stayed it was only because he could count on Ibn Marwan to safeguard their independence.

Ammar seemed hesitant as he walked in, but took his regular spot on the low couch along the wall next to Ibn Marwan's own. Tein followed him and sat nearer to the door.

Ibn Marwan started in full bore before Tein hit the couch. He was not tense. He was angry. "What are you going to do about these rumours? The murder is a sign of end times! The Mahdi will now reveal himself! Again!" He threw his hands up. "How many mahdis have staked their claim? How many caliphs styled themselves so? Or this madman in the street, or that ecstatic? This Shia Imam or that one? How many times is the world going to end? We've had enough mahdis for the end of the world a thousand times over!"

Ammar stood. Tein watched, not understanding.

Ibn Marwan glared at Ammar. "Or it's a sign of a coming attack on the Shia! One of your Shia Imams will overthrow the caliphate!" His venomous sarcasm unlike anything Tein had ever heard from his mouth. "How many pretenders to the imamate are there now?" He stood himself and faced Ammar with his chest puffed out. "You tell me, which 'true imam' will it be? It doesn't matter who wins that pissing match," he taunted, "justice is to be restored to the people once a direct descendant of the Prophet's family leads the caliphate again."

"What are you talking about?" Tein demanded.

Ammar ignored him, addressing Ibn Marwan, his hands out, asking for calm, "With the body staged like Abbas rumours spread quickly."

Tein stared at Ammar. He had not said a word about any rumours. Suddenly, he had a sense of what was coming, and the meeting would not end well for any of them. Tein readied himself to walk out.

"There will be violence on the streets before long," Ibn Marwan replied.

Ammar tried to explain. "The murder *was* staged. But I don't think it's about Karbala or the Shia, at least not like that. Sir, we've only started our investigation. I've interviewed the family and I've got a good lead."

"No." Ibn Marwan wasn't listening, and sat back down.

"What do you mean?" Ammar objected.

Here it comes, thought Tein.

"There will not be an investigation. Too much is at stake. Blame it on a simple matter. A friend killed him over a woman. The shots were an ugly coincidence. Drink. Gambling. Arrest someone and shut it down."

"The lead I got..."

Ibn Marwan cut him off. "The Banu Furat and their men are breathing down my neck. There is no time. Those viziers know the risks more than you do, it seems. And here I thought you were the best investigators in Baghdad."

"We think he *was* killed over a woman."

"Do you know who?"

"We need to investigate." Ammar sat down hard in a way that implied he was digging in for the sake of the case, but Tein was still wary.

"That's where you are wrong. Find someone, anyone, now."

"We only need a few days."

"There is no time." Ibn Marwan placed his hands on his thighs to lean into his words. "It's a fragile peace with you people."

Ammar leaned in. "You people?"

"Your imams of the past may have agreed not to challenge the caliph's power, but not the others. Those other Shia imams and their factions are still making plans to overthrow the government. If this doesn't end quickly, the Shia viziers say the stability of the city, if not the empire, is at stake. All of you will pay, no matter what side you are on."

"The true imams have done what they can, but there are always different factions who want power. Should all the people suffer for them?"

"If you don't want your people to suffer, shut it down!"

"I haven't said I wouldn't." He sat back down.

"Good." Ibn Marwan's voice lowered, mollified momentarily.

Tein had been expecting it, but had hoped it would not come. Was Ammar really going to find another innocent to pin a murder on because he was afraid? There was always some threat looming over the caliphate. Some rebellion fomenting. What else was new? Was Ammar giving lip service, or did he mean to throw the case?

Tein was ready to get up and walk away when Ammar pleaded, "We can find out who did this and keep this chaos under control."

"Listen." Ibn Marwan's voice rose again. "It's your people, Shia viziers, who are demanding we handle it immediately. They know that their own people, you people, have been responsible for the worst unrest this caliphate has seen. Civil war, unrest, entire regions lost, cutting off our food supply, fighting in the streets of Baghdad. You can't get over Karbala! A tragedy, we agree, but move on! Now one of your imams has his eye on all of North Africa, calling himself the Mahdi, of course. Walla! The viziers are Shia and they know the Shia cannot be controlled."

Tein felt Ammar lose his temper before he said a word. He had fought alongside this man since they were boys. They became men together along the empire's frontier. Now they stood together as partners in the Grave Crimes Section. Tein positioned himself to be ready if needed, even though he did not like where it was going. There would be time to confront Ammar later.

Ammar stood again. His voice was calm, but dangerous, punctuating his words as if they were slaps from the side of his sword. "The old caliph al-Muntasir abandoned Baghdad like a coward, retreating to Samarra because of my people? If he had paid his expensive Turkmen soldiers what they demanded, would they have rioted and murdered Baghdadis to prove their point? 'My people' are not why the empire is fractured and outside the caliph's control. If the Abbasid caliphs had lived up to their claims to the Prophet's legacy, enacting the justice befitting the name, serving the people, rather than themselves, perhaps the people wouldn't have to fight in the streets over lost pay and food shortages!"

Ibn Marwan hit back from where he sat. "And the Zanj? That wild son of Imam Zayd was responsible for a slave rebellion!"

Tein bolted off the couch at the mention of the Zanj. Seething, he wanted to take Ibn Marwan by throat. As if the Zanj uprising were a Shia plot rather than the inevitable outcome of years of African men, women, and children enslaved in the harshest conditions and worked to the bone. He took one step toward him, then remembered his Uncle Nuri whispering in his ear when he was a boy, teaching him to control his anger. As the memory slipped away, he checked his stance, loosened his hands, and was halfway out of the room when Ammar countered, "Imam Zayd's son only opened the door for the Zanj. His generals were Zanji, his tacticians were Zanji, and the troops were Zanji."

Ibn Marwan bellowed at Tein's back. "Where's he going? Tein!"

Ammar kept talking, his voice rising, "Even the Zanj women threw bricks in battle! They were more like the warriors who fought alongside the Prophet than any army this caliphate has produced."

From outside Ibn Marwan's office door, Tein heard Ibn Marwan call for him again. "Tein!"

Ammar continued. "They did not take Basra and Wasit, and almost Baghdad itself because a Shia man gave them instructions!"

Nuruddin stared at Tein as he passed while those on the bench waiting sat in shock, listening. Ibn Marwan's last words came through to the outer office. "As the saying goes, the hungry Zanji steals, the sated Zanji rapes. It was no more than that."

Tein made it out the door and into the road. A breeze blew past him toward Solomon's Gates, leading out of the Round City. Tein decided, *This Zanji is done.*

He wondered if he should wait for Ammar or if he should keep walking. He leaned against the jamb of their office door, staring at the Gates in the distance, and waited, feeling like he owed Ammar a word at least. It had only been a moment before someone laid a hand on his shoulder and he reeled around, his left arm swinging through, ready to trap and break the arm of the man who had touched him.

"Hold on!" Ammar had seen it coming and had stepped out of his grasp, holding both hands up.

"I'm leaving." Tein did not apologize for nearly breaking his arm.

"Can you wait for me here?" Ammar pleaded. "I have to finish."

"Finish what? I'm done."

"You mean quit."

"Of course, I mean quit!"

"Okay, okay." He held his hands out again. "I told him the same thing. I told him if he doesn't watch himself that I'd leave and never come back."

"Why did I think he didn't have it in him?"

"I didn't want to hear it, either."

"It's more than not hearing it, Ammar. I'm done taking orders from a man who has that in him. As for the both of you, I'm not framing anyone."

"I told him I was going after you. We'll talk this out."

"There's nothing to talk out."

"Please, just wait here for me." He headed back to Ibn Marwan's office before Tein could say anything else.

Tein had no intention of waiting. He entered the office to retrieve his blue turban, the one he had worn undercover with Saliha when they first fell in love. Then it hit him like a brick. If he quit, he would have no way to support her. Taking off his black police turban, he slumped onto the couch at a loss for what to do. Every possible resolution was considered and tossed aside, leaving him more and more hopeless at the thought of compromising himself so totally for her love. Finally, he remembered his old friend. "Khalil." He said the name like a prayer.

He could work with Khalil collecting debts for the Amir. There was good money it, more than this job. But as quickly as the idea came, he realized it wouldn't work. She would never respect him if he got the coin he spent on her beating up gamblers who had got in over their heads. And he knew he would not respect himself. In the end, he would rather go back to sleeping in the graveyards, but as sure as this world was cursed, he would not ask her to sleep in the graveyards with him. He rooted around behind the couch and found the blue turban, and as he did, he hit his hand hard against the leg of the couch. "Damn it all!"

From outside the door, Ammar said his name. "Tein."

Tein stood, blue turban in hand, and faced him.

Ammar approached, his face drawn. "Ibn Marwan apologized. Well, as much as an apology as he can give right now."

"I care?"

"The situation in the caliphate is dangerous. Qarmati insurgents killed thousands along the hajj roads. They've got control of Bahrain. You know this. Who knows what they'll do next? The caliph and the viziers worry they'll raid the Kaaba itself."

"Raid the Kaaba? That's absurd."

"The real issue is that they want Baghdad. There are Qarmati sympathizers in the Buratha Mosque cursing the caliphs and Prophet's companions."

"So what? You Shia are always cursing the caliphs and companions."

"For God's sake, Tein, the Sunnis curse the Prophet's family."

On a different day, Tein would have laughed at Ammar's comment with a shake of the head because it was true. Sunni and Shia alike were easy with their curses and damning each other to hell. He had heard Sunnis curse Ali and Hasan for not giving up their claim to the caliphate to Muawiya, then curse Husayn in turn for not bowing before the Muawiya's son, Yazid. The Shia cursed Muawiya for demanding it of Ali and denying Hasan and Husayn the same. He had heard it all. But there was nothing to laugh about today.

Tein pressed, "You didn't tell me there were rumours in Shia community about the murder."

"I lied. I haven't heard a thing, but I didn't want him to know. I don't know what the Banu Furat are hearing. Viziers have their spies, but when I saw the family, no one mentioned any rumours. For them, it was all about the girl."

"Go back and insist you are right."

"It doesn't matter if I'm right. Ibn Furat is worried the Qarmatis will use the murder to incite the Shia to protest and then they'll step in and turn it into a rebellion. You heard Ibn Marwan, there are a lot of ways this could blow. The vizier is trying to stop any protest before it starts. One public complaint about this murder and the military will step in. It'll start in Buratha, then spread to Karkh."

The fact of it cut through his anger. Tein's voice was flat. "Everyone is at risk. Your family. Mine. All the people."

Ammar spoke into the momentary breach. "Ibn Furat is afraid if trouble starts, the caliph will destroy the mosque in Buratha first, then let his army loose on the people."

Tein asked in frustration, "Would the Qarmatis find sympathizers?"

"All they need is to get the people angry enough. The Qarmati armies can move in and push them forward. But there are Shia in Buratha, and maybe Karkh too, who side with the Qarmatis. But even without them, it doesn't matter. One protest and the caliph moves in. We can head it off by solving the case."

Ammar was right. He knew it, and he did not like it. Tein sat down hard on the couch and said slowly so there would be no confusion. "I will not frame anyone."

"I told him about my interview, connecting it to Barbahari." Ammar sat down. "But that got him more upset. Now he's got the idea that fighting is going to break out in the streets between Barbahari's men and Shia rebels. I told him we could get the men at the top, not only the recruits Barbahari sends in to do his dirty work."

"I doubt he went for that."

"I tried to explain that if we frame someone, the Shia will smell it and riot for certain. But if we take the right steps, and the people see the caliph putting it at Barbahari's feet, everyone will be grateful. The rest of Sunnis, the other Hanbalis, too, hate Barbahari as much as the Shia."

"And?"

"He told me that the investigation had to go in the family's direction. No one else. Not Barbahari."

"So you want to fake another investigation?"

"No." Ammar looked stricken at the mention of it.

Tein stood again to leave, but he was afraid for their families, everyone.

"We'll investigate it our way. We don't need to tell him what we're doing." Ammar sounded almost desperate.

"And if the murder turns out to be what everyone fears, intended to incite violence?"

Ammar paused a moment too long for Tein's liking. "We'll just have to solve it. We can do it."

"If I'm in, we do it right. Promise we won't frame anyone."

"I promise."

But his promise was not enough. He clutched the blue turban. "I can't do this job anymore."

"Tein."

"That last case. Mu'mina. The job's done for me."

"I corrected Ibn Marwan about the Zanj. You heard me."

"I heard you. I heard him. I don't know if this job ever was for me. You brought me in when I was down. Maybe it would have been better to have left me where I was."

"I need you on this," he pleaded.

Tein kept his eyes on the door. Heaving a sigh, he declared, "When we're done, I'm done." He gave in only to protect those he loved, the people, and the city. But if he had to set someone up for them, even to save the ones he loved, he would hate himself for it for the rest of his life.

"We'll talk about quitting then. Now I need you to solve this case."

8

Zaytuna had put up the last bit of laundry on the line in the back courtyard. Wincing from the pain still stuck in her hips and lower back, she was grateful that she did not have to drag wet laundry upstairs to hang on a rooftop line. But it meant keeping company with the housekeeper, who sat on a bench against the back courtyard wall, cutting up vegetables in her hands and dropping them into a boiling pot. The scent of the cooking meat made her stomach rumble so loudly she was afraid the old woman would hear it, but the housekeeper was too busy talking to hear anything but her own voice. There had been nothing for breakfast, and she did not have even a chink of coin for bread this morning. She wanted to finish this job, get her coin, then get what she needed for herself.

The housekeeper took a deep breath, getting the air she needed to share more of her thoughts about her neighbours.

Enough. Please.

"Her father, you know what he said? He said how disappointed he was that his own daughter would complain to others, not even family, about how her husband's grandmother had been treating them. Can you imagine her doing that? Talking so that her own father had to speak out against her?"

Hunger had sharpened her tongue and as she picked up the empty laundry basket, she was ready to spit back, "And how does repeating it lessen any of the wrongs done?" But an inrush of calm washed through her as the words got to her throat and they fell back into her heart and dissipated. She stood up straight, surprised but also concerned. Where were her words? She searched for them, strangely feeling their loss, rather than enjoying the calm. Realizing, she scolded herself for not letting the words go with gratitude that God had protected her from her own inclinations. *Remember this for next time. Don't snap.* Resolved to be good, she unwound a long piece of her wrap from under her arms and draped it over her kerchiefed head. "Auntie, I'm finished."

The old woman stood. "Let me get your coin." She disappeared into the house, coming back a moment later, pressing the small coins into her palm with swollen fingers.

"May God restore this money to your family."

"May God increase your good works." She inspected the drying clothes, holding up the edge of a qamis to the light. Tension gripped Zaytuna for a moment; she knew she had got that grease stain out, but worried about criticism all the same. She could not afford to lose business. Without Saliha, she was a slow worker, and not everyone liked it. Layla would be with her now she had moved in, but there was no telling if she would be reliable or not. The housekeeper nodded seriously. "See you next week, inshallah. You always do a thorough job." Then she added, "A little slow, but you listen to my old gossip, so I don't mind."

The calm seeped in again, but this time with a touch of sorrow at the realization of how she had misread the old woman. Here she was thinking the woman was a cruel gossip, when really she was only lonely and wanting to be heard. "Oh Auntie, I know I don't talk much, but I enjoy your stories."

The old woman's cheeks brightened, and her eyes twinkled as she reached out and held Zaytuna's hand. "I'm sure you are a good daughter to your mother in her old age. May God bless you both."

Zaytuna did not mention her mother had died when she was only ten and she had lost the opportunity to be a good daughter to her, saying instead, "Amin."

"You go, now." The housekeeper pushed her out the back gate with a pleased look. As it shut behind her, Zaytuna stood in the alley for a moment, not sure where she would go next. There was no more work that day. She was hungry. There was that. She was also exhausted from her dream the day before, not having slept the last night as she held out the dream to God, hoping that He would unravel it in her outstretched hands. But no matter what Uncle Abu al-Qasim had said, Mustafa was before her throughout the night and the longing for him embarrassed her still. She had to go to him.

It wasn't too long until midday. By the time she got to Ibn Shahin's home, Mustafa would be done tutoring his children until the afternoon. *Go, then. Go. I know the dream's meaning for me. Let him decide its meaning for him.*

She wandered through the crowded alleys skirting the market until she reached the bakers and bought a bit of barley bread. An old woman sat not too far off, her legs straight out, with a small mound of dates piled up in her wrap between her knees. Going to her, Zaytuna squatted before the old woman. "How are you, Auntie?"

"Alhamdulillah," she answered, frowning, her downturned mouth deeply set from years of hardship.

Zaytuna's legs felt low and heavy, thick with despair. *This is what the shaykh meant.* She knew somehow the despair was not her own, but rather belonged to the woman. Not knowing what to do about it, she frowned and mumbled a prayer as she handed over her coin for the dates. There was no response in return. "Can I help?"

"You can help by leaving with your dates now you've paid."

She stood and reluctantly turned away, disturbed. This is what it would be to sense the states of others and have no way to help. She remembered the Prophet's advice. *If you cannot help with your hands, help with your voice, and if you can do neither, at least pray.* Her heart swelled as she prayed God would lift the woman's difficulties from her. It felt hopeful for a moment, but she did not know if the hope she was feeling was that the woman's situation would change or simply from having done what she could. She did not like this new state of things and set out for Ibn Shahin's home to see Mustafa, feeling confused and doubtful about his reaction.

She knocked hard on the gate. A young servant boy she had not seen before opened the inset door. "Assalamu alaykum, Auntie."

"Wa alaykum assalam, I'm here to see Ustadh Mustafa."

"He's getting ready to eat with my master. I'll tell the housekeeper."

The boy shut the gate, leaving her alone in the alley, surprised and hurt, as if it were Mustafa shutting her out and not a little one who did not know any better. Either way, what did it matter? It was another reminder that this was not a life she could share with him. If Ibn Shahin invited her in, how would that be? She did not think she could stand another lunch in separate rooms, having to make idle chat with women who condescended to her, then fighting with Mustafa afterwards. The pit in her stomach told her to go. Her eyes pricked with tears. There was no point in staying, even if he wanted her in the end. She walked away.

"Zaytuna!" Mustafa's voice came from behind her.

She kept walking.

Mustafa ran up beside her. "Zaytuna, didn't you hear me?"

Staring ahead, she said, "I shouldn't have come."

"Ibn Shahin has asked you to join his wife and the children to..."

She stopped. "How do you think that would be?"

"Zaytuna, please. That day is in the past. Why must you bring it up?"

She bit back telling him why, wishing she had said nothing at all. Pulling the edge of her wrap around and crossing her arms in it, she searched for the wash of calm she felt earlier, something to guide her in what to do and say. There was nothing. But the pause put enough of a gap between her impulses and her words that she found the space to think. He did not push her. Giving her those few moments softened her to him, and she found the words she wanted. "Can you come with me? I need to share something with you. It's private."

"Of course, wait here."

As he returned to give his regrets to Ibn Shahin, she found a spot on the wall and leaned her shoulder against it, searching within herself for the right words.

He approached quietly this time. "Ready?"

They walked without speaking out of the alley to a small square.

"Come, there's a shop over there that sells chickpea stew. Like when we were children," he said fondly. "I get it sometimes. It reminds me of our childhood."

"Our mothers, God bless their souls, the drums, Tein singing in that beautiful voice he had as a boy."

"Let's eat in honour of the old days."

She winced inwardly, suspecting what would come. They were only ever to be old friends, old loves, old days to each other.

There were stools and small tables set out in front of the shop. She sat down while he ordered, hearing him mention she was his sister, so there was no chatter from the owner about them sitting together. She noted he did not use to have to say such things, not before he was a scholar and had a reputation to protect. The owner came back to the counter with the steaming bowls, each with a quarter round of wheat bread on top. Mustafa took them, placed them before her, then ran back, returning with a clay jug and cups.

"Not like the jug and cup you made for me," she said, hoping to remind him of the love he had for her once.

"No, not like that," he answered softly.

They ate. He told her about what he was teaching the children, how one of them would joke when questioned about uncompleted work, making it difficult to discipline him. "I cannot help myself, Zaytuna. I am charmed by the boy and lose all my authority. If I had a son like that, I couldn't raise him right. May God give me a serious son."

"Amin," she said, sealing his prayer, but with each word she felt more distant from him and knew it would be YingYue who would give him that son, not her.

"What did you want to tell me?"

She closed her eyes and imagined herself telling him about the dream, and listened for some inward guidance. All she felt was guilt at using the very techniques YingYue herself had taught her in order to decide if she should tell Mustafa she wanted to be a wife to him, that she *could* be a wife to him. She grew hot at the thought of it and shifted uncomfortably on her stool, suddenly wanting to stand up and walk away.

"Zay, what is it?"

She opened her eyes, reciting the saying of Muhammad, "'Consult your heart. The soul feels at ease and the heart becomes tranquil with what is right. The soul wavers and the heart is uneasy with what is wrong, even if people have repeatedly held it to be right'."

"The aunts and uncles always repeated this one to us."

"Uncle Abu al-Qasim asked YingYue to teach me more about it. To judge my impulses, I mean."

He brightened at the mention of YingYue's name, and Zaytuna felt sick, but wasn't sure if feeling sick was the same as feeling uneasy. She checked with herself. Her heart was tight.

"It's very confusing. Right now, I want to tell you about a dream I had. But I keep checking my heart to know if I should. I have so many feelings all at once, though. I don't know which of them is my heart."

"What did she say?"

"To think of how I feel in those most pure moments, when I feel God's presence and search for that in my heart. Then I will know if I should go ahead."

"Do you feel that?"

"I don't know."

"Zaytuna, I don't want you to tell me something you'll regret later. Take a minute. Get up and walk if you need to. I'll be here."

She stood, feeling grateful for him, which only increased her discomfort. Out in the square, she walked by a green grocer and pretended to examine the new onions piled high into a mound, but kept her distance so the grocer would not call out to her.

Her heart. She said the name, "Allah," to herself, over and over, drawing out the "a" with quiet breaths, and soon her heart felt present to her. *The dream, should I tell him?* Nothing at first, then little by little the expansive warmth that she experienced in her most intimate moments of prayer settled into her chest and washed through her body. It was the answer she needed, and she returned to him.

The dream poured out to him. She turned away only when she told him how she fell into his arms. "The Mahdi implored you to be gentle with me, because the world was ending." Taking a breath, she turned to face him and saw she had made a terrible mistake. His face was mottled and his mouth gaped. She accused her heart, *You betrayed me.* Then to Mustafa, "I shouldn't have told you," and stood.

He reached out for her, missing her hand. "Zaytuna!"

Standing still, she did not walk away but saw now there were tears in his eyes and she wanted to hold his face in her hands and kiss the tears away.

"Sit, please. Zaytuna." He implored her, then said in a whisper, "My love."

She sat, slowly grasping for the edge of the table, finding herself dizzy from the words.

"I love you." He placed his hands, palms open, to her, on the table.

On a precipice, she asked, "Do you love YingYue?"

"Not the way I love you."

A warm humming rose within her, surrounding her heart and embracing her. She knew it was his love she felt, not her own. But his face bore the mark of the conflict within him. "You love her all the same."

"Yes."

"What will you do?"

"I'm promised to her. We have signed the contract. Everyone knows. Uncle Abu al-Qasim had to intervene to make her father accept me. You know her father did not want her to marry at all, just focus on her devotions." He pleaded, "How can I shame her and her father that way?"

A pit opened within her and sucked the humming down into it, leaving her desperate for a way through to him. "Uncle can intervene again."

Reaching across the table, against all propriety, he took her hand. "No."

She pulled her hand back, putting it in her lap, and held it with the other, comforting it. Her eyes on her hands, watching one care for the other, she wept.

"Zay."

Stop, please, stop crying, she begged herself and raised a hand to pull her wrap around well enough to cover her face and wipe at the tears.

The shop keeper shouted, "Take that someplace else!"

Mustafa stood so quickly, the stool beneath him knocked over. "She's had some bad news. Have mercy!"

The man grumbled, but stood back.

She watched him from behind her wrap as he pulled his stool back up and sat down. That face. It was that way since he was a boy, chin sticking out, lower lip raised into a frown. He was angry with himself.

"I understand," she said, the words coming out in a half-sob. She understood propriety, but she wasn't very good at it. Not like him. He knew how to act in every situation. To him, the contract was unbreakable. And that she should have realized.

"Zay, maybe that's not what the dream means. Maybe the dream has a different meaning? Did you talk about it with Uncle?"

She said, "Yes," although she did not want to explain.

"What did he say?"

"It was about my soul's attachments to this world ending." Then she admitted, "He said what I felt for you was only my body's understanding of divine ecstasy."

"Maybe you fell into my arms because I am safe?"

"No." She stopped, then started again. "Yes, of course he is right. But there is more to it. If that is what my body felt for God, it means my body can feel what I thought it never could. It means I can love you like a wife." Her voice rose. "It means I am a woman. It means I can be loved."

"You have always been a woman. I have always loved you."

"Then leave her!" Her voice was shrill and desperate.

Mustafa looked around, worried someone had heard, then whispered, "I cannot. Please understand."

"Curse propriety!" Standing in a rush, she ended up knocking the clay cup to the ground where it shattered, and then she understood. He needed to hear the dream and say all this so she would know exactly how he felt. Now she could leave her attachment to him behind. *This was necessary.* How could she find God if her heart was secretly searching for Mustafa? Saying nothing, she walked out into the centre of the square. There were five different lanes opening into the square and she did not know which way to go, finding herself stuck in the middle.

He came up next to her. "Please, please don't let this come between us. I cannot be without you in my life."

Turning on him, she tried not to sound angry, but accepting. It did not work. "You have my blessing to marry her. I don't like it. I don't have to like it for it to be right."

He let out of a sigh of relief.

The sigh made her want to slap him and say, "Have some respect for me, for what I'm feeling," but she held it back.

"Let me get you back the main road." He walked toward one lane beyond the square. She followed behind him in silence, her hips hurting, and she realized she was limping like Tein.

On reaching the lane, he pleaded, "My friend, my love. Forgive me."

She felt his love again and closed her eyes as much to stop the tears from coming as to keep from seeing his face, loving her so, and understood the selfishness of putting him in this position. Facing him now, she admitted, "I know you must marry her. I knew better, yet I came. I shouldn't have put you in this position." She took a deep breath. "Please forgive me. I've been turned upside down my entire life and I am only righting myself now. Mustafa, I've been cruel to you all these years. Even this was cruel to you."

"There is nothing to forgive. There has never been anything to forgive." Despite all propriety, he reached out and touched one of her fingers.

An unbearable longing for him gripped her. She fought the desperation to keep fighting for their love, turned without a word, and left.

He called her back. "Zaytuna."

Halting, she waited for him.

"In your dream, what about the dead body?" he asked. "What did uncle say about that? Was it Abbas?"

Her eyes opened wide, her breath catching in her throat. Why would he ask that now? How had the conversation turned so abruptly? A sharp comment nearly escaped her when she understood that he only meant to reach out to her, and her heart cried out to him again. She whispered, "He didn't mention it."

"It seemed significant." His voice trailed.

She pulled her wrap off of her kerchiefed head and wrapped it around her under arms as she did for work. Accepting the meaning of the dream, finally, she said, "It is my soul. Abbas is me. I have to die to my old world, my old loves, in sacrifice for the true love of God."

9

It was an impossible position. They were to hand over somebody, a killer, an innocent, or their community would suffer. If the Shia protested the murder, demanding justice and calling it a warning sign of a coming attack on the community, they would come under the boot of the caliph's army. Any revolutionaries waiting for their moment would use it to their own ends, not only the Qarmatis. Any self-styled mahdi could find enough followers to set things off. He and Tein could expect the worst.

Ammar snatched up the sack holding the murder weapon and asked Tein harshly, "Do you have the arrowhead?"

"In my pocket." Tein lifted an eyebrow at his tone.

They walked towards the Solomon Gates and turned off right before it, going through a wide archway that opened onto a gently sloping road leading down into a small field and stables. As Tein and Ammar reached the field below, they came upon a mounted archer standing by his horse, brushing his hand over the animal's flank, his archer's silver thumb ring well-polished and gleaming in the sun, his lasso at his belt. But he was not regular cavalry usually stationed here. He wore the uniform of the ghilman, Turkmen taken from their families at a young age and enslaved, raised in the caliph's army, and freed on the completion of their training when they took their place as elite soldiers in an army loyal only to the caliph.

"What is he doing here?" Tein whispered, an edge to his voice.

Ammar did not answer, sharing his fear, and called out to the soldier instead. The archer stood at attention. Seeing they were only police, he relaxed his stance.

As he approached the man, Tein beside him, Ammar took the bow from its sack and held it out. "We're from Grave Crimes. We need to know who made this bow."

The archer did not reply but took the weapon as if it were a woman's supple body and said, "What I would do for a bow like this."

"Do you know a craftsman in Baghdad who does this work?"

The archer reluctantly looked away from the bow. "No, but ask there." He pointed to the garrison beyond the stables and handed back the bow reluctantly. Taking his horse's reins, he said, "Arslan will know. Our sergeant. I saw him on my way out."

The man wasn't a lone archer. If their sergeant was in the garrison, the ghilman cavalry was stationed here, close enough to Karkh and Buratha to attack from the river, outside the city, or even in the streets. "Look." Ammar gestured toward the stables. Other mounted archers from the caliph's private army were milling about, and there would be many more. "If the cavalry are here, where are the ghilman infantry being stationed? They'll be the first in the streets. Closer to Buratha, no doubt."

Tein ignored him. "Ibn Marwan made it sound like none of this had reached the caliph yet." He was angry. "The caliph knows and is prepared for the worst. He'll start the worst himself. How do you think people in Baghdad and Buratha will react to the ghilman in the streets? They will fight. No one is waiting for us to solve the case."

"It's worse than I thought. I think we're minor players in someone else's game. No matter what we do, no matter who wins, the people will pay."

"What does that mean?" Tein demanded. "What game?"

"I can only think that the viziers, the Banu Furat, thought they could move behind the caliph's back to protect the Shia before trouble got out of hand. The caliph found out and is trying to outmaneuver his viziers." He put his hand on the hilt of his sword. "There isn't only a battle brewing in the streets of Buratha, but in the highest levels of the caliphate."

"Ibn Marwan didn't say anything?"

Ammar shook his head, angry but keeping it under control.

"Did he think we wouldn't see the ghilman?"

"Whatever Ibn Marwan said, we have to solve this fast."

"Walla, the ghilman will incite the protests and the riots themselves."

"And any revolutionaries will use it to their advantage," Ammar finished.

They walked past the stables to what had been the office for the regular mounted archers. Its large wooden doors were open. Empty crates sat to one side. The archer's sergeant and his men had moved in from their regular barracks and training grounds across the river, pushing out the regular army mounted archers to God knows where. Three older Turkmen with long grizzled beards sat on low couches, talking. One of them was as big as Tein, his long legs sticking out beyond the small table. More bows than he could count hung on a rack along the other wall and what Ammar took to be the tools for maintaining them lay in neat order on a work table nearby.

Tein spoke first. "Assalamu alaykum, we need to speak to Arslan."

The men looked him up and down, then returned to chatting amongst themselves. Ammar waited. It was for Tein to decide what happened next.

Taking the sack from Ammar, Tein stepped into the room and pulled out the bow for all to see. He spoke without waiting for their conversation to end. "We're Baghdad Police, Grave Crimes Section. We need the name of the bowyer who made this weapon or the name of one who can tell us."

The men stopped talking, their eyes on the exquisite bow. The big man lifted his gaze, settling on Tein. He stood up easily, not showing signs of his age, and challenged him. "Police? Since when does the police employ black men? Shouldn't you be guarding the inner gate of the palace with the other eunuchs?" He looked past Tein to Ammar. "Or perhaps this man is your slave?"

Ammar stepped forward, his anger nearly loose and driving his hand to the hilt of his sword, but out of the corner of his eye he saw Tein had changed his stance, telling him to back down.

Then came Tein's mocking laughter. "You ghilman. It took you how long to beat back the Zanj? You still resent the fact that enslaved black men, women, and children rising out of the brutality of the salt marshes could become an army and kill so many of you for so long." He tipped his chin at Arslan. "Old man, you must have been there. Humiliated even in your victory and after so many years, you still can't forget it."

"This man." Ammar stood forward, hand still on his hilt. "This man you insult is a ghazi."

"Ah!" Arslan mocked. "My apologies. So he is the respected warrior and you are his slave? Or his woman? Look at your warrior's face, woman, he didn't like your intrusion on his pretty speech."

Ammar glanced at Tein. There was no mistaking that he was angry, and it was not directed at the sergeant standing before them. The men on the couches were sitting forward, smiling, enjoying every moment. Unable to control himself any longer, Ammar blurted out, "Two ghazis stand before you!"

The men behind him were paying attention, no longer relaxed.

Arslan looked them up and down. "Foot soldiers on the frontier. Paid a pittance. Paid even less as police now. Where's the respect in that?"

Tein took a step toward the sergeant, who did not step back in response. Instead, Arslan held his body like a man who enjoyed fighting. He faced Tein, matching him in height and strength, but said nothing while waiting for his move. Ammar took a step back so he could more easily pull his sword.

Tein finally broke the silence, saying evenly, "I don't need your respect. I need to know who made this bow."

"Let me see it." The old soldier held out his hand, but stood his ground.

Tein gave it to him.

The sergeant turned it over in his hands. "Did the bowyer commit a crime or the owner of the bow?"

This time Ammar remained silent. Nor did Tein reply immediately.

"Do you have a tongue?" Arslan asked, eyeing Tein.

Waiting, Ammar watched the two men on the couch as they shifted their bodies to its edge so they could stand in a moment. One of them stood and Ammar readied himself, but saw that the man was not only old, but had the untested body of an archer who had always been held to the rear of the fighting. He had never been on the lines like he and Tein, who had fought Byzantine soldiers face to face with their weapons, fists, or whatever was to hand in the chaos of battle. Nor was the archer a brawler like Arslan. Ammar liked their odds, but he and Tein wouldn't get past this room once the men outside came to help.

Arslan took a step back but held his position by demanding, "Answer my question."

"Whoever shot the bow killed a man," Tein replied.

The sergeant raised one eyebrow. "A ghazi in wordplay and swords."

He had conceded the ground. Ammar relaxed his stance.

"Do you know the bowyer?" Tein repeated.

"I know the man who does this work." He pointed to delicately painted blue and opalescent scales, like the skin of a snake. "It is the signature of Nurmyrat Didar. He's recently dead, so safe from your accusations."

"Is his shop still open?" Ammar asked.

"Ask for his son, Nurmyrat Adam, in al-Atash market."

Tein held his hand out for the bow. The man gave it over and showed his back as he returned to the couch, making one last statement that they were not worthy of being considered a threat. The detectives gave each other a look, turned their own backs, and left.

Stable boys leading horses out into the field blocked them as they came out into the morning light. The animals were extraordinary creatures of every hue, their reddish brown to deep black coats shining and changing shade with the curves of their muscle and the movement of their bodies in the clear morning light. Staring in wonder at them, Ammar forgot for a moment that ghilman soldiers might ride them into the streets of Baghdad and Buratha and recited God's words, "*And there is pleasure for you in the beauty of your cattle, how the colour of their hides changes in the light of the evening when you bring them in and in the light of the morning when you send them out to pasture.*"

He did not realize Tein had been admiring the grandeur of the animals too, until he said the words that seal the recitation of verses of the Qur'an, "God speaks the truth."

"And all these years." Ammar tucked his thumbs in his belt, leaning back in surprise. "Who knew it would only take the beauty of these beasts to make you a man of faith."

"I've never said I didn't recognize truth in its verses, but that's not the same as having any use for faith." He paused, pointing at the horses. "They are being readied for battle."

The horses were quiet as the boys led them out of the stables, but Ammar knew their aggression and fearlessness on the battlefield. Some of these even had the scars of battle on them, marking them as mounts for the archers who sometimes entered the fray alongside the infantry, shooting their heavy, armour-piercing arrows down into the enemy coming for them on foot with swords, maces, and axes at the ready. The caliph was expecting close fighting in and outside the city. A knot tightened in Ammar's gut. "There's not enough time."

Tein grunted.

Ammar had lied when he told Ibn Marwan that they would resort to pinning the murder on an innocent man if necessary. But now he wondered if it was the right thing to do. Sacrifice one man for everyone. By God, Imam Husayn was given foreknowledge that innocents among his camp, even his family, would be slaughtered when he stepped onto the plain of Karbala. But not one of them turned away from the fight to save themselves. They were all sacrificed for the truth. Is it not the same here? *No*, he answered himself, *not unless you find a willing man*. Perhaps they could find a Shia man with the courage of Imam Husayn. The thought of it made him angry again. He was caught between feeling shame for thinking it and defensiveness at the thought that he should not. There was no telling Tein. He would never agree. Not even if a man came forward. He walked beside Tein in tortured silence as they made their way back up to the Basra Gate Road and out of the Round City.

Once they neared the bridge over the Tigris to the West side of the city, Ammar could not hold back. "What do you think?"

"We'll solve it."

"And if we don't?"

Tein stopped and faced him. "I know what you are getting at. If you want me alongside you in this, don't bring it up again."

Ammar opened his mouth to force the conversation, and Tein cut him off. "Get back to the case." Tein walked ahead and called back to him. "Tell me what else happened at the interview with the victim's parents."

"Aqil ibn Akib," Ammar said, catching up, "the scholar who was visiting the parents, bothered me."

"How?"

"He's a pompous ass."

"What's new there? You always hate the arrogant ones."

"He acted as if he had ownership over the family and, more strangely, they let him have it. He said he'd grown up around them, that they were family friends. But something is off."

"Talk it out."

"The scholar is an Imami, like my family, following the Twelfth Imam. Not Fatihi, following Jafar the Liar's son, like the victim's family."

"But if they are old neighbourhood friends..." Tein replied, sounding impatient with Ammar's reasoning.

"True, they could be. Few refuse to cross these lines for the sake of friendship or business."

"So what is it?"

"There's something wrong."

"We're going to need more than that."

They returned to walking in silence and stepped out onto the pontoon bridge spanning the Tigris. The multi-storied palaces of the wealthy towered on either side of the riverbank. Gauzy curtains moved with the breeze on the wide balconies. The sounds of laughter and song reached them from above. Ammar turned to see two wealthy men leaning over the balconies, watching them. Those men had never had to walk that bridge in their lives. Their servants took them across in skiffs from private landing to private landing or carried them across in a litter.

Along the riverbanks, boys and men in ratty robes, bare-footed, with just scraps for turbans, worked the landings pulling goods out of the round reed boats to carry up to the markets or homes or loading them up for the same somewhere else along the river. The woman in front of him was balancing a burlap package on her head as they crossed over to where the wealthiest of Baghdad lived, including the caliph himself. The question he asked himself, the same one his mother had asked him, pricked at him and he said without thinking, "Whose side are you on?"

"What?" Tein asked.

"Not you. Not about this case."

"Maybe it should be," Tein replied.

After the bridge, they made their way through wide avenues with arched side streets leading to the palaces and estates of the wealthy until al-Atash Market opened up before them. Its grand archways, tiled in patterned blues and greens, led in two directions off the main square. Boys and men in well-worn robes and turbans came in and out of the market gates, carting goods out for the wealthy, taking the coin tossed to them for their efforts, then ran back inside to get more trade. The market rivalled that of Karkh in size and goods, but the sheer number of the wealthy and powerful on the West side meant that those craftsmen and merchants who specialized in the finest goods had their shops here. Not that Karkh did not have its own rich folk, but those who lived near the caliph's palace possessed wealth of another sort.

Ammar grabbed one of the young porters, running back into the market, by his ragged sleeve. "Take us to Nurmyrat Adam's workshop. The bowyer."

The boy did not reply, but gestured for them to follow. He walked at a quick pace, and they hurried to keep up. Because of his old leg injury, Tein fell behind by a few steps, but Ammar knew he would not lose them. The boy wove through the crowds of rich women and men trailed by servants in the fabric and gold markets. They passed housekeepers in the food markets haggling in seeming anger over mounds of dried fruits and nuts imported from every corner of the empire. He led them through breezy courtyards shaded by trees and edged with small tables and chairs where young men served wealthy customers small plates and sweet drinks, then out again into the paper shops where scholars leaned over the boards chatting with the shopkeepers within, and finally to the row of bowyers' workshops. The boy stopped before one, tapped the counter-board, and held his hand out, waiting for his fals. Ammar had no sooner placed the coin in the boy's dirty palm than he disappeared into the crowded market.

Beautiful bows lined racks along one side of the shop, while the back held a shelf of leather-bound books. On the other side, a young man sat at the bowyer's bench while another sat with a nearly finished bow clamped before him, painting a design onto the back with a brush that must have been a single hair.

A much older man, with a trimmed grey and black beard, noticed them and approached. His turban was undyed, but as he came closer, Ammar saw it was made of fine silk treated so that it had no lustre. His robe was likewise simple, in the Turkmen style with lapels also in dulled silk, but with red and black stripes and tied with a sash of the same material as his turban. It was a style of understated wealth that spoke to the success and respect due to the workmanship of the shop.

"Nurmyrat Adam? Assalamu alaykum."

The bowyer returned Ammar's greeting, his eyes already on the bow that Ammar had taken from its sack and handed to Tein. He returned his attention to Tein, pleased. "One of my father's bows and in the hand of a man who, if I am not mistaken, is a warrior. He would be honoured."

"I was a ghazi, but no more," Tein replied, bowing his head. "Now I am police and we're here to trace the person who bought this bow."

The man held his hand out. "If you would, Ghazi, let me examine it more closely?"

Tein handed him the bow.

"This type of horn inlay in the siyah and the snake skin design on the front of the bow was my father's signature, but if made for one person in particular, he would have marked it with their initials." Pointing to three tiny letters and a date worked into the design, he said, "Right there. I'll check for you."

He went to the back of the shop and pulled down one of the leather-bound volumes and turned the pages until he found the one he wanted and chuckled. Turning to his workers, he whispered, "That fool, Utbah ibn Harb. He's let his bow catch him in a crime."

Ammar called across the shop expectantly, "Utbah Ibn Harb?"

Adam returned to the front of the shop, placing the bow on the counter between them. "Utbah ibn Harb ibn Abdulqahhar al-Basri. You have good ears." He considered them for a moment. "Permit me to be frank. He is a spoiled young man of great wealth who likes to come by the shop to pick up arrows for hunting when he is in Baghdad. He could get them anywhere, but he seems to like to examine my bows just to declare them beneath the quality of my father's work."

"How does that go?" Ammar asked.

One worker at the back encouraged the other to speak. He called out, "Tell him about that one time you tricked him!"

"Ah! Just so!" Adam said, shaking his head. "I brought in my father's finest work for him to appraise. My father would never sell it. It was a unique design, but without his signature on it. Utbah declared it unworthy for the trash heaps!"

Tein pressed, "And this bow belongs to Utbah?"

"It was made for his father who died not long ago."

The bowyer did not add the customary prayer on the dead man's soul after mentioning his passing.

Adam picked up the bow again and examined the arrow-pass. "It is well-used and recently too."

Tein asked, "Why would you think that no one else in his family would have used it?"

"If you found it in Baghdad, it likely belongs to the son. The family estate is outside of Basra." He added, "Harb ibn Abdulqahhar only bought his bows here; no bowyer in Basra could match my father's skill. I met him many times. He came here whenever he was in Baghdad and often brought his son, Utbah, with him, even as a boy. There was no love there. More than once he slapped Utbah's face for some real or imagined slight. The boy, then the man, bore visible bruises until the father became too ill to hit him. I recall Ibn Abdulqahhar saying he had only one useless son and had married his equally useless daughters off at a young age. I can only imagine the bow is Utbah's. Unless they had gifted it to another, of course."

"Do they have a home in Baghdad?"

"I recall they stay at a family member's home here. Let me check, it will be in the records. My father would have delivered bows there." He returned to the records. "Yes, Umar ibn Abdulqahhar, on Jasmine Vine Road. Utbah's uncle, on his father's side. If the fool is in town, he's likely to be there."

"Where is that?" Ammar asked with an apologetic shrug, "We are Karkhi."

"Of course. It is off Abd al-Muttalib Square at the rear of the estate of the vizier, Ibn al-Furat."

The suspected killer lived next door to the vizier pressing them to find the guilty man? Ammar choked back a laugh at the irony.

Tein took the arrowhead out of his pocket. "And this?"

The bowyer picked it up. "It is ours. As I said, Utbah ibn Harb bought his arrows here, including hunting arrows with these heads."

"Their names seem intentionally chosen." Tein asked, "Did you hear him speak ill of the Shia?"

The bowyer pulled his head back in shock. "Extraordinary isn't it?

Each one of them named after a child of Yazid, as if to honour the slaughter of the Prophet's family at Karbala. Can you imagine making such a statement! We may differ in our beliefs, but we Sunni and Shia must not disagree on the inviolability of the Prophet's family."

Ammar had not realized until that moment how much Ibn Marwan had hurt him with his insults. He wanted to hold the bowyer's hand and call him brother.

Adam continued, "Utbah ibn Harb's grandfather and father had a virulent hatred for the Shia. Living in Basra, I suppose they had painful experiences. It could have been simple prejudice. He was not a cultured man as I believe we are here in Baghdad, but that is no excuse."

"Did Utbah ibn Harb ever say anything along those lines to you?"

"No, I would remember such an offence. But the man is a wastrel. I doubt he shares his father's hatred for the Shia as it would require him to have an opinion about the world beyond his own immediate needs."

Ammar bowed his head, hand over his heart. "You have been very helpful, thank you."

"Alhamdulillah. God willing, there will be justice. If the matter ends up before the Police Chief's court, I would be pleased to do my duty and confirm what I said." He paused. "But you haven't said what he's done."

"We don't know that it was him," Ammar replied, "but this bow was used to kill a man by the Cemetery of the Martyrs at at-Tibn Gate."

"Of course!" Adam gasped. "We've all heard of the killing. Word here is that the caliph is going to put pressure on the Shia of Karkh and Buratha. They say that the Shia did it themselves to mark a coming rebellion. It seems impossible that they would do such a thing. Is it true?"

"No!" Ammar's voice boomed and Adam took a step back from the force of it. "My apologies." He raised his hand to his heart again to assure him. "I only mean to say that the murder is only a personal matter. I assure you. If you hear people saying this, please object. It puts everyone in Baghdad at risk. The manner of the death is a mere coincidence."

"I understand." Adam then offered, "If that is the case, Utbah may not be the man you seek. Despite being a fool, he is an expert archer. I've heard extraordinary accounts of his skill. No arrow he shot would find its mark by coincidence." He shuddered. "Perhaps Utbah killed the man for sport? The shots a comment on his father's hatreds? Still, I cannot believe that, even of him. He is too stupid to be so clever."

Ammar shot a look at Tein, who was putting the bow back into its sack. Far from dissuading them from Utbah, Adam had made a case against him.

"Did Utbah ibn Harb ever bring anyone by here?" Tein asked.

"Yes!" Adam's eyes lit up. "I remember now. I was surprised. A poor young man, his clothes were quite shabby. He obviously felt uncomfortable. I got the sense that Utbah was showing him off in a way that I did not understand." He put a finger to his lips. "The young man's hair was long. He did not keep his head shorn closely as we all do. It stuck out from under his turban."

The victim did not have long hair. Ammar checked with Tein to see if he had anything, but he shook his head.

Tein said to Ammar, "Could he be tied up with Barbahari's men?"

"They would never permit long hair."

"No," Tein agreed.

Turning back to Adam, he asked, "Was the man dressed like a Hanbali with the turban the way they wrap them?" Ammar moved his hand to show the particular way they twisted a length of turban under their chin.

Adam interrupted. "Yes, I know. No, nothing of the sort."

They thanked Adam again and left the shop, heading back in the direction they came.

Tein spoke first. "Abd al-Muttalib Square?"

The midday call to prayer sounded from the mosques in the city. Ammar replied, "I need to pray. Then let's see if we can interrupt Utbah's midday meal."

10

Tein leaned against the wall outside a small mosque as he waited for Ammar to finish praying, hoping Utbah ibn Harb was their man and trying not to think about Saliha. As long as Utbah had no association with Barbahari, closing the case would relieve the pressure building in both Karkh and Buratha. He suspected there would be a demand to have Utbah paraded through the streets with shit smeared on him and callers announcing his name and crime to those they passed. It sickened Tein, not only because of their last case but watching a crowd throw rocks and shoes at a man already on his way to execution? What good does it do any of them? Even if they found the right man, they were doing the wrong thing.

There had to be something else, some job with no one over him, something Saliha would respect. Zaytuna had it good washing laundry. *No one dies if she can't get a stain out of a qamis. Wash, hang, dry, fold, done. Simple.* He said with an irritated sigh, "Zaytuna."

If only Zaytuna would keep things simple. She tried to embroil herself in every case of theirs, or worse, kept an ear out for neighbourhood gossip, hoping for a mystery to solve. Most often she made something out of nothing and only sometimes made a difference. When she made a difference, it mattered, but he still wished she would stick to washing clothes so he wouldn't have to worry about her.

At least she had not fallen into ecstasy again, the way mother did, since that time in the graveyard months ago. At least that he knew about. But he couldn't be everywhere to make sure she was safe. In his frustration, he wished she and Mustafa would work things out so she would be on Mustafa's watch, not his.

The scent of grilled meat was coming from some place nearby, and his stomach growled, putting him in a worse mood.

Ammar's face fell on seeing him.

"Where does all this end?" Tein muttered to himself. Then, seeing Ammar, he deflected. "It's not the case. I'm hungry."

Ammar relaxed. "Let's eat and arrest the mother's son."

"I smell kabab," Tein grumbled.

Ammar stepped out into a throng of passersby and tapped a porter on the arm, asking directions. He returned, grinning. "Let's go. I have a reliable account of where we can find that kabab."

They turned a corner, then another, passing a tavern along the way, until they reached a food stall in a cul-de-sac. Fatty smoke rose from the grills. It was early yet, but there was already a large cluster of working men waiting their turn. The same number lined the walls, stooped over their food, talking loudly, taking a minute of respite from their jobs. Two men in short sirwal and qamises tied off with matching waist wraps worked the grills while a third slapped flat dough onto a tannur, pulling it off when done and tossing it to a fourth. That man laid the meat on the bread, added fresh herbs, and folded the bread over it all, pulling out the skewer as he handed it over to a customer.

Ammar caught the eye of the one taking the orders and held up two fingers. It wasn't long before they, too, were bent over with bread-wrapped mutton in their hands and hot fat dripping into their beards and down to their feet with every full-mouthed bite. Tein wiped his face with the back of his hand and headed to the basin to wash up. Following him, Ammar joked, "We wouldn't need the trouble of women if we ate that every day."

"That meat calls for a trip to the bathhouse, not this minor ablution!"

The two laughed like old times, but when the moment passed, losing the friendship to the trouble that had grown between them pierced Tein and made him long to forgive Ammar everything. Holding onto the longing for a moment, he gave it fair consideration, and set it aside for the time being. The timbre of his voice softened as he said, "What do you think?"

Ammar heard it and stepped closer to Tein. "Utbah looks good for it."

"Maybe a rich wastrel who has become a true believer? He's taken up his father's mantle and killed one of the Shia his father hates so much? If so, I just hope he isn't working with Barbahari's men."

"That outcome wouldn't quiet things."

"And if it turns out to be true?"

"The public doesn't need to know." Ammar said.

"We can tell them he did it for sport?"

"I can see that."

"And if they parade him?"

Ammar winced.

"That's all right by you?" Tein challenged, the softness gone.

"I don't have the power to stop it, but I'd try."

"Not like last time."

The censure found its mark. Ammar turned away, his voice trailing, "Not like last time."

But neither one of them had the authority to intervene once the police chief had their man in his court and Tein knew it. He wanted to tell Ammar there was no way to avoid doing the ugly work for powers greater than themselves. That this case would make him as guilty as Ammar had been on their last big case. He did not know if he could live with it, but he knew who he couldn't live without.

"Let's interview him," Ammar said.

Tein let himself admit aloud, "We need the ghilman to head back to their own barracks and away from our people."

Ammar nodded, his mouth a hard line.

They headed back into the crowds of the market, where they tapped another boy to get them to the market gate closest to Jasmine Vine Road.

It was closer than they imagined. They were out of the market in moments, making their way along a street with high walls protecting the estates within. The boy stopped at a gate on the corner. Unlike the other one, this boy politely indicated that they arrived. Ammar even had to push the coin into his palm.

Tein slammed the elaborately cast door knocker, then let his fingers trace the carvings in the wood doors. Jasmine flowers, vines, and leaves. It was as if the artisans shaved them into the hardwood with the point of a razor. A small door within the larger gate on the right opened, and a boy stuck out his head with a questioning look.

"Baghdad Police." Ammar paused. "We're here on the caliph's business to speak with Utbah Ibn Harb."

The boy left the door ajar and ran back without saying a word in reply.

"Caliph's business?"

"Why else would he let us in?"

The door opened wide, this time by an older man, a servant dressed in clothes finer than any Tein had seen on the wealthy in the al-Atash market. Thickly embroidered white jasmine flowers tinged with yellow on green vines sprouting delicate leaves covered his pale blue silk robe. It was as if he were gazing up through the flowers at a clear blue sky at midday. Tein did not give a damn about finery, yet the beauty of what amounted to a uniform for the staff of the estate took him in its grasp. He desired it, not for himself, but for Saliha. And wanting it made him feel small, realizing he could never give her a stitch of similar work.

The man asked them to follow him through the outer garden. It was thick with fruit trees, edged by neat rosemary shrubs and, Tein noted, more jasmine climbing the walls. The home's wide double doors were set into a high archway, tiled in a repeating design of jasmine vines and flowers.

Tein quipped, "I'm sensing a theme," but Ammar acted like he did not hear him. He added anyway, "Crude," and felt more the man for it. Saliha liked beautiful things, but there was beauty and there was crass wealth, and this was it. Still, he taunted himself, *And even if all goes well? The threat passes and you leave this job? What then? Will you be able to give her even the small things she finds beautiful?* By the time the servant led into the vast room where Utbah ibn Harb waited for them, Tein was ready to arrest Utbah because he himself could not afford to give the woman he loved what she deserved.

Utbah ibn Harb appeared bemused by their arrival. He stood behind a low-backed couch set among four others in the centre of a room edged with even more couches, each covered in gleaming blue and cream-coloured silk. Sickeningly, the upholstery matched his eyes and skin, their emphasis a seeming boast that they were descendants of the Umayyad caliphs, and made Tein understand the household theme of jasmine flowers set against a blue sky had nothing to do with the name of street after all. If that were not enough, Utbah was dressed down in a roughly woven undyed cotton robe and turban, the only emphasis a red silk sash at his waist. The clothes mimicked what a poor man would wear, but the sash gave an air of elegance that mocked those men, like him, who wore them out of necessity. Tein wanted to take hold of his neck. Then he saw it. A delicate glass pitcher filled with wine, with three glasses set before it, was sitting on an engraved tray before the couch, baiting him. Tein wanted to fill that glass like he had not wanted to in long time. If Saliha would never have him as he needed, and he could never give her what she needed, what use was there in anything?

Utbah caught his glance and spoke, gesturing to the wine, "If you are the caliph's men, there must be wine."

"No, thank you," Ammar answered. "We're here to ask you a few questions."

"The caliph has sent police with questions for me? Is this a prelude to being locked up in the dungeons, never to be seen again? Have I slighted God's man in the palace somehow?"

That comment about the caliph was enough to get him executed if said in front of the wrong man. What made him think he was beyond their reach? Tein nearly responded when Ammar opened the questioning.

"We are from Grave Crimes, and are investigating the murder of a man near the Cemetery of the Martyrs."

"That!" Utbah's eyes widened with explicit interest. "Everyone is talking about it. Baghdad is on the edge of great turmoil, it seems."

"It doesn't seem to worry you," Tein remarked.

"How would it affect me? The caliph's men would put it down."

"You seem to have a short memory. Uprisings are not controlled easily."

"I would be home in Basra before the trouble crossed the Tigris, if it even got that far." He walked around the couch to the table, poured two glasses of wine and held one out to Tein, smiling. "Come now, have a glass of wine. I cannot drink alone."

Tein eyed his slippers, finely tooled deep brown leather and gold embossed, and realized, of course, he would have many boots with perfect soles and there was no way to determine if the prints the watchman saw were his. He was angry that he had not thought to measure them after seeing them for himself.

Ammar stepped in. "The weapon that was used to kill the victim belongs to you."

Utbah sat down slowly on the couch, placing the wine glass back down on the tray. Looking between them, he asked, "Are you referring to one of my bows? A cutpurse stole it off of my horse last week."

"Where did that happen?"

"I was in Karkh, riding on the Basra High Road. It had become quite crowded. I stopped for a moment when a cluster of boys rushed up. My horse, Arib, became agitated and before I knew it a boy had cut the strap to the sheath and the group of them ran off."

Tein asked, not believing a word, "Did you call a watchman over?"

"I did not notice any. You should have more men out to protect us, especially from these gangs of children." He gestured to the sack held by Tein. "Ah, the bow. I would like very much to have it back. It was a favourite belonging to my father. Sad to have lost its sheath, though. It was equally beautiful. How did you know it was mine?"

"The son of the bowyer who made it told us," Ammar said.

"The man has impeccable discretion," he said, raising an eyebrow.

"I don't suppose you have any witnesses to the theft."

"No," he admitted. Then he returned to his earlier mocking tone. "But I can arrange for one of my servants to act as one if needed."

Tein took a step forward, wanting to pick up the pitcher by its slim neck and hit Utbah across the face. Utbah saw and drew back instinctively on the couch.

Ammar moved into the breach. "We'll be keeping the bow as evidence. What were you doing in Karkh?"

"Visiting friends."

"Someone in shabby clothes with long hair?" Tein jumped on it.

"Excuse me?"

"You've been seen with a young man in shabby clothes and long hair."

Utbah seemed confused at first, then his face lit up dramatically. "What an eye for detail Nurmyrat has! I'll be mentioning his propensity to gossip in my circles, to be sure."

"And who is the man?"

Utbah's confidence returned. "I met him the one time. You can hardly expect me to remember his name." He stretched his arm over the back of the couch. "Someone I picked up for fun one day, paid for him to have some comforts I enjoy, then sent him back to his filthy life."

Tein itched to say something he would regret.

"And the friends?" Ammar asked before Tein could speak.

"'Friends', used in this situation, is a euphemism for a lady whose reputation would be ruined should the police arrive at her family's door to question her."

Ammar assured him, "We can be discreet."

Utbah held his wrists out. "I'm afraid you'll have to shackle me and take me in. I would rather go with you than divulge her name."

"If we take you in," Tein said, "you'll give her name to us in the end."

"On pain of death, I will not reveal it." His delivery was strangely flat, giving the declaration weight. But Tein wasn't buying it.

Ammar turned the conversation. "What do you hear about the killing?"

"What everyone has heard!" He grinned sickeningly. "Killed in the manner of Abbas. It seems to be a message to the Shia community of a coming slaughter."

"Your father was not friendly to the Shia," Ammar stated.

"Are you implying that my father killed this man from his grave?"

"We are implying that you share your father's hatred."

Utbah sat forward. "My father's hatred died with him. Let me explain. Perhaps twenty-five years ago, an underling of the late Shia vizier, Ismail ibn Bulbul, denied him a request that ended with him losing a significant importation agreement. Father took the matter to Ibn Bulbul himself, who sided with his own man." He added with a shrug, "Ibn Bulbul's man did not get away with it. He soon found his unmarried daughter was pregnant, and not by her own choosing. As a result, the underling lost his standing in society."

Tein glanced at the bottle again, not knowing if he wanted to hit the man, drink it down, or both.

"Did Ibn Bulbul know?" Ammar asked.

"Of course! My father was a fool. He not only made sure it was known, he spread the word that he did it himself. The vizier made sure that he lost more than that one importation contract. My uncle stepped in and was eventually able to reach an expensive rapprochement with Ibn Bulbul. But my father never forgave him and blamed all the Shia."

The bowyer made it clear the hatred went back to his grandfather. The family names. The Umayyad colour scheme. Tein wanted to call him out on it, but Ammar asked instead, "And how do you feel about the Shia?"

"If they share their wine and women with me, they are my friends as much as any other."

"Your Shia friends?" Tein followed up. "Who are they?"

Utbah's face twitched ever so slightly. "Shia friends? You two are not making any sense."

It was him.

"We *will* find out," threatened Ammar, "and we will find the name of the woman. It will be ugly for all of you if we have to do it this way."

Utbah turned his head and called through an open door to their left. "Abdurrazzaq!" Returning his attention to them, he said, "We have good relations with Ibn Furat and I will send word. This harassment ends here."

A guard arrived before Utbah had finished speaking. The man held himself like a ghazi, but one who had found wealth working for this family. He wore a leather cuirass as battle-worn as Ammar's own, with a dagger at his belt, but over a finely woven short robe with embroidered edges. His sirwal were tucked into expensive, but well-worn, boots. Still, they could be recently resoled. Tein wondered if the man had been paid to shoot Bishr for Utbah.

"Show the caliph's men out."

Ammar cut in before Abdurrazzaq reached them, lying, "It was Ibn al-Furat himself who sent us to you. It seems your father's reputation has stained yours as well. He gave us permission to question you how we liked and come back to him with whatever answer gets the job done."

Utbah held his hand up to the guard to wait. "Because someone stole my father's bow and killed a man with it, I am to be framed for this murder in further retribution for my father's acts?"

Tein kept an eye on the guard while watching for a sign from Ammar.

"You satisfy many political needs," Ammar replied matter-of-factly. "The conviction of an arrogant, wealthy man whose father was a well-known bigot would quiet the Shia of Karkh and Buratha."

Tein told him the truth, getting a sense of the satisfaction people got out of public shaming and not liking it. "You are to be smeared with shit and paraded so the people have a way to spend the anger that has been building. Is that what you want? Help us exonerate you."

Utbah paled, this time having nothing to say.

"If you help us," Ammar said, "we might just be able prove it was not you. We can stop this from happening. While any man will do to quell the violence, we would prefer the right man pay for what he's done."

"I cannot divulge her name. Nor will I give you the names of my friends so that you can shame her through them. If I must suffer for my father's sins, then I must bear it."

If the man was acting, Tein could not tell, but his gut said Utbah was gambling on them backing down. "You're not so flippant now as you were when we arrived."

He looked straight at Tein. "Then, it was a game. This is no game."

"No, this is no game," Ammar confirmed. "You won't help us?"

He shook his head. "I cannot."

"I hope for your sake your uncle can do what you say. But don't bother leaving the city. The caliph can find you in Basra or anywhere else. He has spies everywhere. Ask who would keep your secret? Family perhaps, but all your servants, down to the errand boy? It's unlikely."

Utbah registered the comment, knowing it was true.

"If you leave, it makes you look guilty," Tein added.

"My uncle will be back tomorrow evening and will handle this matter with Ibn Furat directly." He glanced at Abdurrazzaq, obviously afraid. "Show these men out."

Abdurrazzaq moved toward them again, but this time without a threat in his eye. Tein thought he saw some satisfaction there. Was it to see them gone or to see the nephew of this house afraid? Taking one last long look at the wine, he wished he could wash down this case and the loss of Saliha with it and be rid of the fear he would betray himself for both.

When the guard had shut the gate door behind them, Ammar

said, "His family can't protect him. The viziers will sacrifice anyone to stop what is coming."

"In my gut, he's guilty," Tein said, exhausted, unsure if he meant himself or Utbah. "But did you see the guard, his boots?"

"Yes. Maybe Utbah paid him to do it?"

"We have to question him again."

"Right now, Utbah is our best shot."

"Do you see him confessing?"

"Someone knows something. We can use that. We'll get there, Tein. We won't turn him over without proof. Now, who will watch the estate?"

"There's a spot over there where I can watch the main gate and the servant's gate. If he tries to leave the city, I'll hold him."

Ammar nodded. "I'll get reliable watchmen to take your place as soon as I can and watch him in shifts."

Tein settled himself into the alcove to watch the doors and decided to give Saliha what she wanted.

11

The moment the police turned their backs and left, the performance of Utbah's innocence collapsed around him. Utbah ibn Harb was going to be framed for a crime he actually committed. He panicked and ran up the stairs to the suite of rooms he used while in his uncle's home and threw open the trunk at the far end near his bed. Pushing aside several elaborately embroidered wraps, he exposed a wide box containing filigreed gold and jewelled rings, brooches, pendants, and three extraordinary scabbards with ornamental daggers. And his father's letter. He pulled the box out with too much force and threw it on the bed beside him, spilling the pieces out without care. But he paused before the letter, reverentially tucking it back into its place, set the box aside, and dug into the chest. He found what he was searching for at the bottom, a casket holding hundreds of silver dirhams and gold dinars.

I need a purse. He circled the room. *I wore one last night! Where did that maid put it?* Throwing open cabinet doors, he pulled out one piece of fine clothing after another, embossed leather belts, and turbans of every fabric onto the floor. Piles of clothes at his feet, he fell to his knees and wept, pulling his beautiful things around him as if they might hide him from the police.

As his tears passed, he grasped a purple silk qamis lying in messy folds beside him and ran his finger along the taraz embroidery that spelled his name around its edge. He pressed the qamis to his face, wiping away his tears, and took one deep breath after another until the urge to cry again subsided.

Exhausted, he got onto all fours before standing. He pushed the clothing to one side with his foot, as if to convince himself that they did not matter anymore, and revealed several small purses. Choosing one made with plain, strong leather, he returned to the casket. He dug his hand into the coins, grabbing a handful and filling the purse to bursting. Utbah removed his robe and slung the purse across his chest, concealing it under his arm. Already wearing his walking boots, he put his robe back on and searched among the things on the floor for a plain turban and sash, finding a matching pair in faded, rough brown linen.

He sat down on the bed.

Basra would not work. The police would expect it. He contemplated waiting for his uncle. The man despised him but would help him to protect the family name. *Wouldn't he?* But the servants would know, and so would anyone his uncle approached to arrange his escape. Would the servants speak to the police without his uncle's permission? Would the others? He had to admit he did not know and resented them for their questionable loyalty.

It came to him. He would join a trading caravan out of the city. Go beyond the empire. Once far enough away, his uncle could send further funds to him. He could return once his uncle had paid for his innocence. But there would be no walking into the caravan offices to secure passage. The police would question them all. It would have to be arranged outside the city, on the road.

He pressed his arm against the full purse. There would be no difficulty. *Simply walk out of the city.* But provisions, he would need water, food for the road until he found a caravan willing to take him. Stopping at a market in Baghdad, or even a caravansary on the road out, would be too dangerous. *Spies, the police, they'll trace me, know which road I take out of the city.* Horrified, he realized he might even have to sleep on the road. He took one dagger and laid it aside to search through his clothing for a thick winter wrap. Throwing it over and around his shoulders, he commanded his absent uncle, "Get back here, now!"

A servant boy walked by his room carrying a basket.

Utbah yelled, "You!"

The boy came back, eyes down. "Yes, sir."

"Is my uncle home yet?"

"No, sir."

"Come and tell me the moment he arrives."

"Yes, sir." The boy remained standing, trembling in the doorway.

Waving his hand in dismissal, he commanded, "Go!"

The boy ran out of sight, nearly dropping the basket he was holding.

"There's no time to wait," he muttered, pacing the room and wondering if he could take provisions from the kitchen without it being remarked on by the servants. He stopped when he realized, saying aloud with a tremor, "My men." Even if he had to tell them killed Bishr, they would not hold it against him. Bishr had betrayed them as well. He would only have to explain that if he had not killed him, they would all be facing execution for the theft of the tithe. *They have to help me. They can help me escape.*

Putting the last few things he needed in the pockets of his sleeves, he gazed back at the room, his wide and comfortable bed, his finely made clothes in piles on the floor, the exquisitely embossed woodwork and copper lamps, the tile work set into the arched windows, and wondered what his new world would be like. *It will be rough, for a time, but you will have all this back and more. If you are careful.* He turned, leaving his life behind, and walked down the stairs as if he were going out for a night of drinking.

A new female servant whose name he could not remember was coming up the stairs. She turned around quickly so that they would not pass each other, and waited at the bottom of the stairs, eyes on the floor. On another day, he might enjoy considering when he might make use of her for his own pleasure. Today, he only thought of what story she would tell the police if asked. "Lay bread and cheese out for me," he said as he passed. "I will be late with friends and will need it on my return." No sooner had he said it that he regretted it. Every night he had come home drunk, he made his demands on his return, not before he left. He prayed she would not remark on it if asked.

The doors were still open to the front courtyard garden, and he walked through the grand hall leading to it. The gate boy jumped up to get to it before him. Utbah's chest tightened, and he took a step backward and turned around. The police might have left a man outside to follow him. He went up the stairs to a room with a balcony overlooking the street. Hiding behind the balcony's gauze curtains, he saw the black man sitting in an alcove across the street, appearing to sleep. There was no question he could see both the main gate and the servant's entrance. But, Utbah realized, not the market gate!

There was no help for it. He would have to go past the kitchen to reach the gate where they took deliveries. He rushed downstairs. As he passed the kitchen, the clanging of pots and the orders of the cook fell silent. He ignored them, going through the hall to the pantry and the door leading to market gate beyond.

They were used to seeing him. There should be nothing to remark on here among themselves or to the police. He had been down here many times before. First, when he had discovered the lovely Aisha washing pots, her slim fingers already calloused, then as he put her in Bishr's path, using her to draw him into returning even when he did not have butter to deliver.

The two fell in love easily, and through it, he had gained Bishr's trust. She had even brought, Talha, her brother along to join them. He had laughed at the irony of two children of a Sunni extremist thinking they were taking the side of the Shia against their despised father when, in truth, they would serve his goals in the end.

He left by the rear pantry door, giving access to the well, and turned back through the narrow kitchen garden pathway that led to the market gate. Opening it, he looked carefully up and down the road and slipped out. He had only got a few steps when he heard his name called in a whisper behind him. He reached for his dagger, expecting to see the Zanji detective behind him. Realizing he had left it on the bed, he gasped, "God protect me!" As he turned, an immense man came at him with hands outstretched, reaching for his neck. Utbah's knees gave out underneath him and the man caught him as he fell. This would be his end.

"God is protecting you," the man said. "That is why I am here."

Utbah shuddered and looked up, eyes wide. It was the scholar Aqil, his great hands not around his throat but digging into the flesh of his arms as he lifted him up.

"Stand on your own, man." Aqil looked around him. "We have to go."

Utbah stood, still weakened by shock and backed slowly to the gate, not knowing who he feared more in that moment, Aqil or the police.

"I've been following the police," Aqil said, leaning past him to pull the gate shut. "Once I saw they had the bow, I knew they would trace it to you. I waited over there." He pointed to a deep alcove in an estate wall across the street. His voice rose. "I've been behind them all day. Never once did they notice me!" Then he whispered, "I can help you."

Running from one fear to another, Utbah grasped his arm, and whimpered, "They are going to frame me for the murder."

"Yes, of course." Removing Utbah's hand from his arm, Aqil patted him like a child. "First, let me take you off the street and to a room I keep."

He pleaded desperately, "But I must get out of the caliph's reach! Out of the Empire!"

"I can make arrangements for you from there." Then he took hold of Utbah ibn Harb's arm and pulled him along. "We're going back to Buratha, where you'll be safe."

12

—————

"I'm coming with you." Layla emptied the leather bucket of water from the community fountain into the basin.

Zaytuna stacked the cooled bricks that Yulduz used for a makeshift brazier in the far corner of the courtyard. She stood, her hand bracing her back from the lingering pain, hurting inside and out. Now she would have to find the energy to be with this girl, not only tonight, but tomorrow and every day and night after that. They would wash clothes together, eat together, wake up in the morning to each other. Next thing she knew, Layla would crawl in with her at night or follow her to the latrine down the road. Would there be any peace? The incessant chatter. The constant touching. The wanting something from her she did not know how to give.

"Since when are you interested in praying all night?"

Layla held the bucket in one hand, ready to go back to the square to fill it again. "You don't *pray* all night at your uncle Junayd's remembrance gathering," she said breathlessly. "I know what you *do*, you sing songs praising Muhammad, God bless him and peace."

"More than that." Zaytuna pressed her back flat against the wall.

"That's what Saliha told me."

"Saliha has never been there."

"Well, that's what she said." She crossed her arms.

Zaytuna closed her eyes in frustration and considered her options. *What if she is meant for the path and I leave her behind? I have to take her. All right. I'll take her. I'll give her to the aunties. Abdulghafur will be busy, but he'll be glad to see her. I'll barely know she's there.* She waited a moment more to be sure, felt her heart try to expand even in the tight grip of resentment, and said, "You won't make any trouble or complain that you want to leave?"

"I promise."

"I have to talk to Saliha first."

Layla skipped out of the passageway with the bucket.

Before she could get to her door, Saliha called out to her. "I'm napping."

"I didn't even say your name." Zaytuna pushed aside the curtain and stood, head ducked, against the wall in the small room.

"You two woke me up. And I came with you to your uncle's once."

"Never."

"Once. It wasn't long after we first met. You thought it would soothe me. It did. I fell asleep. After, I got up and left."

"Right," Zaytuna said, remembering. "I searched for you afterwards and worried about you the entire way home. So you told Layla what you remembered before you fell asleep."

Saliha smiled in answer and patted the mattress next to her.

"No. My back."

"Is Yulduz here to work on it?"

"She's off visiting Marta."

"I thought it was quiet around here."

Zaytuna chuckled, and noticed the late afternoon light coming through the cracks in her ceiling. "We have to fix that. Mine too. Everyone's roof needs it. When the rain comes..."

Saliha sat up on the mattress against the wall. "Rain's on your mind from your dream? I talked to..."

Zaytuna cut her off. "We can get Layla to get up there with the mud. She won't fall through."

"Good idea. But, Zay, your dream."

"My dream?" She eyed Saliha intently.

"Tein told me about the case he's working on. The body is like you dreamt it." She leaned forward. "Exactly."

Zaytuna pushed off the wall in a quick jerk and groaned from the pain. "I need to speak to Tein. Where is he?"

"Why would I know?" Saliha's tone changed as she threw her hand out in a dismissive gesture. "He's your brother."

Taking a few slow breaths to calm herself, she straightened her back and hips, asking through the pain, "What did he say?"

"He called it a coincidence. Although he used a dinar word for it when a fals would do, but it adds up to it being a coincidence."

"Of course he did," she replied. "Are you meeting him later? I don't have to go to Uncle Junayd's."

"Not go to the sama? Zaytuna bint al-Ashiqa as-Sawda!"

"Saliha, it's about a man's life."

"The man is no longer alive. He's not going anywhere. Find Tein tomorrow at work. I don't know when I'll see him again."

"Not see him again?" Zaytuna had to repress a note of hope in her voice. "Why?"

"We fought."

"About what?"

"What we always fight about." She shrugged. "He wants to make an honest woman of me and I am already honest."

Zaytuna shut her mouth tight, torn between encouraging the two to give up on each other and scolding Saliha for the risks she was taking. She held firm, not letting herself say either, but could not control her tone. "So why is this fight any different?"

"He saw me at the hospital." Saliha teased, "We take our moments where we can." She sighed. "I only wish he would let me come to him."

Zaytuna lost control of herself. "If someone saw you!"

"He should come here!" Saliha sat up straighter. "The neighbours are used to him sleeping here. He's your brother. Who would notice?"

"I would notice, Yulduz, and now, Layla. A child!"

"Oh, how you love to scold. He'll not act on it, don't worry. What other man could restrain himself the way he does? Walla, I guess he inherited something of your mother's ascetic sanctity."

"Saliha!"

"I will wear him down." Saliha clucked with certainty.

"I'm leaving." Zaytuna opened the curtain.

"To find your brother or go to your uncle?"

"Who knows where Tein is? My uncle. I'm taking Layla with me."

"Say a prayer for me!" Saliha called out.

Layla was waiting for her in the courtyard with her best wrap on, but wound around her like a working woman and her face uncovered. Zaytuna's heart went out to the girl, remembering the days when she covered her face like a rich girl and reminded herself not to be so hard on the poor thing. "Mashallah, Layla. You look pretty."

Her brown eyes lit up.

Pointing to her bare feet, Zaytuna asked, "What about those good sandals Auntie Maryam got you?"

The girl dashed into her room and out again, hopping on one foot, then other as she pulled the sandals on. She bent over, examining her feet in the thin, crisscrossed straps. "My feet are so big."

"You are perfect." She held her hand out.

Out of the passageway, Zaytuna turned toward the square, but Layla pulled to the left.

"Why that way?"

"Umm Parviz will see you. She'll be closing up her shop."

"Walla, the woman *asked* me to find out if her husband had taken another wife."

"That doesn't mean she wanted to know, Auntie."

"How was I to know the difference?" She pushed Layla ahead, away from the square, following the girl through the curving, narrow lanes and arguing with herself the whole way. *There are plenty who are grateful for my help. And Salman? I found his stolen coin purse and the boy who did it!* She had dragged the boy by the ear across the square to Salman who, in retribution, bound the culprit to learn hadith with him. *And I got paid!*

Zaytuna slowed, letting Layla get ahead of her as she thought about Umm Parvaiz leaning on her crates stacked high with fresh vegetables. The neighbourhood women gathered around her shop, gesturing and sucking their teeth as she shared her suspicions that her husband had taken another wife. Zaytuna had stood to the side, a bunch of long-stemmed spring onions in one hand, listening as the woman wailed, "If only I knew! It would set my heart at rest. Ya Allah!"

She never asked you.

"I could find out for you, Auntie," she had called out to her.

Umm Parvaiz carried on, ignoring her. "If only I knew!"

One of the women put her arm around her and repeated Umm Parvaiz's call, "If only you knew!"

She never asked you. You did not listen. Now look.

Her gut clenched. She searched for an alley to escape.

Where will you run to get away from yourself?

Layla got further ahead.

Say it!

She stopped walking and put her hand on the wall. Her back tightened into a knot and the pain shot down her leg.

Under her breath, she admitted, "I did what I wanted, because I wanted it. I made that woman's life worse." She sighed. "God forgive me and unravel that woman's troubles."

Far ahead, Layla turned around. "Auntie!"

Zaytuna stood gingerly, protecting her back, as Layla rushed to her.

"I'm all right, it's only my back."

"I should have noticed," she said, taking her hand. "Can you walk?"

"Yes, yes," Zaytuna said too harshly, aiming the tone at herself, not the girl. She prayed silently, *God, open my ears, my eyes, and my heart. Guide me so I know when I should act and how.* Aloud, she recited the blessing on Muhammad, his family, and companions to seal her prayer, "Alahumma salli ala sayyidina Muhammad..."

"...wa ala alihi wa as-sahbihi was salima tasliman," Layla joined, swinging her hand. After, she asked, "Getting ready for tonight?"

"Something like that."

It wasn't long before they were at Junayd's home. Ziri was in place at the door, greeting everyone as they came through. "Assalamu alaykum, Zaytuna." He bowed to Layla in welcome. "Who is this?"

Zaytuna put an arm around her. "My neighbour, Layla."

Layla added, "I wash clothes with her, too!"

"Mashallah!" he exclaimed and stood back from the door.

As always on the nights they held the ritual of music and remembrance of God and the Prophet, the main room was crowded. Clusters of men and women were already sitting on sheepskins laid out around the courtyard in circles upon circles, leaving a space in the centre open to the sky. When ecstasy overcame them, some would rise to dance and turn there. The lanterns were lit, sending flickering light from their niches and the archways visible even though the sun had not set. It would not be until dark that the elaborate patterns from the cut metal lanterns would move along the walls with the slightest breeze, as if they, too, were remembering God and swaying in love as the ritual overcame them.

Her uncle and shaykh was sitting in his place while the aunties were on the far side, close to the kitchen and sitting on sheepskins and chatting. One of Uncle Nuri's old friends sat nearby them in a well-worn robe with a wrap around his shoulders and over his turban, covering his face. Nuri loved the people and since he died, now and again, one would come and sit in his regular place to be with the great saint of Baghdad in spirit. *I am with you*, thought Zaytuna, tasting the sweetness of the memories of sitting here with her uncle, the children leaning on him, until he fell into ecstasy and would stand and sway with divine love.

Putting her hand on Layla's back, Zaytuna pushed her in the

direction of the kitchen. "Go see who is back there. After go sit by the aunties."

Layla walked tentatively ahead of her while Zaytuna watched, anticipating the two young friends being reunited. As Layla approached, Abdulghafur ducked out of the kitchen, holding two large jugs of water, and stopped short. His eyes met hers with surprise, followed by gratitude, then pleasure. Putting down the jugs, he rushed forward and picked Layla up, and to her obvious delight, swung her around before realizing where he was and placed her back on the ground, his face flushed with embarrassment mixed with joy. Auntie Samiha laughingly scolded him and called Layla over to her. She followed, and Abdulghafur picked up his jugs. The two stole smiles at one another.

"Zaytuna." Mustafa's soft voice came from over her shoulder. She turned, feeling like Layla in the air, hoping to find herself in his arms. But he stood far enough away for there to be no misunderstanding his intent.

They stood in silence for a moment, but not the silence of their quiet companionship of days now passed. He was reticent to speak, finally whispering, "Are we still friends?"

"Yes," she replied, despite still wanting more.

Beginning again in the awkward silence, he asked, looking past her to Layla. "You brought the girl?"

"She wanted to come. I don't think I ever told you she and Abdulghafur are old friends. They've had a reunion."

"Oh?"

"He worked nearby her before he came here."

"Oh."

There was silence again for a moment too long.

She broke it this time, remembering his effort to reach out to her before, and talk about what was uppermost in her mind. "Remember, my dream?"

He coloured and turned away from her.

She put her hand out. "Oh, no! Walla! The body, Mustafa, I meant the dead body, Abbas. Tein is investigating a murder just like it."

He gasped in relief. "Yes! I heard about the murder and thought of you. I should have said something to you immediately. Have you talked to Uncle Abu al-Qasim about it again?"

Leaning in, hoping he would understand, she said, "God must want me to help." Then, remembering how she had misread Umm Parvaiz, she retreated. "I'm not sure."

"Zaytuna." He took a half step forward. "Do not get involved."

He was always like this, warning her off of investigations. She kept her mouth shut until an acceptable retort came to her. None did, so she remained silent.

As usual, he could read her silence and pressed on. "This is a serious matter. The man was killed like Abbas." He paused. "Don't you see? There will be political implications. It is said that he was killed to provoke the Shia into rebelling. That Imam in North Africa might want to take advantage. Or the Qarmatis. Everyone dreams of taking Baghdad." Brow knitted with worry, he whispered, "There could be violence. You must tell Tein about the dream, but do nothing else."

"Subhanallah!" Her objections retreated as the dream unfolded before her, all its elements falling into place, and not the places where her shaykh had put them yesterday. The flooding rain. The approaching, encompassing wave. The man carrying the butter sack filled with coins seemed sinister now. The Mahdi carrying the body of Abbas, with Lady Fatima standing beside him with the tablet in her arms. The promise that the end was coming. It was about something more than her own soul. "I'll be able to find him in the morning."

"Tein won't believe the dream is significant. But Ammar might."

She glanced at Junayd. "Could Uncle Abu al-Qasim have been wrong about the dream? He said the dream was personal. It was the end of my world. I thought I was Abbas."

Mustafa coloured at the implication that the shaykh could err, insisting, "He had no reason to interpret it differently. Tell him about the body."

Several men were sitting with Junayd talking, but the

preparations for the sama were well under way. The drums were being corrected for sound by the fires in the kitchen. The call to prayer would come before long. "There's no time, now."

"Come back in the morning, then, but go see Tein."

"I will. Thank you. I prayed for guidance, Mustafa, and here you are saying this. May God reward you."

"Alhamdulillah." He lowered his head with the acknowledgement.

The old humble Mustafa whom she had loved since she was a girl was before her again, and she wanted to fall into his arms. She glanced around to see if anyone noticed and backed away from him, blushing, saying under her breath, "I'm going to sit down with the aunties."

"If you want to talk again, I'm here."

She nodded and returned quickly to the back of the courtyard. Layla was sitting at the edge of the circle of elder women, as close to the kitchen as she could, obviously searching for Abdulghafur. Before she could sit down, she heard her name.

"Zaytuna."

The accented Arabic. It was YingYue. *God, how you test me.* She blinked hard in exasperation and forced herself to turn around. "Assalamu alaykum."

"Wa alaykum assalam, Zaytuna," she said, concerned. "Something is wrong."

"It's nothing. Truly. My back hurts."

"Is there anything I can do?"

Uncle Abu al-Qasim was busy. Auntie Hakima was gone. The murder was more important than her feelings. Perhaps YingYue could help. "The dream I spoke to you about yesterday. Something happened."

YingYue pulled her to a quiet space near the back door. As they passed Layla, the girl looked up at her longingly.

"Stay with the aunties, I need to speak to YingYue."

Layla nodded in agreement, but seemed worried. Zaytuna stopped. Of course, the girl was uncomfortable sitting there with old women she did not know. She held out her hand to the girl. "Come sit with us." Layla scrambled up, taking her hand, and followed them.

YingYue sat down against the wall. Zaytuna sat across from her, her back to the community. Layla nestled in next to her. Everything in her body wanted to push the girl away, but she forced herself not to react.

"Tell me," YingYue said.

"I found out today that the dream may be about a murder. Tein and Ammar are investigating a crime in which the victim was killed as Abbas was killed. Mustafa pointed out that the murder might be political. I hadn't thought of it. Perhaps someone is trying to provoke a revolution. If the Shia protest the killing, revolutionaries might take advantage of their distrust of the caliph." Only then did the more likely scenario come to mind. "Or it is all a coincidence and the caliph is ready to take advantage of it to crush the people. Either way, it's dangerous."

Layla stiffened next to her. She wished now she had made the girl sit apart from them. Turning to her, she asked, "Layla, would you wait for me with the aunties?"

"Don't treat me like a child."

YingYue asked, "And if you hear something that upsets you?"

"I'll be brave."

"There is no telling this one what to do."

"I believe you will be brave," YingYue said to Layla, patting her on the knee. "You must also trust God."

Layla agreed, but drew herself in more closely to Zaytuna.

"YingYue," Zaytuna asked. "Why did Shaykh Abu al-Qasim say the dream was about me, only?"

"It is about you, but it might also be about the murder, perhaps violence coming. Dreams have many levels, Zaytuna."

"What should I do?"

"You should speak to Shaykh Abu al-Qasim again."

"If God gave me this dream, doesn't it mean I am being called to act?"

"You must tell Tein and Ammar about the dream. But you must

also speak to Shaykh Abu al-Qasim."

She hesitated. "But shouldn't the shaykh know without me telling?"

YingYue's cheeks reddened. Her eyes widened as she pulled back. "Perhaps he knows and did not think it was useful to tell you. There is a risk of getting attached to dreams at this level. But also, Zaytuna, remember that he is not God. The shaykh only knows what God lets him know. The rest he knows from his eyes and ears like anyone else. I do not know what he knows. You will know by asking."

"I will come in the morning." Zaytuna stiffened at the correction.

"No, Zaytuna." She leaned in again. "He will be gone in the morning. I was told to be here to greet anyone who might come to visit. He will be back before the evening prayer. Come at that time."

Zaytuna bristled at YingYue being given that responsibility, then pulled herself back from it, answering without emotion. "I will. Then I'll speak to Tein and Ammar. But I can also start asking around, especially about the man with the butter sack. We know who everyone in the dream is but him. He could be important to the case."

"Only if there is no danger." YingYue paused, worried. "The servant of God should act slowly. Do not be rash."

She was tired of YingYue's admonitions, but took the point all the same. First thing, she would go to the police offices to tell Tein and Ammar everything. That would not be rash.

"But," YingYue said, her index finger at her lip. "The shaykh said that as one world ends another begins. One world after another in our lives. He said that you shouldn't worry? Correct?"

"Yes?"

"Perhaps he is prepared for this crisis? This world is nothing but upheaval after upheaval. He has seen a great deal, and he knows we go on despite these losses." She paused again. "Perhaps he knows, but does not want you to worry about that. He wants you to reflect on your lower soul."

Zaytuna stared at her intently, trying to push away what she was saying, but her words were coming at her with the force of water seeping through cracks, and soon the truth of it soaked through her.

"That is most important," YingYue said insistently. "If the violence comes, Zaytuna, how will you be? What will you do? Will you have the wisdom to act," she paused, searching for the word in Arabic, then found it, "to act judiciously or will you act out of fear, anger, and ignorance?"

"What does she mean?" Layla asked.

"If something bad happens, will I follow the commands of the animal in me? When I'm scared or angry, I yell at people. Like when I am mean to you. That's my animal, biting at people from the hole where it's trapped."

Ziri made the call to stand in prayer and they turned to see that the men and boys had laid out sheepskins and rugs and everyone was finding their place.

Zaytuna stood. "Come, Layla, let's pray."

"When is the music?" she asked.

"Afterwards." Zaytuna caught YingYue's attention as she arranged a shawl over her capped head and forced herself to admit aloud that YingYue's advice had helped. "You're a good teacher."

YingYue blushed and lowered her head, pulling her shawl over her face, "God forgive me."

In her sincere humility, YingYue was more beautiful than ever, and Zaytuna wanted to weep.

Layla squeezed her hand and leaned into her. "Let's pray."

The three fell in behind the aunties on the other side of the courtyard. Abu Muhammad took his place ahead of everyone to lead the prayer. While they waited, Zaytuna made a prayer of her own. Holding her heart out to God, her hands open before her, she pleaded, *You gave me a dream leading me to ask these questions. Please guide me. Help me understand what is right. Keep me from being rash.* She felt the reassuring warmth of divine waters reaching her.

As the women were straightening their lines, shoulder to shoulder, she realized what she should do. *The mosque.* She would go to the Shia mosque in Buratha and ask the old women there about the man with the bag of coins. She would bring it all to Tein and Ammar, and after that, her shaykh. *Most gracious, God, You answered my prayer.* Then added another prayer on the success of the last. *Heal my sorrow.*

DAY THREE

13

Ibn Marwan's errand boy was there again, the same rude expression on his face. "The boss wants you," he said in a mocking sing-song voice, and ran before Ammar could hit him. Tein was not in yet, and Ammar was glad of it. He did not know what Ibn Marwan was going to say, and he did not need Tein making good on his threat to leave, not now.

Nuruddin acknowledged him at the office entrance. "It's not good."

No sooner was Ammar at Ibn Marwan's door than he bellowed, "You better have good news! The caliph got word. He's sending the ghilman into the streets of Buratha and the Shia neighbourhoods in Karkh. It's meant to be a show, but it won't be a show before long."

"I know. We saw the ghilman by the stables yesterday."

"You'll see them in the streets today. Where are you on the case?"

"We traced the bow to Utbah ibn Harb. His father hated the Shia. He is our chief suspect. We think he's a bored rich boy, taking up his father's hatred, and hunted down the man for sport. He is a master archer. He could have made those shots."

Ibn Marwan sat up. "Arrest him!"

"Two problems. Utbah says boys stole the bow off of his horse last week and he's probably buying some witnesses to it right now. He also has an alibi. But we have to confirm it. He claims he was with a woman, but he won't divulge her name. I threatened to frame him for it if she can't attest to his alibi, but he didn't budge. Said he'd rather be punished for his father's sins than shame the girl. We think he's lying about both."

"Good. Arrest him."

Ammar ignored him. "We can't prove or disprove the theft. But we don't believe that he wants to protect a woman. Men are only that noble in poems and this man did not have a shred of nobility in him."

"Even better."

"We're going to the Buratha mosque today to ask more questions."

"No! Arrest Utbah!"

"We've only got one chance to get this right. If we arrest him without proof, he'll be sent for execution without it. And what if we are wrong?"

"It doesn't matter. There is no more time! Aren't you listening?"

"Just until the end of the day. That is all I am asking."

Ibn Marwan waited a moment before answering, gritting his teeth. "If you haven't got something reliable for me by first thing tomorrow morning, I'm sending officers to Utbah's home to arrest him."

"I'll have something for you in the morning," Ammar hedged.

He left the office hoping he had bought them more than one day. Ibn Marwan was so angry he forgot to ask Utbah's address. Ammar was not about to volunteer it. If Ibn Marwan did not call on favour from his betters who would be likely to know the name, it would take an extra day for his best men to find out the address, and he and Tein were his best men.

Back in his own office, he paced, waiting for Tein to arrive. They would see for themselves how high the tensions were. First, they had to go back to the house to question the guard. Then they needed to get his mother early and head to the Buratha mosque to question people there. There wouldn't be any time for lunch with her afterwards. She would understand. He hoped.

Tein came in. "The overnight watchman just reported. Utbah didn't leave the house up to when the morning watchman came on duty."

"We need to talk to the house guard, Abdurrazzaq, about Utbah's alibi."

"We should have done that last night. I told you. He'll talk."

"After he showed us out?" Ammar replied defensively.

"We could have cornered him at the gate."

"With the gate boy watching and reporting back?"

Tein did not respond immediately but leaned against the doorway, then said, "I don't trust anything Utbah said. I'll put money on him having Shia friends. I'll put money on that alibi being a lie. And that the guard will give us evidence for it all."

"So now you're a gambler?"

"It's not gambling when it's a sure thing."

Ammar got himself under control. "If we leave now, we can interview the guard, or a servant at least. I want to get to the Buratha mosque early to talk with the men there."

"Get your mother first?" Tein seemed hopeful.

"Sorry, no lunch."

Tein put his hand on his belly. "I'll live." Then, "We'll need a skiff to the lower bridge to make it in time."

"Got it." Ammar shook his arm so that the coin clinked in his sleeve pocket.

They walked as fast as they could out of the Round City to the bridge crossing the Tigris. Despite the lineup of people, they were across and at the home of Utbah's uncle before the sun was far over the wall of the estate. At the servant's entrance, Ammar slammed down the knocker on the gate.

Abdurrazzaq opened it before he could hit the door again. "Utbah will not speak to you."

Tein replied, "We're here to talk to you."

"Yet, I am not here to speak with you."

"You've got aspirations to high society with that patter. You think you're more than paid help to Utbah?"

"I work for Utbah's uncle and I, too, am a ghazi. I know what you get paid and I know what I get paid."

Ammar leaned back, sticking his thumbs in his sword belt, and needled the man. "A fellow ghazi! How did we miss you? Must have been the fine clothes and expensive boots. Not quite what we wore out on the battlefield getting blood on our hands."

"Infantry?" Tein asked.

"I was not an archer if that is what you are implying." His back was up.

"And the morning of the killing. Where were you?"

"Here. And I've got witnesses. A lot of them."

Tein held up his hands. "Ghazi, we need your help."

"And lose this position? I have land of my own now. I'm building a house on it. So, no." Abdurrazzaq began to close the gate, but Ammar stepped in, Tein right behind him. The three men looked at each other with the resignation of old soldiers whose loyalty to each other will inevitably, even if unwisely, come first. "Get out before someone sees you! They'll think I gave you something."

"Step out in the street," Ammar said. "We'll follow and shut the gate."

"Quick!" Tein pushed.

Abdurrazzaq slipped out, and Tein and Ammar followed, shutting the gate behind them. Sighing, he admitted, "Utbah left last night and has not returned."

"How? We had the gates covered."

"Yes, we saw," he said directly to Tein. "There's a third entrance, the market gate."

A curse got half out of Tein's mouth.

"Did he take anything with him?" Ammar asked.

"No, but he dressed the way he does when he's gone for the night."

"To see a woman?"

The guard chuckled, "Not likely."

"What does that mean?"

"He was wearing his rough clothes, a thick wrap. What he wears when he is playing at being a man of the people, not out to charm lovers."

"He says he has a woman he sees, an elite woman he won't expose who can give him an alibi for the murder."

"There's no woman like that right now."

"How do you know?"

"He takes pleasure in sharing details no one wants to hear."

"Even elite women?" Ammar asked.

"Especially."

"How often does he sleep out?" Tein asked.

"Once or twice a week," Abdurrazzaq answered.

"And he uses the market gate for that, too?"

"No."

Tein pressed, "Where does he go when he's dressed rough?"

"I will answer this one question, then no more. It will be enough."

They waited.

"The Buratha mosque." He looked between the two of them. "Now go." He pulled a key out of his sleeve pocket and opened the gate far enough for him to get in, and shut the door quickly behind him.

"Utbah is guilty," Ammar said.

"The guard thinks so and I agree."

"Now he's fled."

"Maybe not. He may be in hiding."

"Let's work with that. The watchmen aren't worth much, but we can at least put out word to be on the look-out."

"And the military watching the roads outside the city?"

"I'd have to petition Ibn Marwan for that. For now, let's get my mother and go to the mosque."

They made their way to the upper bridge over the Tigris and found the footpath down to the landing where several skiffs waited for passengers to be taken to the lower bridge. He and Tein climbed into the first one, settling onto the wood slats, Tein in the centre,

Ammar at the bow. It wasn't a moment before the older boys waiting to carry up goods from the basket boats pushed them out into the river. The boatman pulled the sail around to catch the breeze, and in moments they were moving swiftly past the estate houses along the shoreline.

"West side of the bridge," Ammar called out to the boatman.

"That'll cost more."

Ammar waved his hand to agree. The water glittered with the sun and he squinted, checking their pace against the shoreline.

"Why would he hide in the Buratha mosque?"

"Maybe he's not hiding there, but we'll get a lead," Ammar answered.

A moment later, they skidded onto the landing and a boy helped balance the skiff while they got out. Tein struggled to get his bad leg over the side of the skiff while Ammar handed the boatman the fare and a chink of fals to the boy.

Checking the location of the sun in the sky, Tein said, "Still a long walk, but we've got time."

As soon as they got on the main road in Karkh, they saw the increased military presence. It was only several small groups of three or four ghilman foot soldiers, but they were walking to make their presence known. They wore the short military tunic with cuirasses, swords ready. Two had staffs. Some people gave them a wide berth, while others, men who did not care for this show of power, walked too closely, threatening the Turkmen soldiers with hard looks or even harder words.

"It wasn't like this yesterday," Tein said. "Look," he pointed. "There's a watchman."

Ammar ran up to the man and spoke to him, then met Tein. "He'll pass the word along, but we can't expect much."

"No, we cannot." Tein agreed.

They picked up their pace as they crossed the canal bridge by the hospital and hurried past the regular army encampment. Any other day, the men would be relaxed, some sitting in the sun, drinking from skins, while others practiced sword and shield maneuvers, maintained camp or cooked over small grills. The men were there, sitting in groups as usual, but seeming wary. To a one, they were dressed and ready with their swords hanging from their belts. The only smoke was from the encampment mess.

"They're not out in the streets, but they are at the ready."

The two pushed on to the Ushnan bridge over the Isa canal and into Buratha, but there things were worse. The ghilman were stationed in squares for all to see. Some stood in formation, threatening in their icy stillness, while others leaned against walls menacingly, taking up space like petty criminals. Unlike in Karkh, the people of Buratha were not out taunting the men. Tein and Ammar walked through a square, empty except for a man rushing through and balancing an unwieldy package in his arms.

"Should we get your mother? Is it safe?"

Ammar answered by approaching one soldier, Tein right behind. "We're with the Baghdad police. What do we need to know?"

The young ghilman looked down on him, not answering. An older soldier broke out of a group nearby and called out to them. "What do you want?"

Ammar approached him. "I'm Baghdad police."

"I can see. What are you doing in Buratha?"

"I'm here to see my mother, take her to the mosque. Is it safe?"

"Shia?"

"Shia."

"Then watch yourself. We're only here to send a message. But we've been told that the Shia here are ready to revolt."

"It's not true. There're tensions around the death of a man. But tensions only, there's no revolt against the caliph. I would know."

"We'll make sure that tensions do not become something more. And if you know so much, then you should know whether it is safe to take your mother to the mosque."

"I know you are safe from the Shia. I don't know if the Shia are safe from you."

"Whose side are you on?"

"Right now, my mother's."

The man relaxed his posture. "We won't move unless they move."

"Thank you."

They left the square and the ghilman behind and wound their way through the streets to his family's house. Where there were no soldiers on the side streets, they were as busy as usual. Ammar was relieved. It seemed like the people might ride it out, not do anything to provoke the military.

Opening the gate to the front courtyard, they found his mother bent over at the hips, pinching herbs and placing them in a shallow basket. They could smell mutton roasting in the tannur.

Tein said, "I wish we'd be able to stay to eat that."

"I know, she'll be disappointed."

"Habibi! Bilal!" She called out as she stood, her hand on her back.

"Assalamu alaykum, Mother!" Ammar said as he rushed forward and embraced her. Tein close behind.

"My Bilal!" She took Tein's hands and he bent down to kiss them. Tein was always so tender with her. Ammar was grateful that he never took it badly that she would not use his name, Tein, but rather used the name of the first man to offer to call the prayer, a freed black man, Bilal. The one time he tried to correct his mother, Tein held him back, shaking his head. "You look hungry. Let me find you a snack. Lunch won't be ready until later."

"Mother, we have to go to the mosque early today. Can you leave now?"

She glanced at the back courtyard where the tannur stood, not answering Ammar.

"Can you get Tahirah to finish the preparations?"

His mother put her hand on his arm. "Why, habibi?"

"It's work. I need to ask a few questions there."

She moved toward the side gate where his brother, wife, and children lived. "I'll get her." Then she turned back. "Your father is coming, too. He promised me. But he won't be ready."

Tein gave Ammar a questioning glance as they approached the

house. He pulled the door open for Ammar ceremoniously. "Your father awaits."

With a mock bow in thanks, he walked through, knowing full well his father wasn't coming, but he had to go through the motions of asking him.

His father was where he always was, lying on the low couch with his feet up, napping. He had laid a kerchief over his face to block the light coming in from the rear courtyard window, put in so his mother could imagine she saw the plain of Karbala in the far distance.

"Assalamu alaykum, Father."

He came awake with a jerk, the kerchief falling from his face, his belly straining at his qamis as he sat up. "Is it time to go to the mosque?"

So he was coming. "Are you feeling better today?"

Seeing it was Ammar, not his wife, he started in on him. "There are ghilman in the street!"

"I know." He added, "We're going to the mosque early."

His father propped himself up, wiped his face with his hand, then gestured to the far wall. "Get me some water."

Pouring the water with his back to the old man, he wished silently that he wouldn't come, wanting him to make excuses like he always did for missing the weekly trip with his mother to the mosque.

"What's this about? Why are they here?"

"There's trouble brewing," he said as he handed his father the cup.

"I know that." He drank the cup of water down in one gulp, then turned on his son. "I know what is going on in my own city!"

"What do you think is going on?"

"Why would I tell you?" His father sucked his teeth. "You're not my son, but the caliph's man."

Ammar did not say what he knew he would regret later, asking again instead, "Are you coming with us to the mosque? We're leaving early."

"No." He slid back down and pulled the kerchief over his face.

Relieved, Ammar turned away and saw that Tein had already left them to argue in private.

He was nearly at the door when his father taunted him. "What do you come here for every Friday as if we're those cursed followers of Muawiya, may he find his place in hell. There's no Friday prayer for us until the Mahdi comes!"

Ammar turned around. His father was sitting up again, his face hard. The words slipped out before he could stop them. "I thought you were a man of the taverns, not a man of faith."

It took the old man a moment to register the insult. His face turned red as he yelled, "Get out of my house!"

Ammar shut the door behind him, wishing he had not said it. He knew he would pay for it down the line. His father would tell his mother and it would hurt her to know he had spoken to his father that way, no matter what kind of man her husband had become.

The voices of the women carried to him. Tahirah and his mother were discussing the meal. He put on a good face and went around the back to meet them.

It seemed like Tahirah's belly had grown even more in the week since he had last seen her. Little Qasim let go of her and grasped his grandmother's wrap with a chubby fist to steady himself. The mid-morning light shone brightly on them. The dust rose around Qasim as he pulled back from his grandmother and stamped his feet. Then Ammar's brother opened the gate between the two houses, and put his arm around his wife, kissing her on the cheek. She pushed against him, smiling, her other hand caressing her round belly. Longing for a woman and children stabbed at him in a way he had never felt before, and he turned away to catch his breath. But his mother had seen him.

"Tahirah will take care of it," she called to him. "I'm ready, habibi."

"Father said he will come later," he lied.

Her face fell, but she gave Muhsin a pleading look.

Muhsin said, "I'll try," but they all knew the old man would stay where he was until it was time to go to the tavern.

Tein stepped forward and put out his arm for her.

"My Bilal, you are surely my son, as if I had given birth to you myself. May God bless your mother's soul and may she be happy with my love for you."

"Mother, may I be a good son to you."

She patted him on the hand. "I am blessed with three good boys."

Instead of turning down the usual road, Ammar led them through the side streets and she followed without complaint. The back roads were more crowded than usual as people avoided the major roads and squares, but the square that opened up onto the mosque was full of people. The ghilman stood in its corners, all foot soldiers. They were at attention, but showed no menace. As they passed, the soldiers sized them up, noting his sword and Tein's dagger.

Winding through the crowd as they got closer, his mother craned her head, catching sight of someone. "I have a surprise for you."

"Later, Mother. I have to do some business here first."

"Of course, habibi," she said, satisfied with herself.

Ammar leaned against the wall of the blue and white tiled arched entrance of the mosque to pull off his boots, while Tein slipped off his sandals. His mother stood, sandals in hand with soles facing each other, and headed to the area where the women gathered.

Inside the main entrance, men stood in clusters, chatting. Nearby a elderly scholar sat by a column surrounded by a handful of students, all men but one woman who sat to the side. Beyond them others sat quietly around the columns while a Qur'an recitation circle gathered on the far side, their soft voices in unison, call and response, following the teacher.

"Should we speak to the imam first?" Tein asked.

Ammar did not answer immediately. The scholar, Aqil ibn Akib, who had such propriety over the family, was on the far side of the mosque with a group of young men who were having a heated discussion. Tapping Tein's arm, he gestured in the man's direction. "That's the scholar I mentioned, Aqil ibn Akib."

"I wonder what they are saying?"

"Let's see if we can find out. Maybe they'll mention Utbah."

They split up. Ammar took a circuitous route around the front of the mosque so the scholar would not see him while Tein headed to a column near the men and sat down, his back to them.

Ammar did not get far when he heard his name.

"Assalamu alaykum, ya Ammar."

He spun around, wanting to grab the person for calling him out, but found the imam of the mosque standing before him, his gentle face and manner a rebuke to Ammar's frustration.

"You are here early. Is your mother with you?"

Ammar took a breath. He needed to speak to the imam, but first checked that Tein was in place close enough to listen in on the men, before stopping. "Yes, she's already with the women."

"I hoped to ask you about the ghilman."

"The caliph fears there will be violence because of the way Bishr was killed. What do you think?"

"There are rumours," the imam whispered.

"Tell me. Please."

"I hear people say that the caliph had Bishr killed as a warning to the Shia to resist the Qarmatis. But just as many say it was a warning against putting their hopes in the one who calls himself mahdi in North Africa. Others say it is a sign that the caliph will assassinate our Twelfth Imam." He leaned into Ammar. "Thank God no one knows where he is."

"And rumours of violence?"

"I cannot stop these people from talking." He gestured with his hand out. "You understand that."

"I do. But what have you heard?"

"That the people will fight back."

"If the people protest Bishr's killing, will the Qarmatis use it to get the Shia of Baghdad to join them?"

He denied it, but his face betrayed him.

"How well did you know Bishr?"

"He was one of those boys over there," the imam said, pointing at the group of young men talking with the scholar, Aqil ibn Akib.

"Tell me about them."

"They are all followers of Jafar the Liar, except Aqil ibn Akib, of course. I wish he would not speak to them. He has tainted his reputation enough as it is."

"Really! How so?"

"The scholarly circles in Karkh have banished him. They say he has become an extremist."

"When I spoke to him, he made out he was an important man."

The imam pulled his head back. "On the contrary. He argued with them over the reliability of the agents and does not believe the Imam is at risk, insisting that he show himself." He whispered, "Of course, the people have doubts. It's understandable. But he is making these doubts worse. I have tried talking to him myself, but he will not listen."

"Is he leaving the Twelfth Imam for Jafar the Liar's son?"

"No!" he said too loudly, then lowered his voice again. "You must understand he only speaks out of loyalty to the Imam. But even after the scholars censured him, he continues to insist that all our troubles would end if the Imam would come out of hiding. He does not understand the trouble he causes." The imam repeated, "He will not listen."

"So why is he with those Fatihi boys?"

"He grew up with them. They mourn Bishr together."

Ammar turned the conversation away from the scholar. "A rich young man comes here. Utbah ibn Harb. Do you know him? I heard he might have spent the night here."

The imam's eyes widened. "No, not here. Not ever. But he was friends with Bishr. He prayed with us. He was always very polite, but..."

"Yes?" Ammar asked, expectantly.

"His father hated the Shia. However, Bishr said he rejected his father and wanted to join us, but had to wait for his father to die."

"You didn't believe him?"

"There is something I do not trust about him," the imam said.

"We think that Utbah ibn Harb may have killed Bishr in sport or out of his own personal hatred for the Shia."

The imam gasped. "God protect us from evil things!"

"Have you seen him today?"

"No." The imam glanced around, concerned. "He has not been here since the week before Bishr was killed."

Tein came up behind him. "Assalamu alaykum."

The cluster of young men had broken up. Ammar gave Tein a questioning look as he approached, but he shook his head. "I was just asking the imam about Utbah." He returned his attention to the imam. "If Utbah ibn Harb is not here, do you have any idea where he might be hiding? I am trying to solve this murder quickly, before things get out of control. If what you say is true, there must be another motive for the murder."

Tein interrupted. "What is true?"

The imam replied, "Utbah declared himself a follower of Jafar the Liar's son. He even had an audience with him." He was incredulous. "Why would Utbah kill Bishr in that manner? They were close friends. Bishr was the one who brought him to The Liar's son." He shook his head firmly, "It cannot have been him."

Tein objected. "It was his bow that was used to do it."

"There must be some other explanation," the imam insisted. "I do not trust him, but this?"

"What about a woman?" Ammar asked, "Was there any trouble between Utbah and Bishr there?"

"I don't think so. The families disappointed poor Bishr in love, but I never heard that Utbah also loved the girl." He leaned in. "Wouldn't her family be most likely to have killed him? This is what Bishr's family believes." He gazed at the people in the mosque. "I wish others would believe that as well. It would be best for all of us."

"How can I help?" Ammar asked.

The imam was apologetic. "You are one of us, Ghazi Ammar, but you are also a man of the caliph. I think your help might end up hurting. We need attention turned away from this mosque, not towards it." He scanned the mosque, then admitted, "I don't know how to stop the Qarmatis. God help us. There are several who come here and whisper in people's ears. I fear they will get this mosque burnt down by the caliph's men if we cannot protect ourselves."

The call to prayer came, and the three fell silent as a young man's clear voice rang out and the sound echoed through the arched chambers of the mosque.

Ammar said, "If you can think of anything that might be important, please tell us. But would you keep an eye out for Utbah and send word if he shows up?"

"Of course." The imam hesitated to speak.

"What is it?" Ammar pressed.

"A young woman, Nasifa."

Ammar held his breath. The girl his mother intended for him.

"Her family is very poor, you understand. She has nothing to her name but her character. Ammar, this would be riches." He seemed embarrassed. "Excuse me for saying so. Because of their poverty, they do not expect a substantial dowry. Only a good man and a good family for her to join. I have assured them you are one and no one could ask for a dearer mother-in-law than your own mother."

Ammar bowed his head in thanks. "May God reward you for your kind words and care in this matter." Noting the imam had left his father out of it, he wondered if mentioning his father's drinking and lack of faith to the family would get them to drop their interest in him.

They left the imam to find their spot in the already filling prayer lines. Tein said, "So he was hiding having become a Shia."

"That explains why he lied to us, but not why he ran."

"He feared exposure?" Tein asked doubtfully.

"What did you get?"

"Not much. It was hard to hear them over the Qur'an students' recitations. Mainly, one man said that he missed Bishr and wondered how they would carry on without him."

"The imam said they were mourning him."

"I heard the word 'tithe' but not anything else."

"Did the scholar say anything?"

"My back was to them. I didn't see who was speaking."

"We'll have to talk to his friends. The scholar again, too."

Tein said, "After the prayer, then. We'll ask about the tithe."

"Let's get in line to pray."

"So, who is Nasifa?" Tein asked as they found an open spot.

"Another one of my mother's marriage proposals for me." Ammar glanced across the women's section at his mother and caught sight of a tall, bone-thin woman. Her wrap covered her face but she was, without question, watching them from under its edge. "Zaytuna is here," he said as he turned to face the front of the mosque.

Tein cursed under his breath and stood beside Ammar, ready to pray.

14

"Bilal! You didn't say your sister was coming!" Outside the mosque, Ammar's mother beamed at Tein, her arm firmly hooked through Zaytuna's. "I've been begging you to bring her to me and here she is, alhamdulillah."

Zaytuna avoided Tein's eye, smiling instead at Ammar, who could not deny his mother a thing.

"Alhamdulillah," Ammar replied with forced cheer.

"I thought her back was bothering her, so I didn't ask her," Tein remarked. "Yet here she is. But on the wrong day, Zaytuna."

She smiled innocently in return. "My back's eased, thank you."

Ammar's mother seemed confused. "Wrong day?"

"I was going to tell you on the way home, Mother. Work calls me away."

Her face fell and her hold on Zaytuna's arm grew tight. "It is not just the meal, habibi. We have guests."

"There must be time," Zaytuna said, hoping the day would be saved.

Tein broke out of the group. She watched as he followed a knot of young men who had been speaking together, leaving the mosque square, and wondered who they were.

Then, a solidly built man in scholar's robes and a turban marking him as a follower of the Twelfth Imam stepped into their circle. "Assalamu alaykum!"

Nasifa and her parents were close behind him and joined the group.

"Your mother just introduced me to Nasifa and her mother, we're all to have lunch today." Zaytuna insisted, "Ammar, you must stay."

The scholar turned to Ammar. "Are you not staying for lunch?" He put his hand on the shoulder of Nasifa's father. "Abu Burayr here has asked me to come along. I saw you at the mosque and expressed my hope to speak with you again."

Ammar shot a quick look in the direction Tein had gone. Turning his attention back to his mother, Ammar said, "Of course. We didn't realize you had gone to so much trouble."

Tein joined them again and shook his head at Ammar.

"Everyone here is joining us for lunch." Ammar said to Tein. He gestured toward the scholar, introducing him to Tein and Zaytuna. "Mother is right, we can find the time."

Umm Ammar's grip on Zaytuna's arm relaxed. "My son, may I introduce you to Abu and Umm Burayr, and their daughter, Nasifa."

Ammar swallowed hard as he caught sight of her.

His mother added, "I am sorry Abu Ammar is not with us, he had to stay home. His leg, God give him ease."

Umm Burayr and Nasifa were murmuring a prayer for Ammar's father to be healed when Ammar's brother, Muhsin, came up behind them, smiling. "Assalamu alaykum, we are all here!"

Muhsin took the lead, grabbing Ammar by the arm and positioning him so that he would walk next to Abu Burayr, with Tein and Aqil on the other side. The two mothers fell in beside each other, with Nasifa and Zaytuna on either side. The two old women chatted, and Zaytuna observed Nasifa glance at Ammar without breaking with good manners. She seemed to like him. He was not strikingly handsome like Tein, but women seemed to be attracted to this short, barrel chested, and bull-faced man.

What would draw a man to her in marriage? Was it this? Was it liking the looks of each other? Would there be a man who liked the looks of her?

Ammar looked back, stealing a glance at Nasifa.

She fell into comparisons, every one of which pointed away from the possibility that any man would want her, let alone fall in love with her. Nasifa was petite. She would not tower over Ammar the way Zaytuna towered over most men. Nasifa had a round face with delicate features, unlike her own long face with its sharp, strong lines. But she and Nasifa both had strong, calloused hands. Neither one of them would shy from hard work. That had to count for something with a certain kind of man.

Zaytuna had observed Nasifa when she sat with the two old women before the prayers. Nasifa did not disagree openly when they declared the ghilman would soon leave and there was nothing to worry about, even though Zaytuna caught the traces of doubt on her face. She hoped that in Ammar's company she would speak up and he would listen. She considered the hard truths he faced during their last case and decided he would listen to Nasifa, and wondered if she would find a man who did the same. Mustafa would not marry her. Who else but someone who had grown up with her and had learned to love her despite her faults would ever want a sharp-tongued woman like her? There was little hope.

The men got further ahead and now all she wanted to do was leave. Zaytuna had not yet had the chance to ask the women about the man with the butter sack, but now she felt too heavy with the loss of Mustafa to endure the lunch or ask the questions that had so recently consumed her. The men stopped, waiting for them. She tried not to glance at Tein, but he finally caught her eye. He was not pleased she had come along. *Unwanted by men*, she thought, *one way or another*.

The walls of the family home finally came into view. Muhsin opened the gate, hailing his wife. She came around from the back of the house as they made their way in, wiping her hands on an old wrap tied like an apron around her pregnant belly. Both children ran past her to them, the youngest straight for their grandmother, almost pushing the old woman over. Hasan stopped short and took her hand, kissing it and raising it to his forehead. Umm Ammar patted him on the back. "You're as good as a man now, my grandson." Nasifa's face lit up, likely finding the goodness of the scene promising and imagining herself in it.

Only then did Zaytuna realize Ammar would never live in Buratha. He would leave his wife here with his mother, seeing her once a week, or alone in his small room near the Round City, seeing her only when he wandered in late from a case. *That is not what you've been dreaming of, girl.* Her heart sank into the old acceptance of the bitter realities of life. Isn't this how these things always end? And she told herself it was better that Mustafa did not want her. *Let YingYue live with the disappointment. I am free of it. God wants me for something else.* She reminded herself that she would never find God, if she did not let him go. With that, she pulled herself up and her energy for the case returned, wondering how she would ask the women about the man with the butter sack.

Muhsin went into the house, closing the door behind him, as they all stood together in the courtyard chatting, the scent of roasting meat turning everyone's mood to the company and the meal. Even Tein welcomed her, seemingly forgetting in the moment that he did not want her there. Ammar seemed more serious, which he would, knowing the reason for the lunch, but his eye was more often on the scholar, Aqil, than Nasifa. She wondered why.

Abu Ammar finally emerged, Muhsin behind him. The old man was happy. The one time she had visited, he had not been polite and she knew from Tein about his moods and habits. But now he seemed in his element. He had dressed to meet the guests. When she had visited before, he was happy to sit in his stained qamis without even a robe over it or a turban on his head. Now he stood among them with pride, wearing a brown and blue striped linen robe, tied off with a blue sash, and a brown turban. He waved the group inside, holding the door as they walked in, smiling and inclining his head to all.

They had pulled three low couches around a tray stand covered with a large, neatly embroidered tablecloth. Umm Ammar asked her to watch over Umm Burayr and Nasifa while she followed Muhsin and Tahirah to take care of the food. The women sat together on the far couch, Zaytuna making sure that she was next to Nasifa's mother in case the opportunity arose to whisper a question about the man with the butter sack.

Ammar brought out the pitcher and basin for them to wash their hands, going one by one. Once he reached Nasifa, he took care not to glance at her more than was necessary to make sure the stream of water rinsed her hands. A beautiful blush spread across Nasifa's round face, set off perfectly by the purple floral wrap framing her face. Zaytuna was charmed herself. Ammar was flustered as he moved on to pour water for Nasifa's mother, Umm Burayr. Zaytuna was only just able to hold back a delighted laugh and a teasing comment when he reached her, the last to wash her hands. But when she glanced at his face, the look in his eyes told her he knew what she was not saying, and he grinned in response. In that moment, she wished them well and, despite herself, said a prayer that their marriage would not end in loss and loneliness.

The side door to the house opened and Muhsin came in carrying the bulk of the weight of a tray wider than Zaytuna's long arm, with Tahirah on the other side helping him balance it. Umm Ammar came and sat on Zaytuna's other side as Ammar rushed guiltily to take Tahirah's place. The two men placed the tray, heaped with roast lamb and vegetables, layered on bread, onto the stand. Tahirah and the children found their spots, and the guests pulled the tablecloth over their laps as Abu Ammar said grandly, "Bismillah!" He tore off a large piece of meat and a chunk of bread and placed them before Abu Burayr, saying, "Eat, eat!" Abu Burayr took the first bite and they tucked into the glorious meal before them, the conversation going quiet.

Zaytuna took only small bites at first, savouring the rich flavour of the roasted lamb set off by the tang of sour milk, the sweetness of roasted garlic, and the pungency of rosemary. But Umm Ammar urged her on. Wanting to please her, Zaytuna took a larger portion and made a show of eating it, to the old woman's delight. The conversation came alive again, with the realization these two families would soon be one.

The scholar broke through, mentioning the dead man for no reason, ending with the requisite prayer, "May God have mercy on his soul."

Everyone in the room was jarred into sudden silence. Umm Ammar looked to her own sons with worry. Then they all whispered, "Amin," to his prayer. But no one reached their hand out to eat again.

The scholar glanced from side to side, as if he did not understand their reaction. Zaytuna wondered if he were truly that stupid. Then he spoke again. "The poor boy was caught up in love and killed for it."

Tein gave Ammar a look as if to say, "It's on your head."

Ammar shifted in place. "This is not the place to have this conversation. Perhaps when the meal is over and our guests are on their way?"

"But Umm Burayr here has information that might prove useful to you. I hoped to bring her insight on the matter to your attention."

Replying to Umm Burayr, Ammar bowed his head. "If you would not mind speaking with me before you leave, it would be a help."

Out of nowhere, Ammar's father exclaimed in frustration, "What is all this tiptoeing around? The man was murdered like Abbas. It can only mean one thing."

Abu Burayr asked in a near whisper, "What are you saying?"

"The ghilman are in the streets! The caliph's men killed the boy to start a riot, so they would have an excuse to kill us all. You would think those rich Imami viziers could spare a moment for the rest of us, but they're happy to see anyone who doesn't follow their Imam dead and gone."

Ammar's mother stiffened while Umm Burayr gasped.

Nasifa took her mother's hand and whispered something to her.

Abu Burayr turned red, rising from his seat. "*Their* Imam?"

Before his father spoke again, Ammar interjected firmly, "*Our* Imam, I assure you. I and my family are followers of the Twelfth Imam. If my father has concerns, they are his alone."

Shocked at the rudeness of Ammar's reply at first, denouncing his own father in front of them all, Zaytuna then grasped the girl could not marry him if the families were devoted to different Imams. He had to say it if he wanted to marry her.

His father snorted. "The boy is right, but so am I."

Abu Burayr backed down, looking askance at Abu Ammar, no doubt considering a future attachment to a family in which the father was not to be trusted. His daughter would become this man's daughter, live in this home, and it was plain on his face that he was unsure about the outcome of this meeting.

Abu Ammar stood abruptly, but said nothing, then sat back down hard on the couch. Umm Ammar trembled, and Zaytuna put her arm around her.

Nasifa broke the silence. "If I may..." She dropped her eyes. It was plain that she also understood that his outburst meant he wanted to marry her and was hoping to intervene. Zaytuna hoped Ammar's insistence and his mother's goodness would be enough to convince her father. Before continuing, Nasifa whispered in her mother's ear. Her mother nodded, then Nasifa said to the group, "The killing may have resulted from a more personal matter." She paused. "I mean to say, Bishr was in love with a girl and it went too far."

Ammar asked, "What do you know?"

Straightening her back, she looked him in the eye without blushing this time. "There has been talk for some time. He met with a woman from outside this community. She was not Shia. The woman was immodest and uncaring about the risk to her reputation."

Zaytuna bristled at her words, knowing that Saliha was exactly the sort of woman Nasifa would scorn.

Placing her hand on her mother's arm, Nasifa added, "We saw them ourselves outside the marketplace standing close."

Umm Burayr spoke up. "It's necessary to say it. We saw them in an embrace. God forgive the boy for his sin."

Abu Burayr stared at them both, the displeasure clear on his face.

"The girl, as I reported to you before," the scholar broke in, addressing Ammar, "was the daughter of one of Barbahari's followers. What do you think her father would have thought of this behaviour?"

"How do you know what her family thought?" Tein interrupted.

"It cannot have been a secret," Nasifa offered, her hand at her throat. "Talk travels, even between communities." The remark garnered her a censorious gesture from her father.

The scholar coughed to draw their attention. "It was no sin. The two had married, secretly, using a muta."

The other women at the table gasped at the revelation except Zaytuna, who asked, "Muta?"

Nasifa ignored her question. "God forgive me. I was wrong to suspect them. Even so," she defended herself, her voice rising, "they should not have been open in the streets as it was a secret and invited us to sin in gossip."

"A kiss like that, in public, married or not...," her mother added, reassuring her daughter.

Zaytuna became impatient with their piety and wondered how Tein felt, knowing that he was putting Saliha under the judgemental eye of women like this.

If he felt anything, he did not show it, only asking Aqil, "If it was secret how did you know?"

"I was the one who instructed him how to contract the temporary marriage so they would not commit sin. And God forbid, if she became pregnant, at least the child would be legitimate."

Zaytuna asked again, her tone sharper than she intended, "Temporary marriage? Muta? What is that?"

"The Prophet, alayhi salam, allowed it when men were away at war, and we Shia continue the practice," Nasifa replied with a pedantic tone that only irritated Zaytuna further.

"That doesn't tell me what it is," she snapped.

Tein answered, "It's a marriage contract with a time limit to it, a few minutes to a lifetime, whatever is needed. I don't know how it works, but a couple can contract it privately. That's the point. It can be secret. Men in our unit used it at the front. They had wives back home and were away for years at a time."

Nasifa's father recovered himself from his distress with his wife and daughter and tried to explain, "Imam Jafar said about..."

Aqil cut him off. "The minutiae of temporary marriage, as interesting as they are, are not the point here. The point is that I married them." He spoke to Tein, "Bishr had approached the girl's father, but they threw him out on his ear with threats if he saw the daughter again. The couple had no choice. They were going to carry on without their families' approval. I helped."

There was something in his voice that made Zaytuna uncomfortable, something dangerous, but she shook it off.

"How did the girl get out of the house after that?"

"She left her home." He looked between the two detectives. "She went to work one day and did not return. They married and set up house here in Buratha."

"We need to speak to her," Tein said.

"She left the city." He inclined his head in apology. "I informed her myself of his death and she packed her few things in front of me. I offered to help her, a bed in my home with my family, but she insisted she must leave Baghdad altogether."

Sitting forward, Zaytuna reasoned. "An enraged family would beat the boy to death and throw him into the Tigris. They wouldn't stage it so elaborately."

"Barbahari." Both Ammar and Aqil spoke at once, then looked at each other. The scholar invited Ammar to continue.

"The father was one of Barbahari's men," Ammar explained. "They have declared the Shia apostates. They are brutal. It's not beyond them."

"They are not the only Hanbalis to say so," the scholar corrected with an eye on Zaytuna and Tein.

Ammar jumped in before Zaytuna could object. "But they are the only ones who care enough to do anything about it. Most people let the scholars talk and go on their own way. You know how it is," Ammar taunted. "Is every word you say followed to the letter?"

The scholar acknowledged the point, but it was clear the

comment stung. He said, "Barbahari's men would love to see fighting break out in the city. It would suit them to start a crisis."

"Where does her family live?" Tein asked.

The scholar's eyes brightened. "On the grounds of the vizier Ibn al-Furat's palace! The father is his stable man. Can you imagine? He despises the Shia yet serves and lives on the estate of such an important Shia man in the caliphal administration!"

No one laughed at the irony of it. Despite their explanations, it made no sense. The man with the butter sack in her dream must be significant, and he did not figure into this story. She gasped, finally understanding. "Bishr, what did he do for work?"

"Work?" Aqil asked.

"Was he, for example, a mason, a butter dealer, a street cleaner?"

Umm Burayr replied, "How odd you should say butter dealer! He worked for a butter dealer. I don't remember his name, but he sells his butter and buttermilk to the finest houses directly, not just the city markets. Bishr was a delivery man for him." Her husband glared at her. "This is not gossip," she said, warily. "I saw Bishr driving the cart."

Zaytuna sat back with the satisfied feeling that things were falling into place and she had dreamt about a crucial clue. His work is related to the killing somehow. She thanked God for guiding her to this point and pressed forward. "Ammar, Tein, have you interviewed his workplace?"

Abu Burayr spoke over her, saying to Ammar, "I assure you my wife and daughter keep to their own business."

Ammar bowed his head. "I would assume nothing less, but in this case, I am grateful, as your wife and daughter's observations may help save this community from unnecessary violence. Perhaps God drew their eyes away just this once for the good of us all."

Nasifa blushed deeply at his eloquent defence.

Abu Burayr could hardly object, and now, Zaytuna thought, both families had erred at the meeting, putting them on more equal ground. She turned back to the issue at hand. "Bishr's workplace?"

Tein's mouth tightened with impatience.

Ammar conceded, "We'll head there soon."

The scholar inserted himself again. "It was through his butter delivery that he met the girl. She is a scullery maid in a wealthy household abutting Ibn al-Furat's estate." But as he said the words, his face blanched.

Zaytuna gave Ammar and Tein a look that said, "If you won't ask, I will!"

The two men shared a glance.

Aqil said something significant. Why won't you two follow up?

Before she pressed him herself, Aqil added awkwardly, "I should say," correcting himself, "she *was* a scullery maid. When they married, she left her work." He said to Ammar, "I'm afraid there would be nothing to be gained by questioning the cook. What would they say other than she left their employ?"

"Why didn't she work for Ibn Furat's household?" Tein asked.

"I, I," he stammered. "I wouldn't know."

Ammar gave an abrupt, "Thank you," ending the conversation.

Tein eyed him and Zaytuna wanted to stand up and demand that he continue the interrogation. Of course the man knew!

She sat on her hands instead as Ammar said, "I believe I can say, the government will be relieved to hear that it was personal, even if it served sectarian ends for Barbahari's men. Barbahari is no friend to the caliph." He turned to Nasifa's father and said, with great sincerity and meaning beyond the surface of his words, "If we can arrest someone in time, we might avoid this violence. We will do our best to protect this community and all our loved ones in it. Your family has helped."

The old man replied graciously, "Alhamdulillah."

Abu Ammar reached out to take another bite of food, complaining, "It's cold now, with all this talk."

Ammar's mother's face fell.

Tein put his hand in, taking a large bite. "It's delicious, not cold at all."

With that they returned to their meal, followed by a dessert of fritters soaked in honey, but the conversation had become stilted and limited to chat about the grandchildren. Abu Burayr's voice returned to its earlier gentleness as he spoke fondly of his son Burayr's children.

Zaytuna softened to them again. Of course Nasifa had to keep reputation in mind. They were poor, but had family to shame, and these things mattered. No marriage would go forward without her reputation intact. Their concern for the couple's behaviour in the street was realistic, if a touch judgmental. She sucked at her teeth without thinking. Saliha did not have a family to shame, but she had a job to lose. Zaytuna stared at her brother, wishing he would leave Saliha alone. God knows they could not trust Saliha to protect herself.

After washing their hands again, they gathered in the courtyard to say their goodbyes. Zaytuna watched Ammar and Nasifa as they stole shy glances at each other. Mustafa and YingYue looked at each other like that. And she reminded herself that despite loving her, Mustafa never looked at her that way.

As the group walked to the gate, Ammar's father appeared from the house with two packages wrapped in plain cotton and tied in expensive ribbon draped over his arm. He handed both to his wife, who seemed embarrassed. He whispered harshly in her ear, and she handed them to Nasifa and Umm Burayr, saying, "May they be a blessing."

They took the gifts with pleasure, but wondered at them. This was not typical, not for a first meeting exploring a marriage. The groom's family would give the trousseau with the signing of the contract. Not now. But they thanked Ammar's parents all the same, hands over their hearts. Ammar held back, standing with his brother Muhsin, watching the exchange. Both seemed concerned. This was more than a surprising and generous act. Something was wrong. She gave Tein a questioning look, but he shrugged in response.

Ammar's family walked Nasifa and her parents to the gate. As she stepped through, Nasifa turned and glanced one last time at Ammar. He had been watching her go and turned away in embarrassment.

She, herself, lowered her eyes, another beautiful blush spreading across her cheeks.

Tein remarked to Zaytuna as the family left, "This complicates things."

"It does."

Umm Ammar approached her. "My sweet one, thank you for coming. My home is your home. Your brother is my son, you are my daughter."

The words touched her, and she replied with sincerity, "Inshallah, I will see you again soon, Auntie."

"See you next week," said Tein.

Putting her hand on his arm, she scolded him, "*Inshallah.*"

He said sheepishly, "Forgive me. If God wills."

Ammar gave the two of them a look and broke away from his family, giving his mother and the children a kiss goodbye.

The moment Tein pulled the gate door behind them, Zaytuna demanded, "Why didn't you press him on the girl's employment? We need to know where she worked." She said firmly, "No matter, I can help."

Tein cut her off. "Stay out of this."

"The butter dealer! I knew about that. I have information you need."

"You got lucky," Tein scoffed.

"My dream!"

"Oh!" Tein gestured, palm up, mocking. "The dream!"

"What dream?" Ammar asked.

"Saliha told me." Tein answered for her. "Zaytuna had a dream of a man killed like Abbas and now she thinks she knows the secret to the case."

"You only know where they met because of me." She crossed her arms.

"We would have got there," said Ammar. "But what about the dream?"

"I'll tell you along the way," she said. "Now, where are we going?"

15

Tein blocked Zaytuna. "You aren't going anywhere."

Ammar looked at him askance. If she had something, he wanted it. There was no chance he was going to let Tein's disbelief in dreams and visions, let alone his tensions with his sister, get in the way. He moved in between them. "What about this dream?"

She cast a triumphant glance at her brother.

Ammar sighed at having to be between these two.

She addressed him, but kept her eye on Tein. "The Lady Fatima and a man who called himself the Mahdi led an army, and the Mahdi was holding a body..."

"You dreamed about the Twelfth Imam?" He cut her off. "I heard a preacher say once that he is the Mahdi, the one who is anticipated to come at the end of times. I didn't believe it. But my mother did." He paused, gripped by the implication. "Mother was right."

"The man in my dream was the Mahdi, but..."

"How did you know?"

"I knew. He warned me that the world was ending."

Does she know what she's saying? Does she know what it means? His hands trembled. He raised them as if in prayer, palms open.

"Ammar?" She leaned in towards him.

Her voice was far away and he stared at her, wide-eyed.

Tein interrupted. "Enough of this. You two can stand here and talk about whether her dream is going to solve this case. I'm going to talk to Bishr's family." He left, with a parting shot at Ammar. "When you are interested in what they've said, come find me."

Doesn't he understand what she said?

"Ammar," she said, taking his hands in her own. "Breathe."

He nodded and pulled in a conscious breath, then another, until the trembling quieted and he had control over himself again.

Zaytuna looked down the road where Tein had stalked off. He was no longer visible. "Shouldn't we have stopped him?"

"He'll get lost." Then resentment at Tein for walking away from them burned through the shock of the dream. "I'll find him. In a tavern."

She drew her head back. "He hasn't had a drink in months."

"For Saliha."

"And so?" She stepped back from him, pulling her wrap close.

"A man who quits for a woman will drink again when there's trouble." Zaytuna did not answer. But from her glare, she knew he was right. Then he felt guilty for having said it at all. "I'll find him. Don't worry."

"Good."

"But the dream," he said, and the trembling returned. He crossed his arms over his chest to hold his hands still, but he could hear the frantic edge to his voice. "I don't think you understand your own dream."

"What do you mean?"

"The Twelfth Imam has been in hiding since childhood. There's always been the worry that the caliph would have him assassinated. Just because our Imams have made peace with the caliphate, promising never to challenge their power, doesn't mean that the caliphate trusts us or that we trust them." He paused, unsure if he wanted to say it. It was as if by admitting the doubt of others, he was acknowledging his own. His chest grew tight with every word. "The only connection we have with him are his agents who collect the tithe. They used to bring letters in his own handwriting, but even those stopped. You heard my father. People have been leaving our community for Imams they can see or leaving the Shia path all together. Even so, he won't show himself. My mother remains devoted but my father has abandoned the path."

"Oh." She still looked confused.

He uncrossed his arms, wanting to grab her and shake her. "Zaytuna, your dream confirms the Twelfth Imam is alive."

"Ammar." She drew near, her voice uncharacteristically gentle. "In the dream, I knew the man was the Mahdi. I knew he was a descendant of Lady Fatima. But I don't know if he is alive. I don't know if he has even been born. I don't know if he is your Imam. Lady Fatima was next to him and she is dead. May God be well-pleased with her. It was a dream, Ammar. I don't know what it meant."

"You don't understand what you've seen!"

"Ammar, please."

Until that moment, he hadn't realized the extent of his own doubts. He had walked away from his family and his community as a teenager to make his own way as a foot soldier on the frontier of the empire. He was forever bonded to Imam Ali and Imam Husayn. And it was the stories of the courage and vulnerability of those who stood at Karbala that had taught him how to be a man, not his father. Growing up, this Imam, the Twelfth Imam, did not mean much to him. There were no stories of his bravery on the battlefield to impress a young man filled with piss and vinegar.

When he returned to Buratha as a man, he respected his mother's devotion to the Twelfth Imam and hated his father's resentment of it for her sake, but the "who" and "where" of the Twelfth Imam never mattered to him. It was not until this moment that he realized the presence and power of the Prophet, Ali, his sons, Hasan and Husayn, and the succeeding eight Imams were all here with him now. Their presence was here, in this Twelfth Imam. Grieving for what he had missed all those years but grateful to have it now, he fell to his knees, his cheek on the ground, and wept.

He felt Zaytuna's hand on his back and the soft touch of her voice on his cheek. The sound caught hold of him even though it was no louder than a breath as she said, "Allah," drawing out "a" until her breath was spent. The divine name washed through him, every muscle coming unbound, and his tears released into serene joy. He picked himself up to find her crouching before him, her wrap pooling in the dust, brushing the dirt from his face. He understood in that moment that Tein's sister was more than what he had thought of her. She had something of their mother's power.

Zaytuna spoke like a mother. "Come now, Ammar. The case."

He blinked hard. "The body, in your dream, what did you see?"

"A man dead in the Mahdi's arms, like Abbas. And there was another man, with a leather butter sack full of coins."

"In the dream, you saw Bishr worked for a man who made butter?"

"I think so. But what is the money?"

He shook his head. "I was taught you have to be careful interpreting dreams. You could change its meaning through your interpretation and bring sorrow down on you as a result. I don't want to think about what it means that you saw the world was ending."

"My shaykh said the dream was personal. My world is ending, not this one. But," she added, "my other teacher said dreams can have multiple meanings. With this case, now I think it is a warning that the end of our world as we know it is coming if we don't act in time. I am supposed to go speak to my shaykh again today. I'll ask him."

Grasping her hands, he said, "I believe you. Right now, I have to go find Tein. I'll keep an ear out for any hint of money and we'll find out which butter dealer he worked for." He paused. "Thank you."

"Alhamdulillah," she replied, nodding for him to go.

He offered her a deep bow of his head with his hand over his heart and left her behind.

Unless Tein had waited for him, he would be hard to find. He turned the corner Tein had taken, but which of the alleys branching off from that one street would he have chosen? A public square opened up at the end of the road and he went there. Once in the square he searched for a tavern, but no one was seated at the tables except for the owner, waiting for night to come. At least there were no ghilman. There was no telling which road Tein would have taken, so he turned back to the road leading to Bishr's family and hoped Tein found it.

As the blue door came into sight, Tein appeared, coming from the opposite direction, led by a local boy. Ammar snorted. How fitting that he had stormed off because of his sister's visionary dream and gotten lost. Tein grinned, laughing at himself. Ammar wanted to stay mad at him, but his friend's smile washed it away and when they met at the blue door, he slapped Tein on the back.

Outside the family house, they stood at the curtained door. "Assalamu alaykum." Then, "Baghdad Police. Grave Crimes. We have more questions."

The curtain pulled aside, and there stood the scholar, Aqil, smiling. "Wa alaykum assalam. Alhamdulillah, well met!"

They did not exchange glances, but Tein would consider his presence suspicious as well.

"Please come in."

Ammar entered, Tein ducking in behind him. There was no room to sit in the small room, so they stood along the walls. The parents did not rise. Aqil stood beside them and bent to place his hand on the father's shoulder, but he twitched it off in anger. Aqil stood up, holding his hand as if it had been slapped. "I hurried ahead to tell them about their son's marriage," he explained. "It was my responsibility to inform them, not yours. I had guided the couple to contract it."

That explained why he was here, at least. Then, Ammar asked Bishr's father, "You didn't know?"

"Of course not! We never would have permitted it." He gave the scholar a vicious stare, craning his neck. "Now our boy is dead!"

The mother bent over, whimpering, and called out her son's name. Bishr's father drew her to him, tenderly whispering in her ear but watching the scholar all the same.

"When did your son stop sleeping here?"

The father sat up. "Since his legs grew too long to fit. There's barely any room. You see. But we keep his things and he came to us every day. He never left us. How could we know?"

"I'm sorry, but we have to ask you about his friends again."

Tein stepped in. "There was a rich man who dressed down but his clothes were fine. He was an archer with a beautiful bow he likely carried with him. The man would have come down to Buratha on a horse."

The scholar cut the father off from answering. "Bishr had no friends of that sort! I would have known if he had. I know his friends."

The father stood in one smooth and surprising movement, pushing his face into the Aqil's own. "Know his friends? Were you a friend?"

Ammar and Tein readied themselves to intervene.

"No friend would've married them!"

"I assure you." The scholar stepped to the side, his hands out. "I was protecting him from suffering in the next world. He and the girl were intent on one another. I had no choice."

The father growled, "And if they had snuck around? If they had found some corner to hide in, what would be the harm in that? The girl would never have left her family and raised the alarm! My boy would be alive!"

"But the sin!"

"Damn you and your sin to hell! You killed my son as good as her family did! You were always a brutal, controlling boy, thinking you knew better than anyone else and you've grown into the same as a man. The type to kill a person to save them, that's you! And that's what you did!"

The mother's whimpering turned to wails as Bishr's father grabbed Aqil by the arm, dragging him to the door. Tein held the curtain open, and they watched as the father kicked Aqil out onto the street without resistance. The scholar lost his balance and landed hard on in the alley; the impact knocking his turban off his head. Tein let the curtain go, and they heard him scramble up and leave.

Abu Bishr was breathing sharply through his nose, his anger

barely contained as he stared at the closed curtain, the mother weeping into her hands on the floor behind him. Ammar gave him time to control himself, then said, "We've talked to his friends. But the rich one. Utbah ibn Harb. We need to find him."

The father turned on Ammar. "What do you want with him?"

"After we questioned Utbah, he ran off. He knows something."

"Go arrest the girl's father, her brother!"

"We need evidence," Tein said. "Good reason."

"Good reason? You thugs never needed good reason before!"

"Sir." Ammar tried to calm him. "You can help."

Tein added, "Bishr's friends may come to see you. Utbah may come."

He scoffed. "So what do I do? Hold him here for you?"

"No," Tein said. "Talk to them. Remember what they say. If you can send word to us that Utbah's been here, we'll come back."

The father nodded, but his expression said otherwise.

Ammar said, "One last thing, sir, where did Bishr work?"

"Outside the Cheese Sellers' market. Kamal Ali ibn Abdussalam al-Fassi, the butter dealer." He taunted them. "Is that where you'll arrest his killer?"

"We have to follow up every lead," Tein explained.

He took a step toward them, crowding them out. "Go then! This better end in justice for my boy."

They left, glad to be out into the air of the alley, and did not speak until they got beyond the blue door.

"Which way is the market?"

"This way." Ammar turned and took the lead.

The market gate was smaller than those leading into the great markets of Baghdad, but just as delicately tiled and crowded with curse writers and old women sitting on squares of cloth selling cups of pre-soaked beans and handfuls of fresh herbs bound with string. The crowds were returning after the long lunch and Tein and Ammar pushed through into the market. Ammar approached two young men standing before molded cones of colourful ground spices, while a third helped an old woman. He called out to them, "Ya akhi, where is the cheese market?"

One of the young men bowed his head and pointed further in, tapping his finger twice in the air, then once to the left.

Ammar waved in thanks. They carried on straight past two cross streets and turned at the next. They could see the cheese sellers further down and beyond them another gate. Ammar picked up his pace, not considering Tein's leg, only wanting to get there and get what they needed, including confirmation that Zaytuna's dream was true. Outside the gate, he stopped and turned, waiting for Tein to catch up.

He pointed to a row of shuttered doors. "Closed."

Tein turned back to the nearest cheese seller. "Kamal Ali al-Fassi, the butter dealer. He's closed today?"

"Always in the afternoons."

"You're open."

"He sells wholesale or delivers to the estates." The man scowled. "He boasts he sells to the caliph's kitchens, but I don't believe it. I asked him to take my cheese with him one day. He told me the caliph's cooks make their own cheese. Well, if they make their own cheese, I tell you, then they make their own butter. The man's a liar."

"He'll be open in the morning?"

"Like I said."

"Did you ever talk to one of his delivery men, Bishr?"

"God have mercy on his soul."

"We're investigating," Tein said. "Baghdad Grave Crimes."

"Word is the caliph's men did it. So why would you be asking?"

"Tell people that's a lie." Ammar wondered how far that rumour had spread. First, he heard it from his father. Now here. "It's a lie. The killing is personal, not political."

"So why're there ghilman in the streets threatening our families?"

"Because everyone is ready to riot over this."

"We weren't until they showed up," he said, shrugging his shoulders.

"You're not worried?"

"The people of Buratha will fight."

"There's no need for fighting," Ammar insisted. "We'll find who did it."

Something caught the man's eye outside the gate. He looked past them. "Better hurry."

They followed his gaze. A troop of ghilman were walking towards them, putting on a show, with their swords at their hips and shields strapped to their backs. In front of them, four boys were hiding behind a large cart with a pile of stones between them and more stones in their hands, waiting to ambush the unit.

Tein and Ammar approached the boys, Tein grabbing one by his robe. "What do you think that's going to get you?"

The boy spat. "We'll kill you! We'll kill all the caliph's whores!"

The spit hit its mark. Tein held firm to the squirming boy, while another came straight at Ammar, barrelling into his waist, small arms around him, trying to push him back. He felt the boy grab the hilt of his sword and took hold of his wrist gently, forcing him to let go.

The ghilman walked past them, eyes ahead, except a few who broke rank to mock the police trying to control children. Then, the other two boys came from behind the cart and threw their stones at the soldiers. A stone rang out as it hit a soldier's helmet. He bent from the impact, turned around to see the culprit, then alerted the others.

Ammar released the boy and shoved him forward. "Run!"

Tein pushed the one in his hands toward his friend.

The boys ran.

The ghilman marched on the two remaining boys hiding behind the cart again, stones in their hands.

"Run!" Ammar yelled, but one stood up and threw a stone at him. Ammar leaned to the right and it flew past him.

Tein stepped in front of the boys and turned toward the ghilman, one hand on his dagger, the other out. "Stand down!"

But the other boy cut around Tein. Screaming with rage, he charged at the soldiers, throwing what stones he had left before ramming his body into one. The soldier recovered his balance to grab him by the back of his robe while another took hold of his arm. "A lively one!"

Instead of giving up, the boy fought hard, kicking shins, twisting in their grasp, and roaring. Ammar was behind Tein, rushing to the boy just as the soldier twisted his arm up at a hard angle. Surely he had broken it.

"Stand down!" Ammar yelled, his sword unsheathed.

Tein gestured to him and turned back to find the other boy.

The boy's legs gave out, forcing the soldier to let him go, but he landed a kick in the child's stomach once he was down.

Ammar brought his sword around to the two men. They took one step back, each with a hand up, the other on the hilts of their own swords. One said, "Relax policeman."

The boy moaned on the ground.

Two more ghilman came around to them, their swords ready, when a crowd surged out of the market. Men, even some women, were holding staffs, hammers, and knives, ready to fight.

One soldier yelled a command Ammar could not make out. The troop retreated past Ammar and Tein until they were beside the cart, facing the crowd, shields up and swords ready.

Tein came up behind Ammar, tapping him on the shoulder and pointed to the cart, making a discreet circling motion.

With the armed crowd surrounding the soldiers at the front and side of the cart, they would circle behind it and take up the rear.

Ammar stooped down to help the boy get out of the way, his roaring turned now to groans of pain. Tein searched for the other boy, but he must have run for his life. Carrying the injured one behind the cart with them, they placed him underneath it for safety. Then they moved to the rear, trapping the troop between two ghazis and a crowd spoiling for a fight. One ghilman noticed them and alerted the others. Two soldiers broke with formation to face them.

Armed only with his dagger, Tein chuckled, asking in a voice that Ammar remembered well from the battlefield, "Only two? For us?"

Fear crossed the ghilman's face. *Wise*, thought Ammar.

No one moved, not the ghilman nor the crowd. Enlivened by fear, the old hunger for battle growled in his belly and it took everything Ammar had to stand still, but he held on, waiting until he knew the fight had stopped before it started. The silence of the standoff lasted a moment longer than it should. He had his answer. The fight was over.

The leader barked an order. The men stood straight and sheathed their swords, but their shields remained up. Sheathing his own sword, Ammar begged the people, "Let the soldiers go. No one needs to die today."

On the far side of the crowd, a few men stepped aside but only gave the soldiers a narrow passage to march through. To a one, they stood chests out, hammers and staffs in hand, informing the ghilman whose town they had walked into and that it was the people of Buratha who chose if they lived or died.

The people gave way but their voices rose, offering protests to their backs. "They kill our son like Abbas and now they come to kill us!" Another yelled, "The Qarmatis will handle the caliph's boy fuckers!" Then, another followed. "The caliph pisses himself before the Qarmatis!"

Ammar pulled one man aside. "The murder was about a girl. A family matter. There's no need for any of this!"

"Oh, it's long past that now!" Pointing toward where the ghilman had left the square, he insisted, "It's them! It's the caliph! He'll do anything to be rid of us."

Gripping the man's robe with his fist and pulling him in tight, Ammar hissed, "What about the Qarmatis in Baghdad?"

The man grasped Ammar's wrist without fear until Ammar pushed him away, then he spat on the ground. "You're one of them. A boy fucker for the caliph, too."

Ammar walked away, leaving the man to his insults, but other voices rose and fell, signalling that the fragile peace negotiated by the Imams with the Abbasid caliphate was close to breaking. Qarmatis or not, there would be an uprising before long if they could not get the troops withdrawn.

Tein and another man were crouching beside the boy, having

brought him out from underneath the cart. One of his arms was hanging at a sickening angle. The man stood, calling out behind him. "It's Abu Ardashir's other son, go get him!"

The boy's head lolled as he held his broken arm. An eye was swelling shut and blood stained his qamis. He was shivering despite the heat.

"Where's the bonesetter?" Tein asked the man standing nearby.

"Not far."

"He got kicked hard," Ammar interjected. "We should take him to the hospital in Karkh."

Tein placed the broken arm against his chest. Ammar saw what Tein was doing and pulled his own turban off his head, unwinding it, and handing it to Tein.

Tein sat the boy up, keeping his arm from moving while he and the man beside him used the turban to immobilize it. Then he slid one arm under his legs and one arm around his back and stood.

The man objected. "Don't move the child until his father gets here."

"We're taking him to the Barmakid hospital. He may have other injuries that we can't see. Tell his father to come there."

Someone called out from the crowd. "He's here now!"

The father pushed through the crowd. "Alamdar!" As he reached Tein, he held out his arms. "Give me my son."

"They broke his arm," Tein said as he placed the boy in his father's arms. "He should go to the hospital. They kicked him, hard."

"I'll take him to the healer." Turning his attention to his son, there were tears in his eyes. "My boy! You fought the soldiers like Imam Ali! My little lion! My little lion!"

Someone nearby raised the cry. "Our Little Lion!"

Smiling weakly, the boy leaned his head against his father's chest.

They stood to the side as the father walked with his son past those who remained in the square, now standing in honour of the boy's bravery. Here and there, men called out, "Little Lion!"

"Never thought I'd see police helping the people," a man nearby said.

Ammar replied under his breath, "That's because they don't."

Tein swung his head around, but Ammar couldn't read his expression.

"Let's go," Ammar said, exhausted.

The two walked in silence to the Ushnan bridge crossing the Isa canal and back into Karkh, until Tein asked, "You tired of this, too?"

"I'm not tired of protecting the people from each other or the ghilman."

"That's not what I asked."

"Maybe I'm not ready to answer."

They fell back into silence, passing the barracks and making their way to the Hospital Bridge.

Tein asked, "What's next? We go to the girl's family?"

"It's too late now. It'll be night before we get across the Tigris to Ibn Furat's estate to interview them."

"Tomorrow?" Tein balked. "The ghilman will find any excuse and the people are ready to take them up on it."

"And barge in after dark to arrest them with no evidence?" He objected with finality. "We have to talk a confession out of them."

Tein did not respond, and Ammar knew what it meant. Tein did not want to wait. But it wasn't up to Tein.

"First thing," Ammar assured. "Meet me at the office."

Stopping at the end of the canal bridge and glancing at the hospital, Tein said, "I'll stop here," leaving Ammar to walk on alone, bare-headed for all to see.

16

Saliha had already left work. Tein had sent a boy into the hospital to ask, not wanting to draw Ibn Ali's attention or scandalize Shatha by going in himself, let alone give Judah the opportunity to do her any harm. She had either gone to the market or home. The thought of searching for her in the marketplace was humiliating. He had decided to do what he vowed he would not, put his broken life in her hands. If he was going to give up on himself and give her what she wanted, it would not happen in a public place. The only way was to go to her home and wait if he had to.

As he walked, the late afternoon sun picked up the dust rising from the donkey carts ahead of him, turning the golden light to dun. On another afternoon, a month or more after that day in the graveyard, when he told her he could not be with her unless they married, he waited for her on a corner between work and home and called her to him. She came joyfully. They had found a room easily enough. No one asked questions. Saliha left him afterwards, sprawled on the mattress, his dagger fallen to the floor and forgotten under the clothes she had taken off of him, piece by piece, so slowly, and then her own, that he almost ruined it all with their first touch. Afterwards, he limped to a tavern and sat with a cup of wine that he refused to drink, knowing he had ruined her and betrayed himself. He had not sat in a tavern to drink since.

They continued to meet, but never again like that. As they walked the city together, she would playfully call his attention to nahariyyas hidden down alleys where they might find a room. He refused and she gave up trying.

He knew he was a hypocrite. Agreeing to meet her in the hidden doorways of crumbling neighbourhoods was no better than rooms rented by the hour. Yet he had searched for her in those doorways the way he used to seek taverns to sit in, drinking cup after cup until he no longer saw his mother raped and threatened, his wife and son murdered, and his sister's recriminating face. He thirsted to pour her over his memories. Join the wine of her with the hold of family. The aunts and uncles loving her as he loved her. A child between them. A community around them. There were only two choices then and now: leave and return to her a whole man she could come to trust and marry, or go to her broken in her freedom as she liked and take what dregs he could to make it through the day.

A donkey cart driver yelled behind him and he jumped to the side to avoid being hit, but the man cursed him all the same. The heat of the road bore down on him. He told himself that if their affair ruined her, he would be there to pick up the pieces. They might move to Basra or Kufa, or further, as far as the Maghreb. He would call her his wife, and no one would doubt him. No one would know that there had never been wedding preparations or a wedding feast or that the neighbours had never clapped to the drums celebrating them in the street outside their homes or offered them congratulations marking their right to be with one another and making their children legitimate in other's eyes.

He had heard Saliha's objections. After the violence of her last marriage and her family's complacency in the face of it, no one would ever have rights over her again. But Uncle Nuri had taught him the principal of ithar, never to prefer his own rights over others. She knew that. Still, she would argue that he and Zaytuna were illegitimate, the children of rape, and their mother a scandal. But it wasn't the same.

It was not that no one suspected their mother never had a husband, it was that no one asked. She simply arrived in every village and city with her two children and moved on soon after until finally settling in Baghdad. She told Uncle Nuri, Uncle Abu al-Qasim, and Mustafa's mother, maybe others. While he imagined she did not need to keep it a secret from the other aunts and uncles, she would not have thought it anyone's business either.

It's not the same. He continued the argument with Saliha in his mind, then stopped. The street split before him. To the left, it led directly to Saliha and Zaytuna's home. To the right, the road wound by the Shuniziyya cemetery. Facing the road to the cemetery he said aloud to Saliha, "I am at your mercy," and went to be with the living and the dead.

The low wall of the cemetery and the people who lived there stretched out before him. Woven palm or reed lean-tos covered burrows dug into its thick walls. Begging bowls with little in them punctuated the space between him and the grounds where he too had slept when he had nothing. He dropped chinks of coin in the bowls and stopped before the gate, but did not enter. The twin palms he and Zaytuna had planted and nurtured as children loomed over his mother's grave in the distance. He knew what she would think of this. And all the old resentments he had toward her were as fresh as ever.

She would hold his face and tell him no woman should be bound to any man. But she would not mean in the way Saliha wanted. For his mother, there was no lover but God. She would praise Saliha for having given up on marriage but pray she give up on desire for men as well. And what guidance would she have for him? Her thumb and forefinger would pinch his chin as she drew his face close to say, "Only the fool makes his abode in this world a haven."

"What good has your advice ever been to me?" He answered her aloud.

A labourer in short sirwal and no shirt lifted himself up on the wall beside him, pushed at his teeth with his miswak, and answered him by reciting a verse from the Qur'an. "*Say Allah, and leave them to their useless talk.*"

Tein turned on him. "I wasn't talking to you."

The man leaned back on both hands, rolling his miswak between his teeth, and eyed him, unimpressed. "*I complain to God alone of my anguish and sorrow.*"

"Stop sputtering God's words at me."

"*You prefer this worldly life.*"

Tein shook in frustration and yelled at him, "Nothing but mad people and the dead in this place!" He stepped backward, away from the gate, tripping over himself, and returned to the road.

The man called after him, more insistently this time. "*They preferred the others to themselves even though they had nothing to give.*"

Tein stopped, his back to the man, and whispered, "Ithar."

"*God has preferred you over us,*" the man yelled.

"Uncle Nuri." Tein spun around and ran to his uncle's grave. Falling to his knees on the now flattened mound, dug only a few months ago, he repeated Nuri's guidance to him, whispering it as if it were an incantation that would raise his uncle from the dead. "Ithar. You taught me that to be a man I must prefer others over oneself. But like this, how?" he pleaded. "Do I give her what she wants, or leave her?"

He held his hands out in prayer, though he did not pray. A man of reason would not expect an answer, and nothing came. Turning within to search his conscience as his uncle had taught him, he only found answers of his own making and none worth choosing, leaving him wanting only her. Then, a touch brushed his shoulder and a secure comfort spread through him. The desperation for her slipped away, until the shock of the touch itself made him wrench around.

No one was there. The labourer was sitting on the wall in the distance, still eyeing him. The ones who lived in the cemetery clustered around its walls, attending to their shelters, chatting, cooking. Smoke rose from dung fires and cooking pots on make-shift stone hearths. No children were close enough to touch him and run.

In the distance, a woman stood weeping into her hands as her thin wrap was blown against her hunched body.

Angry at himself, he turned back to the grave. *What was I thinking? Did I think I would see Uncle here? A dead man returned to me? There's nothing.* As if in answer, an icy stream of air snaked through the heat, winding its way around him. Any comfort he felt was carried away with it. His old injury ached more than it should as he got up, brushed the grave dust from his clothes, and headed for the gate. He replied to the wind, "I don't care."

The labourer still sat on the wall chewing his miswak, squinting at Tein and shaking his head. Tein ignored him, hurrying past to the road, but the man called out behind him. "*We hear and disobey!*"

Once in the road, he used his sleeve to wipe the sweat and dust from his face, pressing against his eyes. "Hear what?" he muttered. "Disobey what? You madman!"

There was nothing now but getting it over with and moving on from this suffering to the next. Then he realized Zaytuna might be home. Like the man in the graveyard, she would have her own cryptic nagging to add to this mess. He leaned into each step, pushed forward by his anger until he was not only angry with himself and for whatever he imagined Zaytuna would say, but with Saliha, too, for loving him at all. One furious slap of his sandals after another, he found himself at the narrow passageway before their home. He stopped. Looking toward the square where Salman sat on his stool, his back against the tavern wall and holding court over the drunks, Tein's eyes hardened. His mouth drew tight and he demanded of himself, "Decide."

Before the word was out of his mouth, the call to sunset prayer sounded across the city. He drew himself into the dark passageway, bowing his head to keep from hitting it, and came out into the fading light of day. The courtyard was empty. When had he ever come that Yulduz was not gossiping? That Qambar was not nearby watching his wife with tender eyes? That Zaytuna was not arguing? Or Saliha was not laughing? He waited in the strange stillness, not knowing what to do.

A child's cry rang out as Layla rushed from the room Umm Farhad had left months ago. Tein started at the sight of her.

"Uncle Tein!" She threw her arms around his waist, making him even more unsteady. "It's been so long!"

"Layla." He put a hand on her back and held her to him as if she were life itself, and found his balance in the embrace. She gazed up at him, her grin making her little chin even more pointed and her earnest brown eyes brighter. "What are you doing all by yourself, Layla? And in Umm Farhad's room?"

"Didn't Auntie Zaytuna tell you?"

He shook his head as he pried her away.

Standing back, she squealed, "I live here, now!"

The pleasure in her face and knowing what it meant for her to live here made him glad. But it pained him, too. He knew what she wanted, and Zaytuna would not give it to her.

"Where is everyone?"

She wasn't able to hide her disappointment. "Auntie Zaytuna left this morning without telling me where she was going even though we had a house to do." Her voice quickly turned to childish pride. "But I did the laundry by myself."

He frowned, and she caught it.

"Uncle, I've been washing clothes by myself my entire life." She gave him a matter of fact look. "I don't need Auntie Zaytuna. She needs me."

At least half of that was true. "And Yulduz and Qambar?"

"Yulduz and Qambar are visiting Marta's family outside the city. It's Christian holiday and there's a going to be a lot of food. They wanted me to come with them, but I had to do the laundry and I didn't want Auntie Zaytuna to come home to an empty house."

"With Yulduz gone all day, what did you eat?"

"I had bread and dates this morning and Old Murad gave me a cup of his tharid broth when I stopped by on my way home."

He took her hand in his. "I'm hungry. Would you come with me to get some food? I'd like the company."

"Yes, please!" She ran back into her room and returned with her wrap wound around under her arms and draped loosely over a workaday kerchief, just like a woman who laboured for her coin. He wished it could be otherwise for her, but all their childhoods were the same. Why not her, too? She squeezed his hand and pulled him toward the passageway. "Old Murad's tharid was good. Do you want that? It's beef, but he cooks it for a long time, it won't upset your stomach."

"Old Murad's tharid, it is."

They made their way to the square. Tein glanced to his right as they entered. Salman was on his regular stool and caught sight of him immediately.

"Tein, my old friend, come, come!" He waved them over, using a grand gesture as if he presided over the caliph's own wine house rather than a set of makeshift tables surrounded by stools that seemed like they would collapse under their owner's weight. Layla pulled harder at the sound of Salman's voice. Shrugging at Salman, he pointed to Murad's and let her hurry them across the square. She let go of his hand and ran ahead, giving Murad their order.

Salman's voice carried across to them. "Bring that tharid here to eat. You can't leave a man to sit alone!"

By the time he had reached her, Layla was waiting and the old man was ladling stew over dried bread in two large bowls. He hadn't been hungry before, but smelling the salt and vinegar in the fatty broth made him realize he had been all along. Tein put coins on the counter and Murad handed over two thick unglazed ceramic bowls hardened and sooty from a life of sitting in coals.

"Can we take it over to Salman's?"

Layla stiffened.

Tein leaned down to her. "What's wrong?"

"I don't like him."

"Why?"

She answered sharply, "I just don't."

Tein caught Salman's eye and shook his head, pointing to the table. The two sat down on the stools. As always, Tein's stool was too small for his large frame, and he landed awkwardly, slopping a bit of the bread stew from the bowl.

"Oh, Uncle." Layla grinned. "It's not always good to be so tall!"

He handed her a spoon. "It's not always good to be so small!"

Layla's eye caught something in the distance, and her face lit up. She stood and yelled, "Auntie Zaytuna, Auntie Saliha!"

He stood, too, in time to see Saliha and Zaytuna walking across the square, arm in arm and smiling. Saliha tugged her wrap around her so the curves of her body moved with each step. He shot a look at Salman who was taking her in with a hungry stare. She knew what her walk would do to every man there, but he knew it was for him alone. And he knew it meant that she wasn't angry with him anymore, but he wasn't sure if that made what was coming worse or better.

As they approached, he gestured to the table. "Sit, you two." Then held up two fingers to Murad and pointed to them.

Zaytuna protested. "That lunch, today, Tein. I'm still full."

"You were at lunch with Uncle Tein?" Layla asked petulantly.

"Speak for yourself, Zay," Saliha protested. "We had a busy day at the hospital and I only had some dried fruit and nuts that the pharmacist shared with me."

"Ibn Ali?" Tein asked, fearful they had spoken about him and the inappropriateness of their relationship. Ibn Ali would do no such thing, nor would he sit with her, compromising his own reputation as well as hers.

Saliha nodded, offering no explanation.

Old Murad held out two more sooty bowls, and Zaytuna took them. "We'll bring these back tomorrow."

Layla followed, picking up her bowl and spoon. Tein moved to object, but she corrected him. "It's getting dark."

Saliha had already left with her bowl, and Layla followed with hers and the spoons under her arm.

Only Zaytuna stayed to say, "Pay the man," then left to catch up with the others.

As Tein reached into his sleeve to get the coins from his pocket, he realized he had given them all to the poor at the cemetery.

"Bring that tomorrow, too," Old Murad said.

Tein thumbed at the women walking away. "What just happened?"

Unsmiling, he replied, "Women just happened."

The three were well ahead of him, turning the corner out of the square. A customer had arrived at Salman's. Another drunk was swaying towards the tavern. As he passed by Salman, he lifted his hand in greeting, but the tavern-keeper had his back to him.

By the time he reached the courtyard, they had laid out the bowls and spoons on a reed mat. Saliha emerged from her room with an unlit oil lamp and a short, thin cut of dried reed. "Layla." She handed the reed to the girl. "Go ask Auntie Ilham to light this for us."

Layla jumped up, took the reed, and ran past him through the passageway.

Saliha sat down, leaning her back against the wall, one leg tucked underneath her, the other knee up with her arm draped across it, gazing at him in that way she had that made everything so much harder on him. "Aren't you going to sit?"

There was space beside her and she meant that he should sit there, not caring what the others thought. Zaytuna cursed-well knew already, and Layla might as well, if this was to be their life now. Saliha watched him as he moved towards her and stood over her for a moment. Her long black hair hung loose out of her kerchief and spilled over her shoulders, all but covering the low slit in her qamis. She gave him a look that was an invitation to more, and he nodded once in reply. Then she leaned forward, saying to Zaytuna, "Give me one of those spoons." He sat down hard next to her, leaving little space between them.

Layla returned holding the burning reed, cupping the flame so it would not go out. She knelt before the oil lamp and lit the wick, making sure the flame had caught before blowing out the reed, sending tiny red embers floating toward them.

The girl tucked her legs underneath her and, spoon in hand, said, "Bismillah," for them all. Zaytuna ate despite her protests.

"You ate with Uncle Tein?" This time Layla tried to sound as if it were nothing.

Tein answered her, avoiding Zaytuna's eye. "We were on a case and Zaytuna helped us. If it hadn't been for that, we would have invited you."

"I understand," Layla answered, but it was clear she did not.

Finally, looking at Zaytuna, he asked. "And you two? Where were you coming from?"

"After I left you and Ammar, I found Saliha and we strolled through the market. She took me to look at fabric for a new wrap."

A whimper arose from Layla. Saliha rushed to answer. "Would you like to come with me when I buy it?"

But he noticed Zaytuna's face turned hard at the whimpering and Saliha's consolation. His sister did not like having to think about Layla's feelings, and he wondered if she would say something to hurt the girl. Instead, she stood. "I'm exhausted. I'm going to sleep for a while before my prayers." Pointing at Layla, she said, "You need to sleep, too. We have a big day tomorrow. And remember to pray."

Pleased with Zaytuna's nagging, Layla agreed, and she rubbed her finger to clean the last bit of food out of the bowls before taking them to the water basin.

"Are you sleeping here?" Zaytuna asked him.

"Are Yulduz and Qambar coming back?"

"They would have been here by now, don't you think?" She looked up. "There's no crossing the city at night. They're likely sleeping with Marta's family. Be back tomorrow."

"I'll sleep out here."

Saliha's hand brushed his hip. "I'm tired too," she said, standing and raising her hand to her mouth in an exaggerated yawn.

Zaytuna came out as Saliha was retreating to her room with her oil lamp. She threw her blanket at him. "See you in the morning, brother."

Layla disappeared into her room with a wave. "Goodnight, Uncle Tein!"

The blanket sat at his feet, while the oil lamp burned from within Saliha's room, sending her shadow against the curtain. He stood, and clutched the blanket to him as he watched her silhouette. She pulled her qamis over her head, turning so the outline of her body played across the thin cloth of the curtain. Then she pulled the strings of her sirwal in one long gesture until they dropped to her feet. He gasped without realizing and he saw the shadow of a hand waving him to come to her.

Pulling the curtain aside, he found her waiting, unclothed, her skin glistening in the lamp's glow. He was too tall for the room and his turban brushed against the ceiling, forcing him to tilt his head to one side. She put her hand to her mouth to stifle a laugh as he removed his turban and skull cap. Still smiling, she hooked her fingers into his belt and tugged him closer, loosening it and letting the belt and dagger down slide to the floor. Unlike that last and only time, she did not slowly tease his clothes from him, but eagerly pulled them off, pushing his robe off of his shoulders while he untied his sirwal, and giggled in a whisper at their haste. Finally, she gestured for him to bend down so she could help him get his qamis and undershirt over his head. But he had to fold himself over so awkwardly that she tittered as he stood straight again, imploring him with her eyes not to laugh himself.

There was no chance of it. From the moment he pushed the curtain aside, he had given up loving this woman as he wanted. He let her take him down, drawing him to her mattress on the floor. Vulnerable to whatever she chose, he lay before her, straining from the unexpected joy of giving her everything. Sitting beside him, she saw it on his face and shook her head, insisting that he hold on. Then she did finally laugh. The trill of it must have sounded into the courtyard, and he worried Zaytuna would hear, knowing what it meant. She put her hand over her mouth and shook with the effort of holding back more.

There was a cough. Neither of them moved, holding their breath, eyes wide. Then another.

"Yes?" Saliha answered.

"Yulduz is here, Saliha." It was Qambar. "She would like to speak to you."

"A moment." She gave him an irritated look and pulled on her qamis and dragged her wrap around her. She pointed at him to stay on the mattress, out of sight. He rolled to his side and grabbed his clothes, pulling them on as she took the oil lamp with her into the courtyard.

He could not hear Yulduz's words, but the tone was clear. Saliha did not respond. He stood, unspent desire turned to anger.

"Come out. Be a man," Qambar said.

This was what he had warned her about. Her neighbours had caught them, and they would soon be the subject of gossip if Yulduz had her way. This was on him, all because he was not man enough to deny himself. He fastened his belt, then took his turban in hand with him to where the frail old man stood, waiting. Zaytuna was beside him. Only the thought of leaving Saliha alone to face them stopped him from pushing past into the street.

Qambar said, "I don't need to tell you what you've done to her. If she's not wise enough to understand on her own, you do."

He waited for Zaytuna to add her own criticism, but she stood silent and it made him only angrier at himself for it.

"I don't want to see you here again," he continued, "that is, until you two marry."

Zaytuna did not object, but he did not expect her to. She was right.

"I'm an old man," Qambar said with a touch of sadness in his voice. "So if you want to fight me, I'd lose in body. But you'd lose in honour, like you have already lost so much tonight."

The truth was Qambar was more of a man than he would ever be. The old man gave up his family and his community to elope with his love, Yulduz. He did not abandon her just because he was Shia and she was Turkmen, or use her for his own needs, then leave her to carry alone the burden of the world's judgement. Tein stood ashamed before Qambar's courage in love and to face him like this. "I'll leave."

Layla came out of her room, half-lit by the lamp, looking as if she had been frightened awake. "What happened!"

"Nothing, Layla," Zaytuna answered first. "Tein is leaving. He was saying goodnight to Qambar."

Yulduz and Saliha approached. Saliha's face was unmistakable. She was furious, but held back, looking at him expectantly. What did she want from him? To argue with them? Tein was only grateful that they had intervened before he told her, not only in body but in words, that he belonged to her, no matter the consequences. "I'm sorry," he whispered to her and left.

Yulduz stepped in front of him, blocking his way, and looked him up and down before spitting at his feet. "I expected this of you."

She was right. Although only indirectly, he had played his part in her friend's suffering. It lay at his feet as much as Ammar's. Now he put Saliha at risk because of his weakness. Useless. No good could come from him. He walked out of the passageway, turban still in his hands, and turned right toward the square. There was torchlight ahead, and he desperately hoped Salman's tavern was still open.

17

The room was dark. The bodies kneeled in lines, thigh to thigh, knees to backs, all facing a featureless wall, all in perfect silence. Despite there being no gaps between one body and the next, there was space for Utbah to walk among them. He searched the faces for someone he recognized, not knowing why he was there. In the third row, he found his father and his chest ran cold with fear. In a deep-throated whisper, he cried, "I thought you were dead!"

His father strained to lift his head, neck muscles taut as ropes. By sheer force of will, he drew his chin toward his son until his face followed and Utbah could see his burning fury. The mouth on his father's face cracked open to speak, but the words arrived without his tongue moving. "Where do you think I am?"

Utbah's palm burned. He drew closer to his father until he was nearly standing over him. "Hell?"

"This is not hell, boy," he replied with a with a screeching disdain that was and was not a perfect echo of his father's voice. "This is the isthmus between the world before and the world after and the after is hell."

Sorrow for the old man struck him. "Ask God to forgive you."

"Why? I am proud of all I have done," he answered with familiar conviction.

Utbah wept.

"Did you get my letter, boy?"

"My uncle gave it to me," he answered through tears.

"Then you know." His father's face stretched into a rictus grin.

Utbah frantically searched the darkened walls for a window or door to escape and tipped backwards, his arms flailing, but did not fall. There was no way out.

"Despised by all." His father recounted the letter's contents as Utbah's arms spun round like waterwheels. "You lived only on the promise I made to your mother whom you poisoned in the womb. You inherited only the basis of the law. Wretched parasite."

"Father," he begged.

"Oh, how delicious a tormentor is God that you come to me in my grave to tease me so pleasurably with your simpering face!"

Utbah righted himself.

His father turned his face up, each muscle and tendon tightening until a scream of extraordinary pain unleashed and his grin transformed into gaping terror.

In that, Utbah found his strength and answered him. "Your letter is precious to me. If I have a moment of remembering you kindly, the urge to pray for your soul, I only need to touch it to return to myself. It is the talisman of my strength." Crouching until his face was even with his father's own, he licked the old man's twitching skin. "God is on my side."

The walls of the room fell away to nothing, and he drifted from it back under the blanket of sleep until a voice and a sharp push against his shoulder woke him.

"Up."

Utbah turned over against the wall, reaching for blankets that weren't there, trying to pull himself back under.

"Up." This time, a hand on his shoulder pulled him back. He opened his eyes. Coming awake, he saw only darkness coming through the cracks in the reed roof overhead, then he turned over to see the lamplight casting shadows on a man's face, transforming it into the gruesome mask of his father's tortured grin. Utbah gasped and scrambled up against the wall.

"Nothing to do but sleep all day?" The scholar leaned against the wooden door to the windowless room.

The horrific mask transformed into Aqil ibn Akib's eager face, and he remembered where he was, a filthy room in Buratha, hiding from the police. "For God's sake!" He pulled his wrap close. "I could not sleep worrying that the police would find me here."

"And they did not. I told you that I knew how to protect you."

Utbah pulled himself together to face Aqil. It seemed he had no choice but to use him. Aqil was fearsome, the most brutal among them, but he was also an ass. *You can control this ass and make him carry the burden of your escape. You do not have time to indulge your fear. Later, in the caravan, you play the woman. Now, be a man!*

"I don't know why you did it," Aqil said, "but you have brought the ghilman to Buratha. You have forced matters in a way I never imagined." He stood away from the door, becoming excited. "If there are riots, if his people are threatened, the Twelfth Imam will have to show himself." His voice rose as if he were giving a sermon from the minbar. "He will not leave us to be crushed by the caliph's men without a word."

Utbah sat forward, not understanding. "What has happened?"

"The ghilman, the caliph's own soldiers, are in the streets. The people of Buratha believe they will soon be under attack and they will fight."

"What does this have to do with me?" He had to crane his neck at an uncomfortable angle to look up at Aqil, the tendons in his neck straining.

"Bishr's death, man!" He threw up his hands. "Did you intend for those shots to land as they did? A work of art! No one knows what to make of it! Everyone has a different theory, but all agree that the caliph will use it to crush us once and for all."

"Sit down! I can't keep looking up at you like this."

Aqil settled down across from him on the rotting reed mat, inclining his head. "Again, we have you to thank."

Finally, what Aqil was saying got through to him. There would be chaos. The Shia would feed off each other's conspiracies and be crushed. Who could rival the ghilman? It changed everything. He could go home to his uncle. No one would care about Bishr or anything else once there was fighting in the streets. If there were lingering doubts in the police, surely a bribe to their sergeant would resolve them. My God! This was more than he had hoped for, and he blurted out, "Ah! I see!"

But the implication of Aqil's speech took a moment longer for him to grasp. *He knows I killed Bishr.* He became suddenly hot and he tore his wrap off as if it were choking him and loosened his robe.

Aqil thrust forward in an offer of help. "What's wrong?"

In a moment of animalistic fear, he saw himself pressing his fist into the scholar's throat and wanting to hear the rasp of his last breaths. The vision returned him to himself and he slapped the scholar's hand away, protesting, "He was our friend."

"Yet, you killed him."

"Never." There was no confiding in this man. Bishr insisted Aqil join them in the robbery, arguing that he had known him since childhood and their goals, in essence, were the same. But Aqil had put himself into the centre of every conversation, disrupting Utbah's careful plans, and then exposing the robbery in a careless boast at the mosque one day. Only his quick response, turning Aqil's boast into praise for the unknown men who exposed the corruption of the agents, saved them.

"Why run, then?" Aqil returned to his seat, leaning against the wall.

"I never should have." Utbah took measured breaths, trying to feel his body as his own again. The scholar offered nothing in reply, and he rushed into the disturbing silence to explain. "Only the guilty run."

Aqil raised a mocking eyebrow. "Excuse me?"

"What don't you understand?" He leaned forward. "The police want me for a scapegoat. I did not do it. I panicked and ran."

"But you did it. Why would I come for you otherwise?"

The scholar said it so plainly that it nearly knocked him back and he asked without thinking, "Were you there?"

"No." He shrugged, as if it did not matter at all.

Utbah countered to cover his mistake. "One moment of losing control and I have placed suspicion on myself. Even you believe I killed my friend, and in such a despicable fashion...." Pausing, he lowered his voice, hoping to catch a note of sorrow, "...as if I were my father."

Aqil offered only a knowing stare.

"If you are certain I killed him, then why did you come? Surely, you would prefer to see Bishr's killer face justice?"

"It is what Bishr would want. This is not for you. The coming war honours his death. The people of Buratha will not give up. They will fight and our plan will move forward." He paused. "But, before all that comes to pass, other matters are at stake."

There it was. *If I fall, they all fall.* The change in situation and Aqil's admission released him. If caught, he might reveal how they planned and executed the robbery of the tithe and give up every last one of the men involved to the police. Utbah said firmly, "I must return to my uncle. He can speak to Ibn al-Furat. If the police cannot find the killer, my uncle can pay them to frame someone else." He threw out his hand with emphasis. "And we will be free to enjoy the reward of the chaos."

"You cannot leave. They have eyes out for you everywhere."

"My uncle will handle this, I assure you. He can buy me time until the fighting begins and they forget all about me. Who will I be to them when there is blood in the streets?"

"You are certain your uncle's money can turn the investigation away?"

"What is money and influence for if not this?" he snapped, then stood, wanting to leave. It was dark. He could make his way back to his uncle without discovery. "I must return." Shaking out his wrap, he draped it over one arm and brushed away the bits of filth that had adhered to it from the squalid room.

"I gave Bishr and Aisha this room." Aqil stood. "It was their marriage house, such as it is, and the place they conceived their child."

"Pregnant? May God give her a son." He sneered. "Your kindness must have meant everything to them."

"I shared what I had." The scholar bent his head in a gesture of humility meant to imply that Utbah, with all his money, had not.

A tremor ran through him. *Bishr's wife, Aisha.* Bishr must have revealed his dream to her and the planned meeting at Imam Musa al-Kazim's tomb, and she, in turn, revealed it to the scholar. Even if this fool kept his mouth shut out of self-preservation, would the girl? She could expose him before he was safe, arrested before the fighting even began! Aqil was muttering on about Bishr and Aisha, her pregnancy, and all he had done for them, making Utbah's hands itch to shut his mouth for him. A vision of Aqil and Aisha as chattering mice rose before him and he imagined himself biting off their heads and tasting their blood.

Aqil's voice broke through. "You're panting like a dog!"

Without thinking, Utbah reached across and grabbed Aqil's robe with both hands, as if he could physically dominate this brutish man, and demanded in a voice he barely recognized. "Where is Aisha? She didn't go back to her family with a heretic's child in her belly!"

"She fled the city." Aqil pushed him off easily. "I helped her escape, just as I will help you!"

Aqil was lying. He could smell it and knew, somehow, that Aqil was hiding the girl just as he was hiding him. Probably in the room where they made their plans to rob the tithe. Utbah took two controlled steps back and draped his wrap around his shoulders, thinking. When he left him alone tonight, he would not escape to his uncle's but lie in wait for Aqil to go to Aisha and kill them both. He had left his dagger behind and needed a weapon, but that could be remedied. There might be a cooking knife here or a neighbour would have one. Or perhaps something heavy to hit them with? Then he thought of it, remembering his desire to push his fist into Aqil's throat. He would strangle them both with his sash. The weapon was with him all along. Aqil was strong, but strong men also need to breathe. The plan was perfect. "Alhamdulillah," he said, relieved, but not for the reason Aqil would think. "If she had remained in Baghdad and the police found her, all would be lost. Your involvement in the robbery would be exposed as well."

"Yes, alhamdulillah." Aqil's eyes fluttered. "But she assured me before she left, she would never give us up. She loved Bishr but also our cause."

"Oh?"

"If you won't accept her loyalty, accept that she will not speak for her own protection, but more so for the right to be the one to raise her child."

"If you help me find her, I would be glad to send her the funds necessary to establish her new life."

The scholar stiffened. "It would be only fitting since it was you who took her husband's life."

"Leave me to my own fate, then." He shrugged and walked toward the door. "I am returning to my uncle's home."

"Go then, see how far you get without my help." But instead of opening the door for him, Aqil blocked his way. "I have been following the police, intervening in their investigation to find out what they know. In fact," he said with a smug look, "I have been insisting that they follow up on the matter of Aisha, telling them it must have been her father or brother who murdered him."

"You will lead them to her!"

"I told you." Aqil widened his stance, his bulk blocking the door entirely. "She left Baghdad!"

"What have you done?"

Aqil stared at him defiantly. "She left because she feared the one who murdered her husband would come after her."

"I did not kill him," he answered through gritted teeth. "But you are going to get me executed with your meddling. You were like this from the start. Now get out of my way. If I can get home before the police find out I've left, I will be safe."

"I'm afraid not."

"What do you mean? Move!" He pushed the scholar aside with such force that he slid along the wall.

But Aqil easily caught himself, exclaiming, "They know!"

Utbah forced the door open but stopped halfway through. "What are you saying?"

"The police know you left."

"What?"

"They came looking for you at the Buratha mosque." He slowly moved on Utbah, took his arm in hand, and led him back into the room. "They found out about your connection to the mosque. That you and Bishr were friends, that you spent time with the rest of them."

"Why didn't you tell me this immediately!"

"Don't you see? It is too late. You must leave Baghdad." Aqil shut the door. "I queried the caravaners asking about passage."

"You revealed me to the caravan offices as well? My God! The police will question each one of them." He pushed again toward the door, but the scholar forced him back.

"Not you. I did not ask for your sake. There is a caravan leaving Baghdad for Cairo in three days. You can continue on beyond the caliphate into the lands held by the Idrisids in the Maghreb or even Umayyad Spain. But I need money to pay them for the passage. And I can, after you leave, help arrange for your uncle to send whatever you need once you are settled."

The man would not get out of his way. Utbah wanted nothing more than to kill him now. He touched his sash as a reminder of his plan. The only way out of this room and back to his uncle's to wait out the danger was to concede to whatever Aqil wanted, then follow him and kill them both.

He would send his uncle word using a boy from the market. Abdurrazzaq would send someone to rescue him and hide him some place acceptable until it was safe. In the coming street battles, they would count Aqil and Aisha among the dead. All of his enemies dead. The Shia offering their bodies for the ghilman to slaughter as if this dingy town were Karbala. This was greater than anything his father imagined.

He fell into the ease of it. He would have destroyed the Shia and could return to his old life. Utbah thought again of the softness of his bed, the breeze blowing in off the Tigris in the morning, and a servant bringing him whatever he desired. As the memory of old comforts touched him, he lost the immediate hunger for Aqil and Aisha's blood, but not the certainty that it must be done. Feeling the fat purse under his arm, he lied. "I didn't bring any money with me. Get me paper and a pen. We'll send a message to my uncle. He'll send the money immediately."

"Good!" Aqil's face lit up. "I'll send it with a package so the police won't suspect." Aqil moved away from the door to get his leather sack, although he was keeping an eye on Utbah as if he would charge the door. Pen case and a leather notebook in hand, he pointed to a board leaning in the corner to use as a writing surface.

Utbah took up the pen and dipped it in the small ink pot within the case. The board teetered on his knees at an uncomfortable angle. He lifted one knee higher to block Aqil from seeing his words, but the man stood over him, watching. He would have to write his request cryptically, but in a manner his uncle was sure to understand. Beginning with the required opening words, he traced the lines slowly to give him a moment, then began:

By now, you are aware that I am in trouble. By God, I am innocent of this crime. I need your help. I must escape the reach of the Abbasid government. An ally has offered to secure anonymous passage in a caravan beyond the empire.

He looked up at the scholar as if to ask, "Good?"
The scholar nodded.

I need funds for the trip immediately. Once I have arrived, I will contact you to arrange for the transfer of my wealth wherever I settle. God willing, the police will find their man and I will be free, but for now, they are trying to frame me for the crime. Please give the delivery boy as many dinars as you can spare from the household coffers.

Hopeful that the scholar would not guess the hidden meaning of the words and that his uncle would, he wrote,

May God protect you and forgive me for bringing undeserved shame upon your household and name, as my father did, forcing you to go to Ibn al-Furat to make your name good again.

"Will that work?"

"Yes, conclude now. I'll send it off with a boy."

Utbah finished the letter and handed the page to the scholar, who laid it aside for the ink to dry, and checked his bag. "There is no string or clay to seal it."

"Are you that simple? Pick a boy who cannot read to carry it!" Utbah snapped, then regretted it.

Aqil frowned at his tone and held his hand out to Utbah to help him stand. Once up, Utbah drew the scholar into an embrace, whispering, "I am sorry. You can imagine I am upset."

The scholar pushed him off and opened the door to leave. "Stay here."

Utbah closed the door except for a crack and watched the scholar go. When Aqil was far enough ahead, he adjusted his wrap to cover his turban and face, blew out the oil lamp, and slid out to follow.

The scholar crossed the square and went into the marketplace. Some shops were still open despite the hour. The light of oil lamps and torches cast flickering shadows over the stalls of piled nuts and dried fruits. Utbah watched as Aqil stopped at one, pointing at what he wanted. The shopkeeper scooped dates into a small bag, then retreated to the back of his shop and came out again with the dates wrapped as a gift in cloth with ribbon. Money changed hands.

Aqil asked the man something. He invited the scholar in, and he spread the letter out on the counter. Borrowing pen and ink offered by the shopkeeper, he wrote something on Utbah's letter and, after waiting a moment, tucked the rolled letter deep into the wrapping. The shopkeeper waved a boy over and Aqil placed the package in the child's hands, spoke to him and made the boy repeat it back.

Instead of going back to the room, Aqil went further into the market. Utbah slipped out of shadows and followed at a distance. At the sight of a watchman's torch, he tugged his wrap down further and pretended to inspect the offerings of a shop. By the time the watchman passed, he had lost Aqil and hurried after him, looking up and down each cross street. Three corners away, he saw him standing in front of a food stall, holding up two fingers. Within moments, the cook handed over two battered pots nestled on a hanging tray. He adjusted his leather bag, took the tray, and doubled back. Utbah slipped into the space between two shops and fell in behind him as he passed.

Aqil left the market and crossed the small square familiar to Utbah from their days planning the robbery. It was only five paces in length and barely that in width, with several narrow alleys leading from it. He disappeared down the alley to the right. There was no way to follow without being noticed. Utbah held back, watching until he entered the room. But he remembered that there was a passage on the other side of the alley. Utbah crept forward and hid, near enough to see shadows against the curtain from the oil lamp, but too far to hear what was going on within.

A woman's shape moved in front of the curtain. *Aisha is there. This is it. You must kill them both now.* He untied his sash, ready to throttle Aqil from behind. Given the man's strength, he had to attack in surprise. First Aqil, then the girl. But he could not make himself do it. His feet were stuck in place. *You killed a man,* he admonished himself. *What is it to kill again?*

He expelled a harsh breath, sash taut in his hands, and forced himself out of the passage as Aqil emerged bearing only one pot. Instead of confronting him, his chest tightened, and he drew back further into the passage. *When he passes, fall on him from behind.*

Holding his breath, he waited for the scholar to cross. Instead, Aqil's footsteps sounded from the far end of the alley. He stuck his head out. Aqil was gone. "Curse him!"

"Who's that?" A man's voice called out from behind him in the passage.

A shot of terror propelled him into the alley, and he dropped the sash. Unthinking, he pulled back the curtain of the room. Aisha scurried against the back wall from where she had been sitting with the pot of stew. Her eyes were as wide as her mouth, open in a silent scream. She reached for her wrap, dragging it over her belly as if it would protect her unborn child.

Utbah kicked the pot aside, spraying the stew onto the dirt floor and bent down, lifting her into his arms, her wrap falling away. He whispered in her ear, "God is on my side."

He trapped her arms against his chest, and still she did not scream. As she squirmed, he hiked her body up, one hand grasping onto her bottom as he covered her mouth and nose with the other and pressed hard.

Then the fighting began. She bit into his palm, but instead of letting her go, the pain shot a bolt of pleasure through him, heightening the sensation of her body moving against him as she struggled. He ground his groin against her as she twisted away. Her efforts to breathe under his hand weakened. It took all he had not to lift his hand and press his mouth against hers to suck the last bit of her life into himself. Slowly, she wearied and went limp. As she slipped from his grasp, the mound of Bishr's baby pushed against his groin and the terrible awareness of what he was attempting came up on him like vomit and he dropped her.

She fell and came alive, gasping.

Aisha crept toward the door, but he stepped in her way. The right thing would be to finish her and go find the scholar, kill him too, and return to his uncle. Utbah picked up her wrap to press against her face, but it rubbed painfully against the bite on his hand and he dropped it. The perfect arc of her teeth stood out on the pale skin of his blood-smeared palm. He licked the blood, hoping it would arouse him, but there was nothing in it but copper tingling on his tongue.

Frustrated, he dragged Aisha away from the door by the arm. She shook uncontrollably and covered her belly with her hands. His father would not have hesitated in such a moment. Yet here he stood, unable to act. He reached under his robe and pulled so hard on the purse of his father's money that the leather thong snapped, releasing it into his hand.

Utbah tossed it to her. "You have enough there to go anywhere in this world you like and start new." He threatened her with a power he wished he had control over, but did not. "Go, or by God, I will find you in Baghdad. There is no one to stop me. Not the police. Not Aqil ibn Akib. You cannot hide from me."

He paused in the doorway, wanting to scream in agony at the mess this had become. The letter would be at his uncle's by now, and Utbah prayed he was putting plans into place to save him. He could sneak back home through the market gate in the dark. Then his uncle would send men to kill the scholar and Aisha, too, if she did not leave. For what his uncle paid him, Abdurrazzaq would do it. There must be a way out. He dropped the curtain behind him and headed toward the small square and a road that would lead him out of Buratha and across the Tigris to his uncle's home.

But as he came into the square, he ran into a soldier holding a torch and took a quick step back. Three ghilman filled the small square. One of them grabbed him by the arm before he could retreat. "What are you doing out at this hour?"

"Visiting my cousin." His voice cracked. "I, I brought her food."

"Where do you live?"

He could not admit where he was going and fearfully pointed in the general direction of the room where Aqil had hidden him. "Through the market. On the other side. Not far."

"We're watching you!"

He left in that direction, but the sound of their boots was always behind him and he did not dare turn along the road that would lead him out of Buratha. A pair of watchmen hailed him to stop, but one of the ghilman called out to them, "He's ours!" The black-turbaned watchmen acknowledged them and carried on. The ghilman close behind him, watchmen nearby, he had no choice but to return to Aqil ibn Akib's room. As they approached, the light of the oil lamp was visible through the gaps in the door.

He gave the ghilman one last fearful look before opening the door to find Aqil standing before him.

"Where have you been?"

"I needed air," he said weakly. "I took a walk."

"Sit!" Aqil barked.

Utbah sat.

Aqil stood over him. "Lost your sash?"

DAY FOUR

18

"I bn Marwan wants you." Ignoring Tein, the boy spat the message at Ammar then ran off, document rolls under his arm.

"I'm going to slap that boy one day," Ammar promised.

Tein winced. "Leave him. Life will slap him without you."

"Let's go." Ammar stood at the door, his hand on the frame, looking toward Solomon's Gate.

"Wish we could walk out of here?"

"We are. We're not going to see Ibn Marwan."

"No?"

"He'd only command us to arrest the first man we saw on the street. We would end up telling him we're still investigating and asking him to hold on. Maybe he'd agree, maybe he wouldn't. Better not to go."

"This is a first." Tein adjusted the belt around his robe, tugging hard at his dagger. Ammar had never balked at challenging Ibn Marwan before. He hoped Ammar was finally losing his taste for the job and they would leave together. It was over with Saliha, so there was no need to sell his soul to this brutal empire to give her what she wanted. He snorted at the thought of it. *I nearly sold my soul to her last night to give her what she wants. No more.* He threw his shoulders back. "What's that verse, *'You may love a thing, but it is bad for you'*?"

"Come on." Ammar turned towards him. "You remember that one. Our sergeant recited it day after day on the battlefield. *Fighting is enjoined on you despite it being hateful. But perhaps you hate a thing that is good for you and love a thing that is bad for you. God knows and you do not.*" His face fell. "Is this about the job?"

Tein shook his head, but Ammar did not seem to believe him.

Still looking concerned, Ammar said, "You lead the questioning."

Ammar meant it to be generous, but Tein wasn't in the mood to be granted a concession from on high, and replied, "I'd planned on it."

"A lot is riding on this. If one of them turns out to be the murderer, it'll be better for us. Getting evidence on Utbah, let alone a confession, isn't going to be easy. I hope it's one of them."

Tein only grunted in reply.

Only when they had reached the gatehouse leading out of the Round City did Ammar ask, "What's wrong?"

Tein shrugged beside him. "I'm tired. Last night."

"Last night?"

Not sure if he wanted to say it or not, he said it anyway. "Saliha."

"What happened?" Ammar asked without looking at him.

"I gave in to Saliha and we got caught. That old man, Qambar, stood barefooted and bent with that worn out turban on his head, and told me to be a man and marry her. He is more a man than me."

"You'd be a good husband. I don't understand her."

"I do, but she doesn't understand me."

"So what's next?"

"Long nights with a jug of wine."

Ammar chuckled uncomfortably.

"I drank at Salman's tavern afterwards. I had a few. I rolled home, sober by the time I got to my room and made a vow. I'm done with her. I won't be what she wants. I won't try to force her to be what I want. She's a free woman, but that means I'm also a free man."

Ammar replied by putting his hand on Tein's back for a moment.

He had to force himself not to flinch under Ammar's touch, too much like pity for his taste. Gratefully, there was no more talk as they crossed the bridge over the Tigris into West Baghdad and made their way into the al-Atash Market.

Ammar strode ahead of him into the market, passing by the boys hawking their services, and they found their way out the other side to Jasmine Vine Road. The walls of Utbah's uncle's house came up on their left. The market gate door of the estate was obvious now, and Tein was angry with himself for not having noticed it the first time. Then came the servant's gate, and after that the main gate. A watchman sat slumped in an alcove across from it.

The man was trying to blend in, but loiterers were few and far between in this neighbourhood. The servants were well aware of their presence and, no doubt, Utbah was, too. How obvious he must have been on the watch for Utbah that first day. Ammar walked over to the man and bent over, speaking for a moment. The man brushed off his robe, pulling his wrap back from his turban, and stood on guard.

"I told him there was no need to hide."

Tein wanted to lay the blame on Ammar, but there were no grounds for that. Ammar was not in charge of him, even if he thought so. Failing to notice was on him, and he vowed there would be no more failures.

They turned the corner and the walls of Ibn Furat's estate stretched into the distance. It must have been as large as a village and reminded him of police chief's court held in a palace with grounds of endless pools, fruit trees, flower gardens, grand rooms meant to hold a hundred people or more with thick rugs laid end to end.

"The stable gate." Ammar gestured.

Two guards stood outside it dressed in short robes and narrow turbans, easy for fighting, and armed with swords and daggers for close work. The gates were wide enough for five horses to ride in abreast and embossed with interweaving designs of vines and flowers, but nothing like the ostentation of Utbah's uncle's home.

Ammar turned to him. "I pray this breaks the case."

Tein hoped the same and approached the guards with a mood as sharp as his dagger, ready to get what they needed. He hailed them. "Assalamu alaykum."

One replied, "Wa alaykum assalam."

"We are with Grave Crimes in the Baghdad Police. We're here to speak to the stableman, Umar Abu az-Zubayr. Can you get him for us?"

One of them looked at him, then Ammar, judging them for a bare moment before opening the small door inset into the gate and sticking his head in, speaking to someone just beyond. Then he shut the gate door again, returning his attention to them. "He'll be along."

The other guard chuckled.

Ammar asked, "Care to let us in on the joke?"

The guard looked over at the other one, checking, then said, "We call him Ibn Hayd, but not to his face."

The harshness of the insult surprised Tein. It was no small matter to say a man was conceived while his mother was menstruating. It must have shown on his face because the first guard offered, "We all hate him, even his own wife and children."

"Except," the other guard broke through. "His second son, az-Zubayr Ibn Hayd. Turning out to be just like the father."

"And his daughter, Aisha?"

"A beautiful girl! She left, though. Works at Ibn Abdulqahhar's estate."

"Left here with a small bag and never came back." He sighed, thinking of her. "There isn't a man among us who didn't have a high hope for her, despite the idea of having a father-in-law like that."

The other man winked in agreement.

"She must have enjoyed the company of you men when her father wasn't looking," Tein said.

One guard sniggered. "She kept her face covered when her father was around, but the second he was out of sight and one of us was within her eye's grasp, she let that wrap fall away so we could see the whole of her. Mashallah! 'God is beautiful and He loves beauty'!"

The other guard shook his head. "Lost to us, forever."

Ammar followed up. "You haven't seen her since?"

One shrugged, then looked at the other, who answered, "No."

"You said only one of his sons is like him? What about the others?"

"One is too young to tell. He may be like the father, yet. But the eldest, Talha, he hates the old man. You can see it on his face. He keeps his mouth shut, does as he's told, but you can see the hate on him. Works the stables with his father, but sneaks out whenever he can."

"Where does he go?"

They both shrugged this time, but one suggested, "A tavern! Wouldn't you if you had a father like that over you?"

The gate opened. An imposing man with a hard face, and dusty from work, stood just inside. Tall and broad, the man looked like he could carry a horse on his shoulders. Tein wanted to fight him.

Ammar approached. "I am Ammar at-Tabbani, Grave Crimes Section of the Baghdad Police. We are investigating the death of Bishr ibn Dalal ibn Hasan and need to ask you a few questions."

"A Shia heretic investigating the death of another Shia heretic." He said it with an air of exhaustion, but his body was relaxed and ready to fight.

Caught between defending Ammar and reminding his partner that he was wrongly leading the questioning, Tein gave the man a look that said he would be the one to finish him.

Abu az-Zubayr mocked them. "This one your dog? He's ready to bite me for your sake."

Ammar stood back, giving Tein a concerned look.

"Would you like to discuss your daughter in front of the guards?" Tein asked, an edge to his voice. "Or should we follow you inside?"

Abu az-Zubayr's face showed he realized Tein would not be above sharing details about his daughter in front of these men. He shifted his weight, seemingly giving Tein ground. "You a ghazi? I know the look of a man who has fought on the ground. Not like this coward here." Abu az-Zubayr thumbed in Ammar's direction.

"We both fought on the frontier," Tein replied quickly, taking the bait and regretting it.

"I don't believe it." He looked Ammar up and down. Then said to Tein, "You, honoured ghazi, I'll answer your questions, not his."

"He comes with me." Tein took several steps forward until he was halfway through the gate and within striking distance.

"On your head," Abu az-Zubayr said, conceding for that one moment.

They followed him through the gate onto a field with an expansive fenced in area for horses to be exercised. Men worked around them, one walking by with a spade over his shoulder. The stables were close, with a small house attached. Fruit trees and a large willow shaded the house from the sun and swayed in the breeze. A low couch was set out underneath it. As they drew closer to the house, Tein heard a stream nearby. It was a peaceful scene.

Abu az-Zubayr faced them. "Let's do this and be over with it."

"You call the Shia heretics," Tein taunted, "yet you take your livelihood from one. What would Barbahari think?"

He sensed Ammar's disapproval, but ignored it.

Abu az-Zubayr shrugged it off. "Where is your religious proof that a Muslim cannot work for a heretic?"

Tein pivoted. "Proof is why we are here."

"Proof my daughter killed that Shia piece of shit?" He scoffed.

"No, that one of you did."

The man's stance changed. "Ghazi," Abu az-Zubayr warned, "watch your words."

In response, Ammar stood ready to pull his sword, and Tein was ready with his dagger and fists. "What did you do when you found out your daughter wanted to marry a Shia boy?"

"We told him and his family that it was finished."

"And was it?"

He nodded sharply. "We finished it."

"And what if Bishr and Aisha decided it wasn't?"

"In that case," he said plainly, "we would have killed them both."

"And Barbahari would give his permission for that?"

"Barbahari?" He pulled his head back, obviously confused by the question. "Why would I need his permission for anything? Do you think I am his slave?"

"Why would you follow him if not to do his bidding?"

At this, Abu az-Zubayr took a menacing step toward Tein, then suddenly grinned. "I understand now."

"What do you understand?"

"You're the caliph's whore. Not interested in the life of a Shia boy. You're here to find proof against Barbahari so the caliph can execute him. That's the proof you are looking for."

There was movement from inside the house. A woman's head popped out and back again, then two young men came out, both as big as their father. The elder brother leaned on the doorjamb, his long curls hanging out from underneath his turban, while the younger one came to stand beside his father. Tein glanced at Ammar, who had seen him, too. The one with the curls was the young man Utbah had taken to the bowyer. Talha. And he was wearing boots that did not look like he was about to muck out a stable.

"That would please the caliph." Tein turned his attention back to Abu az-Zubayr. "But perhaps we get you for the murder of the Shia boy?" He tipped his head toward the son standing next to him. "Or this one here?"

The younger son's face flushed. He took an unpracticed step forward to charge Tein, but his father threw his arm out, blocking him, and bellowed, "Get inside!"

The son opened his mouth to object, but did not move.

"Inside," his father said coldly, raising his hand.

The son took a step back, his protective rage eaten up by fear of his father. He took several steps backwards, not turning his back to his father until he was out of striking distance. Going into the house, he clipped his elder brother hard enough on the shoulder that Talha had to take hold of the doorjamb to keep from falling.

The father watched the scene, then returned his attention to Tein, exasperated and ready to end it. "I did not kill that boy. My son did not kill that boy. I don't care who killed the boy. God arranges things with His own wisdom and saved my girl with his death."

"And Barbahari had nothing to say about it?"

Ammar shifted uncomfortably beside him.

"Barbahari, Barbahari! Who is he to me?"

"You are one of his followers."

"You mean the man who will not permit a bad word to be spoken about al-Hallaj who preaches lies about God in the streets?" He snarled, "This al-Hallaj has built a makeshift Kaaba in his home and does the pilgrimage there rather than go to the holy city of Mecca as commanded by God, glory to Him, and taught to us by the Prophet, peace and blessings on his companions." His voice rose. "He is nothing but a Qarmati! The Law is nothing to al-Hallaj and Barbahari allows for this Shia heresy!"

He did not know that al-Hallaj was still in Baghdad. Tein wished the man were in front of him so he could shake the lunacy out of him. A claim like that was sure to cause riots, get him and anyone associated with him killed. Every move he made put his Sufi family at risk. He only hoped Uncle Abu al-Qasim was aware of it and had warned the aunts and uncles to stay away from him. If Uncle Nuri were alive, God knows he would stand by al-Hallaj and get killed for it.

The father took a step toward Ammar. "This al-Hallaj is one of you! This is what you people do! You tear down the walls of Islam. If any of you are left standing, Islam crumbles before us."

Ammar did not budge.

Tein stepped forward, hands out. "He follows no one's teaching but his own. He claims no one and no one claims him."

"Barbahari claims him." The bitterness was unmistakable.

"Why?"

The man shook his head, his tone changing. "They studied together when they were young. Barbahari says he knows what is in al-Hallaj's heart and to leave it to God's judgment, not to risk the wrath of God by even thinking ill of him."

"You've left Barbahari's circle, then?"

"What does it sound like to you?" The man said it so sorrowfully that if Tein was not aware of the harm Barbahari and his men did, he might feel for his disillusionment.

"I have to ask you about your daughter."

Abu az-Zubayr did not reply.

"Where is she?"

"With us."

"Can we speak to her?"

"She's had enough talk with men. She'll not see another stranger's face until she meets her husband on her wedding night."

They would be looking to get her safely married, not waiting for a good match. With scandal hanging around her neck, it would be a family that needed a woman to help around the house. The marriage would be for the help of the mother, not for the son, but he would get what he needed from her all the same. Tein asked, "Did she say who killed her man?"

"Not her man," he growled.

Tein conceded, a hand up. "Did she tell you who killed him?"

He called back to Talha, still leaning in the doorway. "Come."

Talha walked toward them warily.

"Tell them why Aisha said the Shia was killed."

"It was nothing," he mumbled.

Did he not want to answer out of fear of his father or because he had some allegiance to whoever did it? If Utbah killed him, then that crew of young men might be involved, too.

"Tell them," his father pushed.

Talha looked around for a way to escape. His father glared at him. He flinched and stammered, "Bishr had, he had a secret and someone killed him so he wouldn't tell it."

"What was the secret?" Tein stood up straight.

"He never told her."

"How is that possible? They were in love."

"That's what she told me!"

His father positioned himself between them. "My son does not lie."

"How is your archery?" Tein asked Talha, sensing Ammar come alive at the question.

"You think we shoot arrows from the backs of those horses?" Talha scoffed. "We feed them, we groom them, we exercise them."

"My boy was with me in the stables the day that filthy Shia was shot."

"He knows more than he is saying."

"Only what his sister told him. Now go."

Ammar stiffened beside him. He would not like what was going to happen next. But how in this cursed world were they going to get what they wanted otherwise? They did not have time to wait for Talha to sneak out one day and ask him then. If his father beat his son or kicked him to the street for this, then so be it. "Your son was friends with Bishr. He introduced your daughter to him."

The father's face became strangely impassive, as if a stupor had come over him. His breathing deepened, his great chest pulling smooth, full breaths. But the son was moving, knowing an explosion was coming. His eyes darted between the two of them before landing on his father. He grasped his father's arm. "It's not true!"

The father's arm twitched. It was only a slight shift, but his son let go as if his father had jerked his arm free.

"It's not true!" Talha repeated, backing up toward the house.

"Leave." Abu az-Zubayr said to Tein.

But Tein went on, not caring where it he would lead, "Bishr's father told us about his son's friend, Talha. The son of a follower of Barbahari. He described the long curls. He told us Talha took his sister, Aisha, along with him and that was how the two met. When you refused Bishr, Talha also left his Shia friends behind."

"He was with me the morning of the shooting. Leave."

"Talha knows what the secret is. Your daughter knows. We can't solve this murder without finding out. There will be violence in Karkh, in Buratha, if we can't solve this case." Then he said, regretting it the second it came out of his mouth, "The ghilman are ready to slaughter the Shia."

Tein saw Ammar readying himself out of the corner of his eye and put his hand on his dagger.

Abu az-Zubayr bellowed, "Then her ruination had purpose! Her honour was martyred for God's plan! Let them all die!" Abu az-Zubayr made his move.

Ammar unsheathed his sword before the man had finished and brought the flat of the blade against the father's chest. "You'll be the first to die if you take another step."

Abu az-Zubayr looked down at the blade, his fury uncontained, and swung his right arm around, taking hold of the sword by the blade itself and wrenching it from Ammar's grip. Tein was on him, pinning his arm to the side and pushing him back, chest to chest, roaring, trying to catch him on his heels and give Ammar time to pick up his sword. But the father only staggered back, regaining his balance. Ammar crouched to retrieve his sword when the younger brother tackled him, driving him off.

Talha rushed Tein, grabbing his robe in his fists. Tein head-butted him, dropping Talha on the ground. But his father was already there. The power of the man's fist slamming into his gut doubled him over, and he turned with his hands up to protect his head from the next punch, forcing a cough to get his breath.

The punch never came. The guards and workmen had hold of the father and his sons and were pulling them back as Abu az-Zubayr's wife ran from the house screaming, her wrap slipping off onto the dirt behind her.

Abu az-Zubayr's chest was heaving, his hand dripping blood from where he had grabbed Ammar's sword. He watched Tein like a caged animal while his wife rushed to her sons, who were being held by guards and still posturing for a fight. Tein, his dagger at last in his hand, drew shallow breaths, wanting more, but a guard from the gate blocked him. "Enough, man. Go."

"We're going," he said in a growl and showed he meant it by placing his dagger back in its sheath. He signalled to Ammar, who had picked up his sword with his weak hand and was putting it back in its scabbard with as much dignity as he could muster. The two retreated backwards to the gate, the guard beside them, until it was safe to turn. As the guard shut the gate behind them, he said, "Did you at least get what you needed?"

Tein did not reply nor look at Ammar. He knew what he had done, and he did not need to see it on Ammar's face or worse, hear what he had to say about it. Instead of admitting that he had put Talha's life in danger for nothing, he turned on Ammar. "Have you had enough of this job yet!"

"You did that in there!" Ammar demanded, "What were you thinking?"

Tein rushed him, trying to push Ammar over, but Ammar stepped out of the way and Tein stumbled then caught himself. Instead standing back with regret, Tein spat on the ground. "You knew who I was when you pulled me into this job. You thought you could save me. Look at you. The saviour of me!"

He stalked off, turning at the corner where Utbah's uncle's house was and heading back into the market. There was a tavern tucked into an alley just before the kabab stall. Tein found it, settled down on a stool big enough to hold him, and leaned back against the wall.

He slapped a chink of coin on the table, wanting a jug of wine, but called to the proprietor for nabidh instead. Ammar would be there soon, and Tein wanted at least two cups in him before he had to listen to him talk. Thankfully, the clay jug arrived quickly. He swallowed a cup in one furious gulp, then another, and his sore gut warmed from it. Not as good as wine, but good enough to dull the edge on him.

Ammar sat down as he poured a third cup. "I've done worse, Tein."

That was cursed-well true, but that did not make what he did right and he drank his next cup in three smaller gulps, laughing bitterly to himself. It was the practice of the Prophet to drink water in three gulps and, who knows, maybe long-fermented nabidh, too. The shock of the slanderous thought gripped his throat with frozen hands and pinned him back against the wall. How far had he fallen to disgrace that man? He pleaded with the Prophet's memory, "Forgive me."

"We got all we were ever going to get."

Tein looked straight at him, not saying he meant the apology for the Prophet. A man who, like Ali, was the model of the man he wanted to be and could never live up to. He retched into a cough.

Ammar raised his hand to the owner. "Water. And get a boy to bring us some bread and stew?" He turned back to Tein. "Tell me."

Taking another cup to wash down the sour nabidh at the back of his throat, he let out a gasping sob and put his head on the table, weeping. Ammar placed his hand on his shoulder, and Tein felt no pity this time, only the comfort of their long friendship. Leaning into it, he shuddered. "Saliha."

19

Zaytuna stood in front of the butter dealer's warehouse, holding her wrap closely around her. It was early morning; the sun was just rising, but the men were already hard at work. The wooden shutters were strapped back, exposing a space wide enough for four shops. Men stood over yellow clay jars half as big as themselves, thrusting the churning staff up and down. One man was dressed only in sirwal rolled up to his knees. Sweat glistened on his shoulders and arms, heightening the lines of his muscles as they moved with every plunge of the staff. She looked away. But their banter and the sound of the staff slapping the milk carried out to the street, bringing the image back to mind.

She grew hot but pulled her wrap even tighter, reciting the saying of the Prophet as if it were a prayer, "The first look is for you, but the second is against you." Thus armed, she turned back to observe the shop, but avoided looking at that one man.

Another worker called out a warning to a boy carrying an amphora of butter to the delivery cart to watch where he was going. The boy turned to listen and tripped, but corrected himself in time. He handed the unglazed ceramic jar with its fat middle and narrow ends to the man in the cart with relief. Two other men were at the far end of the shop, away from the finished butter and the churning, clarifying butter over wide, shallow pans set over coals. An older man in fine but simple working clothes walked among them, watching over their work and sharing some joke with them. He was broad-shouldered with deep brown eyes, a wide forehead, and a thick reddish-brown beard shot through with grey that grew in beautiful waves, framing a warm smile that made her feel like laughing along with them all. The last twinges of pain in her back softened. He reminded her of descriptions of the Prophet Muhammad himself, and it put her at ease. She loosened her protective clutch on her wrap and approached.

"Assalamu alaykum." She yelled over the din. "Sir!"

It took a couple of tries before the man turned, and only then because one worker noticed and pointed her out. The man was taken aback, as if he recognized her, and made his way out of the warehouse, tugging on his robe to straighten it. He put his hand over his heart and bowed his turbaned head. "Wa alaykum assalam. What can I do for you?"

He smiled again, careful not to hold her gaze too long. For once, she accepted the respect of the gesture, feeling strangely safe with him, knowing somehow that he would never say or do anything to harm her. Calming waters reached her, expanding her breast until she thought she might emerge from the waters to fly. She fell into silence, unable to remember why she was there or what she had wanted to say. Instead, she wanted to touch his cheek and look into his soft eyes that still held the spark of laughter he had been sharing with his men.

"I am at your service," he prompted politely when she did not answer. But his ruddy cheeks had flushed even more under her gaze and she blushed in return, realizing her desire showed on her face.

"I'm, I'm sorry," she stammered, and turned to leave.

He spoke before she could turn around altogether. "May I offer you a glass of our buttermilk?"

Wanting nothing more than to sit with this man and allow him to make her happy, she nodded, her heart beating hard in confusion.

"Perhaps you might consider our buttermilk for your household?"

The question hit her like a slap, returning her to herself. Her thumb rubbed over the callouses on her fingers and she remembered what she looked like, who she was. Nothing more than a worker in someone else's home, here on business. Not a woman. She stopped him. "On second thought, maybe another time. I am not here to buy for a household."

"No?" The disappointment was clear on his open face.

She told herself it was only because he had lost a sale and she returned to her purpose. "I won't take much of your time. I came to ask you about the delivery man who was killed."

At the mention of Bishr, his eyes glistened with tears. "May God have mercy on his soul and give respite to his family, among whom we count ourselves."

"Amin," she said, a sigh catching in her throat at the sincerity of his grief. In that moment, she realized she had not prayed for Bishr beyond the required words. She had not felt his loss or considered what he meant to those who cared for him. He had been only a mystery to be solved. A body in a dream.

Shame overcame her and gripped her into a rising panic. Bishr, a man with a name, had only meant something to her for what he meant about her. Because of him, she wondered if she was something more than a broken woman who misstepped every way along the Sufi path. So she prayed for him, full of regret, that he find his grave wide, with a gentle sun shining on him, grasses swaying in the breeze, and a cool stream nearby, all heralding his acceptance to paradise when the day came.

Misunderstanding her expression, he asked, "You were a friend of our Bishr, too?"

"No. It is only the tragedy of it." She used the edge of her wrap to wipe away her tears.

"Please." He gestured toward a table with stools nearby, then to a boy within. "Take a moment for yourself."

She took the chair, allowing his kindness, even if wrongly placed.

The just risen sun warmed her, and she raised her face to it with her eyes closed, letting it caress her, and she forgave herself. Taking a deep breath, the expansive calm returned, and she looked at him. He had taken a seat across from her, but at a respectable distance.

The boy came and handed them glasses of buttermilk from a copper tray with a comical, flourishing bow, leaving her chuckling. Her "bismillah" before taking a sip emptied her to taste the buttermilk's sweet tang. It was like none she had ever known before and she teared up again, but this time at the beauty of the simple things in this world and then again, as she drank the last sip, at the small losses of every passing moment. Then, without warning, she felt the beauty in that too, and she gasped. "Alhamdulillah."

"I am so glad it pleases you," he said, misunderstanding again.

"I am intruding."

"You are no intrusion," he replied softly.

"I am helping with the investigation of his murder."

His eyes brightened at her declaration, not to mock her but with unexpected pleasure, and he begged her to go on.

"The police wondered if he met his killer through his deliveries." Her voice gained in strength. "They want to know if he said something to you that would suggest any trouble."

"You work with the police?"

"Yes, I help them at times."

Leaning forward and putting his hand on the table, next to his glass but no nearer, he replied, "He said nothing to me. He may have mentioned something to the others. I can ask for you."

She thanked him, realizing she had no sense how she would approach the men and ask them herself.

He stood but then sat down again, wrinkling his brow. "Do you typically interview women? My apologies. I am intrigued. I have traveled the empire and I have never heard of a woman who worked for the police."

"I, I," she stumbled, not knowing what to say, not wanting to lie before God, but also not wanting to lie to him. "I do not work for them," she admitted. "I help them if needed." She wanted to tell him more. Still unsure of herself, she added, "More often, I help in my neighbourhood if a matter arises that does not require the attention of the police."

"Family concerns?"

She winced inwardly, thinking of Umm Parvaiz. "Yes, at times."

"Do you find the men and bring them home?"

"I inform the wives, but they sometimes wish they had not asked."

"Is it not always the way? We think our lives are made of one thing only to find they are made of another and, in the end, wish we had not known. Perhaps sometimes it is better to go on in ignorance." He paused, looking at her for an answer. "Or is knowledge, with all its responsibilities, preferable?"

His voice carried a note of pain, making her wonder if his wife had been unfaithful. Although she could not fathom why a woman would leave a man such as this. "Did your wife stray?"

His brown eyes, so full of expression, held her own. He answered her with a look of confusion and relief that she understood him, but only replied aloud with the verse from the Qur'an. "*With every hardship there is ease.*"

"Are you still married?" she asked, realizing she was afraid of the answer. Either yes or no.

"No," he said, and readied himself to stand again. "I understand she has happily remarried. I remain alone."

His reply left her struggling between relief that he was not bound to a woman and fear of what it meant. But she reminded herself that he only saw her as a servant and her attraction to him was nothing but the wake of confusion following the dream. She pinched the soft spot between her thumb and forefinger to rouse herself from her foolishness.

He went to speak to his men for her.

As she watched him question them one by one, they turned to look at her, one incredulous, the others merely surprised. To a man, they shook their heads in response. Disappointed, she not only had nothing to bring to Tein and Ammar but also she would have to say goodbye to this man.

He stood on his return. "I am sorry, but no one knows anything, and I am afraid I must return to work."

Looking at him one last time, she marvelled at how she felt so at peace in his company and wished he felt the same. In answer, the calm washed through her again, taking with it her self-doubt, and buoying her to a place where she could see the terrain of her life. And she thought in wonderment, perhaps the butter dealer is meant for me. My old world is ending. She saw herself happy there, and pulled her wrap over a cheek to cover the shock that such a thing was possible, and walked away, unable to even say goodbye.

"Wait," he called after her.

She stopped, not knowing what she wanted him to say or what she should say. Without a word, she turned and let her wrap fall away from her face and body so he would see her. *This is who I am*, she said to him inwardly. *You must decide.*

But he did not look at her. Instead, he stood with his arms clasped at his waist, his head bowed, his body offering her the greatest respect. "I am here if you have any further questions," he said tentatively, "or if you would like to sit and chat with me again."

The shock of his last words exploded into a thousand tingling sparks. He wanted her. The surrounding air had thickened and was drawing her to him. *Your old world is ending*, a voice within her reminded. *Come to your new world.* But she resisted, afraid she could not inhabit a world in which she was happy. "No," she replied hoarsely, refusing it, and released herself into the thin air of her old world, running back home to safety.

It was not until she had crossed the bridge into Karkh that she realized she was on her way to Uncle Abu al-Qasim's and was already nearing the cemetery. She wondered if the old woman in the burrow was there. Bare feet stuck out here and there from underneath woven palm lean-tos placed against the cemetery walls with begging bowls out, praying for a chink of change. But none matched the woman's brown and gnarled feet, making Zaytuna wonder if she had died.

She wept as if the old woman had truly passed and walked into the cemetery, finding herself on her knees before her Uncle Nuri's grave and praying for the souls of the dead, including her own. A gentleness encompassed her, holding her in its arms, and she wept on its shoulder until it lifted her, one hand directing her toward her mother's grave under the two palms in the distance.

Approaching her grave, she placed one hand on the palm she had claimed as her own, Tein's beside it growing at an angle and leaning away toward the cemetery gates. Her mother's body near, Zaytuna prayed that her soul be raised up to the shade of God's throne on the Last Day when the sun would bear down on them all, unrelenting. A voice came up from within her on a wave of peace that drowned her in its unaccountable joy. Then the voice faded in her ears and she did not hear herself recite:

A deluge will appear,
   as the heart's clouds disperse.
The sun of the truth revealing a vista,
   concealing that we abide with God there.

Waking, her cheek in the dust of her mother's grave, her fingers caught in the wrap that she had wrested from her body when she fell into ecstasy, she sat up, then stood. Shaking the dirt out of her wrap, she wiped her face with an edge, then wound it around her, ready to speak to whoever would advise her at her uncle's home.

The cemetery road leading to Junayd's neighbourhood was busy with people. Donkey carts rattled by, raising dust in the coming morning heat. One animal stopped to bray, and the driver urged it on, gesturing wildly. Children ran, weaving through men and women carrying goods or walking empty-handed as they chatted. But none of it touched her; she walked lightly, as though her body had expanded beyond itself, and again she enjoyed the sensation that she could fly if she would only touch off in the right way, a way she had not yet discovered. The butter dealer's eyes revealed themselves to her again. But this time, she wanted him without fear. She had not even asked his name, and yet she felt unaccountable love for the man, uncomplicated by the tangled attachments, doubts, and recriminations that were the fabric of her love for Mustafa.

Ziri opened the door at her uncle's home after her first knock. His eyes widened at the sight of her; he said nothing other than the required greeting but followed her in through the vestibule and into the main reception room where he touched her elbow, directing her to the secluded place where women washed themselves for the prayer. Once alone, she removed her wrap and her kerchief, letting her braid, with its thick matted strand strung through with her mother's bead, fall free. She touched the bead. Breathing into the call to God's blessing, "Bismillah," she used a cup to take up water from the barrel and began her ablutions. The cold water washed away the dust into the basin and fixed her to both the earth beneath her and the sky above. Awake, she stood and went looking for guidance.

Auntie Hakima looked up as she appeared in the courtyard and cupped her hand, calling Zaytuna over to her spot near the kitchen. As she approached, pots clanged against one another in the kitchen and a girl giggled. It was Layla. Abdulghafur's voice answered her, teasing. A wish passed through her that the two would marry and he would take Layla from their house, relieving her of responsibility. The wish left her sore-hearted and ashamed of wanting to be rid of the girl. But instead of reproaching herself so harshly as she always did, she caught sight of the deep fear that drove the desire and held it out to God to take from her. Auntie Hakima followed her glance toward the kitchen and tugged her down. "Leave those children to their joy and sit with me."

She took the old woman's hand to kiss as she kneeled and the scent of roses enveloped her. Auntie Hakima's dark and wrinkled face was framed by a wrap so startlingly white that the woman seemed to have dressed herself in a fabric made of light.

"My daughter." She smiled.

Zaytuna pulled her head back in surprise. Somehow, her missing teeth had been restored and where her remaining teeth had been darkened and stained, they now glistened like pearls. "Auntie, your teeth."

Auntie Hakima raised her hand to her chin and massaged her jaw. "Uff, another one of them has come loose. I should go get it pulled before it makes more trouble for me." She patted Zaytuna's leg. "Good reminder."

"But..." Zaytuna stammered, not understanding her.

"But what? Listen to me now."

Silenced, she stared at the old woman, wondering at the change in her.

"Your uncle has told me about your dream, but I knew before he said so." She looked across the courtyard at Junayd with an impatient expression. "No need to recount it."

"Oh..." She was drawn away from Auntie Hakima's transformation to her own situation.

"It didn't use to be that a woman on this path had to pass through love of a man first before she arrived at God's doorstep, but times change." Auntie Hakima propped her elbow on her knee, and her sleeve fell back from her arm. "We might roam free, if that was our way."

Her face took on a cast of nostalgia so sweet Zaytuna wanted to follow her there, even though she and Tein had lived the hardships of it themselves with their mother. Instead, she was surprised that the mere mention of an ecstatic woman's life on the road did not bring old resentments over her childhood, each demanding to be attended to with bitter thoughts and sharp words.

"Troubled by men, to be sure," Auntie Hakima continued. "But we called the people to us in the streets and the graveyards, whispered to them about our Lover, and drove them mad with love to God Himself. We were free so that no creature could come between us and God." She poked Zaytuna's knee with one finger. "We're to follow a middle way now! It seems all the young companions are to be married." She looked over again at the uncles and younger men sitting with Uncle Abu al-Qasim, and added sharply, "Whether or not it's a good idea."

The old woman could only mean YingYue and Mustafa. Contradictory feelings presented themselves and Zaytuna took each in hand. She wanted their marriage to be a failure so she could have

Mustafa for herself, finally. And she wanted it to work so she could be free for the brown-eyed man she had run from in fear. Holding them tight to herself, suddenly Auntie Hakima's old white wrap became yellowed and dingy again and her teeth were stained and missing as they were before. Zaytuna trembled.

The old woman picked up her shaking hand and held it still. "Everything is changing. We are to be like the scholars. We are to fit in. I understand the risks. We frighten people with our loving God so deeply and could end up back before the High Court answering to charges of heresy like before." She sighed. "He's not wrong. And without your uncle Nuri here, who will stand up for us and save us from the executioner?" Tugging Zaytuna's hand, she asked, "But I wonder where all this is going? Will there be a day when the men say to us women that God will not love us unless a creature of this world, one of them, approves? Will the gates of Paradise be barred to us without a husband's permission?" Auntie Hakima gripped her hand so hard that her fingers hurt, sounding the way her mother did when angry at this world, for God's sake, "The idolatry! Zaytuna! The idolatry!"

Zaytuna would not accept it. She considered the aunts and uncles she had grown up with and the brothers and sisters on this path and refused to believe they would make a man the lord of a woman's salvation instead of God. "They would never."

"Of course, they would not. But I fear what will come after us. This middle way is meant to stop us weeping and wandering, so we fit in with the rest of the Muslims. Nothing will be the same." She let go of Zaytuna's hand and slapped her own thigh, drawing herself out of her worry. "Enough of that. Now, your dream." Auntie Hakima looked around her as if other women were sitting among them. "You are not the only one."

"Not the only one?" Zaytuna's heart sank. Was there nothing in the dream for her alone? Have they all dreamed of the butter dealer? The Mahdi and Lady Fatima? Abbas?

"You all are having dreams that this life of asceticism is ending! You are a woman who can love a man now. So we must talk about it."

"Oh!" She blushed with embarrassment and secret relief that others did not share her dream and that the old woman read that part of the dream as she did. "Why now?"

"Why now, you?" Auntie Hakima replied brusquely, "You've been untying those knots in yourself, starting to live for God's sake, instead of your own pain. But there's still too many of those knots left."

She hung her head.

"Now stop that. You are not only becoming a woman who can love a man but also a human being who can love God."

Lifting her head, she asked, "How?"

"God's guidance comes not only in dreams with signs that need reading, but the world, too, girl, the world! Your soul! This world and your soul are filled with signs that need reading." The old woman leaned forward until she was so close that Zaytuna could smell her breath. "You need to learn to read."

Zaytuna ventured, "I think I understand the part about men. The change is..."

Auntie Hakima held up a hand. "No need to say it."

"I understand that part of my world is ending."

She gestured for Zaytuna to go on.

"But when I spoke to YingYue about the dream, she said dreams can have many layers of meaning. Why Abbas? Why the body, like that? Did she tell you there was a man murdered just like Abbas? Tein is investigating. My dream fits it. Perhaps there is more to the dream than me being able to love a man?" Then she added cautiously, knowing that Auntie Hakima would only say it was her pride. "Maybe I have the secret to solve it?"

"YingYue told me. So, have you solved it?"

"No," she admitted. "I think because I don't understand the dream. I thought it meant one thing, then it seemed to mean another."

"This work you do, finding things out for people. What comes of it?"

"Sometimes good ends."

She glanced toward the kitchen and Auntie Hakima agreed, "Just so."

"Sometimes bad ends."

"And do you know why one ends one way and one another?"

The answer came to her without thinking. "I don't always know how to read the clues before me. I don't always listen to the meaning behind the words people say."

"*We shall show them Our signs on the horizons and in their own souls until they know that We are the Real*," Auntie Hakima recited. "God is showing you the signs so that you will learn to read them. Listen to me. These investigations are a distraction, like all things of this world. You are thinking about murder or men who've run from their wives and not thinking of God, whose Names and Attributes are speaking to you concealed in each act." She recited from the Qur'an again, "*God is the One who acts*, girl, not these people." The old woman pressed her leg with a forefinger again, but this time so hard it felt like a pinch. "Read the signs on the horizon and in the souls."

"I don't understand," she complained.

"I have to spell it out? Abbas, may God be well pleased with him, went to the river to bring the children water. Abbas is you. The children are those you help. The water is God's justice, a tributary of His ocean without shore. You must struggle to bring water to the children and die to this world to do it."

She replied, "I understand," but she only understood she would fail, just as Abbas was killed before he could get the water to the children.

"There is a body here in this world?" Auntie Hakima broke through her circling thoughts. "Just like the body in your dream?"

"Yes."

"Look from a body that conceals to God who reveals."

She did not understand again and became distraught.

"Uff, you've always been a hard nut." The old woman pushed. "Zaytuna, there is nothing in this world other than God! There is a place, an overlook, from which you will see it all, Zaytuna. Climb to it and take in the vistas before you. Then you will have your answer to yourself, these men, that murder, and whatever else troubles you, leaving you at peace with God."

Confused and heartbroken, all Zaytuna understood was that she was to have a man but not be an investigator. The one thing other than worship that gave her life and made her feel that she had something to give, she was to give up. Her eyes pricked with tears.

Auntie Hakima stood. "Enough of that."

Zaytuna got up to help her, trying to hold back her tears, and put out her arm to support her. Auntie Hakima raised her soft, wrinkled hand to Zaytuna's cheek, saying, "You're a dutiful daughter, but you must release those knots," then left her and joined the men sitting across the courtyard.

Once the old woman's back was to her, Zaytuna turned toward the kitchen to find Layla. She wanted nothing more than to grab the girl and walk home, listening to her jabber on about nothing so she would not have to hear her own thoughts. But as she turned, she nearly tripped over the girl, who had come without her knowing and was sitting behind her.

Layla looked at Zaytuna and said firmly, "You can fix anything, Auntie. You always could. You can solve this murder and anything else, so it ends the right way, not the wrong way. You just need to read the signs."

"Didn't you hear what she said?"

"I heard the whole thing. I know what she said. I know *exactly* what you're thinking, Auntie Zaytuna, and you're wrong." The girl stood and held her hand out. "Now, let's go home."

20

U tbah half woke in the early light to a boot on his back.

"Get up."

Instinctively, he rolled against the wall, raising his arms to protect himself.

"What are you doing?"

Coming fully awake, he realized where he was and coughed to give himself a moment to recover, then rolled back to face Aqil. "I was trapped in a dream. Announce yourself like any decent man. Do you kick your family awake every morning?"

The scholar mock bowed in apology.

"Get me a cup of water!"

Aqil poured the water, handing the cup to Utbah with a flourish. "Sir."

He accepted it with a sour look and anger that he had not killed him last night. Utbah said with his last shred of hope, "My uncle's money should be here soon." *And a way back home.*

"Oh, it is." The scholar smirked. "One of your uncle's servants brought it just before the call to prayer."

He sat up, confused. "But I did not hear anyone."

"Not here. I added a message to your letter instructing that the money be brought to my home. Much safer."

His uncle had agreed to help, but would not know where he was hiding. "The servant. Was it my uncle's guard? Tall man in a leather cuirass?"

"It was."

His uncle had sent Abdurrazzaq to get him after all. Thank God. He continued on as if it were nothing. "Pure muscle. Not a sensible thought in his head. I am surprised he found your home at all. But I suppose it was the only safe way to get money across the city at that hour."

"He seemed bright enough to me. Since I could not trot you out in front of him, he had me describe what you were wearing to prove it was not a ruse."

"Of course, my uncle would need assurance," he said calmly. But his thoughts were running wild. *Abdurrazzaq must have followed Aqil to this room! He must be just outside, ready to pull me out of this misery and back into the fold of safety. I'll have him kill Aqil on the spot, shut his mouth forever.*

"I can go to the caravaners today for you." Aqil patted the bulge of a large coin purse under his robe. "You will be safe before long."

Utbah placated him. "I appreciate your foresight and planning."

"I think of everything." He added with frustration, "If only people would listen."

The comment had hit its mark. He inclined his head. "I am in your debt." Then Utbah looked down for a moment. "Aisha, has there been any word from her?"

"So interested in her welfare."

"Of course, I am." He examined Aqil's face for any sign he had been to check on the girl and found her gone, but the man was giving nothing away. For now, his primary concern was alerting Abdurrazzaq. "I am hungry, and I need to stretch my legs. Perhaps we can go to the market."

"I would have thought that you had enough of a walk last night, but, as it turns out, I need you to come with me."

"To the market?" Utbah did not like his tone. Something was behind it.

"First, yes. Then I am taking you to my home."

Utbah nearly cried out with pleasure. If the guard were not here, then he would be watching the house. Aqil would die. Then he realized the scholar's family would be there and they would witness the killing. Would they have to be killed, too? "Your wife and children? They are prepared for guests?"

"I sent them to my sister-in-law's home in Najaf this morning. They won't return for several weeks."

Relieved, Utbah stood. "Your home, where is it?"

"Near the Ushnan Bridge to Karkh."

Aqil opened the door, but first gestured that Utbah should cover his face with his wrap. He draped it over his turban, hiding his face like a woman, and they set out into the busy streets. Every time he had the chance, he pulled the wrap away and looked for Abdurrazzaq, but there was no sign of him. If he were there, surely he would approach or signal him somehow.

The scholar led him through one unfamiliar alley after another until they emerged into a square he knew too well. Two of the men he led in the robbery of the tithe were lifting the great shutters of the butter dealer's shop up and strapping them to the wall. He whispered, "Why did you bring me here?"

"You must want to say one last goodbye to your men before you leave the city for good."

"There is no need." He paused, wondering now if the men would welcome him after all, and found an excuse. "If the police were to question them, they should feel at ease saying that they have not seen me. Please, let us not put them at risk."

"A fine sentiment, but are you not concerned that they might blame you for Bishr's death?"

He stepped back into the alley, out of sight. "Why would they think that? I know this is your obsession, but surely they are not so stupid?"

Aqil followed him back into the alley, putting a hand on his shoulder. "Don't worry, your secret is safe with me."

Glaring at him, Utbah said, "Your sense of humour escapes me."

"Come." Aqil led him back down the alley, through another and into a smaller square leading to the market. "Remember when I joined you late in the planning? The men were unhappy, saying that you fought with them over their plan for the robbery. They never respected you."

Lingering resentment over the men's elaborate proposals came back to him as if it were yesterday, and Utbah forgot himself. "Not only that," he complained. "They had not even considered a robbery. Every plan they had to expose the Twelfth Imam as a figment of the agents' imagination was more ridiculous than the last. It took immeasurable patience to convince them that robbing the tithe was the best answer. Arguing theology with people?" He rolled his eyes. "Money is a different matter. No one wants to feel robbed. You make people doubt their leaders on the matter of money, they will doubt them on everything else."

"Said like a man who knows nothing of theology," Aqil postured.

"A sore spot." He raised an eyebrow. "You all could never have pulled this off. One of them wanted to rob the agent using a butter delivery to his home." He turned toward the scholar, touching his arm. "Recall at this point, we did not know yet if the agent in Baghdad collected all the tithes meant for final distribution. But they wanted to show up there with a butter delivery and rob him. Then drive away, ever so slowly, in a donkey cart." His eyes were wide. "Absurd!"

The scholar did not commiserate. "The location of the tithe aside, it was an inspired choice. They mocked you for not knowing."

"Knowing what?"

"The first agent, Uthman ibn Said. After he died, rumours spread that he disguised himself as a butter dealer and hid the coins in a leather butter sack to deliver the tithe."

The thought of being mocked for something so arcane burned

him. "And for this poetic gesture we were to get caught, all of us, piled up in a donkey cart, as we congratulated ourselves?"

"Perhaps not." He shrugged.

"Yet with my plan," he said, pleased with himself, "we robbed the tithe in the most simple manner, in the dark of night, no witnesses."

"It was a better plan," Aqil conceded. "To be honest, the men's skill surprised me, following one agent to another, lying in wait, until we found the main agent in Baghdad." His chest puffed out. "Imagine if I were to walk into those scholarly circles that shun me now and tell them I know the name of the agent closest to the Imam and they do not!"

Utbah, remembering the thrill of the robbery, got caught up in Aqil's imagined revenge. "And you tell them that you, yourself, held a knife to the agent's throat!"

He put a hand on Utbah's arm. "Remember how we trapped him outside the city? A man travelling alone is always at risk, but what a coward! My one blade at his neck. Surrounded by men, he handed over the bag without a struggle. He should have been willing to die for it."

"It was a satisfying night."

Aqil put his arm through Utbah's and they walked together for a moment in the memory of that night as if all was right in the world. Then he sighed. "All is not lost. If we take care."

The comment returned Utbah to the present moment, and he pulled his arm out of Aqil's, looking around furtively again for Abdurrazzaq.

"Let's get some bread and cheese for now." Aqil walked toward a cheese shop. "We have dried fruits and nuts at home. I can bring us hot food at midday."

Utbah hung back as the scholar made the purchases. Then he turned to Utbah, saying, "I do not have a basket to carry our things." Aqil put a chink of coin into his hand and pointed, "Go there, around the corner, there is usually a woman with baskets to sell."

He took the coin and thought again to escape, but assured himself that Abdurrazzaq would be waiting at Aqil's home. It would end there. Utbah turned the corner and bought the basket.

On his return, he held it out to Aqil.

"No. You carry the basket. It is your breakfast. I am not your servant."

Utbah wanted to throw the basket on the ground, but did as he was told. Aqil gestured to him to take the two palm frond baskets of cheese from the seller. The seller looked at the two strangely, and Utbah pulled his wrap further over his face, then placed the cheese in the basket.

Aqil asked cheerfully, "Bread?"

Leaving the market, Aqil hurried, and Utbah struggled to keep up with him. The scholar mocked him, "Do you spend all your time sitting on fine couches that you are out of breath?"

"And you," he said, hoping to insult him, "performing manual labour gives you endurance?"

"Wrestling," he said with a hint of pride in his voice. "I was not always a scholar, but I keep up with it still, despite the demands of my study."

Utbah hoped Abdurrazzaq would be waiting at the house and silently followed Aqil through the alleys to the wider streets until they were close to the Ushnan Bridge and before his home. The padlocked door was solid, but unpainted and chipped. Successive rains had worn away at the mud bricks of the outer wall. He supposed the scholar thought this neighbourhood was a step up in the world. "Pitiful," he said under his breath as he scanned the road for Abdurrazzaq.

"What?" Aqil asked, turning the key in the padlock.

He had no answer, sinking into the realization that Abdurrazzaq had not come to save him. He was alone.

The door opened onto a bleak courtyard. There was only a small tannur with a long-handled copper pan hanging beside it and a covered barrel of water in the corner nearby.

"Fired brick walls within, plastered roofs, and all the rooms are ours," he intoned as if the home were a palace. He pointed to a curtained door furthest from the water and the tannur. "We have a latrine, although I am afraid we empty it ourselves when the dung collector comes." He squinted with pleasure. "You will have to clean up after yourself in there. I imagine you have servants to wash your ass and rinse the latrine for you. Not here." He pointed to another room. "You will sleep in there."

Utbah pushed back the curtain to the room. There was a clean bedroll laid out on fresh reed mats, with a wool blanket folded at the end. The relief of a clean and comfortable bed, no matter how humble, overwhelmed him. Looking back at Aqil, he said with all sincerity, "You are very kind." But as he heard his own voice say it, it sickened him. The man had worn him down when he was at his most vulnerable, and now here he was simpering over a clean bed. Rushing out of the room, he burst into the latrine and retched bile into the sluice. Emptied of weakness, he resolved it would end here and left his sick for Aqil to rinse away.

In the courtyard, he rinsed his face and beard at the basin, wiping his mouth dry with the back of his hand and giving his beard a resolute tug. Aqil was waiting with a cup of water and a solicitous look on his face. But the bile burned in the back of his throat and he took strength from it. He was the man who organized the robbery of the tithe. The man who killed Bishr. And he would bring down the Shia. The tables had turned. He would humiliate Aqil. Tell him how he used him and all the men to destroy their own community. Then it would be over and he would walk out. Find some way to contact his uncle. Go into hiding under his uncle's care. Abdurrazzaq dispatched to kill Aqil. The police held off by the sway of his uncle's influence. Then there was only waiting for the people and the ghilman to begin the slaughter. A perfect plan.

Utbah pulled his shoulders back and announced to Aqil's expectant face, "I killed Bishr."

Aqil was expressionless, only drawing the cup back to hold with both hands against his chest.

Utbah had him. Aqil had not known for certain that he had killed Bishr until this moment, and he sighed with pleasure at the effect of his revelation. "I aimed my arrows at his chest," he spoke into the silence. "One missed, hitting his water sack. Then the other his eye. You must understand, I have not missed a shot since I was a boy. My father used to taunt me even when my hands were too small and clumsy to hold a child's bow properly." His eyes widened. "Yet it spurred me to be a better archer than he ever was, than anyone might hope to be. And I am. All to say, Aqil, I could not have missed. And the open, bleeding wounds on his arms? Aqil. Aqil. Listen to me. I did not cut him. God aimed the arrows. God sliced open his arms. God, as it turns out, is a poet."

Aqil took a sharp intake of breath and let it out slowly. Then he said only one word, but his voice caught on it all the same. "Poet?"

"Yes." Utbah leaned in, savouring what would come. "Bishr saw your Imam. Your precious Imam in hiding. He was going to tell the world that Muhammad, the missing son of al-Hasan al-Askari, your Twelfth Imam, is alive. Bishr would have ended this confusion among you once and for all. Yet God declined. God is on my side. What poetry! Bishr was Abbas. He fought his way to the river to bring you all life, and I took him down before he could return with your succour."

The scholar dropped the cup. It broke into shards at his feet, staining his boots. Looking at his empty hands, his knees gave out, and he fell to the ground. He pressed his hands onto the hardened clay of the courtyard to keep from collapsing. Then he wept, his body shaking. It went on and on. Utbah enjoyed every moment, letting it unfold in its own time. Finally, Aqil lifted his head, his face stained with tears and dirt. "Why?"

"To see you all ruined once and for all."

"Bishr could have healed every rift," he moaned. "He could have attested where the agents refuse and the scholars deflect. Led us all to the Imam's door. United us all. Every Muslim would have seen the Imam's light." Aqil got up on his knees, crying out, "Not only the Muslims, all would stand behind him!"

"How?" Utbah mocked, "Think, man! Would the followers of Ismail and Zayd turn and join him? The Sunnis? They did not follow his father or the fathers before him, Imams they *knew* existed!"

Aqil shook his head in horror. "It is my fault for thinking I could work with you Fatihis. It was my mistake thinking I could turn the robbery my way and force the Twelfth Imam out of hiding." He moaned, "My fault."

"Is that what you were after? I wondered why you were with us. You hoped for a double-cross? How ironic!"

"I hoped the robbery would make the Imam show himself and all would be well. The scholars would accept I was right, the Imam would be with us, and the community would be healed." Looking up at Utbah, he said, almost unbelieving, "You Fatihis, you got what you wanted."

"I'm no Fatihi!" Utbah looked at him incredulously. "I am Yazid in this poetic tale! But I have done Yazid one better. I had plans to crush you one by one, but God is the best planner. He directed my arrows and now the caliph has an excuse to destroy you all. The empire itself will destroy every last Shia. I will have started it."

"You have no idea what you've done!"

"Oh, but I do."

"How did Bishr find the Imam? Did he follow the agent to his home?"

"Excuse me?"

"Did he say what happened at the meeting? What did the Imam say?"

"Meeting?" He pulled his head back. "Oh, I am sorry! I have led you astray. There was no meeting in this world. There was a vision, a dream." Leaning over Aqil, he said, "The Imam and Fatima approached him on a plain with an army behind them. The Lady Fatima even carried a tablet in her arms with the names of the Twelve Imams written on them! She showed them to Bishr and commanded him to never doubt. The man told Bishr that he was Muhammad ibn al-Hasan. He was the Mahdi, the one anticipated to come in end times, and that the world was ending. Your Imam, the Mahdi, was holding the slain Abbas in his arms!" Utbah stood up straight, his hands on his hips. "I told him the dream was meaningless, but it was a visionary dream. It was a dream of his own death and the end of the world of the Shia!"

"I don't understand." The scholar sat up straight. "A dream?"

"Yes."

"But that is not the same thing."

"I agree, but I could not let it get out. The people would be swayed. He would have gathered followers around him."

Aqil brushed himself off as he stood. "Exactly."

The moment was slipping away.

"You did the right thing. It was a false dream. Don't you see? Your arrows did not miss. He told you this dream before you shot him? You were simply so affected by his account of Abbas that you shot him thus! Your heart's aim was true no matter what your eye wanted."

"That is not what happened!"

"I and my teachers do not accept dreams as evidence," he taunted. "But it seems that you do!"

Utbah took a step back.

"You haven't ruined us at all." Aqil took a step towards him, his muscular body threatening. "We would have pitied Bishr."

"What good is your pity when your community is dying in the ruins of doubt?" he countered, taking a step back. "It seems you only joined us to force the Imam to show himself because you and your scholars cannot reassure the people."

"It is true," Aqil conceded, his confidence turning to anger word by word. "Our scholars hold that endless quotations of hadith will assure the people that the Imam exists and is watching over us. Over and over they remind the people that the Prophet Muhammad foretold there would be Twelve Imams from his family line. The Imams, themselves, reassured us. As if this is enough! But the scholars brook no discussion! No argumentation!" He took step after step towards Utbah, leaning in to him, seething. "What has their reassurance done? Nothing!"

Aqil had trapped him against the wall. Utbah glanced toward the door leading to the street, not seeing how to get past him.

"They sit by the pillars compiling traditions," he sneered. "It is reason, theology, that is our way out of this mess. But even where there is theological argumentation, it has no teeth. I told those old men. I showed them my reasoning!" He grabbed hold of Utbah's robe with both hands, spitting in his face as he spoke. "I told those old men that if they did not use my theological proofs for the existence of the Imam, then the only answer would be to force the Imam out of hiding! They told me to stand down. But I would not stand down. And they cast me out of their circles!" He released Utbah, raising a finger to the sky. "Since the scholars would not act, I did." He looked around the courtyard as if he were searching for something. "There is still hope."

Utbah moved carefully along the wall to get a clear shot to the door. But the scholar caught his movement and stood in his way again, gripping his shoulders.

"Bishr is dead. The caliph's men are coming to crush the Shia. And the Shia of Karkh and Buratha will fight to every man, woman, and child." The scholar came so close Utbah tasted his sour breath. "The Imam will not leave us without his guidance. He will show himself to end the bloodshed." Aqil pushed Utbah aside and raised his hands in prayer. "He will lead us!"

Utbah ran for the door. He jerked on the handle, but it would not open. Only then did he see the padlock fastened on the inside. He turned. Aqil was standing behind him, holding up the copper pan by its long handle with both hands, ready to swing.

"Yazid!" Aqil yelled, and he swung the pan, hitting Utbah on the side of the head.

The pain cracked through his skull. He tasted vomit and slumped against the door.

21

Ammar pushed the chickpea stew and bread toward Tein. "More."

"Mother hen." Tein slurred the words, but he wasn't drunk as all that.

He thought Tein had been drinking wine, but when he poured another cup, he saw it was nabidh. It would take a lot more than a jug of nabidh to touch him. But if the man wanted permission to weep for losing Saliha, Ammar wasn't going to call him out.

"Let's clear this case," Ammar said, "then talk about what to do next."

Tein hailed the tavern keeper for more, but Ammar shook his head when the man came toward them. The sun wasn't too far up in the sky, but they were on the wrong side of Baghdad. They should have gone there first. But he did not expect Tein to blow the interview with Aisha's father, the interview. It did not matter now, unless they could prove that the son or the father could use a bow with that kind of skill and then break their alibi. After Tein left, he had questioned the guards, but they insisted the family was within the walls of the estate that morning. They were not watching every exit, though. They swore, too, they had never seen them using a bow.

"It's a long way to the butter dealer. Pull yourself together."

Tein put his hands on the small table and pushed himself up straight until his shoulders were back and his chin up. "I need water."

Ammar poured the last of the water and signalled to the tavern keeper to bring them more. "Where are we in the case?"

Tein sopped up more stew with the bread. The tavern keeper returned with a jug of water and Tein poured himself one cup after another. Ammar wanted to roll his eyes at the pose of sobering up, but let it go. After the third cup, Tein took a deep breath and settled in. "Bishr was killed by a skilled or lucky archer."

"Right."

"The most likely suspect is Utbah ibn Harb. He has the skill and the opportunity, but no motive. He is a Shia. But why would he kill his friend?"

"Maybe he was in love with Aisha?"

"That would make sense. If the placement of the shots was accidental and the bowyer says that's unlikely."

"Even the best archer is going to miss, especially in a heated moment. In the interview, Utbah mentioned a woman he didn't want to expose. It could be Aisha. The best lies always have a bit of truth to them."

"If we assume his motive was to kill Bishr over Aisha, is he planning on marrying her? How would that work in their worlds?"

"If he could get away with pretending he was Sunni," Ammar said, "Aisha's father might have approved. He would be lucky to get her off his hands now. And that wealth?"

"We assume Utbah left Baghdad to escape arrest."

Ammar nodded. "Aisha might have gone with him."

"The family is lying about her being at home."

"Remember the guards said they hadn't seen her."

"The father or the younger brother? Maybe Talha killed Bishr on his father's command? Talha's got fine boots."

"We need to ask if anyone on that estate has seen them with bow and arrow. But none of them are going to speak to us again."

There was no hint of embarrassment in Tein's voice that he was responsible for that outcome. But Ammar knew he was feeling it and wondered if the nabidh was over his failure in the interview, as much as Saliha. Whatever the case, they still needed to question people on the estate and he just made it that much harder. "The guards have never seen it. I asked. But that doesn't mean anything. Everyone in that estate hates the man, maybe they've seen something the guards haven't."

"You and I aren't going to get it."

"Zaytuna."

Tein did not reply at once. Maybe he did not like it, but it was the truth. Finally, Tein said, "If there are no other options."

"We also need to get word to Ubaydallah that the father is not a follower of Barbahari anymore and that Barbahari's sympathies with al-Hallaj are creating discord with his followers."

"Can it wait, or do you want to send a letter now?"

"There's no time to stop. It can wait." Ammar stood.

Steady footsteps echoed around a corner and a contingent of ghilman marched past the road leading to the tavern.

Tein stood, no longer pretending to be drunk. "Even on the West side of the city? They are expecting the worst."

"We need to take a skiff to the Lower Bridge."

"There's no time otherwise."

They emptied their coins onto the table and found they had enough. Once out of the market, they hurried to the river bank and down to a landing where several boatmen were lined up for fares. No one was waiting. They rushed to the first skiff. But before they told the skinny boatman where they wanted to go, he shook his finger at them.

"Taken?" Ammar asked, looking around.

He shook his head. "I don't take police in my boat."

Ammar's temper flared. "What?"

"Every last one of you is a mother's son." He shrugged. The man did not look strong enough to maneuver his own boat in the strong current of the Tigris, yet he was not afraid of them. Tein chortled, and Ammar swung his head around and glared.

Tein signalled to the second skiff and got in before Ammar said a word.

Sitting in the front of the boat, Ammar wished it would go faster, even though it was already moving swiftly. He looked back at Tein, who was watching the bridge coming into view.

Ammar jumped out as a man dragged the skiff up onto the landing. Tein followed, pulling his bad leg over the side. As they rushed up to the road, Ammar told him, "There's no money for a cart. It wouldn't be any faster."

Tein slapped his leg. "Walk. I'm good."

Ammar was relieved. At this point, he would have to beg more money out of Ibn Marwan tonight or beg his landlord for more time.

Tein kept up with him as they made their way through Karkh to the Ushnan Bridge, then across into Buratha. The midday call to prayer had not yet come. Ammar said, "We'll make it."

"We've got time. They said he closes before the afternoon prayer."

"No, he closes when all the butter and buttermilk has gone out for delivery. Hurry." He kept his eyes on the road ahead, not wanting to think about how Tein's leg was holding up to all this walking.

They cut through the market in Buratha, Tein only falling behind a few times, and there it was. Still open. They stopped to catch their breath.

A man with the bearing and clothes to be the owner or manager of the place slapped his hand on the side of a donkey cart filled with amphorae of butter packed in a bed of dried grass. The cart left, and the man returned to his shop where three workers were drying off churning staffs and putting away the work for the day.

Ammar hailed him. "Kamal Ali ibn Abdussalam al-Fassi?"

He looked up and hurried out of his shop, approaching with a wide smile. "Baghdad police?"

Tein looked at Ammar as if to ask, "When is anyone happy to see us?"

"Your colleague was here earlier today," he said, excited. "I suppose she did not reach you in time. We cannot help. But I am so pleased to meet you all the same."

"Zaytuna," Tein said in a flat voice.

"Is that her name?" he asked, brightening even more. "She did not offer it and I did not think it was right to ask."

This was not welcome. Tein's reservations aside, she was useful but should not be investigating without their say-so. First Tein ruins the interview in the morning, now this. Ammar said, "We'd still like to ask you a few questions. We've come all the way from Rusafa."

"Please! I would offer you some buttermilk, but everything is packed up and shipped for the day. I wish I could share it with you. My milk comes from only one family who grazes their goats with alfalfa. The butter and its milk is fit for the caliph."

"I hear you sell to the caliph," Ammar remarked.

"When his cook requests it. One waits for the call," he said. "One does not offer it to them." He looked toward the cheese shops. "No matter what people think."

Ammar remembered the resentment of the cheese maker and how he held it against the man. "I am Ammar at-Tabbani and this is my partner, Tein ibn al-Ashiqa as-Sawda."

He drew his head back as if he suddenly realized he knew Tein and recited, "*Wa at-teini wa az-zaytun wa tur is-sineen, wa hadha baladi'l-amin, la qad khalaqna al-insan fi ahsani taqwim.* You are her brother. I can see it now. Your parents were inspired in naming you two. By the fig and the olive. Are you twins?"

"Yes," Tein replied, but no more.

"Your nasab, though, it refers to your mother. She is a great lover of God? She must be an impressive woman."

Tein sounded impatient. "She passed away when we were children."

"May God have mercy on her soul." Kamal Ali held his hands up in prayer for her.

Ammar stepped in, hoping to keep the conversation open. "Did you hear her preach?"

"Sadly, no. I am new to Baghdad, well, to Buratha, only these past six years." He bowed his head to Tein. "I am sorry that I never had the chance. It explains the nobility of your sister's character."

Ammar did not dare look to Tein to find out how he was taking his last comment. "We haven't spoken to her today. Can you tell us about your conversation?"

Kamal Ali took a step toward them, dipping his head again, and Ammar realized he was blushing. What in God's name had happened?

"Your colleague, Zaytuna..." He said her name reverentially. Ammar finally looked at Tein, who returned his unspoken question with a stony face. Kamal Ali continued, "She asked if Bishr met his killer through his deliveries or if he mentioned any trouble to me or the men. I am afraid he did not."

"How was he as a worker?" Tein asked.

"Always good, until the past month. He missed three deliveries. I spoke to him about it and he told me his wife was ill from her pregnancy and he needed to stay by her side. I found someone to take the deliveries for him at the last moment. But I explained in the future that he would need to send word so that the carts do not go out late."

Tein and Ammar looked at each other. She was pregnant.

"Was he friends with any of the men here?" Tein asked.

"All of us are friends here, like family."

A man came around the corner, bringing a large wet copper basin back to the shop. Tein nudged Ammar. But he had already seen him. He was one of the young men at the mosque.

"Can we speak to that one?"

On seeing whom Ammar wanted, Kamal Ali called out. "Amru!"

Amru put aside the copper pot and said something to another worker standing nearby. The man picked up a linen rag and took the pot from him to dry. He hurried to them, sleeves still rolled up, looking worried.

Kamal Ali said, "These are Baghdad Police. They have more questions about Bishr's murder. I hope you will help them."

"You two were friends?"

"We're all friends here." Amru crossed his arms.

"Outside of work."

"We talked sometimes."

"Where?"

He shrugged. "At the mosque, around. We talked."

"Talked about what?"

He shrugged again.

Kamal Ali observed him like a disappointed father. "Please help these men. Bishr's murder must not go without justice."

Amru turned on him. "Bishr got justice. He died a martyr!" Then he realized what he said and looked back at the shop.

Stunned into silence, Kamal Ali turned to Ammar, who closed in on Amru, saying, "Like Abbas."

The young man swallowed hard, looking like he wanted to run.

Out of the corner of his eye, Ammar noticed the one Amru asked to dry the pot for him had stepped out of the shop and was leaning against the wall, watching and listening.

Tein said to Amru, "You look like you've got something to get off your chest. If you didn't kill him, you're not in any trouble."

"I didn't kill him!" He put his hands out in protest.

"We don't think so either," Ammar assured him. "Tell me, Amru, what can we do for you?"

"Do for me?" The defiance returned. He was mocking, incredulous. "What could Baghdad police do for me? I know all about you, the Shia who whores himself to the caliph against his own people."

"Amru!" objected Kamal Ali.

Tein put a hand on Kamal Ali's shoulder, whispered something that calmed him, and the man stepped just out of the circle.

Bishr's friends were up to something, but what Ammar did not know. Whatever it was, this one thinks it led to the killing. "Whatever trouble you got into, I can protect you. My people come first. Not the caliph. Even if what you did led to his murder. We only want the man who shot the bow."

A flash of relief passed through Amru's eyes before they turned stubborn again, and he answered Ammar with silence.

"The people think someone killed him for being Shia and they are ready to revolt. The ghilman will come down hard."

"Buratha will fight them!"

"And many will die, including your family."

"Imam Husayn's family died at Karbala. May God be well-pleased with them."

Ammar took a deep breath. "This doesn't need to be Karbala. Think of your mother. Your mother can live instead of die."

The boy did not answer, but his face changed at the mention of his mother. Ammar had him.

"I'm not telling you more than this." He paused, then looked back at the shop. "You promise none of this comes back on us."

"The police chief only hears what I tell him."

"It was Utbah ibn Harb. Bishr brought him to us after he introduced him to Aisha. The way it sounded to me, Utbah pushed the girl on him. Aisha worked in the kitchen at his uncle's estate. Aisha told my wife that Utbah made her go out and meet the delivery every time. Then once they liked each other enough, he gave them a place to be alone in the house. Bishr fell for her hard, and he trusted Utbah because of that. But we never trusted him."

"Did you witness the killing?"

"You wanted my help. You got it." He talked like something bitter was in his mouth. "Who forces a kitchen maid on a delivery man? What game was he playing? We warned Bishr but he wouldn't hear it. Then we've got this rich boy around, making plans for us."

"Making plans?"

Amru's eyes widened. He had stumbled. "Telling us what to do, always wanting us to go hunting with him so he could show off his skills."

Ammar let it go for the moment, asking, "Archery?"

"Yes."

"That doesn't sound so bad. Did any of you like it?"

"Aisha's brother, Talha. He liked it, followed Utbah around like a pup. Utbah bought him gifts. Fancy boots that are good for nothing but sitting in a litter and being carried around. He was learning to use the bow, too. But once Bishr went and spoke to Aisha's father to marry her, we never saw them again."

Tein asked, "How good an archer was Talha?"

"He couldn't hit Solomon's Gates from one pace away." Amru laughed derisively. "For all his being a pup to that dog, he didn't learn a thing."

"It doesn't sound like you and Talha were friends," Ammar said.

"Bishr pushed him on us, too." He shrugged again.

"Maybe he killed Bishr?"

"If you want him for it, take him. You can make anything stick."

Tein followed up, "So you think only Utbah could have made those shots that killed Bishr?"

"Only Utbah."

"But why Utbah at all?"

"It was him. That's all you need."

"What else were you all up to?"

"Nothing. We work hard here. There's not much energy for anything after work." He bowed to Kamal Ali, hand over his heart. "I'm sorry for my outburst, sir, I was afraid."

Kamal Ali put a hand on his shoulder. "Of course, son."

Utbah was probably long out of Baghdad. If he killed Bishr, they were no closer to knowing why. "One last question."

Amru tipped his chin up, "Ask."

"Was Utbah sincere in becoming Shia."

He let out an angry laugh. "Walla! No! I told Bishr not to take him to see the Imam. But once he did, we were stuck with him."

"You didn't tell us what plans Utbah had for you all."

Amru shook his head. "He was playing us."

"How?"

"You said that was your last question."

Ammar ignored it, "You were too smart to get played."

"Bishr wasn't smart enough, or Talha," Tein said.

"No. They weren't."

Ammar said, "Whatever those plans were might lead us to Utbah."

"I told you already. He wanted us all to be like Talha."

"All right. But if you want the ghilman out of Buratha, I need to know where Utbah is. We'll arrest him, and be done."

"Police, if I see him, I'll bring him to you. But he hasn't been around here since he killed Bishr. He's sitting in that estate of his drinking wine and sneering at the likes of us."

"Tell a watchman if you see him. And, thanks."

Amru warily acknowledged the thanks and went back into the shop. He passed the man who was leaning against the wall, looked at the pot and spoke sharply to him. Amru grabbed the linen out of his hand and got to work.

Kamal Ali was aghast. "I did not know. I would have told Zaytuna if I had. At least the boy has spoken now."

Tein eyed the shop. "Your men trust you?"

"Yes. I believe if you pay men well, if you treat them well, they will work hard for you and remain loyal."

Tein smiled. "Is it true?"

"It has been, so far, by the grace of God." He paused, shifting to a more formal posture. "I would like to speak to your father, if I may."

"My father?" Tein pulled his head back. "I don't understand."

"I would like to speak to your father about your sister."

"We don't have a father."

Kamal Ali's eyes softened, as if he wanted to reach out to Tein. Then he said, formally again, "Then, I would like to speak to you."

"Speak."

"I would like to arrange a meeting with your sister in the proper manner to discuss the possibility of marriage."

Ammar raised his eyebrows, expecting Tein to snap at the man, but he smiled instead, grinning so his back teeth showed. "I would be glad of it."

"I am in your debt." He bowed his head, paused again, and looked into the distance. "I have only seen a woman as beautiful as she once before."

The man was serious! Ammar looked between the two, unbelieving.

"And where was that?" Tein asked.

"In Egypt, I saw a depiction of a Nubian queen, a pharaoh's wife, or a pharaoh herself. I fell in love with her instantly. Your sister is her mirror. Zaytuna has the same noble beauty and intelligence. She is as beautiful as the light that shines from her eyes, her cheekbones as sharp as her mind, and her lips as inviting as..."

Tein held up his hands. "All right. I understand."

But the man was agitated and blurted out, "I will marry her, or I will marry no other woman in my life."

"If you love my sister, do you think she will marry on my word?"

"By God, no!" Kamal Ali's back straightened. "She is a woman who must answer for herself and I would not accept her without it."

"I'll arrange for you two to meet again," Tein agreed. "If she is willing and under the appropriate circumstances. We can go from there."

Kamal Ali put his hand over his heart, looking on the verge of tears. Ammar did not understand. He had come to respect Zaytuna, but she was no great beauty and nothing was sharper than her tongue.

"I thought I would never see her again and prayed to God. Here you are! Alhamdulillah."

Ammar wondered if the man was going to weep with gratitude.

"Don't worry." Tein put his hand on Kamal Ali's shoulder. "I'll come back. We need to clear up this mess first. It may be a week or so. But I'll come back." He paused. "I would be proud for you to be my brother."

"Inshallah!"

They left Kamal Ali in the square, his hand still over his heart.

As they reached the edge of the square, Ammar asked, "Did you just marry your sister off to that man?"

"If she agrees, she'll be off of my hands for good. He's rich. He's obviously a good man. She shouldn't refuse."

"You can't force her. Not Zaytuna."

"No one can force Zaytuna. But if she's smart, she'll agree."

Ammar chuckled. "I don't know if she's smart in the way you want."

As they turned out of the square, they heard running footsteps and turned. The worker who had been listening to their conversation was coming up fast behind them.

He stopped, breathless. "Listen to me. Ask about the tithe. Ask why the poor Imamis around here have money." He turned away, but Tein had a fist of his robe and pulled him back.

"What are you talking about?" Tein demanded.

The young man put his arms up, afraid Tein would hit him. "The men who work here used to talk about the tithe, but whenever I got close, they stopped. Then my Imami neighbour had money he shouldn't. Then it was more than my neighbour. All the Imamis have money they shouldn't. Ask about the tithe."

Ammar remembered Tein heard them talking about the tithe in the mosque. He asked, "Are you one of them? Fatihi?"

"No, I'm Ismaili."

"So why are you telling us this?" Tein let go of him.

"I'm obligated to do the right thing. A man has been killed. I must speak." He ran back to shop.

"Ammar." Tein's eyebrows were raised.

"Where did my father get the money for those gifts?"

"Exactly."

"We're going there, now." As they hurried to his parents, Ammar thought of Zaytuna's dream. The butter dealer with the sack of coins. *She led us to this.*

22

"Where did you get the money for those gifts, Father?" Ammar's mother tugged at his robe to get him to leave his father alone.

His father ignored him, leaving his feet up on a stool, and continued to look out the window into the distance.

"I am not leaving until you tell me."

Still looking out the window, his father said, "Woman, add more meat to the pot, we'll be feeding your son and his crow."

"There will be no more money where that came from," Ammar said.

Abu Ammar spun his head around. "What do you mean!"

"We're not asking you to return it, Father."

The stubbornness in Abu Ammar's eyes softened at the news, but his voice held firm. "If you've made sure of things, you don't need me."

"Bishr died for you to have that money." Ammar took one step closer. His mother moaned and put a hand on his arm to stop him. "It's full of sin. Every fals. You can cleanse it by telling the truth."

"Full of sin!" Abu Ammar burst out laughing.

His mother pleaded, "My son, my son!"

"Mother, please. Leave us," Ammar said without turning to her.

But Tein clasped her hands. "What is it, Auntie?"

Only then did Ammar face her. "Mother, you must tell us about the money. You cannot carry the sin of this with him."

"Truly, the boy was killed because of it?"

He needed to tell her it was true to save her life. But he could not lie to her. "Mother, I..." he tried again, wanting to say it in someway that would not lay heavily on him. At a loss, he looked at Tein, pleading.

Tein took it on. "The money is the answer to the murder. If we know who gave it to Abu Ammar, it will help us find the killer. We cannot take the money back. There's no worry that anyone will come for it or that you'll be in any trouble."

Abu Ammar kicked the stool out, sending it across the room. Ammar's mother jumped with a shriek, pulling her hand away. "I'm warning you, woman!" he yelled. "Don't you say a word! You'll see my hand for the rest of your days if you do!"

She gasped, slapped her hand over her mouth, and ran outside, Tein following her.

In that moment, Ammar understood for the first time what her life must be like every day living under this roof. He had never respected the man for his temper, but also he had never given a thought to what it meant for her. His father ran a strict house and Ammar left for the frontier as soon as he could, but he never saw his father lay a hand on his mother and she never complained about him. His brother and sister-in-law lived next door. The grandchildren. But she was still alone with him much of the time. Ammar's selfishness took hold of him and he directed the anger he felt for himself at his father, leaning into his face, coldly threatening. "Never speak to my mother that way again."

The old man snorted. "Boy, she's my wife and I'm your father."

"I'll take her from you." He stood and gave the old man his back, leaving to find Tein and his mother, furious that there was nothing he to do about it. She would never leave his father, not even to live next door with his brother and his family.

Outside, his mother and Tein stood by the low wall at the rear of the house, staring into the distance. Tein's arm was around Umm Ammar. She leaned on him for support.

Ammar touched her shoulder, and she let go of Tein to face him. Her eyes were red-rimmed from weeping and she frowned, the downward edges of her mouth making deep creases in her face.

"Mother, you must tell us."

"How can I disobey my husband even for my son?"

"It's not for me, Mother, but for the life of another. You aren't required to obey anyone if it's sinful or if it would harm another." He paused, taking her hand and kissing it. "You taught me never to obey if there's sin in the command."

She sniffed, nodding. "It was the tithe returned to us. I told your father that he should give it back to you and Muhsin, as you paid it, but he said it had to be a secret." She grasped his hand. "He used it to buy presents for Nasifa and her mother and I thought that was as good as returning it to you since it was for your engagement."

Ammar clenched at the assumption that the engagement was going forward without his say and his voice had an unintentional edge to it. "Who brought it to the house?"

She pulled back her hand in rebuke. Worse, she answered Tein instead of him. "It was a young man with long hair."

Tein asked, "Big like me? Curly hair?"

"Yes."

Ammar called her back to him, his voice softer. "What did he say?"

Accepting the apology in his voice, she replied, "God forgive him," maybe meaning Ammar as much as the boy. She looked between the two of them. "He said the tithe was being returned to us because the Twelfth Imam does not live. The agents don't deserve our money. And we don't deserve their lies. It was a gift from their Imam to us, that their Imam was calling us to the true path of the Fatihis under his protection and guidance."

Knowing her devotion to the Twelfth Imam, he imagined how

hard it must have been for her. He took her hand. "Did he say anything else?"

"No. He handed it over and I took it to your father."

Ammar looked toward the adjoining house. "You should stay with Muhsin and Tahirah until Father calms down." He looked at her closely. "Mother, is he like this often?"

"No, I am always good. I never disobey him. He has his moods, but never has reason to harm me. But how I will answer for this?"

Rage burned through him, barely contained. He sensed Tein's fury answer his own. It was the only thing that kept him from going inside and dragging his father out into the courtyard. "I'll speak to him," he said through tight lips.

"No, please, habibi."

"I'm taking her to Muhsin," he told Tein, ignoring her plea.

He put his arm around his mother and they walked to the gate that opened onto Muhsin and Tahirah's outer courtyard. "Muhsin!" he called out, bringing his mother to their door.

His brother came around from the back, wiping his hands, while Tahirah opened the door, her youngest clinging to her legs.

"Assalamu alaykum," Muhsin said. "I was milking the goats. If you aren't in a hurry, I can send you home with some."

"Wa alaykum assalam. I only want to leave Mother with Tahirah."

Tahirah held her hand out to Umm Ammar. "The children were just asking for you! God is gracious!"

After the door shut behind them, Ammar said, "Father threatened her."

Muhsin's face took a cast of a man ready to fight. "Tell me!"

"Said he'd hit her if she spoke to us about the money."

His brother gave a hard look towards their parent's house. "The tithe."

"You knew?"

He asked sincerely, "Was I supposed to tell you? He spent the money on your woman. I considered my part to be a gift to your future marriage. I didn't think it was a secret."

Ammar held back spitting out, "She's not my woman," because somewhere inside him, he knew he liked the sound of her being so. *But not without my say!* He looked over his shoulder. Tein was watching and Ammar waved him over impatiently. As Tein approached, he barked at his brother, "Tell us."

"I heard bandits robbed the Imam's agent and were returning the tithe to the Imamis in Buratha. One day a man came and gave the money to Mother. I didn't see it."

Tein whistled and stood back.

Ammar objected. "No one reported it!"

"Why would our scholars report it? It would only sow more doubt in the Imam. That would only serve his enemies. They did the right thing."

"Is this widely known?"

"People talk. Father mentioned that men at the tavern say the agents are corrupt. But he has doubted for a long time. The robbery was only confirmation for him. It has raised doubts for others, though. Tahirah told me one of her friends said that if the Imam were alive, God would not allow the tithe to be robbed."

"What did Tahirah say?"

"She reminded them of Karbala and the struggles all the Imams carried in the past. This is one more. We must hold firm that Imam Muhammad ibn al-Hasan is alive and his guidance reaches us through the agents."

Grateful to her, Ammar said, "She did well."

"Worse." Muhsin put his hand out, calling Ammar's attention. "Many who never doubted before now believe that the Ismaili caliph in North Africa is the Mahdi."

Ammar saw it laid out before him. The killing now looked like something beyond their abilities to resolve.

Tein asked, "The one set to take North Africa?"

"Yes. If he can take North Africa, restoring an Imam, a son of the Prophet's line to leadership of even one part of the caliphate, whoever that man may be, people will believe him to be the Mahdi."

Ammar asked Tein. "Is that what this is all about? Were the

robbery and the killing planned to coincide with the taking of North Africa? Inspire an uprising here so that this Mahdi not only takes all of North Africa, but the centre of the caliphate itself in Baghdad?"

"All this?" his brother asked. "I don't understand."

Tein replied, "Bishr's killing and the robbery may be related."

"God protect us from evil things!" Muhsin exclaimed. "Now I understand why the caliph put troops in the streets." He continued with urgency. "If the robbery and killing were meant to inspire an uprising, it must be the Qarmatis. The Ismailis denounce them, but not too long ago, they were in the same camp. Have they joined each other again? Is the plan for the Qarmatis to take Baghdad from their position nearby in Bahrain while the Ismaili Imam takes North Africa?"

Tein turned to Ammar. "Ibn Marwan lied to us. He said we had to find a suspect fast before the Shia protested the killing, protests the caliph would misunderstand as an uprising."

"Ibn Marwan had to know." Ammar thought of their sergeant that first day he pulled them onto the case. He was frantic, detailing the threats to the caliphate past and present. Now Ammar thought of his ugly speech that day, Ibn Marwan was most worried about the Ismaili Imam in North Africa and the Qarmatis in Bahrain. "The Abbasid caliphate is weakened as it is. That's why the viziers wanted Ibn Marwan to frame a suspect. End it. This isn't about crushing protests in Baghdad over the death of one man. This is about the fall of the caliphate itself."

Thinking it through, Tein added, "So what the viziers really wanted was to stop protests in Baghdad and Buratha from turning into a breeding ground for an uprising. Why keep it from the caliph?"

"Because they hoped to protect their fellow Shias in Baghdad and Buratha. If the caliph found out, he would send in the ghilman. And he did. Whether or not the protests turned into an uprising, the caliph would make the Shia pay." He paused as the horrible consequences sank in, making him want to rush into the street, sword drawn. "Solving the case won't fix this."

Tein replied, every muscle in his face taut, "We don't know that."

"Everyone should be ready to go at a moment's notice, Muhsin. Walk out the back here and around Baghdad itself toward Samarra. The caliph will retreat there. It will be safe. Wrap your turbans like Sunnis. If you have to talk to anyone, don't give them your names. Watch how you pray and what you say."

Muhsin's face blanched. "The Shia of Buratha won't fall for this. I don't hear any talk of protests, let alone revolt among my neighbours or at the market. They only fear the ghilman and will fight if they must. Is there anyone here who wants a revolt? We only want to raise our children in safety. They can call us to revolt, but we will not answer."

Muhsin sounded sure that the Shia would not take the bait being laid out for them. Ammar wished it were true. "We were told that there are men at the mosque who talk about revolt. They might be on the inside, urging on protests, hoping to turn them into more."

"Ammar. Listen to me," His brother pleaded. "No one is talking about protests. And those men are always making trouble at the mosque. We'll ignore them as we always have done."

"Be ready to leave all the same." Ammar reached out. "But Mother."

"I'll have her and Father ready to go."

"I mean today. I've never seen Father threaten her before."

"Mother knows how to handle him."

"That's no way for her to live."

"And you have something to say about that?"

"I'm her son, as good as you."

"Her son who sees her once a week."

Despite knowing Muhsin was right, Ammar snapped, "If you are the dutiful son, what are you doing to protect her?"

"She is with us every day. Father knows I am watching him."

The shame of not having paid attention or been there to protect her at home silenced him.

As he turned to leave, Tein beside him, his brother said to his back, "If the end you fear does not come and you marry this girl, come back here to live. Take control of this household and watch over your mother."

Ammar kept walking as if he had said nothing. His brother had always been naïve. He took after their mother. Fine for a woman to believe the best in people and that a good came from every wrong, but a man has greater responsibilities. A man cannot turn away from the realities of the world. As much as he hated to admit it, he was like his father. Suspecting the worst. Frustrated by the demands of family. A hard man when he had to be. But his brother never had to kill men hand to hand and have their voices whisper in his ear while he slept. At least, Ammar would not turn away from coming danger. He would protect his family in a way his brother could never do.

Out of the gate, Tein dismissed him. "You can give up. I'm going back to the mosque to talk to the imam."

"And that will stop the coming war?"

"You don't want to hear it. But your brother may be right. If the case is connected and we can solve it, there's still a chance."

He wanted to tell Tein he was as naïve as Muhsin, but he kept his mouth shut. The people needed a warning to escape, and those who stayed needed guidance to prepare to fight. There was no point in the case now.

"Get your mind off what might happen and back into the case."

It came out. "And what if the people protest? And the Qarmatis are there to turn it into an uprising?"

"I never took you for a man who would give up."

Tein said it like he was done with him for good. Ammar fumed. The man cursed-well knew that kind of accusation would work on him. He needed time to wrap his head around it. Tein gave it to him. They walked in silence as he brought himself around to reasoning it was wiser to do both. Solve the case fast and be ready for war.

When he was ready, he said, "Utbah is involved in the robbery."

"I agree." Tein started to speak, but held back.

"What? Say it. It might be important."

"You aren't going to like it."

Ammar stopped, pulling him back by the arm, and realizing it was not about the case, glared a warning.

Tein said it anyway. "Are you going to marry Nasifa?"

"Right now, I'd rather there be a war." Ammar walked off, keeping a few steps ahead of Tein. He did not want another word from him.

He should marry Nasifa and be like Muhsin. The good son. The man who milks goats. The thought of going back home unmanned him. But the thought of Nasifa did not. Nasifa had the opposite effect on him, and he did not want to admit that he had not thought about a woman like that in a long time.

He had his share of women along the frontier, never caring to marry like Tein. Eventually, he became ashamed of paying for women or charming frustrated widows in the borderlands into indiscretions. A widow he left behind spat on him as he walked out her door, cursing him and screeching that he was a man with no honour. "All that warrior talk you used to bed me! Husayn, God be pleased, wouldn't've let you fight beside him!" The truth her sword, she was the warrior and he the vanquished. He swore off women for good. It would be marriage or celibacy, and he chose celibacy.

Yet here was a woman who stirred him. Quick-witted, observant, willing to challenge her own father and do it without being disrespectful. She might be the woman who could hold him to account. A woman he would want to have an account to hold over him. A woman he wanted to do right by enough to marry.

But there was no going home.

He did not realize how long he was mulling over the question of her until Tein said, "That silence says a lot."

"You tell me how I can marry her."

"War aside, you mean?"

Ammar bristled. It was no joke.

Tein shrugged. "You contract the marriage."

"You know what I mean!"

"All right."

He gave Tein a sideways glance. "Barring war, where would she live?"

"Exactly what Muhsin said. Another reason to quit the police."

"And what would I do living in Buratha with my wife and parents? How do I support this wife of mine?"

"Make butter for Kamal Ali?" Tein was serious. "We'd get paid fairly. It's near your parents and my sister and Saliha are just over the bridge."

Ammar scowled. So much was wrong about working for the police. Low pay, daily frustrations, every error dogging him when he tried to sleep at night. Worse, the people's distrust. And now this case out of their hands. A voice prodded him. *Whose side are you on?* He waved it off. He was not willing to live without the edge of this job. Thinking through a problem. Getting to the end. It was as close to battle as he could get. And distrust or not, they found justice often enough. Churning butter was mindless exertion to empty ends and it surprised him Tein was considering it. But none of that mattered now. There was no "barring war." It was coming.

They turned a corner. Regular troops were leaning against a wall. One grunt was at a nearby tavern, talking to the keeper and gesturing to his friends. Ammar said, "It's not only the ghilman now."

"Drunk and ready to fight."

"What do you think of a coming war now?"

Tein ignored his question. "The mosque isn't too far ahead."

As they came up on it, the heights of its tiled facade seemed fragile to Ammar for the first time. The small chips in the stuccoed mud brick seemed to warn of imminent collapse. How did the imam of the mosque let it get this far?

The imam appeared, walking out with a shopping basket in hand, his wife beside him. Ammar rushed over, all his frustration directed at the man. "Why haven't you undertaken repairs on the mosque? One hard season, one flood, it'll wash away like the western walls of the Round City!"

The imam's wife pulled her wrap over her face and hid behind her husband while he scolded Ammar for the rudeness of his approach, "Wa alaykum assalam!"

Still angry, he noticed the imam's wife cowering and relented, giving him the required greeting. "My apologies. Assalamu alaykum."

The imam spoke to his wife. She took the basket from his hand and went on without him, but kept her eye on Ammar as she did. The imam countered. "And you? What are you doing about the soldiers?"

Tein cut in, drawing the imam's attention. "We need your help."

"What can I do to stop what is coming?"

"Tell us who was involved in the robbery of the tithe," Tein said.

"You heard about the robbery." The imam's voice trailed.

"Yes," Ammar said, "and we think Bishr's murder is connected."

The imam looked between the two, objecting, "If so, the theft was the work of the Qarmatis. They killed Bishr!"

Ammar felt vindicated, but Tein broke in. "How do you know?"

"Who else would do it? All the Shia communities fight. We all disagree. But we people still gather to pray in this mosque. We live and work together and even marry." His voice rose in indignation. "Only the Qarmatis take our disagreements to such violent ends!"

"Is this just your suspicion?" Ammar asked.

"It is obvious!"

That was not enough. "Did Bishr and his friends talk about the tithe? Any word about the agents? Utbah ibn Harb?"

The imam looked around as if someone might be listening.

"What?" Tein asked.

"Utbah ibn Harb. This morning I overheard him being mocked in the marketplace. But if the Qarmatis are behind it all, what would you want with him?"

"What did you hear?" Ammar asked.

"The scholar, Aqil ibn Akib. He was buying dried fruits and nuts from Imad earlier, only two shops down from where I stood. Imad taunted him, saying that he turned his rich friend into his woman, following him around holding his basket."

Ammar glanced at Tein, who asked, "What makes you think he meant Utbah ibn Harb?"

"Aqil responded using his name. He did not even speak back to the insult. Rather, he insisted Imad must be mistaken because Utbah ibn Harb left the city for good."

"Aqil and Utbah are friends?" Ammar's voice rose.

"I was not aware of it until today. Bishr and Aqil grew up together. He circled around Bishr's group, but I had the impression the other boys did not like Aqil. I rarely saw them all together. I would not have thought he knew Bishr's friends well enough to know their whereabouts."

"This scholar," Ammar said to Tein, "how is he involved in all this? He is everywhere we go, sticking his nose in."

Tein turned back to the imam. "Where does Aqil live?"

"He had a room in Buratha, but mentioned he recently moved. I would think he would move close to Karkh, by the Ushnan Bridge or in Karkh itself. Most Imami scholars have settled in Dar as-Silsila. Despite being cast out of their circles, he would want to be near them. He is a man certain, always, of his own righteousness, God forgive him."

Ammar turned to Tein. "He kept pushing the girl and her family. He was trying to put us in the wrong direction."

"Time to talk to his old neighbours and Imad."

"Imad first." Ammar put his hand on his friend's arm. Maybe they could solve this in time after all. Ammar bowed his head in thanks to the imam. "God protect you. If you hear anything else, please send word."

The imam prayed, "May God reveal the killer and protect us all."

They left, striding through nearly empty main roads, Tein keeping pace despite his now visible limp. While some people ducked their head around corners to see if any military were nearby before crossing a square, others, even women, walked boldly, spoiling for a fight.

Turning into one of the arched entrances nearby to the dried fruit and nut sellers, Ammar called out, "Which one of you is Imad?"

Two of the sellers looked the two up and down and ignored them, while the third gestured he was across and one over. Imad leaned against the back counter of his shop, surrounded by barrels of perfectly mounded cones of dates, dried melons, raisins and nuts, giving the other shopkeeper a dirty look.

Ammar drew his attention. "You spoke to Aqil ibn Akib this morning about his rich friend."

"Utbah ibn Harb." He said the name as if he had something they wanted and would make them work for it.

"The ghilman." Tein was impatient and stood in front of the barrels, ready to kick them aside and take hold of the man. "You can help us get them out of Buratha. You need to talk. Now."

Imad was unimpressed, answering only in the moment before Tein would have followed through with his threat. "The brute was buying cheese from Ibn Butrus and his rich friend was acting like he was the one getting his ass slapped in that pair. A rich one like that holding a basket and taking orders." He shrugged. "I always took Aqil to be the bottom. It's the big ones who beg for it." He leaned over, eyebrows raised, smiling. "I wonder what the wife thinks. She lives alone in that one room with their children while Aqil saunters around spending money on his lover."

"Where's the room?" Tein demanded.

Imad stood up, smiling, having gotten what he wanted. "My boy will take you there." He signalled behind him. A skinny young man in good working clothes came out from the back of the shop. Imad said a few words and the young man waved for them to follow. Ammar noticed he had hennaed a feminine design onto his wrist and wondered how he survived working under that man. He led them briskly out of the market, but as they passed the market gate, a man came running up behind them.

"Wait!"

All three turned. It was one of the shopkeepers who would not answer them. He stopped in front of them, breathless. "I heard what you said about the soldiers. I can help. Aqil ibn Akib bought dates from me two nights ago. My boy delivered them to an estate in Rusafa. He asked me to wrap them as a gift and tucked a letter inside."

"What estate?" Tein asked.

"On Jasmine Vine Road."

"That letter was for Utbah's uncle," Ammar said to Tein.

"Anything else?"

"No."

Tein grasped the man's arm in thanks.

Their guide took that as a signal to go and continued on, walking so fast Ammar strode to keep up. Tein straggled behind, but made it around each corner in time to follow them to the next. Stopping short in a small square, their guide walked to a door, pointed to it, and without a word, ran back to the market.

Tein caught up as Ammar called through the curtain. "Assalamu alaykum, Baghdad police."

There was no answer. He tried again. Tein gestured to him to go in. Pushing the curtain aside, he stuck his head in, pulling it quickly out again. "Empty, but there's blood."

Tein held the curtain back so there was enough light to see. Rotting reed mats covered the floor. A bedroll stained with blood hugged the back wall. A stew pot was on its side, its contents sprayed across the reed mats.

"That's a lot of blood," Tein said.

"Whatever happened here, the neighbours heard it."

Tein turned around to begin the questioning and found a man standing directly behind him. The man was short but sturdy and held his own. "That whoremonger is not coming back to us. Walla, I'll stand him down!"

"Who?"

"Aqil ibn Akib!" He carried on without prompting. "Always entertaining his friends. Then he keeps a woman here for his use. Then he sells the woman to one of them. We heard them tussling in there. The girl played at objecting, but he got what he paid for."

"When was this?"

"Last night. The girl was screaming. The women went to her. My wife got to her first. Whatever he did, he killed that baby in her."

"The blood." Tein said.

"Where is she now?" Ammar asked.

"A woman took her."

"Would your wife know?"

The man hesitated.

"She can lead us to Aqil ibn Akib and he'll never be back."

"Good." He returned to a room next door.

A moment later, he came out again with his wife. She was a beautiful older woman, nearly double her husband's height and girth. The kind of woman men called with appreciation "a fattened camel ready for slaughter." Ammar was struck by her heavily kohled eyes and the boldness of her step. Pulling her wrap aside for them to see her face and even more of her figure, she did not wait to be asked. "I don't know where she's gone. Marwa sent for a midwife, but she got here too late. Barely able to walk even with one hand on the wall from the bleeding and pain. God protect her, at least she wasn't too far along, but I hope she found her way to someone to care for her or she'll be in trouble. We tried to stop her. I gave the poor thing a spare sirwal and wrap to wear. She gave me a coin in return."

"Shh!" Her husband glared at her.

"Don't you give me that," she scolded him. "These men aren't taking my gold from me, and neither are you. The evil eye is already on me! Go back to the room if you have a complaint!"

Her husband stuttered, unsure how to react in front of them.

What did the man expect? Ammar thought, *A woman like that you have to pay for one way or another*. He ignored the man's feelings and asked his wife, "Did she say her name?"

"Aisha," the woman answered.

Neither of them said a word. This was the beginning of something. In the silence, the woman's gaze settled on Tein as if she would take him for herself, slowly. Her husband shifted in place, looking away, pretending not to notice.

Ammar was used to women's reactions to Tein, but there was no time for this. "Your husband said she left with another woman."

She tucked her head back, turning her attention back to him. "Where would he get that? He was in our room. And I saw her walk away, alone." She pointed a hennaed hand at the far end of the alley. "That way."

"The man who was there," Ammar asked. "Did you see him?"

"Hasan startled him, but said it was too dark to see his face. But we all heard him. He talked like a rich Baghdadi."

"Hasan?" Tein asked.

"He's not home. But he told us a man was hiding in his passageway. Hasan scared him, said the man ran into Aqil's room. That's when we heard them and she wasn't enjoying it."

"Aqil ibn Akib wasn't there?" Tein followed up.

"No, only the rich man and the girl."

"Ho!" Ammar looked at Tein. This was something. The girl was Aisha and the man could only be Utbah. He trusted the woman's judgement. Utbah raped her, then gave her money, a lot of money.

"Was she ever here before? With another man?"

"Not that I saw."

"How long was she there?"

She looked at her husband. "Two, three days?"

"Yes, she came in three days ago," he said with authority. "I remember. I heard a woman weeping."

"And the dinar?" Tein asked.

The woman admitted, a hungry expression on her face, "She gave it to me out of a leather purse. A purse filled with them."

"How many of those did she give out?"

"One to everyone who helped."

Ammar thanked them, and they retreated to their rooms, the woman giving Tein one last long look before letting the curtain fall behind her.

Once out of the alley, Tein said, "She isn't with her family after all."

"Utbah took a purse of coins to escape. Came to find her. Rapes her when she won't have him. Then gives her the purse out of remorse."

"It's hard to imagine that man having remorse, but without money, he can't escape on his own."

"He could have had more money on him. Two purses."

"If he had money, he would have left Baghdad, Ammar. Why else would he put himself in the hands of Aqil ibn Akib for protection?"

Ammar nodded. "It's the only explanation for his submissive behaviour in the market. Unless they are lovers, but I thought the shopkeeper was mocking."

"You and I both know the difference. It was mocking." Tein frowned.

"Utbah killed Bishr to have Aisha for himself." Ammar was desperate for it to be true.

"Hold on." Tein disappeared back down the alley. Ammar followed, but Tein was already heading back. He gestured back toward the alley. "The Ismaili who works for the butter dealer hinted that Bishr and his friends were behind that robbery. I forgot the neighbour said men were meeting there. Well, they just identified Amru and Talha among them. So they were planning the robbery in Aqil's room. It seems like the murder has no connection to the robbery except that is how they all knew each other."

"That sounds right." But Ammar could not accept that an Imami scholar would rob the agents of his own Imam. "What's in it for Aqil?"

"Greed?"

"But they gave the money back to the people."

"All of it?" Tein asked. "Maybe he held some back for himself? Why else would he protect Utbah? He's covering his own involvement."

"He put a lot of effort into getting us off track. He was afraid we'd find Utbah and that would lead us to the robbery, exposing him."

"Utbah is in Baghdad." Ammar shook his head, unbelieving.

"All that money. Why wouldn't Utbah leave the city? Why go to her?"

Not looking at Tein, Ammar said, "A man will do anything to get the woman he wants in his hands."

There was a pause. Only when Ammar faced him did Tein say, "Yes," owning the word.

"We have to find out where the scholar moved." Ammar pushed past the moment, wishing he'd said nothing at all. "Utbah must be there."

"There's no time to go door to door to find him," Tein said, frustrated. "No way to track down Aisha either."

He was right. Even if Ibn Marwan allowed it, they were only a few reliable watchmen. The rest were useless men paid a pittance to keep the peace and report back if they could not solve a problem with threats or their fists. There was no chance of a widespread search.

"She'll take that money and leave Baghdad for good," Tein said, worried. "There's nothing for her here, not with that family, not with what she's done."

"She'll be safe." Although there was no way to know that, Ammar tried to reassure him, knowing what he was thinking. "Aisha has more money than the likes of us will ever see."

"If she doesn't get robbed."

"God protect her." There was nothing they could do but pray.

"Our best shot is to talk to Utbah's uncle about the letter. Let's hope Aqil ibn Akib mentioned where he's hiding Utbah."

"We have to tell Ibn Marwan. It's personal. We can prove it."

"We've got to arrest Utbah first, deliver them a man accused," Tein said. "That's the only way to end this."

"He's in Baghdad. We'll get him."

23

"Ghazi Ammar is in Ibn Marwan's office. They're yelling." The errand boy smirked, then ran off down the arcade, his arms full of paperwork, and disappeared into the crowd.

Tein barely glanced at the boy as he leaned on an arcade pillar outside the office, keeping the weight off his bad leg and his eye on Solomon's Gate in the distance. There was no chance he would go to stand by Ammar while he dealt with their sergeant. When the case was done, he was not going to go in there to tell the man he quit, either.

"Kamal Ali," he said aloud, continuing to think his plans through. *He's our way out. Zaytuna will marry him. I'll work for him. I'll get up early every day and walk Saliha to the hospital. I'll make butter, then walk her home. Good pay. No trouble. If she'll marry me.* He straightened up as another voice within him said, *She won't.* The reminder made him unaccountably tired. He slid down the pillar and closed his eyes.

"Tein!"

He opened his eyes with a start, not knowing how long he had been sitting there or even if he had fallen asleep. Hand on the pillar for support, Tein stood to face him. Ammar rushed through a stream of people coming and going, waving a rolled-up document in his hand, but there was a look on his face that said there was more. "We have a letter to get in to see Utbah's uncle! He'll have to talk to us."

Tein stiffened. "What is it?"

"Ibn Marwan has a scapegoat."

"What!"

"The idea came from one of Ibn Furat's men. They have the name of a man who is awaiting sentencing by order of the High Court for some imagined crime against the caliph. If we don't find the killer in time, they'll parade him through the street as our guilty man. Then, execute him publicly."

"They can't do that!"

Ammar did not respond.

Tein knew they could, though, and asked through clenched teeth, "What does 'in time' mean?"

"We have until tomorrow night if violence doesn't break out. They'll parade him the morning after tomorrow. There's been scattered violence around the city, but so far it's contained. Nothing worse than what we've seen. If we can't bring the killer in by then, that man will take his place. The police chief has signed off on it."

Tein grew hot and pulled at his robe. "I won't do it."

"We've got no say. The High Court and the Police Chief. Their men. Not us. They won't let us anywhere near it."

"I'll tell the people." His heart was beating out of his chest. "I'll go into Buratha and tell the people it's all lies."

Tein's eyesight sparked around the edges. The last time he felt this way was when he ran from brutalizing a poor woman and her child with his questions. He ran from them down to the canal and into the reed bed, only to find his uncle Nuri waiting for him.

"Ithar," his uncle had told him that day. "To be a man is to sacrifice yourself for others." This job was not that.

Ammar put his hand on Tein's shoulder, either to steady him or make him accept it. Whichever it was, it was no good. Tein choked out, "I won't."

"If we can't do it in time," Ammar promised, "I will go with you to the mosque in Buratha, and we'll ask the imam to permit us to address the people. We'll tell them ourselves if we are certain who killed Bishr. If not, we'll tell them we don't know. We'll expose it all."

Tein grasped Ammar's wrist and pulled his old friend into a desperate embrace, taking deep shuddering breaths until he felt himself again.

Ammar stepped back, rubbing an eye with the heel of his palm. "They'll execute us for it. Better to die with honour than to live in shame."

"Will the people believe us?"

"They'll believe the caliphate lies to them. We've been holding the short end of that stick for well over two hundred years."

"But," Tein said, realizing what might happen if they took this stand, "if the people protest because of what we say to them, the caliph will clamp down on them and the Qarmatis will make use of it for their uprising. We've told the truth and nothing changes. We've made things worse. For what, our honour? Maybe we should tell them now?"

"How does any of this work?" Ammar asked, becoming angry. "The whole point is to keep them from protesting. They'll protest if they know before. They'll protest if they know after. Either way, it will get violent and we will fail them."

"The only way is to find the killer in time." Tein said it with confidence but despaired of the outcome. He took Ammar's hand for a moment. No matter what, he was grateful his friend had returned to him. The old Ammar, willing to stand for good at risk to his life. Like their days on the battlefield, there was no man, other than the Prophet, himself, or Ali, the Lion, whom he would rather fight beside and die.

"We can solve it, Tein. Let's go." He slapped him on the back. "We even have money for horses!"

They walked hard, straight through Solomon's Gates. As they passed, Tein put his hand over his heart in greeting to the gates, hoping it would not be long before he never had to pass through them again. With that, he felt the strange assurance again that all would be well. They would find the killer. Saliha would marry him. Zaytuna would be safe. There would be an answer.

Once out of the Round City, Ammar turned to the left toward the farrier and dug out the coins from his sleeve pocket.

Tein pulled back, seeing the horses. His leg hurt from all the walking they had already done that day, but riding a horse would not rest his leg any, and taking a cart would be too slow. "It's not far," he said. "Let's walk."

"What?"

Tein pointed at the coins. "I want my part of that to get back."

"We'll have to keep the same pace. The day is getting long."

Tein challenged him with a boast. "Can you keep up with me?" He charged ahead, pulling his leg harder than he had in years and feeling every bit of it. A spasm shot through it such that even his toes curled, but he did not slow, even on the pontoon bridge.

They garnered curses as they walked around those trudging in two directions across it, burdens on their heads or strapped to their backs. The man who governed the line to cross on the other side gave them a dirty look as they stepped off, rushing to the road leading to the al-Atash market. Through the market gates, Tein bumped into a man here or there as they wove through the crowd, his gait making him clumsy.

Out the other side and onto Jasmine Vine Road, it was easy to see the market gate tucked into the estate wall. Its arch was hidden by vines, and the door unpainted and plain, but he scolded himself again for having missed it.

Nearing the main gate, Ammar hailed the watchman, observing the house at the corner. The man was standing at attention in the shade of a willow growing within the walls of a neighbour's estate. On hearing Ammar's call, he rushed over, proud in his thin black turban. "Ghazis, sir!"

"Who has been in and out?" Ammar asked.

"I haven't seen your man. Only a group of older women with a servant behind them came in and out today." He paused. "I tried to monitor all three gates and saw servants come and go from their entrance and the market gate. But I can't guarantee that I didn't miss someone."

"I understand. Is the uncle there?"

"Bahadur relieved me when it was time to eat just after the midday prayer and said there was nothing to report. I haven't seen him."

"You're sure his uncle is home?" Tein asked.

"I didn't say that, sir. I said I haven't seen him coming or going."

Ammar grasped his arm. "Good work. What's your name?"

"Ahab ibn Ishaq, sir."

Leaving him, Tein said, "Give his name to Ibn Marwan," but did not say the rest. *To replace me.*

Ammar understood him well enough and slammed the knocker down on the plate in response, as if he were pounding the gate with his fist. Tein leaned against the wall, grimacing as he took the weight off his leg.

The gate opened. It was the same older servant who opened the door to them on that first day. But this time, instead of being officious, he was afraid. A boy inside carrying a sack dropped it when he saw them and hurried off.

Ammar thrust the letter towards him. "For Umar ibn Abdulqahhar. It's urgent, about his nephew."

"He is not at home, sir."

Tein put his weight back on his leg, almost collapsing, and grunted through the searing pain. "Get Abdurrazzaq!"

The servant ran, leaving the gate open.

"Utbah did it."

Tein put a hand on the wall again and bit back the pain. "We're close."

The servant returned, hurrying, but only came partway to the gate, waving them in.

Closing the gate behind them, Tein spied a bench near to where Abdurrazzaq was waiting for them. Ammar saw it, too, and walked over to it, calling Abdurrazzaq over. "If you know how to find Utbah, tell us now."

"Utbah's uncle, Ibn Abdulqahhar, is taking care of it."

"What is that supposed to mean?" Tein grunted as he sat down.

"The vizier, Ibn Furat, demanded Umar Ibn Abdulqahhar go to him. I accompanied him early this morning. A secretary met us at the gate and brought us into the garden, but no further. The secretary informed him that the police had found Utbah guilty, and he had run to avoid arrest. Ibn Furat promised to destroy Ibn Abdulqahhar's business and strip him and his family of their lands if he did not hand Utbah over."

Ammar looked at Tein, angry. "Ibn Marwan told him we suspected Utbah." He turned back to the guard. "Ibn Furat wants Utbah turned over to him, not the police?"

Abdurrazzaq did not answer, but glanced at the letter in Ammar's hand.

"We know Utbah sent a letter here," Tein said.

"How do you know? I didn't think those watchmen would notice. All but that one out there now were no good. We got Utbah's uncle out this morning without being seen easily enough."

Ammar demanded, "What was in the letter?"

"I didn't see it. But Ibn Abdulqahhar railed that Utbah as good as confessed. Utbah asked him to intervene with Ibn Furat and wanted money to be sent for his escape until it's all cleared up."

"There must have been an address to send the money."

"Ibn Abdulqahhar didn't tell me. He dismissed me at Ibn Furat's this morning and hasn't returned. My guess is that he gave the address to Ibn Furat's men. They may already have him."

If he only "as good as" confessed, they still needed to get an explicit statement of guilt out of him. If not, it would be no better than framing him without other evidence. Tein gave Ammar a skeptical look.

Ammar caught it and replied bitterly, "The vizier is not interested in a confession. Utbah's as good as convicted without proof."

Abdurrazzaq looked between the two, confused. "You don't think he is guilty?"

"Everything points to him," Ammar explained. "But we won't turn suspects over to the police chief for trial without evidence. A reliable witness, a confession, or other proof."

"You think the vizier's men don't care if he is guilty?"

"Correct," Ammar replied.

For a bare moment, Abdurrazzaq smirked.

"You'd prefer they get him even without evidence," Tein accused, the pain in his leg making it impossible to control his temper, even from where he sat useless on the bench. "You going to live with that?"

The guard sneered. "Don't threaten me, Ghazi. I'm the one who told you to go to Buratha when I shouldn't have said a word. Now the city might explode, all because of this middling piece of shit. He's capable of it. I don't care who finds him. Let him die to save the city."

"If he is in Buratha," Tein said, "he's being hidden by a scholar, Aqil ibn Akib, in his home. We don't know where it is. You can get us the address. It's got to be on that letter."

Abdurrazzaq crossed and uncrossed his arms.

"Why wouldn't his uncle just pay Ibn Furat for Utbah's innocence? Why turn his own nephew in?" Ammar asked.

"With destitution hanging over his head? Either way, the man hates Utbah as much as we all do, maybe more." Abdurrazzaq choked out a baleful laugh. "His uncle has known him longer."

"You don't understand." Ammar changed tack. "Ibn Furat already has a man to be scapegoated for the crime if we can't find who killed Bishr by tomorrow. He doesn't need Utbah."

Abdurrazzaq crossed his arms again, thinking. "All right. Maybe I can get that letter and help you find him. I want to see him arrested, but you're right, he should confess."

"Where is the letter?" Ammar demanded.

"I didn't see him take it to Ibn Furat, but it could have been in his robe. If I can't find the letter, it'll be there. We can question Ibn Furat's first guard. He's an old friend, he'll tell me. If Ibn Furat hasn't sent his men out yet, we can get there first." The guard reached his hand out, grabbing Ammar by the forearm. "You can lay first hands on him. Wait here." The guard disappeared into the house.

Tein tried to stand, but fell back down on the bench.

"I can go with the guard, Tein. We may have to go door to door searching for Utbah."

"I'll be fine. I've been in pain before."

"I know you can take the pain. But your leg doesn't care."

Tein stood up, stifling a scream into a protest. "You can't stop me."

"I can. Like it or not, I'm still your superior. You need to get back to your room and rest your leg. Take the money for the horses, get in a cart, and go home. If he can find the address, Abdurrazzaq is coming with me. I'll have Utbah in a cell overnight. You and I can question him together in the morning."

"I'm coming! I'll lay hands on him myself!"

"If you can keep up with us, come. If not, make your way home. We aren't waiting for you."

Tein grunted in agreement and lowered himself back onto the bench.

Abdurrazzaq rushed out. "The letter isn't there. Let's go to Ibn Furat's."

By the time the two men had got to the gate, Tein had only lifted himself off the bench. He made it out by carrying his hip high and dragging his leg. But once there, he saw they were already around the corner. Tein pursued them, wincing and grunting with every step, but when he reached the long high walls of Ibn Furat's estate they were already inside.

"Curse this leg!" He fell against the wall, sliding down to wait for them. The pain overtook him, the spasms wringing beyond his leg through his body, finding their way up his neck to behind his eyes until it was all he could do to keep from weeping from being so useless.

"Ibn Furat's men haven't left!" Ammar and Abdurrazzaq came out a moment later. "Utbah's uncle is still in there. Ibn Furat finally agreed to see him. We can't get a look at the letter, but Abdurrazzaq spoke to his friend." Ammar turned to Abdurrazzaq. "Tell Tein what you told me."

"The letter did not give the exact address. It only said to search for a blue door near the Kufa Road side of Buratha."

Tein raised his eyebrows. "Why so vague? And near your parents, Ammar? Why so far away from Karkh? The Imami scholars live there."

It was clear Ammar did not believe Abdurrazzaq, either, but he equivocated. "It's a strange choice, I agree. But the blue door fits. His last home had one." He paused, resigned. "We have nothing else."

"The first guard said he's been told to get his men ready to go," Abdurrazzaq said. "We're leaving now to beat them there. We'll go door to door until we find him."

Tein was angry. Abdurrazzaq was leading them astray. He gave Ammar a look that said, "Watch him."

"Meet me at dawn in the office. We'll get the confession together." He paused, nodding that he understood Tein. "If there is one to be had."

Tein watched them go. Forcing himself up, one hand bracing his thigh, the other on the wall, he made it around the corner and into the marketplace. The worst of the pain receded as he lumbered along, taking care, but it only made space in his mind for the worst of his thoughts.

Everyone and everything seemed against them. Yet if they did not find Utbah and get a confession, a man innocent of the crime would die for it. There was no letting it go by telling himself the man was guilty of something worthy of an execution. In the High Court, he might only be guilty of heresy or caught sight of one of the caliph's women by accident. Even if it were something much worse, nothing warranted this. How could it be right to sacrifice him for the sake of saving the others?

A name came to him in answer. *Khidr.*

He did not like the story when Uncle Abu al-Qasim taught it when he was a child and he did not like it now.

Khidr took Moses on as his student with the agreement that Moses would not complain, no matter what happened. But when Khidr staved in the boat of a poor fisherman, then killed the young son of a pious family, and finally rebuilt a wall for villagers who refused to feed them, Moses could not hold back. Khidr reminded Moses of their agreement and let him go, but not without an explanation: An army was seizing all the boats along the river and Khidr had saved the poor man's only source of income. The child would grow up to be wicked and he killed the boy to spare the pious parents. The orphans' parents had buried their inheritance under the wall. Khidr rebuilt it to protect the children from the greedy villagers.

While the other children sat rapt, Zaytuna argued with their uncle. "So we can destroy things and kill children if we think it will help others?"

Tein kept his own thoughts to himself. To him, the story was a harsh reminder of the choices he had to make protecting his mother and sister and his ultimate failure to save his mother's life.

Junayd leaned in to Zaytuna in that way he had that could make the children tremble. "So you are Khidr?"

She sat up, still defiant. "It's wrong."

Gently releasing her, he repeated, "I asked if you are Khidr."

Only then, in the shadow of his gentleness, did she back down. "No."

"God informed Khidr directly of what was right. Even Moses, God bless him and peace, did not have Khidr's knowledge at that moment. You are not Khidr. It means you should trust God, Zaytuna, should someone stave in your boat..." He put his hand on hers to comfort her. "...and you lose your mother." But she shook off his hand, burst into tears, and ran to hide in Uncle Nuri's lap across the courtyard. Tein watched as Nuri nodded to Junayd that he had her. But he wondered why it was on him to protect his mother and sister like Khidr without God telling him what was right.

He stopped, leaning hard against the gritty mud-brick wall, finally understanding. *I am not Khidr.* He would do his part to find the killer in time, but it was not on him to condemn an innocent man to save others. It was not on him to decide the risks for the people. The people deserved to know and decide for themselves. They would choose to protest knowing the risks and fight the caliph's men or stand down. They would choose if they wanted to join the Qarmatis' cause or drive them out of Baghdad. It was not his burden to bear alone. "Ithar," his uncle had said to him that day in the reed beds. "Ithar means to sacrifice yourself for others. To give up your rights over others." And with that, the burden of protection, to be the one who decides, lifted from his shoulders. He repeated to himself to he would never forget, *I am not Khidr.*

The spasms in his leg released. He was light, as if he could touch off and fly. Walking again, dizzy with new clarity, he emerged from the shops into an interior market square. Still unsteady, he kept close to the wall of the square, putting his hand out when he needed.

A man rushed past him, knocking his shoulder. Tein looked to see who had hit him and realized a crowd was forming. Men and women, servants, porters, shopkeepers, even the rich in their finery were streaming into the square, moving as a wave to a man climbing up on a platform.

It was al-Hallaj. Tein's body became heavy with fear. His leg spasmed. *This is the last thing we need.* Everything this man said came to no good. It was not too many months ago he and Ammar had to control another one of the riots al-Hallaj incited with his public preaching. The man could not help but spew his ecstatic fantasies that skirted the edges of heresy. The city was ready to blow and al-Hallaj did not care that he could spark a war. It was how it always was. He made his wild speeches and others paid the price, most especially his own aunts and uncles in the Sufi community. The High Court could not tell the difference between the Sufis and this camel foaming at the mouth. Tein hated him and his hatred drove him into the crowd, despite the pain heightening in his leg again.

As he pushed aside one person after another to get to the platform, they hurled insults and complaints at him. "Off!" "Stand back where you were!" One man yelled, "Mother's son!"

Tein wanted to slap his chest and announce his proud lineage through his mother. *I am Tein ibn al-Ashiqa al-Sawda!* He *was* an unmarried mother's son, but was no bastard.

He kept on instead, determined to pull al-Hallaj off the platform and make sure he never said another word.

But al-Hallaj addressed the crowd before Tein could get to him. Dressed like a ghazi in a short tunic and turban meant for close fighting, al-Hallaj held the crowd with the majesty of a great warrior. Tein readied himself. But instead of unsheathing a weapon ready for battle, al-Hallaj swayed before the crowd. Recognizing the cast of al-Hallaj's face from his own mother's bouts of ecstasy, Tein knew nothing could stop what was coming. He only hoped to pull the man off the platform in time to avert a riot.

"God!" al-Hallaj cried. "You who have made me drunk on Your love and let me wander on the shores of Your nearness, You are One, alone in the solitude of eternity."

"What is that about being drunk?" A woman near Tein cried out. "That man is saying we should drink wine! God protect us from evil things! Stop him!"

Tein tried to pass her, but the crowd had become immoveable. He found himself boxed in on all sides.

A man answered. "Shut up, woman! He doesn't mean wine!"

The crowd responded to the man as if it were a signal to surround her, but as they did, a narrow path opened, leading to the market wall to the side. There was no way to get to the woman. Tein left her to her fate and took his chance to get out and pull down al-Hallaj before things got worse.

Continuing from atop his platform, al-Hallaj called out, "There is no one to witness You. Nothing is above You to cast a shadow on You. Nothing is below You to support You. Nothing is ahead of You to limit You. Nothing is behind You to overtake You. You are both the Witness and the Witnessed."

Tein crept forward along the wall until a porter was in his way. The man complained to his friend. "It's only the Throne Verse. What's so special? I thought he healed the sick. I came here for a healing." The porter cupped his hand around his mouth and yelled. "My friend here has boils. What can you do about that!"

The crowd nearby him laughed in return and other voices called out, asking for miracles and healing, while still others tried to quiet them so they could listen.

All the while, al-Hallaj kept on. "Do not return me to me after having robbed me of me! Do not show me my soul after having shown me there is no other than You!"

Tein tried to get the porter to move, but crowd crushed in even more towards the platform, blocking his way now even along the wall. There was no way to reach al-Hallaj.

Then al-Hallaj pleaded, "God! Increase my enemies in your cities and those who clamour for my death!"

Cries rose in reply, and bodies behind Tein fell forward in one movement. He flattened himself against the wall, avoiding the worst. His head well above the crowd, Tein bellowed at al-Hallaj. "Stop!"

And al-Hallaj stopped. He searched the crowd, craning to find the voice. Then he saw Tein and smiled. It was a quiet smile that softened his features.

Where was the majestic warrior pleading to God for his enemies to kill him? The man on the platform Tein had despised for so long transformed into his friend, his brother, his father, his teacher. His teacher's eyes opened wide in astonishment. He gasped. Despite the din and crush of the crowd, Tein heard it as if he had whispered in his ear. Then there was silence. And there was no pain. The ground came up underneath him and held him as if he were a tree rooted to that spot from before the time people had ever walked this land. Rooted, his head and arms lifted like branches and leaves seeking the heavens, Tein gazed at those around him. They were frozen in place, mouths half open, a fist raised here, a head thrown back there, a grimace held, a taunt half-uttered, all in utter stillness. His gaze found its way back to al-Hallaj, who leaned in and whispered to him across the crowd. "Hu."

Two letters, "ha" and "waw," that, when said together, pointed to God's essence alone. The aunts and uncles taught that the word spoke to a reality so encompassing that it erased the possibility of creation itself. There is nothing real but God alone. No self. No other. The two letters alighted on him, enveloping him. He breathed in their purity. He breathed out their wholeness. And he collapsed, lost to himself in an ocean of blackness.

Tein woke up on the ground to deafening noise and a sharp kick to his back. All he could see were legs scuffling for purchase to ground punches thrown in the fight above or kicking shins and the bodies of the fallen below. It was impossible to stand. He was still against the wall and rolled over onto his hands and knees to protect himself, and from there, found his way up. As he stood, another kick landed on his bad leg. His knee collapsed, but he recovered in time and crept along to the market gate leading out of the square. The sundown call to prayer rang out as he reached it. He joined the stream of those escaping and found a place to stop and catch his breath.

Guards and watchmen rushed past them. Shopkeepers disappeared into their stores. Porters scattered. Wealthy men caught in the fight, their expensive robes and wraps filthy and torn, turbans awry or missing, ran in the opposite direction at the sight of the guards swinging their staffs. The square emptied, leaving only the guards and watchmen spoiling for action. And al-Hallaj was nowhere to be seen.

Blood dripped down Tein's face and into his beard. He reached for the tail of his black police turban to press against the cut, realizing only then he had lost it, and turned his back on the square, uninterested in finding it again. He was free, unafraid, certain that he would do whatever was needed, no matter what came. Searching within himself, he wondered at the change. Only then he remembered the shattering "Hu." What had al-Hallaj done to him? He stayed with the thought for a moment, then shrugged it off. It did not matter. He did not want to know and only hoped the man would leave Baghdad until the threatening storm had passed. Using his sleeve to wipe away the blood, he limped out of the market and toward the river for a skiff to take him down the Tigris to Saliha, to ask her to marry him, again.

24

Tein stopped in the passageway. A breeze carried Yulduz's teasing and Saliha's laughter to him. He felt as much as heard the love in their voices. Straightening his gait as best he could, he went to meet them in the courtyard.

A single oil lamp was lit, sending faint light across the circle of faces moving in and out of shadow with every gesture and smile. They turned as one toward him.

Saliha rushed to him, Layla right behind her. "What happened?"

"I got caught in a riot." He could not say more. "It's nothing serious. Where is Zaytuna?"

"Where is the blood coming from?" Saliha insisted.

"It's fine."

Layla answered his question. "We were at Uncle Abu al-Qasim's earlier, but she left again. She didn't say where."

He wondered if she was out investigating. The old irritation and worry over her came up on him, then just as quickly retreated.

"The blood on your clothes, Tein."

He had not even thought of what he must look like. "You know how the face bleeds."

Layla ran into her room without a sound as Qambar and Yulduz brought over the oil lamp. "Here." Layla returned, holding out several clean rags.

Saliha took them with thanks and bent down to wet them at the basin. "Yulduz, hold that lamp closer so we can see."

"Let the man sit," she replied, placing a hand on Saliha's back.

Giving him a desperate look, Saliha begged his forgiveness, only making him want to kiss her cheeks and eyes, then her lips, to see her smile again. But he nodded instead and reached out to use the wall to get down, his back and leg aching with the effort.

"Oh, Tein." She reached out to support him as he sat.

Qambar took the lamp from Yulduz and held it close to Tein's face.

"You've got a split lip. And a cut over your eye." Saliha ran her fingers tenderly across the small curls of his closely shorn head. "You've lost your turban."

"He's not bleeding anymore. Let's clean him up." Yulduz bent over to examine him herself.

"Anywhere else?" Saliha asked him.

"Bruises on my back and my leg, I'm sure, but nothing's broken."

Giving him a light smack on the arm, she said, "What are you complaining about, then? This is nothing!"

"I'm just looking for attention." He touched her face, smiling.

"Let's wash those wounds."

"I'll get what I need for a salve in the morning," said Yulduz.

Layla tucked in beside Saliha, holding out a small jar of soap. Saliha took a finger full of it onto the rag and worked it into the cloth, then cleaned and rinsed his wounds.

He gazed at each one of them. Saliha's touch was an embrace, the light held by Qambar a hand reached out in kindness, Yulduz's clucking, a mother's care, and Layla's worried face, his own child's love. He loved them all, wanting only his sister beside him.

"Habibi," Saliha whispered as she wiped away his tears.

Layla broke the spell in her small voice. "What happened, Uncle?"

There was no point in waiting. He had to tell them and ask them what they wanted. "You know a Shia man was killed. There are rumours about why it happened and people are becoming angry enough to protest. Or at least the government thinks so. There is a risk that the Qarmatis in Bahrain hope to turn the protests into an uprising here. The caliph has sent his troops into Karkh and Buratha to prevent it. But you know how Baghdadis are. We don't take that kind of pressure easily. The people of Buratha are the same. The troops might just spark the fighting themselves. All to say, if we cannot find out who did it in time to satisfy the people that there's been some justice, there could be bloodshed and the fighting would spread beyond Buratha and into Baghdad."

"You will find out, Uncle." Layla announced, taking Yulduz's hand.

He acknowledged her sweet confidence, but went on. "The government has a way out if we fail. They have a man being held for another crime who they will use as a scapegoat for this killing. They'll parade him in the street and take his life in a public square."

Qambar asked, "What will you do?"

He looked at Qambar, then the others in turn. "I have no right to decide for you. I can keep quiet about the man being framed. Or I can preach it in the streets. What do you want?"

Yulduz slapped her thigh. "So you're not one'em after all!"

Qambar offered, "Imam Ali, alayhi salam, said, 'I showed myself while others hid'."

"We fight," Yulduz declared.

"Yes," Saliha said, but he saw the fear in her eyes. "We fight."

"And the children?" He looked at Layla.

"What have the children always done in this life?" Yulduz pulled Layla to her, putting her under her arm. "They hide, they fight, and sometimes they die like the rest of us."

Layla held tight to Yulduz. "Why can't we tell the caliph we don't want the man killed for us *and* refuse to fight?"

"That might be hard to do. The people could appeal to the governor's men, but I think it's too late for that. They'd have to go into the streets. The caliph's soldiers will be there, waiting for something to go wrong so they can attack. Even if only a few protesters become violent, all the people will suffer for it."

"I see." Her voice trembled. "I will do my part."

"All to save the life of one man? A man you don't know?"

"His life is not a high price for all our lives together," Qambar said. "But it will be for each one of us when we stand alone before God on the Last Day." He held out his hands in prayer. "May it not come to pass!"

Saliha said, "I know you, Tein. You'll find the killer."

Layla hid in Yulduz's embrace. The old woman patted her back. "It may not come, girl. But we'll be with you if it does."

"You know what we want. That's done," Qambar said. "Tomorrow is another day. Inshallah, the day you find the killer. As for tonight, if you two haven't married, Tein'll have to leave or sleep with Zaytuna in her room."

Tein faced Saliha. "When I got up from being knocked down in the riot, it came to me." He paused, waiting for encouragement before he went ahead. None came, but she did not stop him, either, so he came out and said it. "We can contract a temporary marriage."

She jerked away from him.

Qambar interjected. "Wait, wait. Yes, this would work. Please, my daughter, listen. There's something to this."

She stopped, crouching beside Tein, and considered Qambar with narrowed eyes. "And what would that be?"

"Please tell her," Tein pleaded.

"A man and a woman contract a marriage for a specific length of time. They have to contract it again each time they want to be together."

"What's the purpose of that?"

Yulduz chortled as she walked away, taking Layla with her, saying over her shoulder, "Use your imagination!"

Saliha burst out laughing at herself, giving Tein hope. "This is something Shia do? I've never heard of it."

"I saw Sunnis do it on the frontier," Tein said.

"Is that how you married Ayzit?"

"No." He winced inwardly. "Ayzit and I married the...," almost saying "the right way," but corrected himself in time, saying instead, "the other way."

She sucked her teeth, knowing what he did not say, but returned her attention to Qambar all the same. "So I could marry him for a night?"

"Yes."

"And does he have rights over me during that night?"

Qambar hesitated. Tein didn't know the answer himself and closed his eyes for a moment, afraid of what the old man might say, then found himself, again, relaxing into whatever would come.

"I don't know," Qambar admitted. "You'd have to ask a scholar. All I know is that if you become pregnant, the baby is legitimate, and he has to pay to support you both. And if you marry the same man over and over, there is no waiting period between each marriage to determine if you are pregnant. I know that. I saw it done." He paused. "And the neighbours know you are married if you want to tell them, so there is no talk."

"You want to tell them?"

"It's up to you. It can be secret."

"I wouldn't mind you all knowing," she said to him.

Qambar bowed his head in acknowledgement.

Tein stopped her before she could agree. "Maybe I will have legal rights over you. But what say do these scholars have over us, Saliha? When have either of us cared what they think? I declare here before Qambar and anyone who will listen that I want no rights over you." He took her hand. "I love you because you are your own woman."

He could not read her expression, but she did not pull her hand away.

"If the marriages are only for the hours we are together," she asked warily, "then no one, not you or anyone else, could claim during the day that you have a say over me?"

Qambar answered for him. "That's how I understand it."

"I need him to say it, Qambar." She turned to Tein. "You won't have the right to protect my reputation, either?"

"Your reputation is your own." It did not change the risks she faced. But he meant it and he'd be there to defend her if necessary. "You decide who knows. I'm here for you, if you need help."

"We all are," Qambar assured her.

"How do we contract it?" Her tone was clipped, but the words were a balm on his wounds.

A reluctant sigh escaped from Qambar. "Before we go on," he addressed Tein. "I've never asked before because it's not my business. But Saliha is family to me. I must act as her father and ask. If you are an unbeliever, you cannot marry her. Or maybe it is more honest to say that I will not help her marry you, if so."

"We don't talk about that." She brushed it off, sitting down beside him again. But he heard in her voice that it had mattered to her all along, and he had not known.

"You may not talk about it," Qambar said, "but I won't help otherwise."

"I understand," Tein said, but did not answer immediately. He would lose her on this alone. But he would not lie. Then a whisper resounded within him, expanding his heart until he thought he could not bear it. The two letters pointing to God's essence, "Hu." His eyes closed and he could not stop himself from swaying and speaking from the sound. "There is no 'god' for me to believe in because nothing exists other than 'Hu' to give that reality a name." The words closed, the swaying stopped, and he opened his eyes. Saliha and Qambar were staring at him, open-mouthed.

"What does that mean?" she whispered, afraid.

Qambar nodded his head slowly. "I suspect Zaytuna would know. But I think their mother would say something like it from all the stories I hear about her." He straightened up. "It's good enough for me. I'll help."

A stone dropped into his heart and closed around it. He sounded like his mother. It made him want to stand and declare that he believed in nothing if believing meant he was like her. The woman who abandoned him and his sister to please herself in ecstasy with

God, leaving him afraid, always watching for the next threat to them, from his earliest days?

"Hu." The whisper encompassed him again, wanting in, but he pushed against it this time. It did not relent. Finding its way around every resistance, it washed through him, leaving him overwhelmed by the certainty that he could carry whatever would come, even if it meant finding his way back to his mother. He was safe. *Is this why you left us?* Fearing he would abandon those he loved to chase after the intoxication of God's shelter, he grasped Saliha's hand and pulled himself away from it to her.

"Tein," Saliha said, concerned.

He came awake to her voice, and it took every bit of him to hold back from taking her in his arms.

But Qambar was satisfied with him and called him, "Son."

"Are they going to marry?" Yulduz yelled from within her room.

Qambar ignored his wife and addressed them. "I might get it wrong."

Nestling against him, Saliha scoffed. "Is a scholar here to check?"

"We don't write anything down." He sat with them. "Saliha, you offer yourself to him according to Qur'an and the way of the Prophet for a dowry price and without either of you being due inheritance for whatever time you choose. Then he accepts."

"That's all?" Tein asked.

"All I remember," he hedged.

Yulduz came out and pulled Layla's curtain aside. "Come out girl, those two are going to marry."

Layla burst out of the room. "I heard! I was listening!" She ran to them, falling to her knees. Her eyes lit up like stars in the night.

Tein only wished that Zaytuna were there, even if the marriage was for a night. "Let's wait for Zaytuna."

"Why?" Saliha objected. "You are making too much of this. We'll have to do it over and over again. It's nothing."

The declaration should have hurt him. But he understood for her it had to be nothing, or it could not be at all. He leaned into her. "Then offer yourself to me, woman."

In a sing-song voice that made light of it all, she said, "I offer you my body according to the Qur'an and the Sunna for whatever chink of coin you've got in your pocket and without inheriting from each other from right now until sunrise tomorrow."

Sheepishly, he reached into his pocket and found one fals. It was all he had left after paying for a skiff and a cart to get there. He held it out to her. "I accept."

"You'll make a wealthy woman of me." She plucked it from his hand, kissed it, and raised it to her forehead.

Layla lifted her head and let out a ululation into the night sky. Yulduz joined her while Qambar clapped as if there were music all around them. Then they heard women from houses nearby returning their call of joy.

"What is going on?" Zaytuna was standing in the passageway.

A cold breeze cut through the warm night. She eyed each one of them sitting clustered by the water basin and oil lamp.

"Quiet, you! Tein's been hurt," Saliha snapped.

She rushed to him and bit back at Saliha. "Why are you ululating, then?" Crouching in the circle, she asked, "My brother, what's happened?"

"I got caught in a riot. Nothing that won't heal."

Layla exclaimed, "Tein and Saliha are married!"

Everyone fell silent. Zaytuna stood, stone faced, took a few steps to her room, turned to glare at them, opened her mouth, shut it, and went inside.

"I'll handle it." Tein tried to stand, every bit of his body hurting. Saliha was beside him, offering help, but he shook his head.

"She'll feel bad in the morning, Uncle Tein," Layla assured him.

Placing his hand on her head, he said, "I know."

As he pushed open the curtain to Zaytuna's room, a sharp pain shot through his back. He had fractured a rib, after all. He took a deep breath, as much to prepare himself for her anger as to make sure there was no blood in his chest, and coughed into his hand. No blood. Tein took it as a good sign as he stepped inside the dark room. "You are afraid of something. Tell me."

"Afraid?" Her voice rose, but the expected lecture did not follow.

"It's a temporary marriage for one night," he answered. "Layla was happy. She doesn't understand."

"One night?" she said bitterly. "There will be more than one night to this. Layla understands just fine."

She was right. Layla understood. He and Saliha were as good as married or better. They would never have the luxury of taking love for granted. Of course there would be trouble, but what was life but rising and falling land to walk? "I'm sorry. You're right. We should have waited for you."

"Waited for me?" He did not need to see her tears, he could hear them in her words. "What good would that do for what I feel?"

"Tell me what you feel."

"Where is Tein? Who is this brother asking me what I feel?"

"I will never leave you. Never again." He tried to make light of it. "Not unless you want."

He hoped for a loving jibe in return, but there was silence. Then it came out. "You live near the Basra Gate. She'll go with you. I've lost both of you, now. You left me and now you'll take her from me."

Saliha's voice cut through the curtain. "Who are you to decide that?"

Stomping over to the curtain, Zaytuna pulled it aside. "You're married!"

"For one night at a time." She took Zaytuna's arm and pulled her out into the lamplight of the courtyard. "Only for the nights we want. I'm not going anywhere."

"She'll live here?" She swung her head around to Tein, who was wincing as he ducked out of her room.

"Yes."

Her shoulders slumped with relief.

The courtyard was empty. Qambar, Yulduz, and Layla had gone inside their rooms. Not to give them privacy, but no doubt because they did not want to manage his sister's temper. They were listening all the same, so he gave them and her something to hope on. "Who is to say, though, sister, that you won't marry, too?"

"Mustafa marries YingYue in two days." Her eyes were pained. "Why mock me?"

"No." He shook his head slowly. "Not Mustafa. I mean Kamal Ali, the butter dealer you spoke to this morning. Ammar and I saw him today. He declared his love for you and asked me to arrange a meeting with both of us to discuss marriage."

She pulled her wrap over her face. "You mock me, again."

Taking her hand, he pulled her back to face him. "He said you have the face of a queen he saw painted on a monument in Egypt."

Her knees buckled slightly. She searched his eyes to find the lie.

"He impressed you, too," he said gently.

Saliha stepped closer. "What is this? You've never mentioned him."

He did not know if she meant the question for him, Zaytuna, or them both, but Zaytuna replied, her breath still high. "I only just met him."

"Would you like to meet him again?" Tein asked.

"I've been sitting in the Shuniziyya Mosque asking myself that question for hours." Then she answered with certainty, "Yes."

"I'll take care of it." He shook her hand lightly.

Putting her arm around Zaytuna's waist, Saliha tugged her into an embrace, but said nothing.

Zaytuna held her tightly, then let her go to face Tein. "What is happening with the case? What did Kamal Ali say about it? I knew I didn't ask him the right questions."

"We're in a bind, Zaytuna." He moved over to the wall to lean against it. "We believe Utbah ibn Harb is guilty, but we still have to find him and get a confession. I was telling them before you came back that the government has a man to scapegoat for the crime. He's innocent of it, but it will satisfy the people and keep the city from exploding."

"Tein," Saliha pressed, "ask her as you asked us."

"If we cannot solve the case in time, would you want that man to be executed so Baghdad does not fall into fighting, maybe even a war? Or would you want the truth exposed?"

"I know what is at risk. Tell the truth."

"Consider what it means."

Saliha said, "It would be one man's life for all our safety."

She looked between them, surprised, then recited, "*To have killed one person is to have killed the whole world.*"

"We all feel the same, but we needed to know from you."

"That you even had to ask!" She turned to Tein. "What can I do?"

"Nothing for now. Unless you happen to know where Utbah is hiding."

"How do you know he is in Baghdad?"

"He sent his uncle a letter confirming it. Ammar is searching for him tonight with his uncle's guard. They know the general neighbourhood but not the house. I'll meet him at the office first thing. Hopefully, Utbah will be in a cell and we can get his confession."

"And if it isn't him?"

"We'll keep searching for the guilty man no matter what."

Zaytuna pulled her head back. "How do you know it was a man?"

"The bow. It would take an extraordinary woman to shoot it."

"Maybe you should search for an extraordinary woman!"

"Should I put you in manacles now?" he joked.

"I am serious." She pulled back.

"You're right. But all the evidence points to Utbah."

Saliha tugged at his sleeve. "I wish you could come with me to the hospital in the morning. Shatha needs to know about this marriage. I'll need her on my side if I am going to keep my reputation and my job. You tell Ibn Ali. I respect him."

Zaytuna's face marked the realization. "You'll be safe from recrimination now!" She clucked. "This is the first you've ever hinted you were worried about it!"

"Of course I was worried! I wasn't going to tell you that. Let you all push me into doing what I won't do."

Zaytuna took it as an affront, but Tein waved the two off before they could argue. "Not on my wedding night."

Mollified, Zaytuna withdrew whatever she was prepared to say next.

Turning his attention to Saliha, he said, "I wish I could come with you." He did not add that he wanted the pleasure of informing Judah, but she did not say he could, and he hoped telling Shatha and Ibn Ali would be enough. For a moment, the old fury at Judah tugged at him, but he slapped it away. He would pound the man if it came to that, but it would not be his rage driving his hands round the man's throat.

"I'll walk there with you," Zaytuna said to Saliha. "I don't have a job in the morning. Layla can come help me with something." She paused, saying awkwardly, "I need to go to the market."

She was hiding something, but he could not hold himself up any longer to find out what it was. "I need to rest."

Raising her eyebrows, Saliha pushed Zaytuna back toward her own room. "Goodnight, my friend. We'll walk together in the morning."

Zaytuna put her hand over her mouth and ululated with joy, her eyes crinkling at the corners and, again, the neighbour women returned the call.

Ducking into her room, Saliha's hand was on his back as she followed with the oil lamp. The curtain closed behind them. She placed the lamp on the box at the far end of the room, then returned to embrace him, careful of his wounds, kissing him on the corner of his mouth that was not split. He pulled her closer, despite the pain.

Chin on his chest, she looked at him seriously. "I may offer my body to you one day at a time, but I offer you my love to the end of my days."

"I accept," he said breathlessly, his heart expanding beyond what he thought he could bear, and restrained a grunt of pain as she pulled him down to the bed.

DAY FIVE

25

"You missed all the excitement last night. Men are searching for you."

Utbah sat up quickly. His skull throbbed and he wanted to vomit. He lifted both hands to cradle his head, but one hand jerked back suddenly. Aqil had manacled his wrist to a chain on looped iron stake driven into the fired brick wall. Bile came up in his mouth. Instead of swallowing it back, he spat it at Aqil and wiped his mouth with the back of his free hand. "Men? What men?"

Aqil ignored the question and retrieved the piss pot. "I apologize for having to restrain you, but you should not have tried to leave." He disappeared into the latrine for a moment, then returned without it to rinse his hands beside the basin. Staying just out of Utbah's reach, he drew in close enough to examine the contusion on his head. "It's no longer the size of an ostrich egg. More of a chicken egg, now." He smiled, satisfied with the contusion's progress. "By tomorrow it will be a pigeon!"

Utbah squinted in pain in the morning light. "What men?"

"Your uncle's men. Who else could they be? The one who came here to give me the money was not among them, though. They knocked so loudly, I was surprised you did not wake up. I assured them the address they had was in error. I even opened the door wide to let them in and see. They took that for innocence and left."

His uncle's guards were here. He tugged at the manacle and moaned. Then he realized they would report back to Abdurrazzaq, who would know it was a lie and return to kill Aqil. Maybe Abdurrazzaq was waiting for Aqil to leave the house? Or perhaps waiting for the two of them to come out together? Yes, he was certain of it.

"Do not worry. We are safe here, for now."

His fury contained by the confidence that Abdurrazzaq was just outside the door, he asked, "When do we leave for the caravan?"

"Later." Aqil's eyes narrowed. "You should not have harmed Aisha."

"What are you talking about?"

"I brought her a meal after I incapacitated you. She was gone."

Aisha left.

"Not only gone," Aqil continued, "but the neighbours complained to me. In fact, they nearly beat me believing I whored her to you." He stood back, offended. "I barely got out with my life! But not before they told me she lost her child after you attacked her."

A spark of arousal caught fire at the memory of her body writhing for its life against his own. "I remember."

Aqil recoiled at his tone, and came back at him, challenging, "This was what you did on your 'walk'? You attacked her. The child is lost because of you. Were you trying to kill Aisha or rape her?"

"I wanted to kill her, but let her go because of the child. She lost it anyway." He shrugged. "I should have followed through."

"Why? Why would you harm a woman with child?"

"Bishr told her about the dream."

"He did not!" the scholar insisted.

"So you say." Utbah shut his eyes against the light.

"They said she had a great deal of money."

"I gave her enough to escape Baghdad," he snapped. "And, if she is careful, she will never worry about money again. Why are you so concerned about her?" He cradled his head with his free hand. "She has been more than compensated for the pregnancy."

Aqil pulled up a stool and sat across from him. "What were you trying to do, pushing Aisha and Bishr together?"

"It started as a little fun." Utbah sat back, leaning against the wall, watching him and shielding his eyes from the sun, the throbbing in his head manageable. "Him a Shia boy. Her a child of Hanbali extremists. I wanted to see what would happen."

"Did you know they would fall in love?"

"You should see your face. Did you love her yourself? She is quite beautiful."

Aqil frowned in disgust.

"She was beautiful. Bishr was handsome." Utbah shrugged. "These things are inevitable."

"Love is not inevitable."

"Love is only a mask for lust." He sighed at Aqil's naivety. "I wondered if he would fuck the honour out of her and he did."

"My God!"

Utbah laughed, but the spasms made his head throb worse.

"Why did you befriend him?" Aqil demanded. "Why wasn't ruining their dignity enough?"

"To hear about it, of course. I plied him with questions until he related their meetings. There were many a night's pleasure from his tales. I had to imagine the parts he was too proper to mention, but it was enough."

"My God, you are beyond all that is good," Aqil gasped.

"So sanctimonious! Look at this house!" Hand pressed against his head, he spat at the scholar. "You kept your portion of the robbery meant to be given back to the poor souls who paid it out. Is that piety?"

"I would have given the tithe back once I fixed this. Once the Imam showed himself. The scholars would praise me. They would hold me up." He slapped his chest. "I would have the wealth I deserve. Then, I would have returned the tithe. But not to the people, to the Imam himself, by my hand."

"And the money my uncle sent? Where is that? Free me if you are so pious and loyal. Let me have the coin and face my fate," he insisted. "I will not tell them about the robbery. But even if I did, who would believe that an Imami scholar, a man who has devoted his life to the Twelve Imams, would rob one of them?" He hissed, "It is me they want."

"Stop! I can still fix this!" Aqil stood. "If they would have listened to me, nothing would have gone wrong!" He glanced at the door. "I told Bishr not to trust you. The men told him the same, but he would not hear of it. They only followed you out of loyalty to him."

"Bishr was loyal to us both, it seems." He sat back again and closed his eyes partly. "Loyalty was his weakness."

Aqil threw his hands up. "How did you get him to trust you?"

"I listened to his heartache over Aisha. They could never marry without permission from the families. He begged me for money for them to run away together. I put him off and begged him, instead, to tell me the stories of Karbala." He opened his eyes again to give the scholar a sickening smile. "We wept together and he promised to take me to his Imam." Enjoying the effect of his words, he leaned in to say, "He was the one who brought up the complaints about the agents and the imams. I suggested he rob them and take some of the tithe for himself to escape Baghdad with Aisha."

"You used Karbala. You used him." Aqil turned away. "He was my friend. We were boys together. No one was kind to me but him."

Enjoying the sight of the brute nearly driven to tears, he pushed harder. "At first, he was taken aback at the thought of even committing a crime. But he worked his way around to convincing himself that a robbery would solve his problems and support the cause of his Imam. Did you know that? Your pure friend Bishr." He paused. "Until that cursed dream, his plan was to keep his portion of the tithe so he and Aisha could be together."

"God have mercy on his soul. This has fallen to pieces." Aqil paced the courtyard. "It is on me to clean it up." He turned to face Utbah. "As always, on me!"

"Yes, on you." Wanting to get him out the door and into the hands of Abdurrazzaq, he said, "Fix it, then! Better, take me to the caravan now." He lifted his manacled arm. "Unlock this. I cannot go a chained man."

"Later. And only then, if you go to the caravan quietly, will all be well." He pulled back his robe, exposing a dagger on his belt. "This will be at your back the entire way. Do not cross me."

"Free me now. What does any of this matter?"

Aqil grimaced at his question, then fell into thought, finally saying, "What does it matter? Exactly! Too much has happened now." He paced again, his eyes wild. "The fighting! The robbery, the murder, all of it will be forgotten when the fighting starts."

"Yes, yes. I know that!"

"That is the answer of what to do with you."

"What to do with me? The caravan! I'll no longer be your trouble."

He dismissed Utbah with a wave of the hand. "Not now."

"What do you mean by that?"

"Be patient. I have a meeting tonight. I am to speak." He disappeared into his room and came out a few moments later, patting the coin purse under his robe and wearing a plain brown turban, wrapped so as not to signal loyalty to any Imam. "I have the money. I will fix everything." He crossed the courtyard to another room and came out again, holding the dates and cheese they had purchased the day before. "Eat this cheese before it turns. Nothing but old bread, though." He put the food down and pushed it over with his foot.

"So you will take me to the caravaners tonight, after you return?"

Ignoring him, Aqil returned with the piss pot. Then he brought over two jugs of water and some rags. "Do your best."

"When will we go?" Utbah pressed.

Aqil turned on him. "Are you listening? Too much has happened now! Only I can fix this. I alone will decide what to do with you."

Utbah sank back against the wall. His head throbbed again in full force. My God. How could he not have seen it? Aqil alone thought he could save them all. The scholar meant the Imam. This was not about a cover up but Aqil's plan to save the community of the Twelfth Imam by forcing the man to come out of hiding. At first, that had meant robbing his own Imam, thinking he would surely come out to strengthen his weakened people. Now that plan had failed, what did Aqil have left?

The Shia must come under attack by the caliph's men to force the Imam to come out to save them. Aqil was planning on inciting the riots himself. He would not sit and wait to see if protests turned into fighting. Aqil would make sure of it.

And Aqil would make sure of him. If fighting broke out in the streets, no one would think of Bishr or the tithe. He no longer needed to help Utbah get away to cover up the crime. Aqil was planning on killing him and dragging his body into the street when the fighting came.

But Abdurrazzaq is outside, he told himself. *Stay calm. Abdurrazzaq will kill Aqil the moment he walks out that door.* Then a voice of terrifying doubt crept in. *Did he follow Aqil to you the day he came to deliver the money? Did he remain at Aqil's house waiting for you? He was nowhere to be seen. What makes you think he is outside? Your uncle has abandoned you!*

All his planning to destroy the Shia and he would die at the hands of a mad Shia scholar! The fear that gripped him released into convulsive, desperate laughter, ending finally with him doubled over, coughing. He would die in this hovel. Aqil would drag his body into the filthy streets of this shit hole town to be trampled under foot by fighting men and escaping families. Tears streaming down his face, he mocked himself, lamenting, "What an ignominious end!"

Aqil took a step toward him. Utbah shot forward. The manacled arm held back, the other stretched out, swiping at Aqil's leg. He grasped enough of Aqil's sirwal to tug hard, but Aqil kicked his hand away.

"Have you lost your mind!"

"Have you?"

"What do you mean? I am here to help you! You see! This is why I had to hit you and chain you to the wall. I cannot trust you to know what is best. God protect me from fools!" He straightened his clothes, then glared at Utbah in disbelief. "What am I to do with you?"

"Kill me? Is not that how you will fix this?"

Aqil did not reply immediately. "If I must." He sighed, as if he were thinking it over. "If the fighting starts before I can take you to the caravan, I will come back and release you. You must run from here and never come back. Baghdad will forget about you, about all of us, when the Imam shows himself."

Utbah promised, "I will." But Aqil was lying. The man would kill him. He was sure of it.

"Good. Now I must go. Everything depends on this meeting." Aqil turned to leave, pulling the key to the padlock from his pocket.

"What is this meeting?" he called after him.

Aqil turned back. "An uprising! I will be a Qarmati for a night and call the women to action! Since the men are cowards and will not act, I am certain that once stirred, the women will. They will shame their men into action. If the men will not fight on their own, I will start the fighting for them." He left, shutting the door hard behind him.

The padlock clicked shut. Utbah turned around to inspect the iron spike that Aqil had hammered into a joint in the brick wall. With both hands, Utbah pushed and pulled at it until tiny bits of mortar in the joint loosened. At the sight, he shook the spike violently, his body screaming.

26

Tein leaned against the wall, watching Zaytuna and Layla follow Qambar in the dawn prayer. Slowly they emerged as outlines in the brightening blue light, then into distinct bodies bending and bowing, moving as one. He sighed at the beauty of it, forgetting that it used to irritate him. A feathery touch on his cheek drew him away. Saliha. He grasped her around the waist and pulled her to him. "Marry me again tonight?"

"Perhaps," she whispered, her voice trailing into desire. She held her finger to her lips, then pointed to those in prayer. They sat, legs tucked underneath them, heads turning to the right, then the left, making their closing greetings to the angels.

Yulduz came out of her room and passed by them, clucking with pleasure. "None of that, now. You're not married as of first light."

"Sunrise," Saliha corrected.

"My apologies." Yulduz bowed her head.

Qambar and Zaytuna took their time with their personal prayers while Layla watched Zaytuna and mimicked her every move. Saliha left his side to remind Zaytuna that they would need to leave soon. He steeled himself for Zaytuna's inevitable sharp reply.

"We have to go," Saliha whispered.

"I understand," she answered quietly, her voice catching with emotion.

He raised his eyebrows, surprised.

Footsteps sounded through the passageway, and a watchman's voice reached them even before he emerged, holding a letter rolled in his hand. "Ibn al-Ashiqa!"

Zaytuna stood up. "I'll take it." She pointed. "That's him there."

"Ghazi Ammar at-Tabbani sent it," he said and left.

Zaytuna scanned it in the dim light as she walked over to Tein. "They couldn't find him. They went door to door and found a second room rented by Aqil. He's no longer there. Ammar says to meet him at his parents in the morning, no later than duha."

Tein snorted, stifling a laugh to protect his rib.

Saliha eyed him strangely. "What is there to laugh at!"

"I didn't tell Ammar I would come here, but he guessed."

"Ah," Saliha said. "But you don't have to meet him until mid-morning? You can come with me to the hospital."

Saliha returned to her room, and he followed her in, watching as she pulled her blue and white wrap around her.

"I took your last bit of coin with my dowry last night," she said. "Want a loan to go to the baths?"

"And what will you do?"

"I have to do my ritual bath before I can wash any bodies. But I'll use the bath at the hospital. God willing, there won't be any bodies to attend to right away. If so, they'll have to wait and Shatha will be mad."

"Keep the coin."

Her brows knitted. "All this talk of dowries makes me wonder how you're going to afford me night after night?"

"I'll ask for a job churning butter with Kamal Ali. He pays well. Do not fear." He said it as a joke, but liked the idea of it more and more. *What are the chances I'll be asked to frame someone, decide who is guilty, who lives or dies?*

She smiled.

"What?"

"Does he have his men churning by spinning the jars, swinging the leather, or," she paused, "thrusting the staff?"

"I'm liking this new marriage more and more."

They left her room to find Zaytuna standing outside, arms crossed, but happy. "Maybe you two should move to another place. I'm not sure we can all stand this day after day."

Saliha walked by, dramatically pulling her wrap over one eye in Zaytuna's direction and whispered, "Jealous."

Rather than teasing Saliha back, she only shrugged. There was something behind Zaytuna's eyes Tein did not recognize. First, she was not angry with Saliha interrupting her in prayer. Then making a joke of them moving? Now unwilling to return a jibe? What is going on with you, sister?

Qambar came out, a spare turban in hand. "It's wrapped a bit too tight for you, I imagine."

Taking it gratefully, Tein unwound the old green cotton with him, Qambar holding the wind of cloth as he wrapped it messily, but firmly around his head.

"That'll do." Yulduz came up beside Qambar, approving.

"Layla!" Zaytuna called out. "We're leaving and I need you."

The girl scrambled out of her room, her wrap wound under her arms and loosely over her head, and caught up to Saliha.

Tein took Zaytuna's hand. "Sister, you don't need to come with us."

"I said I have to go to the market. Layla's coming with me."

"Work?"

"Work."

"Not the case?"

This time, she spun on him. "I said work."

"There you are. I didn't recognize the other one talking to me."

She drew her head back. "What do you mean?"

"Nothing." He followed her through the passageway and out into the alley. His whole body hurt from sleeping on one side all night to protect his rib and lying half on and half off of Saliha's narrow mattress. But he was unwilling to leave her and stretch out more comfortably in the courtyard. If he only had one night at a time, he would not lose a moment of it. But watching her ahead of him, swinging her hips for his pleasure, distracted him from the pain.

At the Karkh market, Zaytuna held her hand out for Layla to come with her, and they disappeared within. He could not imagine what she needed to buy; the houses supplied the laundry soap. Saliha drew up beside him, brushing her hand against his own, and he left the thought there.

By the time they approached the hospital, the sun was over the horizon. Saliha walked ahead of him so they would not be seen together, then pulled back, waiting for him. "We go in together."

"We're not married right now," he warned.

"We aren't going to hide anymore."

He pulled her back. "Let's wait until we talk to Shatha."

"No." She took his hand, and they walked through the arches of the wide front entrance, through its foyer, the men's and women's wings on either side, and into the courtyard at its centre. He glanced to his left and right, then past the courtyard, looking out for Judah or Ibn Ali, but saw neither.

A cool breeze swept through, rustling the leaves of the lemon and bitter orange trees planted in a line at its centre and sending fresh air into the wards. A young man comforted an old woman in a black wrap drawn around her in grief as they sat on the bench before the fountain. An orderly left the women's ward with a basin, heading toward the passage at back of the hospital leading to the pharmacy, surgeries, and corpse washing rooms. On recognizing Saliha, his eyes darted to Tein's hand in hers and started at the sight of it, blushed, and turned away.

She stopped him in a clear voice. "Ibn Muhammad, congratulate us. We've been married."

Caught imagining the worst, the orderly blushed again, more deeply this time, and quickly uttered his congratulations before hurrying on his errand.

Tein tugged her back for a moment. "That's not what you wanted. You didn't want to be married."

"I'm not."

"But I thought you didn't want them to even think we are married. That I have rights over you."

"If I have to, I'll explain it to them, and so will you. We never had a reason to be ashamed and even less so now."

He understood better what she wanted and was humbled by her courage, falling in love with her even more for it. Hand in hand, they walked through the courtyard to see Shatha.

The pharmacy door was open, but as they passed, he saw Ibn Ali was not yet in, and he was glad. He was not ready to speak to him. Shatha first. Saliha urged him along and they passed the oculist, the bonesetter, and the surgeries. But still there was no sign of Judah, only one of the young medical students preparing for a patient.

The door to the women's and children's corpse washing room was closed. Saliha glanced at him. "Ready?"

There was a lump in his throat but underneath his worry a deep settledness held him, assuring him that no matter what happened, they could bear it. They would live their lives honestly among these people or not be with them at all.

Saliha pushed open the door a crack. "Assalamu alaykum, a man is with me. May we enter?"

"Come," Shatha replied. As they entered, the thick-set old woman stood at attention to see what matter needed addressing, her hands clasped over her belly. If she was surprised to see Tein with Saliha, she did not show it. Instead, she returned Saliha's greeting. "Wa alaykum assalam." But then she started in. "Now, I've tolerated you two because you're a widow, Saliha. You're no young thing who doesn't understand the uses of men. If anything, you understand their uses too well. But this is beyond what I can accept."

"Auntie," Saliha tried to interrupt.

"You're a good washer, Saliha. Your heart and body are in it and you are quick and smart about the work. I don't want to lose you. But this? You can't show up here like this."

"Auntie, listen."

She put her hand on the bench where they washed the bodies.

"What could you say to make this right? I need him to go and you to be more careful if you want to stay on. There's only so much I can do to protect you."

"Protect me?" Saliha's tone changed. "You've been protecting me?"

"Who keeps that Dr. Judah from ruining everything?" She pointed at Tein. "Do you think it's the threats of that one?" She pulled her shoulders back. "I'm the one who speaks for you. I'm the one who is heard. Dr. ar-Razi himself heard me on your account."

Tein stepped forward. "Dr. Judah, he..."

"Yes. He went and complained about her to Dr. ar-Razi. But Dr. ar-Razi asked me and I told him that no one had any say over her but me." She puffed out her chest as she remembered. "I told the great director of this hospital that you were my business and no one else's. The great man bowed to me and left. This is my place and that devious ass, Dr. Judah, has no traction here."

Tein burned with shame. All this time, he thought he was the one protecting Saliha from Judah. That it was his threats that kept Saliha safe. It stung, but he pulled himself up to meet it. He heard his Uncle Nuri speaking to him as if the old man was before him, not as a half-remembered sentiment uttered months ago when Tein was reeling in shame from not being able to save the world. "You have sacrificed yourself for others your whole life. But you believe you know best what you should have done then and what you should do now. That makes you someone who thinks he owns a bit of this world, or should, and tries to control it."

You never had control over anything.

Saliha left his side to embrace Shatha in thanks, but the old woman pushed her off uncomfortably. "None of that." But Saliha kept hold of the old woman at arm's length. Shatha looked past Saliha to Tein, her shoulders hunching forward as if she might push him out like a wrestler in the field. "Now, you. Leave."

"Auntie," Saliha said, "we're married."

The woman's shoulders visibly softened. But she did not congratulate them. Instead, she let go a deep sigh, grabbed Saliha by the wrist and shook her arm as if she were a child being scolded. "You could have said that when you first came in, woman." She smiled at Tein. "It's good you've done the right thing."

"But Auntie," Saliha interjected. "Not the way you expect."

"I don't understand." The old woman took a step back.

"It's a temporary marriage. We'll marry each night we are together. The marriage will last that night only. I stay my own woman during the day."

Shatha burst out with a hoot that echoed in the room, ringing off the copper basins, and covered her mouth, hearing the noise she had made. "You walk a thin line! People out there won't accept that! That's for the Shia folk, not us."

"Men did it at war," Saliha objected. "I can do it."

"It's not for us."

"It's for me," she said firmly, ending it.

"I have to give it to you. You are a strong woman. And he seems to love you for it. But what are you going to tell them out there?"

"I'll tell the truth."

"What does that mean?"

"That we are married when we are together."

"You are going to say all that?" She raised her eyebrows. "That's a lot of words in your mouth."

"What should I say, then?"

"Nothing. It's no one's business and I told Dr. ar-Razi that."

Saliha glanced at her in astonishment.

Tein wanted to embrace Shatha himself and tell her, although it made no sense at all, that he would be proud to stand beside her on the battlefield.

Shatha pulled Saliha back to face her. "So if someone asks, tell them it's none of their business. No one needs to know the details but who you choose to tell and the marketplace inspector if he asks!" She laughed. "But I'm glad you told me."

"Thank you for defending me." Saliha took her hand. "Thank you for believing I'm good enough for this work. I love it. I've never felt like what I did truly mattered until this."

"I had a woman work for me who was pious as sin itself and it showed in her work." Shatha brushed at her clothes. "She would cluck at a stray hair on a woman's head in the street but had no tenderness for those in our care. You do. Your goodness shows in how you care for these folks. You matter to them. It's time for you to have a black sash, so all can see that you've left your apprenticeship here." She gave a quick bow of her head to Saliha, then eyed Tein. "Now him. He needs to leave, we'll have to be at work soon."

"He can go. But, Auntie, uh, I need to use the baths."

Shatha hooted again. "Go! Go, woman, before we are needed."

Leaving her, Saliha pushed Tein out the door, grinning. But his face fell when the door shut behind him. He had to tell Ibn Ali. He respected the man and wanted the man's respect in return. Maybe Shatha was right. There was no need to say a thing. He asked himself whether Saliha wanted him to tell Ibn Ali now and turned to knock on the door of the corpse washer's room.

Saliha opened it. "Goodness! I was afraid it was a body arriving."

"Do you mind if I tell Ibn Ali about us?" he whispered.

"I said so already! Please tell him." She took his hand for a moment, then closed the door with a wink.

The sense that all would be well settled on him again, and he turned back to the pharmacy with confidence. Whatever Ibn Ali thought, he would at least be able to face the man in all honesty, although he hoped he would be happy for them to have found a solution. Tein tentatively stuck his head in the door.

Ibn Ali's narrow sleeves were rolled up as always when he was working, but this time he sat at a desk writing with a large bound volume open beside him. Tein hesitated to bother him. It might be important. But Ibn Ali saw him and put his pen down. "Tein! Assalamu alaykum. Here on a case?"

"No, I have news. Can you spare a moment?"

He stood, putting the paper he was writing on aside and closing the volume, marking his place. "The courtyard?"

They found a spot on a bench under the trees.

"My situation with Saliha has become regularized."

"I am not certain I understand."

"She will not marry. You know that. But we found another way."

"Ah."

"Temporary marriage."

"Yes. It is not ideal, and certainly unusual for us Sunnis. But as I recall, Abu Yusuf discoursed on this matter last year." He looked up, remembering the day. "Several Sunni legal scholars upheld it as a right even as most prohibit it. Ahmad ibn Hanbal himself equivocated on the matter, preferring we do not, but not prohibiting it all the same. It offers her protection and that matters most." He put his hand on Tein's back. "May God bless your union, bless you, and unite you both in goodness."

Tein hesitated, then said, "It is ideal. Ideal for us."

Ibn Ali inclined his head. "I am happy for you both. My apologies."

"No need. I only wanted to make it clear. We will renew the marriage every time we are together. She is her own woman."

"And you, your own man?"

"I would happily bind myself to her to the end of my days."

"This is for her, then?"

"Yes, and that makes it right for us. I cannot bind her to me, not if she does not freely choose it. Now she can choose, each time, if that is what she wants. You know what marriage means for women."

"I do, but it all depends on the man. She must know that you can be depended upon not to exercise your rights over her in any way that would displease her, let alone harm her."

Tein glanced at the back of the hospital. "She knows that because I am respecting her choices now."

"I am curious, though. Temporary marriage is not like standard marriage regarding the rules of remarriage?"

Tein faced him, worried that Ibn Ali knew something Qambar did not. "What do you mean?"

"She does not need a waiting period in-between each divorce to determine if she is pregnant, after which she must marry another man, consummate with him, divorce, then wait another three months before marrying you again?"

But as Ibn Ali spoke, a hand smoothed over the doubt and he answered with confidence. "The man who instructed us on how to contract it said, no, and we aren't looking into it any further. When Zaytuna would ask too many questions, the aunts used to tease her with the verse, *Do not ask about things which, if made plain to you, may cause you trouble.*"

Ibn Ali inclined his head again, but Tein could see he still considered the matter to be a problem and doubt nagged at him again.

This time, Tein reminded himself of Shatha's guidance. No matter how much he respected Ibn Ali and, he admitted, sought his approval, it was not any of his business. "It's right for us, Ibn Ali. I wanted to share the good news with you. That's all."

Ibn Ali put his hands on his thighs and stood facing Tein. "It is not for me to say. Although, you have piqued my interest. I may ask Abu Yusuf the next time I see him, but I'll not share what I learn unless you ask. I don't suppose you planned to come, but we have cancelled our meeting at Baraqan's paper shop today."

Standing himself, Tein replied, "Good idea. Things might be difficult for a while. There might be serious violence."

"Yes, I've been watching things closely. We all have. I sent my wife and children to her brother outside of Baghdad." He paused. "If I can say so, the caliph is overreacting. I hear what they say in the marketplace and here at the hospital. There are theories about the murder that land at the caliph's feet, to be sure, but I hear few wanting revenge, let alone speaking of revolt. Most worry about their livelihood, the safety of their families. They will fight if they must, but they do not want to fight."

"I agree. When there is trouble, it feels to me more like the people are reacting to the ghilman in the streets than anything else."

"Do not misunderstand me," Ibn Ali said. "The caliph has reason to react as he has, especially with this Ismaili Imam in North Africa and the Qarmatis holding Bahrain and the Hajj roads."

"What do you think will happen?"

"I tell you the caliph will lose more of North Africa than he supposes. This fight will go straight through to Egypt and the Abbasids will eventually lose it all. Walla, there will be an Ismaili caliphate."

"Truly?"

"The Abbasid caliphate is weakened on all fronts and I hear that this Ismaili Imam is a brilliant strategist. He has an army of men who believe in his divine right to lead. If he is successful, it will inspire men here."

"I can imagine he hopes for it. Do you think the Qarmatis and this Imam have joined forces? They were one community not long ago."

"The break between them is too severe," Ibn Ali replied with certainty. "The Ismaili Imam denounced them in no uncertain terms."

"But an alliance between them for the sake of taking Baghdad?"

"No. By all accounts, this Imam is a principled man."

"I hope you are right. If so, our challenge is what it's been all along. Find the killer before the ghilman push the people too far."

"And will you find him?"

"We're working on it." He decided he should begin telling the truth here and now. Perhaps Ibn Ali could warn others. "There is a man the police chief will declare guilty and sentence to parading and execution tomorrow morning if we cannot find the killer."

"A scapegoat. The caliph assumes the Qarmati and Ismaili revolts will inspire the Shia of Baghdad, even though there is no evidence that they will. That is concerning."

"Only it is the Shia viziers who have come up with the scapegoat knowing the caliph may act precipitously on his fears alone."

"I am glad I sent my family away, then." He scanned the hospital wards, then back to the pharmacy. "Dr ar-Razi has called a meeting for later today. I imagine he wants to prepare us to care for the injured."

"Ibn Ali." He paused. "Ammar and I won't accept the scapegoat. We will tell the people the truth."

Ibn Ali asked uneasily, "You have confidence they will not react with the very protests you are trying to avoid when they understand the nature of the betrayal?"

"No. But it is not for me to choose for them."

"I see. If you do not mind the observation, there is a connection between the way you speak about Saliha's choices and your reticence to choose for the people."

"Yes." Tein checked the location of the sun in the sky. He would need to leave soon to reach Ammar in time.

"This is unwise," Ibn Ali began. "Reason would dictate..."

"Ibn Ali, please forgive me. I have to go. The case."

"Yes, of course. But you cannot be sure you have the will of all the people, Tein. God willing, it will come to nothing and we can enjoy discussing this ethical quandary when the trouble is peacefully resolved."

"God willing," Tein replied as he left, but he would do everything to avoid it. It was one thing to listen to these men debate philosophy and ethics, but another to put his Uncle Nuri's guidance and all that he experienced under their critical eye. There was no explaining any of it. Not to these men and, frankly, he did not want to look too closely at it himself.

He came out of the coolness of the hospital into the increasing heat of the morning and set out across the Hospital Bridge. His leg still ached and was dragging. There was nothing he could do about it, though, but at least his fractured rib did not hurt any more than it should.

The barracks on the other side of the canal were no longer crowded with off-duty regular infantry. Maybe they were out patrolling? That would come to no good. He quickened his pace as much as he could. It hurt to take the deep breaths necessary to walk faster, and his leg was beginning to spasm. He hoped they could take Utbah without a fight.

When he reached the Ushnan Bridge, crossing the Isa canal, he saw a water seller at the foot on the other side. A woman and girl crouched down, drinking from his cup. It was Zaytuna and Layla. What were they doing heading into Buratha? Why would she bring the girl with her on the case? Even Zaytuna, in her zeal, would not put the girl in any danger. Then he remembered how odd she had acted this morning and held back, giving her a chance to get well ahead of him. She was going to see Kamal Ali, the butter dealer, with a chaperone of her choosing.

27

Ammar was waiting impatiently outside the gate of his parents' house. As Tein rounded the corner, his leg seemed in better shape today. When he got closer, Ammar noticed the cut over his eye and the deep black of a bruise. While it had been an exhausting night searching for Aqil ibn Akib's house, Ammar was undaunted. Today was their last day. And Tein better be ready for it.

Walking ahead to meet him, Ammar asked, "What happened?"

"I should ask you that."

"You've been in a fight."

"There was a minor riot in a market square at al-Atash. Turnips were half-price and I got caught in the rush. I'm fine."

"Good." Tein could walk at least. They had a lot of that ahead of them. "After Abdurrazzaq left, I kept searching. Just before first light, I finally found the room where the scholar lived with his family, and sent you that message. He told the landlord yesterday he wasn't coming back. But he did not say where he was going. No one else knows, either."

"Did Ibn Furat's guard lie to Abdurrazzaq about the address?"

"Or did Abdurrazzaq lie to us?"

"You've had time to think about this. What's your take?"

"Abdurrazzaq wants to find Utbah so the uncle gets the credit for bringing him in. Or he wants Ibn Furat's men to find him for a similar reason."

"He can't be protecting him."

"Or the uncle is playing both sides. He wants Ibn Furat to believe he's helping, while really he's trying to help Utbah escape."

"That works."

"But there's news. Utbah was in the room where Aqil's family lived."

Tein took a step towards him. "What?"

"Neighbours said he moved his family out last week and had a man fitting Utbah's description in there for the two days before he left for good. They heard arguing, but the room has a door and no windows, so nothing specific."

"Not one nosy neighbour to listen at the door? If this were Baghdad, you could count on that."

"Maybe they don't want to admit it. But listen, the neighbours said Aqil told everyone his father died, and that he bought his family a whole house with a courtyard. And get this, he boasted they had a latrine."

Tein whistled. "Didn't he grow up next to Bishr's family? The room with the blue door? Other than the luxury of a door, that's not the neighbourhood of a father with wealth to pass on unless he was hoarding it. I can't see how Aqil inherited a fals."

"I went to the mosque and nearly pulled the imam off his prayer rug to get some answers. He said Aqil's father died years ago. More than that, he said even his extended family is poor. But Aqil always had airs. The imam said he paid for the wooden door at his parents' room. The landlord said he paid for the door there. Ask me the colour of that door."

"Blue."

"You were supposed to ask me," Ammar cracked.

"So now we're searching for a large house with a blue door."

"I walked half of Buratha. Nothing."

"At least the sudden wealth permitting him to move into a whole house confirms he was in on the robbery."

"First, the sin of robbing the tithe. Second, the sin of covering up a murder. What kind of man is he?"

"No surprise those Shia scholars told him to never come back."

"Good men." Ammar was surprised to hear himself say it, never having had any respect for scholars. But if these men noticed an unscrupulous student among them and got rid of him, they could be trusted.

"I should have made the connection." Tein sounded angry with himself. "If Amru and the others were meeting in Aqil's room to plan the robbery, they may still be in contact. Let's head to Kamal Ali's now."

Ammar jumped at it, angry with himself likewise, even though it would likely amount to nothing. "Why would Amru tell us? It would be a confession."

"If the agents don't report the robbery, he's in no trouble."

Ammar did not reply. If Amru or the other men admitted to the robbery, he had no choice but to report them to Ibn Marwan, no matter what.

"Aqil must have boasted about the location of the new house."

"The neighbours said he didn't. All I got was they used a donkey cart to move their things. But no one remembers anything specific about it, markings on the donkey or the cart."

"All right. The carts first, then Kamal Ali's." Tein started walking toward the centre of Buratha, then turned back, shaking his head. "Where is the nearest market gate to that room? We need to question the cart drivers."

Ammar caught up with him and pointed to a street up and to the left. "This way, but listen."

"I should have been out there at dawn to question them."

"Listen! I asked Muhsin. He went and came back already. Nobody in the first shift remembered him. But we still need to go back and interview whoever is there now." Ammar settled in, matching his gait to Tein's. "We can't spend the entire day waiting for drivers, though."

"A watchman?"

"I sent word. We'll see if anyone shows up."

"I wonder if we hadn't pushed Utbah," Tein said, "would he have stayed put at his uncle's? He's the kind of man who thinks he's untouchable. We could have arrested him out of his home."

"That's on me." Ammar took the criticism head on. "I made him afraid he was about to be framed for the murder."

"We've both made mistakes on this cursed case." Tein waved it off. "Me butting heads with Aisha's father, not to mention missing the third door at the uncle's estate."

He may have dismissed the mistakes, but Ammar could tell Tein was still carrying the weight of them. He was, too, and gave Tein a brotherly slap on the shoulder.

Tein jerked forward, wincing.

"What?"

"Fractured a rib. Nothing I haven't fought with before." He held up a hand. "Just don't slap me like that."

Ammar gave Tein a look of apology, but he cursed-well hoped they would not get into a fight he could not handle alone. They took another turn, this time onto a main road. Ghilman marched along it, swords at the ready. The largest of them had a staff and was swinging it threateningly as passersby gave them a wide berth.

"I've had enough of this." Even with a noticeable limp, Tein strode up to the man with the staff. Ammar tried to stop him, but Tein shot him a look that made Ammar stand back. It was the face Tein wore in the depth of fighting, when his body knew what to do before he knew himself. Ammar cherished the feeling, but was not sure if he could trust where it was leading Tein now.

"You there," Tein called out.

The ghilman turned around. Ruddy faced and spoiling for a fight, he held his staff at the ready. Their sergeant pushed by him, saying a word under his breath, and the soldier stood back, putting his staff to his side. Approaching Tein, he demanded, "What's this?"

"Baghdad police," he said firmly, but calmly. "What are your orders?"

It was not the tone that Ammar expected.

The sergeant tucked back his head. "My orders? What are your orders?"

Tein conceded, "We're trying to find the man who committed the murder that started this mess so the government can parade him. The people will see everything is under control, show that the caliph is on their side. But the way you all are acting, you're telling them the caliph is against them. It's provoking."

"Our orders are if we see men gathering, or so much as look like they are conspiring, we're to step in and beat them down until they stop."

"We don't hear anyone conspiring. People are afraid of what you'll do and they are ready to defend themselves."

The sergeant crossed his arms. "We have our informants."

"Informants?" Ammar asked, incredulous. "People of Buratha?"

The man mocked him, "Some people would prefer peace under this caliph than the chaos their neighbours think is more pious."

Tein took a step back, instead of a challenging push forward. "Who here wants chaos?"

"There are Qarmatis at the Buratha Mosque."

"That's it?" Tein replied. "Qarmatis go there?"

"Qarmatis have always prayed at that mosque," Ammar objected, "along with the rest of us. It doesn't mean anything."

"Us!" The sergeant tipped his chin up at him. "Now I understand," he said and gave his attention to Tein.

"Is there any imminent trouble?" Tein asked.

"Nothing today." He shrugged. "But that might change."

Tein stood forward, hand over his heart, and thanked him. The sergeant turned without a word and the troop continued marching.

Ammar and Tein followed close behind, with Ammar not grasping the change in Tein. He went from fighting Aisha's father to weeping at a tavern table to this? Maybe he and Saliha were able to resolve things? But this seemed like something more. He eyed Tein warily.

"What is it?"

"You're different." It hit him. Tein was done with the job and at peace with his choice. "I get it. You've quit."

"I told you I was quitting."

"Yes, but you were still fighting with yourself over it. You were coming up with reasons to be angry about the job. Now you're done."

Tein stopped walking and grinned, then laughed, open-mouthed so the back of his teeth showed, then stopped short, bending over with his hands on his knees. "My rib," he choked and took a few slow breaths to stop the spasms of laughter and catch his breath.

Ammar stared, wondering if he had lost his mind.

Finally, Tein controlled himself and stood upright. "I'm done with everything. It's true, but not only this job."

"What does that mean 'done with everything'?"

"To be honest, I don't know what I mean. But you don't need to worry. I'm here to see this through to the end, even if we can't solve it. I'll stand beside you to tell the people the truth."

"I need you," Ammar admitted.

"I hope you'll leave the job with me when this case is over."

"And churn butter," he replied skeptically.

Tein started walking again. "If that's where we end up."

Ammar did not reply at first. Ibn Marwan had shown his hand. There was no going back, no pretending that he and Tein could follow their own conscience the way things were. Of course, things were easier before joining the police. Maybe Tein remembered those simpler days and wished for them. "Not like the old days," he said, "when they pointed us at the enemy and we held our swords."

"That's what I mean," Tein objected. "We did the caliphate's bidding then, too. Calling us ghazis as if we were Muhammad's companions fighting the Meccans. We've always been pawns in someone else's game."

"And if we hadn't been with Grave Crimes to investigate this crime?"

"It's not all on us, Ammar. I'm doing my part. But what makes me think that someone else couldn't do it just as well? And maybe someone else would have done it better? Maybe someone else wouldn't have made the mistakes I did?"

"What if I like this work despite everything?" It was all coming out, and he was glad of it. "I like the challenge of finding out who committed a crime and the justice I can bring to the lives of the victims. I will not be happy churning butter, Tein."

Tein said, as he strode ahead, "We'll find a job that does all that, but without the caliphate forcing us into corners we can't get out of without betraying ourselves."

He said it with such confidence that Ammar almost believed him, but insisted all the same, "I can talk to Ibn Marwan. I can negotiate a way for us to be independent."

"You do that." Tein kept walking.

They continued on without speaking. Ammar's mind was busy turning over the possibility of leaving this job, and it looked wrong from every angle except one. His family. If he left, he could marry Nasifa and build a room onto his parents' house for her. But he set his family and Nasifa aside for the time being. He would not marry her for his parents' sake, let alone his own. And the fact was that Ibn Marwan knew he needed them. If he threatened Ibn Marwan, he was sure he would get the changes he wanted.

The busy square opened up in front of them. The main thoroughfare to the Buratha market let out onto three smaller streets leading to alleys on the opposite side, one of which led to Aqil's room. There was a long line of donkey carts waiting for fares. If they did not find the right man now, there was not much chance. Drivers picked up a new fare wherever they dropped off the old one. The chance that the man Aqil used had a regular spot here was thin. Muhsin had tried in the morning when the regulars for this neighbourhood had started their day and failed.

Ammar approached the first driver while Tein started with the last one. "Assalamu alaykum. Baghdad Police, Grave Crimes. We're trying to find a family. They used a cart from this location to move about a week ago. The man of the family was an Imami scholar, wore their turban. Big man, thick neck, like a wrestler. Wife and two small children, not a lot of things to move."

The man shook his head. "No, but I'll ask around." Ammar had just opened his mouth to tell him where to send news when the man interrupted him by spitting on the ground at his feet. "And when I find him, I'll tell him to hide from you fuckers of dogs."

It stung, but he left the man to his insults and turned to the next driver. This one gave Ammar a wry smile at his approach and shook his finger, telling him not to bother. The next one was asleep in his cart, his head propped up on a moth-eaten blanket. Ammar tapped the side of the cart.

The young man jerked awake, wiping the spittle from the corners of his mouth with his thumb and forefinger, then dragged his hand down his shaggy beard. "Yes, sir! Where to?"

"I'm sorry." He glanced at the front of the line. "There are two ahead of you, still. Baghdad Police. I'm asking about a family you may have moved."

The driver sat up, irritated at being woken for nothing, but listened. There was no sign of recognition as Ammar described Aqil and his family. The next driver was the same, followed by an insult from the driver after. Tein met him in the middle, shaking his head.

"We tried."

"Kamal Ali?"

"After we search for the house with a blue door." Ammar sighed.

"Aqil's a scholar, he'd want to live someplace that makes him feel important," Tein said. "He'd want to be around them even if they no longer respect him."

"The important Shia scholars are in Karkh now."

"Where in Karkh?"

"Tein! That first day. What neighbourhood in Karkh did the witness who heard the thump of the arrows say he worked?"

Tein's face brightened. "Dar as-Silsila!"

"Right!" Ammar remembered. "That's also where Aqil said he studied. It's got to be Dar as-Silsila."

"Okay, let's check with Amru. If we get nothing, we head to Karkh."

"While we are at Kamal Ali's, we can ask about work," Tein added wryly.

But Ammar did not find it funny and walked on, mouth tight.

They entered Bakers' Gate where the loaves of every kind were stacked into towers. Ammar pointed to the street that would lead to the cheese seller's market and finally to Kamal Ali's shop. Tein got ahead of him, remembering the way, and Ammar fell behind.

How is there justice without police? he grumbled to himself. *Those drivers. They hate me for no reason other than being police. But if any one of their family were murdered, they wouldn't spit on me then. They'd beg me to find the killer.* He wanted to remind Tein that all the Imams, including Ali, a man Tein admired and sought to emulate, had worked with the very caliphates that were trying to destroy them. Sometimes you must work with those in power to protect your people. Imam Ali's obligation was to the people first, even when some resented him for trying, even when one of them killed him for it. Would Tein say that Imam Ali had no conscience? He wanted to grab him and demand an answer, but Tein was already nearing the Cheese Seller's Gate and had turned the corner. Ammar had to hurry to come alongside him.

"There's no way to question Kamal Ali's workers without it coming out that we suspect them of the robbery," Tein said once Ammar caught up. "They may lose their jobs, even though they're safe from prosecution."

"We can't help it." He paused. "And if they give us an admission, we're obligated to report them."

"Report them for an unreported crime?"

Ammar said bitterly, "Let Ibn Marwan cover it up. Do the bidding of the viziers and the agents. But I'm going to do my job and report them. You don't have to stand by me for that."

Tein did not speak, but there was no question he had something to say.

"Say it, Tein."

"This is the job you are fighting for? The job you enjoy so much because you can exercise your mind and get some justice?"

Ammar watched him closely. Tein had said his piece. It was the last word Ammar wanted to hear. He would talk to Ibn Marwan, lay down his demands and show Tein they could change things. Tein would come back. The job would go on.

Tein called out. "Ya Kamal Ali!"

Kamal Ali was bent over a churn alongside one of his workers, a young man in a blue turban, and stood on hearing his name, grinning when he recognized them. The worker beside him stood. One of the young men from the mosque. He tugged the sleeve of another man in a yellow turban. Ammar recognized that one from the mosque too, but did not see Amru anywhere. The two whispered to one another, but did not make a move to run.

"Assalamu alaykum!" Kamal Ali asked, "Is there any word from your sister?"

"Wa alaykum assalam, good news." Tein put his hand over his heart. "But that is not why we're here."

"May I have the good news first?" His eyes twinkled.

"She's interested. I imagine you'll see her soon."

Kamal Ali clasped his hands, pleased. "How can I help you?"

"We suspect some of your employees robbed the Twelfth Imam's agent of tithe and gave the money back to the people."

"That!" His ruddy face paled.

"It seems like Bishr and his friends did it and Bishr was killed over it."

Reaching out and grasping Ammar's shoulder, Kamal Ali asked, "Did one of them kill his friend?"

Ammar answered. "I can't say for certain, but all the evidence points away from your employees. One of them may know where the killer is hiding, though. Is Amru here?"

"He has not been back to work since the day you questioned him. I feared he killed his friend. I am relieved to hear that is unlikely."

Tein said gently, "You should have told us he disappeared."

"But what if it were only a coincidence? Perhaps he is busy with a family matter? It happens sometimes with the men. With due respect," he said apologetically, "I was not prepared to call for the police on a suspicion."

Ammar saw Tein smile in understanding out of the corner of his eye. It angered him, and he said forcefully, "We need to speak to any of your workers who were close friends with Bishr."

Kamal Ali agreed, but unhappily.

Tein stopped Kamal Ali. "The questioning could lead to your men being arrested for the robbery. Do you want to take us to them? You can deny it to us. We would ask them anyway, but at least you will have protested."

"Either way, it will be on my head. I want to hear what they have done from them and take my stand from there."

The three approached the workshop, Ammar positioning himself so he could block their escape through the market if they tried.

Kamal Ali spoke quietly to the two men Ammar had recognized. Their backs were up, but they were not looking to run.

"You two!" Tein called out. "We have a few questions."

The one in the blue turban did not move, and gestured to his yellow-turbaned friend to stay put. "You have something to ask, ask it right here."

"If that's how you want it." Tein shrugged, moving in closer. "We know you robbed the agents."

Ammar was behind Tein, still eyeing the routes of escape.

The blue turbaned man shrugged in return. "What of it?"

"You aren't afraid of being arrested for it?"

He scoffed. "The agents haven't reported it. We'd have heard."

Ammar and Tein did not reply.

"Is there a crime if the victim does not complain?"

"Yes," Ammar answered, "if the police chief decides."

"The police chief and the viziers and the caliph himself, they are going to bring this to court?" Standing with his legs spread and shoulders back, he said with confidence, "The whole of that corrupt caliphate relies on the acquiescence of the Imamis to caliphal power. It's the only way the caliphs can claim to be legitimate rulers of all the Muslim people. No one will say a cursed thing to put the Imamis at risk. They'll bury the story, not us."

It took all Ammar had not to step forward and remind him that one caliph after another had been holding the Imams. They had no choice but to broker peace. Who were these people who did not understand their sacrifices?

Ammar's objection must have been plain on his face. The young man spoke directly to him. "Yes, the Imams of the past, the ones we share in common, worked with the caliphate from their hiding places. But no more hiding. No more deals. Where is your Imam? Ours shows himself. And he'll never give into the caliphate." He turned back to Tein. "The police chief won't decide to hear our case."

Kamal Ali had taken several steps back, gaping at the speech. "Yaqub, Wahid, I took you both for honest men! Neither thieves nor revolutionaries!"

Yaqub ignored him as Tein came in closer, asking, "And the murder?"

"That was Utbah. Amru told you."

"That's not evidence. Amru didn't see it himself."

"When do police care about evidence?"

Tein grimaced. "And I suppose you didn't do it because you'd admit to the killing if you had, just like you admitted to the robbery?"

He sniggered, glancing at his friend in the yellow turban who did not seem as confident and was now eyeing avenues of escape and finding none. "No, we would not." Turning back to Tein, he said, "The police chief will decide *that* case." Yaqub became serious. "But walla, it was not us."

"Where's Amru?"

"You two spooked him. But I can tell you Amru did not kill Bishr."

Kamal Ali audibly sighed in relief, but was clearly still in knots over the revelation of men he had trusted.

"And Aqil ibn Akib," Tein asked, "was he involved in the robbery, too?"

Yaqub's eyes widened with pleasure. "Can you imagine it? An Imami robbing his own Imam's agent. He thought he was using us. We used him."

Ammar called out. "Using you, how?"

"You'll have to ask him that. I've said enough."

"He's hiding Utbah," Tein said. "We need to know where he lives."

The one in the yellow turban, Wahid, said, his voice cracking, "He's got two rooms. One off of Bakers' Gate. The other off of Sughayr Square."

"He's moved," Ammar replied.

The two men looked at each other, surprised. Yaqub said, "He keeps his family in the room with the blue door. You sure you tried the right place?"

"Yes."

Tein said to Ammar, "They don't know."

Ammar left them and walked into the square. Tein said something to the two men, but Ammar did not hear it. Then Tein and Kamal Ali joined him.

"If you have anything else to ask these three men," Kamal Ali said, "ask it now. They no longer work for me." He bowed to Ammar and Tein in thanks. "Unhappy news, but I am grateful to know. I will give them their pay and more to tide them over despite everything. If they are not honest men, they have been honest workers."

Ammar glanced at them. Yaqub understood what was coming or chose to leave himself. He was rolling down his sleeves, and Wahid followed. He turned back to Kamal Ali. "Do you know where they live in case we need to speak with them again?"

Kamal Ali nodded.

Ammar and Tein thanked him and headed out of the square.

Making the question a jab, Tein asked, "You don't want to arrest them?"

"I'll report them. That's all."

Tein grunted. "One more thing. If those men believe the robbery would never be reported, then why would Aqil hide Utbah to cover up his role?"

"I don't know," Ammar replied, "but we're going to find out."

Something drew Tein's attention. "Look." He pointed at the furthest market gate.

Ammar scanned for signs of the scholar or Utbah. "Is it Aqil?"

"Zaytuna and Layla."

"What's she doing here?" Then he understood. "Oh."

"Yes," Tein replied, "Layla is acting as her chaperone."

"Let's not embarrass her. Cut through the market."

They took the nearest market gate and had passed the cheese sellers when he saw Nasifa. A flood of warmth enveloped him, drawing him to her. She was wearing a dingy wrap, so washed out the pattern was only a shadow and it made him wanted to forget the case and take her to pick out whatever her heart desired and drape it over her head himself to see her smile. He became uncomfortable. This was not what he thought he wanted.

She rushed to him, breathless. "Ammar, Tein, assalamu alaykum, I didn't know how to find you! Your mother and Muhsin said you were searching the city. I walked, praying, and here you are! Alhamdulillah."

Wanting to pull her into his arms, he took two steps back instead, even holding out his hands to block her approach. "What's wrong?"

She stopped short at his gesture. Her smile faded, and she responded coldly. "I came to tell you there is going to be a meeting tonight for women only. The speaker will discuss the robbery and insurrection. It must be the Qarmatis. What if they reveal the evidence you need?"

"How do you know this?" he asked.

"Our neighbour, Maha, asked me to come." A smile returned to her lips. "I led Maha along, telling her I hoped for revolution, too."

"At a meeting for women only?" Tein asked, looking between them.

"Shia women have always stood beside men in battle," she explained. Then to Ammar, "They must want us to urge our men to revolt against the caliphate. I'll report back what I hear."

"It won't be safe." Ammar took a step toward her. "You can't go."

Her chin up, she challenged him. "I suppose you would have advised the Lady Zaynab not to accompany her brother, Imam Husayn, to Karbala?"

This was not the daughter who respectfully disagreed with her father at lunch. He was dumbfounded. Nasifa was the embodiment of Lady Zaynab. A woman who gave no quarter. A woman who challenged Yazid in his own court. Not the woman he had imagined. His attraction to her turned into something more.

Tein tapped him, gesturing toward the square. "Zaytuna."

He understood, and without thinking, he reached for Nasifa's hand. "Come with me." Her own hand came out to meet his, the tips of their fingers brushing, and their eyes met. The whole of the market came to a standstill around them and Ammar saw himself kneel before her, taking her hand, kissing it and bringing it to his forehead. She gazed at him with eyes so loving and lips so sweet that he vowed to give his life to her. Then, just as suddenly, he remembered where they were, the impropriety of touching, and pulled his hand back, burning with the realization that he loved her and would marry her no matter the cost to himself.

She turned away, covering her face with her wrap.

Tein coughed. "Zaytuna."

"Go!" Ammar urged.

Tein led the way back to the square. He and Nasifa followed, but he took care not to glance at her.

"Zaytuna!"

She was almost at Kamal Ali's shop and turned to them in surprise. Layla tugged on her hand, saying something, but she did not answer. Instead, she seemed horrified. Ammar felt awful for her.

Kamal Ali had seen her and was walking towards her, but they reached Zaytuna before he did, and he retreated.

Flustered, she stammered, "We were... Uh..."

Tein interrupted. "It's fine, sister. I'm happy to see you here. This is about something else. We have a job for you on the case. Do you want it?"

She glanced at Kamal Ali approaching, down at Layla, and then back to Tein, Ammar, and Nasifa. "Yes."

28

Tein addressed Zaytuna. "You go with Nasifa. Listen. Ask questions, but don't do anything."

"What will you be doing?" Zaytuna asked.

"We'll be searching door to door for Aqil's house until then. If we can't find him, we'll wait outside the meeting for you," Ammar replied, glancing at Nasifa with concern. "If we don't show up, then we found him, so there is no need for you to attend. Go straight home."

Ah, thought Zaytuna. They had updated her on the case and asked her to go only to protect Nasifa. She nodded her head so Ammar would know she would watch her. His face relaxed.

Layla tugged on Zaytuna's hand excitedly. "Can I go?"

She shook her head, and Layla made a face.

Nasifa explained to Zaytuna where to meet so they could enter together. "They won't let you in if you aren't with me. I can't go except that my neighbour invited me." She was excited, clearly not understanding the risk involved. But Zaytuna admired she wanted to be there at all and wondered what Ammar made of it.

The four said their goodbyes. Zaytuna watched as they walked away, both Ammar and Nasifa taking one last glance at each other.

Layla said, "Ammar and Nasifa are in love."

"I think so." She eyed the girl. "You and I need to talk."

Pulling back on Zaytuna's hand and frowning as if she had done something wrong, Layla objected. "I've been good."

"Yes, you have been. This is about me. I have to tell you about why you are with me and what we are about to do."

"Is it a case?" she asked, jumping up and down.

"Layla, stop." Zaytuna let go of her hand. "The man who owns that butter shop. He's the one Uncle Tein said wants to marry me."

"But what about Uncle Mustafa?"

"He's marrying YingYue," she replied more sharply than she intended.

"You could be his second wife. You love him, don't you?"

"Not like that, I don't." She turned her head away from the girl to keep from schooling her on the matter.

"But the Prophet, alayhi salam, he had lots of wives. You love the Prophet. It's no different."

"The day a man in this world is the Prophet, I'll be his second, third, or fourth wife and I'll gladly bear up under the trouble these marriages inspire even in the best people. But there will never be another man like the Prophet, alayhi salam wa rahmatullahi wa barakatuhu."

"Not even Uncle Mustafa?"

"Especially not Uncle Mustafa," she said, recalling all the times in which he had betrayed the Prophet's example while believing he was upholding it.

"Auntie, that's not very nice."

Zaytuna accepted the girl's scolding in Mustafa's defence. She had a point. Mustafa had seen his errors and changed, but there was no guarantee he would not err again with all the infuriating confidence of a religious scholar. *He's YingYue's problem now*, she thought with satisfaction, but the satisfaction was mixed with loss all the same. She explained, so as not to confuse the girl, "I only meant that there is no chance for Uncle Mustafa and me any longer."

The girl looked toward the butter shop. "What do you want me to do?"

"Listen in and tell me what you think later."

"Can I ask him questions? I know you very well."

Zaytuna squeezed her hand. "One or two, so make sure they are the questions you want to ask the most."

When she glanced across the square, Kamal Ali was standing at attention, waiting for her. She admired his broad forehead, the wave in his beard, his aquiline nose, the tinge of red to his skin, and his gentle smile. It did not escape her that he shared these features with the Prophet and she hoped his character would bear the same traces.

He came out to meet them. "Assalamu alaykum, Zaytuna." Bowing warmly to Layla he said, "Assalamu alaykum, I am honoured to meet you. I am Kamal Ali ibn Abdussalam al-Fassi."

"I am Layla bint Zaytuna," she said firmly.

Zaytuna restrained herself from correcting the girl. Why was Layla using her name as her nasab as if she were her daughter? Would he misunderstand? Zaytuna turned her attention to Kamal Ali. "She is my neighbour and I care for her like a daughter. All the women love her. She has many mothers."

"But only one whose name she takes!"

He meant it as a compliment, but it bothered her all the same. Layla's hand had become clammy in her own, and she guessed the girl must have felt her stiffen. Zaytuna pulled her in close. "It's a good nasab," she said. "Thank you." Layla softened against her and she wondered at this girl who could be so forgiving despite everything that had happened to her. Zaytuna turned to Kamal Ali. "She's my chaperone today."

"I am honoured," he said. "I will send someone out for sweets."

Layla jumped up a little at the mention of sweets, and the three made their way to the table where she had sat with him that first day. Zaytuna put down her basket beside the table and sat expectantly. Kamal Ali called a boy over and whispered to him, placing some coins in his hand, and he ran off into the marketplace. He relayed something else to a worker who crossed the shop to a shelf of flat-bottomed pottery jars. Only then did Zaytuna see he was short three workers and wondered where they had gone. Kamal Ali emerged from a back room with three glasses on a tray while the man returned with a small glass pitcher filled with buttermilk.

Kamal Ali poured the buttermilk into the glasses with a flourish. She smiled. This was where the young boy who worked for him had gotten his comical presentation of the buttermilk. Kamal Ali finally sat down with them, saying, "Ya bismillah!"

Layla giggled as she drank the buttermilk down in one gulp, leaving a trace on her upper lip. She wiped it clean with her sleeve. "I've never heard anyone say it that way, with the 'ya' first."

"I grew up in the city of Fas in the Maghreb. This is how we say it."

As she took small sips of her own buttermilk, as delicious as the first, Zaytuna wondered at how far he had travelled and what he had seen, especially in Egypt, thinking especially about the queen on the monument, when he leaned forward and asked Layla a question.

"What do you do during your days, Layla?"

"I wash clothes now with Auntie Zaytuna. My parents left me to do scullery work in one house, but my master kicked me out because I tried to help a friend of mine after my other friend died and he didn't like that, so Auntie Maryam took me in, and it was good there except I had to pretend to be nice to Zaynab and I don't like her at all." She took a deep breath, sat up, her back straight. "It's better to be my own woman, with my own room, like I am now with the aunties and Uncle Qambar."

He sat back, smiling at the girl, and glanced at Zaytuna long enough for her to see the concern in his eyes. "It sounds as if she has lived a whole life in just a few years."

Zaytuna shrugged, a crevasse opening between them. "Most of us had by her age. Not you?"

"My father had four wives at all times. Each family had several rooms, on different floors. I had three full brothers and twenty-seven half brothers and sisters of all ages. My elder brothers' wives even lived with us with all their children. My memories of those days are sweet. All my father's wives were mothers to us all. We had seven grandparents to share among us, too. There was always plenty to eat. It was warm in winter. Cool in summer. We fought, but made up quickly. The only shortfall was my father's time."

"Oh?"

"There was never enough time for all his children. We longed for him and, so, without meaning to, he broke our hearts. May God forgive us our longing and rest his soul."

"Amin," she said as she should and took another sip of the buttermilk. But she wanted to get up from the table and leave. This man would never understand her. He had never known what it was like to be hungry or not have a safe place to sleep as a child. He grew up loved, unafraid. Would he want a wife like her when his own memories were so happy? His only sorrow a father who did not have enough time for him? Bitter disappointment caught hold of her. *Of course*, she thought, *this was never going to work.*

Layla asked him, "Is that why you left home?"

"No," he replied, returning his attention to her. "I only left because I liked to wander. I was always running away from home to discover new parts of Fas as they built it up into the surrounding hills. My brothers always had come find me and drag me home by my ear." He chuckled at the thought of it. "So despite loving my family, I set out when I was not much older than you are and traveled the empire."

The boy returned with three small copper bowls balanced on a hanging tray in one hand and a package wrapped in cloth in the other. He went to the back of the shop first, and came back, placing three bowls of pudding with three small copper spoons before them, again with a similar flourish.

The boy retreated, returning with a bowl and pitcher of water, and held the pitcher for Layla first, winking at her. Kamal Ali sucked his teeth, and the boy corrected himself, offering the basin and water to Zaytuna.

Zaytuna was not sure if she should admit she had never seen such a pudding. It was translucent, firm, scented with lemon and rose and topped with finely chopped walnuts. But Layla had already picked up a spoon in her fist and was quickly devouring it. Zaytuna took up her spoon, watching Kamal Ali to see how he held his, and tried to do the same but got angry that she even tried and went back to her own way, holding the spoon, like Layla, in her fist. But that did not work either, because the spoon was too small. She huffed aloud in frustration, only to see that Kamal Ali had put his spoon aside.

"I usually eat my faludhaj this way," he said, eyeing Layla and stuck two fingers into the bowl, pulling up a bit of the jellied pudding and popping it into his mouth. "Try it," he said to Zaytuna, smiling.

Understanding full well what he was doing, she agreed to the kindness of it and scooped up the pudding with her fingers. Closing her eyes, she held the pudding on her tongue for a moment as she tasted one delicate flavour after another. Sweetened rose, lemon, and, she recognized with pleasure, quince, something she and Tein only had when they snatched them from public fruit trees. But there was something else in it, a deep scent that filled her with longing.

"It's very tasty," Layla said.

Zaytuna opened her eyes. "What's in it?"

"It is made with starch and sugar, roses, quince, lemon, and a touch of musk. It is only for the most special occasions. People can become addicted."

"I can imagine," Zaytuna said, and picked up the spoon, no longer worrying about getting it right. She brought the spoon to her mouth, asking, "Where do you travel from here?"

"I am through travelling," he said. "Buratha is my home. I only long now for a house filled with a family to love." He glanced at Layla, making sure that Zaytuna understood the girl was welcome in his home, too.

The boy came back with the pitcher and bowl, retreating again after they had washed their hands to get two packages wrapped in cloth.

Kamal Ali took them from the boy and handed Layla the small package, and gave Zaytuna the large one. Layla tore hers open without waiting, revealing a beautiful oblong headscarf of stripes in every colour imaginable. The girl moaned with pleasure, her eyes wide, and held one end of it to her face. Zaytuna touched it, the edges were bound with tiny, perfectly regular stitches of thread as delicate as the cotton itself. The scarf was so sheer a light breeze could carry it away and she sighed at it, mainly because the girl would never take the delicate thing off and it would rip straightaway.

It was her turn now and Zaytuna gasped as she pulled back one edge of the package, then the other, revealing a wrap in the same delicate cotton. But hers was the blue of the sky just after sunset, with block printed pink, blue, and red flowers similar to those she had admired on one of YingYue's wraps. A flower that was a rose within a rose within a rose. Iridescent butterflies floated among them, searching for nectar. A drop of water appeared on the cloth and she glanced up at the sky, clutching the fabric to her to protect it from the rain, when she realized it was her own tear.

"It's beautiful, Auntie Zaytuna." The girl touched the embroidered edge.

Still clutching it to her, she faced him without wiping away her tears and said, "I cannot marry you."

Layla gaped at her.

He took a deep breath, but did not reply.

"I am not the woman who can wear such a thing." She opened herself to him. "You have mistaken me for someone else. It is too beautiful, too delicate." She stood. "Look at me." She put the wrap down on the table and held out her calloused hands, already wrinkled and worn like an old woman's. "Look at my hands."

He stood with her. "I am looking. I have seen."

She picked up the wrap and held it out. "This is what you think of me?"

Reaching out and touching one edge of the wrap, he said gently, "This is who you are. This is who I see."

"You don't know me." She laid the wrap back down on the table and woefully shook her head. "I can't follow you into the rooms of fine people even if you dress me like this."

"What rooms?"

"People will come to visit. I will be made to visit them. Women will want to chat about fine things. My people are the poorest of Baghdad. My people live entire families in single rooms or in the walls of the cemetery, not homes with floors for whole families, who never worry about food to eat. I have never known fabric like this except to wash it with the utmost care in the homes of the wealthy."

"Who are these fine friends of mine? My people are the people of Buratha. I sell butter to wealthy homes, I do not eat with them. And if I did, I would give them all up so that you would share each meal with me and invite whomever pleased you."

She touched the wrap, wanting to sit again but unsure. How could he be telling the truth? What sort of man is this?

"Zaytuna, will you sit?"

Layla tugged at her, imploring, and so she sat.

"You must have seen women in wool wandering the roads on your travels," she said to him. "Some maybe with children behind them, doing menial labour for a place to sleep and something to eat?"

"Yes."

"That was my childhood."

His eyes offered her understanding that said more than words. There was not a shred of pity in them, only that he saw, and she was grateful for that. All right. She would try. Start again. Make her demands. See if she was the woman he thought he wanted, after all.

"I will never give up working on investigations."

"I was first enchanted by your beauty, then by your spirit and your mind. I would only want you to do as you like."

"It is one thing to admire such a thing in a woman you desire, but another if she is your wife."

He raised one eyebrow, saying matter-of-factly, "If I wanted a wife who never leaves her home and only has gossip and talk of the goods of this world on her tongue, I know where to find her."

"You wife was a woman like that?"

"I have been married twice before."

"Tell me about them."

"In both, after the first year of romance, there was nothing to say to one another. Of course, they had their social circles. We rarely saw each other." He paused. "The most recent one ended the way I mentioned. The first ended when she tired of me and asked to be released."

"And you released them both."

"Why would I hold a woman who does not care for me? They left with their dowries in their hands and much more."

"Do you have any children?"

"Children never blessed my home."

"Tell me what you want."

He sat forward, intent, no longer gazing away from her out of propriety. "I want a companion who captivates me with her conversation and her interests, who seeks justice for those who need it, who will join me in noticing those in need and alleviating their situation."

"And what about a wife who follows the Sufi path?"

"I have sat with the Sufis. They love the family of the Prophet, as I do."

"Yes. Our path is their path. The Prophet, alayhi salam, said, 'I am the city of knowledge and Ali is its gate'."

"Then, our paths are the same."

"You are Shia?"

"What does it mean to be Shia or Sunni?" he replied. "My mother was Shia and my father Sunni. But I am emotionally drawn to the Shia and am most comfortable among them, which is why I live in Buratha."

"Which kind of Shia?" she asked, hoping he was like Ammar only because she knew nothing about the others.

"I've travelled too much. I've visited and lived with every kind. In Mecca, I met Abu Abdallah ash-Shi`i, the representative of the Ismaili Mahdi. He was with a group of Berbers from Kutama and I sat with them for a time. I was closest to joining him. He is a man of great charisma. Their Mahdi will establish an empire in North Africa, I am sure of it. But I am not a joining man. When I find myself joining a community, I wander away from it."

"And when you join in marriage?"

He laughed. "This is why you are perfect for me. This kind of question. How will I ever become lazy if you are beside me?"

"You like a sharp-tongued woman?"

"When I was young and sleeping on the road with other travellers one night, I heard a man tell a story of a great woman. He advised me that only a great man could bear the weight of such a marriage. I never forgot what she said when she found her husband sleeping all night instead of standing with her in prayer."

He lifted a finger, changed his face slightly, and the woman was before her. "'Get up', she said to her husband. 'Get up, you heedless man! Get up, you idle oaf! I swear you will not enter the Fire on account of me! On the piety of your mother, pray that God has mercy on you! Do not slack, for God will decide your case!'" He relaxed and became himself again.

Zaytuna burst out laughing and Layla, too, saying, "Oh Auntie Zaytuna, she's just like you!"

He smiled in return. "I have longed to be the kind of man who is honoured by such a woman. I would gladly take her prodding."

But Zaytuna wondered if, in the company of a man like this, she would snap and prod and asked, "And if I soften in your company and all that is left is this woman you see here who uses your money to help the poor?"

"I would welcome her. That such a woman would also have the face of a Nubian queen of Egypt? God will have blessed me beyond what I deserve."

Zaytuna stopped. "A Nubian queen?"

"You have her face. I fell in love with her when I saw her painted on a monument in Egypt. Then you arrived, investigating for the police, and every bit of you carrying the power, posture, and beauty of that noble woman."

Up to that moment, she had only recognized their Nubian mother in Tein. Never in herself. She had believed she had nothing of her mother in her but her height and long face. In her mind, Zaytuna had always been the rapist's daughter while Tein belonged to their mother, having her deep, russet brown skin. But here was this man telling her none of that was true. She was a Nubian woman. A queen. And beautiful. She wanted to believe him more than she wanted to run from him. Taking hold of the wrap on the table, she stood and drew it around her. Once fully draped, she pulled her old one off from underneath, and felt easy.

"I will marry you," she said as she folded the old wrap. "But first you must come to a wedding tomorrow night at my uncle's home where the Sufis of Baghdad gather. It will begin after the sunset prayer. Get there in time for the prayer. This is my community. No one can part me from these people or the path. If you love them, you can love me. If you will support my path, I will support yours."

He stood, overwhelmed by joy, his eyes glistening. "I will be there."

She took Layla's hand and bowed to him. He bowed, hand on his heart, in return.

"One last thing," she said.

"Whatever you wish."

"I will be your only wife. My dowry will be to spend whatever I like on the vulnerable of Baghdad for the rest of my days."

"We shall put that and whatever else you want in your contract," he finished with an eager flourish. "I will sign anything!"

Near tears again, she told him how to find Uncle Junayd's, then left, running from him in a state of agitated joy and dragging Layla behind.

"Auntie, Auntie! Slow down!"

Once they were out of the square, Zaytuna stopped, putting down her shopping basket, but still holding her old wrap in her arms. She asked breathlessly, "Layla. Can I do this?"

"Do what, Auntie?"

"Can I be happy?" The question was too much to bear. Happiness was beyond anything she imagined for herself. And she placed all the weight of it on the girl's answer.

"Oh, Auntie!" Layla threw her arms around Zaytuna's waist. "Yes!" She leaned back, eyeing her seriously. "I think you should marry him.

But," her tone changed, "only because you cannot be with Uncle Mustafa, right?"

It was a slap in the face. Her answer was worse than a simple, "No." She wanted to drop the girl's hand and stalk off. But Zaytuna made herself whisper, "Allah," sighing the divine name until she had the wherewithal to reply evenly. "I will always love Uncle Mustafa, but that's over."

"But if YingYue and Uncle Mustafa got divorced," Layla pressed, "would you marry him? Because if you marry Kamal Ali and they get divorced after, it's too late for you."

The girl would drive her to tears. "Why are you asking this?"

"I want to make sure you are sure, Auntie Zaytuna."

Zaytuna took a breath, wiped away a tear, and accepted that Layla was right. Looking into the distance, she asked herself if she should marry Kamal Ali, even if Mustafa were free and wanted her, and listened to her heart. Calming waters flowed beneath her, rising and washing through her, the hushed sound of grasses in the breeze surrounded her, and the scent and taste of sugared roses consumed her. She knew then with certainty and vowed to not doubt this man that God had brought her and whispered, "Alhamdulillah." The certainty ebbed until the noise of the bustling alley returned her to Layla and her question.

Stooping down to the girl, she replied as she put her old wrap in the shopping basket with the other things. "Uncle Mustafa and I love each other. But even if we were free for each other, I can't be what he needs me to be. I would have to give up what means most to me. I would have to learn how to be a lady, so I don't shame him in scholarly circles."

Layla acknowledged her answer, whether she accepted it was no matter. "Let's go see if Auntie Saliha can come out and chat for a while."

"Are you going to tell her?"

"Yes."

Every step through Buratha, then over the canal bridges into Baghdad and to Saliha, she sought the certainty that had overcome her. It lingered within her and she touched its edges as if it were a miracle unseen to all but her and kept tethered to this world through her prayers alone.

At the entrance of the hospital, she pushed Layla to go in and get Saliha while she waited outside in the sun. She stood close to the wall, beside the wide arched entrance way but far enough away from the guard, who eyed her strangely. She pulled her wrap over her face and gazed at the coloured light shining through the tight weave of the fragile cloth.

"My God, it's beautiful!"

Zaytuna pulled the wrap away from her face at the sound of Saliha's voice and could not help but smile. "It'll be ruined by the end of the day."

"Layla told me, but I didn't believe it." Saliha picked up the edge and examined the embroidery. "You don't want to know the price of such a thing." She giggled with pleasure at the enormity of it. "Come inside. I don't have much time. We can sit by the fountain. A proper lady like you, standing out here in the street."

Oh, that was why the guard wondered at her. Women who wear wraps like this did not wait in the road. They may walk through one, but they never stop long enough to garner gossip. She shook her head. "No, outside is fine. I need to get Layla home. Maybe we can pick up a job today before I have to go out again this evening."

The girl sulked beside her, but she ignored it.

"Layla says you're set on marrying him."

"Kamal Ali."

"This is rash, Zaytuna. Your whole life, there is no man for you, even Mustafa, who has always loved you. But now that Mustafa is getting married and after speaking to a man once, you've accepted his proposal." She cocked her head, her voice sharp. "It is a beautiful wrap, but when did you ever care for beautiful things?"

Instead of coolness of flowing water, the scent of roses, and the hush of grasses, a winter damp crept up and rotted away the hope she had and returned her to her proper place, a woman who was not to be loved. An ugly woman, never to feel beautiful. She did not cry, but her face settled back into carrying the weight of a life bereft of knowing how to hold and be held. Pulling her hand back from the miracle of love, she let it go and, without a word, turned and left them, taking the cemetery road home.

"Zaytuna!" She heard them calling, then Layla's bare feet slapping the hard earth as she ran up behind her. The girl took her hand and tried to pull her back. "Auntie. Where are you going?"

But she ignored the girl, her hand limp in Layla's, and walked ahead without a word, feeling the gravel and pits on the road through her thin sandals, the dust caking her calloused and cracked feet, and the tug of her delicate wrap dragging on the road. She stopped only when Saliha took her by the shoulder and forced her around.

"Zaytuna, my God, forgive me."

She collapsed in Saliha's arms and to the ground, finally weeping. People stepped around them, some cursing them to get out of the way. Saliha cursed back, then returned to her, pulling the wrap away from her face, and wiping her tears away with her thumb, whispering, "You do love him."

"This wrap."

"It is beautiful, a gift like no other. I'm so sorry."

"He told me its beauty is who I am. What he sees in me."

"Oh my beautiful, Zaytuna, yes. Yes, it is. Yes, you are even more beautiful than this wrap. He sees it, too." Saliha pulled her close, and they wept together in the road with Layla standing guard.

29

Zaytuna searched for the edges of the certainty she had touched so briefly, but they were out of reach. By the time she and Layla made it through the passageway home, she was leaning heavily on the girl and only wanted to sleep. Removing Kamal Ali's wrap in the courtyard, she looked away as she shook it out, not wanting to see where it must have ripped or where the dirt ground into it from the road. She folded it gently and pushed aside the curtain to her room. Layla lingered at the door for a moment before coming in and pouring water into Mustafa's cup for her. Accepting it, she drank deeply and thanked her, then said, "I need to lie down."

"I'm going to stay here for a bit, Auntie. You sleep."

Accepting that, too, she lay down under the girl's caring eye, wanting the company, and wondered if that meant she had not lost the right to be loved.

Zaytuna slept and dreamt.

She gazed across a vast meadow of swaying tall green grasses and blooming wild carrot. In the distance, a fawn wandered away from its mother and slowly pushed through the meadow to her, sniffing tentatively, its brown, damp nose twitching at her, its soft, round eyes searching her own. She lay down on her side and called the fawn to her. The animal nestled against her, and they slept.

The sound of footsteps outside. Her name called. She woke up. Layla lay in her arms, snoring softly. Zaytuna untangled herself from the girl and kissed the back of her head. "Daughter, wake up."

Layla sat up bleary-eyed and crawled over to get a cup of water for herself. "My bed is more comfortable, Auntie. You can sleep in there with me." She added tentatively, "If you want. Sometimes."

"Sometimes," Zaytuna replied, meaning it, and, with that, her lost certainty was within reach again and she took hold of it for good.

"You two sleeping?" Yulduz's sing-song voice carried through.

"Be right out," Layla answered, putting the cup back in its honoured place, and scampered out to them.

They had slept the day away, but she was not too late to meet Nasifa. Zaytuna took her old wrap out of the basket. There was one prayer to make up and one to do on time before leaving.

In the courtyard, Qambar pulled out a reed mat from their room and lay it out for them to sit, while Yulduz put out a jug of water and Layla dates.

Squatting in front of the basin to perform her ablutions, Zaytuna whispered, "Bismillah," as she cupped water into her hand. The drops soaked into her skin, deepening the colour and making it more supple. She thought of Kamal Ali's face, his eyes, his lips, and wanted to go to the baths to be scrubbed and oiled. "God forgive me," she whispered, remembering she was washing up for prayer, and shook the thought of Kamal Ali out of her mind. "Bismillah," she started again, this time keeping her mind on God and not a man.

Yulduz and Qambar had Layla between them and were fussing over her. Once standing in prayer in her room, she found their voices were fine companions, rather than irritating her as usual. She prayed in a state of gratitude and ease, reciting verse after verse from the Qur'an wishing she could remain in the feeling even longer.

She sat back, gave her final greetings to the angels on either side of her, and held out her hands in supplication. "Whatever will be with Kamal Ali, I leave in your hands. I could not have designed it. I will not try to direct it. If we are to be companions, let it be easy. If not, let that be easy, too." She drew herself up to face what was ahead of her, straightening her back. "Tonight, help me read the signs, like Auntie Hakima said. Help me listen and understand. And keep us safe, especially Nasifa." Then, remembering the comfort of Layla in her arms and hearing the soft conversation outside, she added, "And bless this family and our daughter."

She steeled herself and went out to the courtyard. "I'm off."

"To your uncle's?" Qambar asked.

"On this case for Ammar and Tein. God willing, it will all be over tonight, and we'll be safe."

Yulduz said, "Tell your brother I'm praying for him."

It was a first out of that woman's mouth but she did not call attention to it, nor laugh; they all seemed to be changing and she thought it best to let it go unremarked, as if they had always been accepting of one another.

"I'm going to say a lot of prayers for you tonight, Auntie," Layla said. "I hope you are the one who catches him!"

"Inshallah, it'll all be over with no one getting hurt."

"Amin," said Qambar and held his hands up in prayer as he whispered to himself, then wiped his hands over his face.

Once in the alley, she settled into a breathing meditation, saying one word of "There is no god but God," with each step. She felt the familiar waters of divine love wash through her, little by little, as she walked. Soon the sounds of the alleys and roads she walked fell into the background and she turned from alley to alley, then onto the road to Buratha without thinking. As she passed the cemetery, the waters rushed through her with such strength that she stumbled and stopped reciting in order not to be overwhelmed and fall into ecstasy where she stood.

"Daughter!"

She turned toward the voice and the old woman she feared had passed was sitting in her place by the cemetery wall, half tucked under her lean-to. Hurrying to her, she grasped her soft, but calloused, hands. "Auntie, I've looked for you," she said as she kissed the woman's hands and brought them to her cheek.

"I see you're leaving that cell you had locked yourself up in."

Doubting herself despite everything, she asked, "Have I, Auntie?"

"You are nearly there." The old woman winked. "You've got the tips of your fingers on the outer edge of peace with all that has happened and all that will happen." The old woman stared hard at her. "Doesn't mean any of it is easy, mind you, but I can see you're not fighting every bit of life that comes your way anymore."

"I don't want to leave you Auntie," Zaytuna glanced down the road, "but I have to be in Buratha before the sunset prayer."

"About that." She leaned back against the wall. "Listen."

"Listen?"

"Out there and in here." She tapped her chest. "That's where you'll find the names of God. There's divine gentleness in a fawn's call for its mother. Divine tenderness in a man's gesture of love. And the sound of divine vengeance in the voice of a man denied recognition and control. Listen for the signs in the voices of the people and you'll hear what they want and know when and how to act."

The answer unfolded the mystery in Auntie Hakima's advice to her to read the signs of God. She kissed the old woman's hands again and stood, waiting until she was in the road to brush the dust from her knees. Rushing past the hospital, she wanted to embrace Saliha and tell her all was well. That would have to wait. By the time she crossed the canal bridges and reached the meeting place, it was almost time for the call to the sunset prayer and she prayed she had not missed her chance. She corrected herself, remembering the old woman's advice, and took a breath as she rushed through an alley. If I miss it, that was the right thing and, inshallah, I'll know what I should do.

Reaching the square, she gasped, "Alhamdulillah." Nasifa was still there.

"Assalamu alaykum," Nasifa said under her breath. "Don't be obvious, but look over at that tavern when you get a chance."

Zaytuna pretended she was searching for someone around the square and found Tein and Ammar. in the tavern pretending to be drunk If they were here, that meant they had not found the scholar's house and this meeting might be their last chance. Ammar had switched out his black turban, and was no longer wearing the military tunic and cuirass, but he still had his sword. She assumed Tein had his dagger, although his hands were enough in most fights. Tein slumped over to one side, leaning against the wall, a clay cup in his hand.

Clusters of women were coming into the square from the alleys surrounding it and headed towards a passageway between a green grocer and a stand where an old woman sold bone, dung, and thornbush for fire. "So many women are coming. I'm surprised."

"Women's meetings are always crowded."

"Did you find out who is speaking?"

"No. My mother only lets me go to the ones run by women where we listen to the stories of Karbala. This is new to me."

"I'm glad you came to us. Inshallah, we'll find something out tonight."

"If it weren't for Maha, the neighbour, Mother would never permit me. Still, it took some convincing." She squeezed Zaytuna's hand. "Really, you must come sometime to a Karbala meeting with us. The women who came to stand with Imam Husayn were very brave. I think you would see yourself in them, Zaytuna."

Zaytuna thought of Kamal Ali and wondered if this is where her life was headed, going to Shia meetings, becoming part of that community. She was not sure what it meant for her and replied, noncommittally, "If God wills."

They crossed the square and entered the passageway, finding themselves suddenly stuck in the dark behind the women in front of them. The two finally made their way in, spilling into an already crowded courtyard. Oil lamps hung from the arches, sending scattered light over women as they stepped over one other, finding a place to sit in any gap on the floor. There was a fabric screen set up, dividing the room to the right. An older woman with a commanding voice called to them from the far side.

"Maha," Nasifa whispered. The woman had spread out her legs out sideways against the wall to hold their spots and was waving away others trying to get her to move as if they were not worth the effort. They made their way over to her, careful not to step in laps.

"God reward you," Nasifa said as she settled down next to Maha. "This is my friend, Zaytuna. I mentioned her to you."

"Assalamu alaykum," she said as she slid down the wall next to Nasifa and pulled her legs in tight as women crushed in around them. "Why the screen?"

"A room full of women?" Nasifa looked at her quizzically. "Not all the women may be comfortable with men seeing them."

Maha lifted an eyebrow. "And to protect the speakers from our eyes."

It irritated her. As if the women were not sufficient chaperones for each other. There had never been a screen in her Sufi community, but she thought of Auntie Hakima's worry about changes taking place and she feared they might come to be.

"The women can be worse than the men sometimes!" Nasifa agreed.

Maha leaned in. "The men who took back the tithe will be here tonight. They have to be protected from those who might turn them over to the police or the thugs hired by the agents to punish them."

"Agents' thugs? Took back? Maha! I've never heard you speak this way."

"Why are you here, then? You said you longed for revolution. I would not have invited you if I'd known you were loyal to that Imam. I thought you were only playing the part for your parents sake!"

Zaytuna jumped in. "She is close. When she told me about the meeting, I swore I would come with her so she could hear the truth herself. She can bring it to her family and tell them."

Maha nodded in approval to Zaytuna, but then threatened Nasifa. "Your family did not take the tithe back. Don't think we all didn't notice."

"I, we, I mean..." Nasifa stammered.

"Your father is known to be loyal."

Nasifa gripped Zaytuna's hand.

"We don't broadcast our business. Your mother would never have let you come to meet me if she knew we had turned against the Imam." Maha sniggered.

"When, Maha?"

But Maha ignored the question, turning to speak to another woman who had tapped on her shoulder.

The call to prayer sounded through the city, and Zaytuna made to stand. Nasifa tugged her down, hard. Only then did Zaytuna notice that none of the other women were standing.

Nasifa whispered. "We perform the two evening prayers together."

"Because of the meeting? Like joining two prayers while traveling?"

Nasifa shook her head in disbelief, but took care no one heard her explain. "There are five prayers. But God enjoined us to pray only three times a day."

"God says that in the Qur'an, I know, but the Prophet, alayhi salam, prayed each of the five at different times, not gathering the five to pray in only three times."

"He did both. No one ever taught you this? It eases the burden on the believers." Nasifa said, with a touch of scolding superiority behind it.

My God, Zaytuna thought, *are these people even Muslim?* She vowed to ask Mustafa about it next time she saw him and hoped that Kamal Ali did not pray this way. If he did, he would hear from that sharp-tongued woman he wanted so much if they were to be married. He would never do it again!

Nasifa pointed toward the screen. "They're coming!"

The women turned their attention to the screen as a door opened behind it. The light of an oil lamp they carried revealed the distorted silhouettes of two men appeared on the screen.

One man coughed, then a voice boomed out from behind the

screen, "Assalamu alaykum! Oh, sisters and daughters of Karbala! May God grant you all a rich reward. The day of fighting the armies of the caliph has arrived."

Nasifa put her hand over her heart and sighed with the women in the room. Zaytuna did not understand.

"He is quoting from our master Husayn's speech before Karbala."

"I have brought before you today the man who exposed the corruption of the agents! The man who returned your tithe to you!"

One woman called out, "Takbir!" And others joined her in the call.

The second man spoke haltingly at first, trying to find his voice. It was low and powerful, as if he were speaking from deep within his chest. He said with an emotional power that even moved Zaytuna. "Our Day of Ashura is coming! Our plain of Karbala is here!"

Zaytuna looked around her and moaned along with the women, "Ya Husayn!" Within, she prayed, *God help me find this person who has betrayed these good people and put us all at risk. Help me listen. Help me read the signs.*

"The time of the Imams appeasing the false caliphs from within their hiding places has passed. Now we stand. The Mahdi is coming!"

The women gasped, and Nasifa shook her head with concern.

"Have we not suffered enough under these caliphs? The caliph and their courtiers taking everything from us in taxes we cannot pay and giving nothing in return. They vie with each other in building tall houses along the Tigris to shame us as we cross the bridge with our bundles on our heads, our burdens on our backs."

"I carry too much, brother!" one woman cried.

"They laugh at us from their balconies!" another called out.

"Yet," he said sorrowfully, but with a note of resentment behind it, "our Imam is content to remain in hiding while we suffer!"

It made sense they would resent the Imam for not showing himself if they needed him. But there was something else behind his tone. She remembered the old woman's words at the cemetery, "...A man denied recognition and control." *There's something there*, she told herself. *Listen!*

A woman in a black wrap pulled around to cover her face objected. "The caliph would kill him if he showed himself!"

"How do we know that?" another woman asked, but kept her head down, not wanting to draw attention to herself.

"He has knowledge of the unseen! He knows. That is enough for us!" The woman let her wrap fall away and looked the other up and down. "You, whoever you are, do not!"

"Sisters! Sisters!" The first man called out.

The second man gestured for the first man to be quiet and turned toward them. "If he had knowledge of the unseen, how did he not foretell that we would rob his agent and warn him to escape?"

"He intended for the agent to be robbed," she shot back, but there was uncertainty in her voice. Her voice rose again, "He is our Moses, hidden so that he would be safe to lead us to justice from under the thumb of Pharaoh when the moment comes!"

The man behind the screen asked, "And when will he decide that moment has come? When you are dead and buried from hunger and loss? Why is your Moses not here to lead you?"

An old woman stood, her back curved with age, and held onto the back wall of the courtyard to steady herself. She said with every bit of strength she had, "Unseen to us, he will always guide us! He will live until the end of all our days. Then, he will return to us as the Mahdi!"

Maha yelled, "Stop your bleating, you old goat!"

Other women joined in, cursing her.

The man who introduced the speaker tried to calm the room.

Zaytuna whispered in Nasifa's ear. "Live to the end of all our days?"

She leaned in. "I don't know what the scholars say, but I've heard some women say he will be long-lived."

"Long-lived?" Zaytuna could not hide the skepticism in her voice. "You believe he doesn't die like the rest of us?"

Nasifa snorted in offence, before cupping her hand over Zaytuna's ear to whisper sharply, "Of course he dies like the rest of us. Just like us, when his time comes. God decides his time as God decides our time. Don't you believe in Khidr, who drank from the well of life and will not die until this world ends? Don't you listen to stories of the man who guided Moses!"

An objection lit onto her tongue, but she held it back. Nasifa was right. It nagged at her until she saw her criticism was not about them at all, but about her worry over marrying a man who worshipped like them. She would have to sit down with Kamal Ali and discuss it before she signed any marriage contract. In fact, she vowed to put in her contract that he could do as he liked, but he would never have a say over her own practice. But to take those fears out on these people? Then her guilt brought her around to Qambar. He prayed with them at home five times a day. Their way and not his own. It broke her heart that this old man she and Saliha loved so still felt he had to hide his practice from them. She took Nasifa's hand in a gesture of apology. "I was wrong."

Mollified, Nasifa said more kindly, "Another woman told me to ignore it. I should ask at the mosque, see what our imam says."

A hush came over the crowd. The speaker recited the verse in a mesmerizing cadence. "*We wanted to confer favour upon those who were oppressed in the land and make them leaders and make them inheritors.*" He took a deep breath. "The time of the Mahdi is upon us and if Muhammad ibn al-Hasan will not stand forward and will not lead, he has forfeited the right to be called 'Imam'."

Still standing, the old woman said, "I will not listen to another word of this!" A younger woman got up, held her elbow and whispered to her. But the old woman shook her head and began stepping over those seated, treading on them even as they leaned back to make space for her. But not one of them cursed her for it. Instead, hands rose to support her and a child got up to guide her out.

Nasifa leaned into Zaytuna. "I would leave, too, if we were not here for good reason. God protect us from evil things!"

The speaker taunted the old woman as she walked out. "Why has your Imam not come out of hiding to guide you? Why has your Imam left you in this state of confusion?"

"I am not confused. Look at yourself when you use that word," she said, and disappeared into the passageway.

The speaker tried to take back the room. "Abu Said Jannabi in Bahrain. You know his name! He has established a state in the Mahdi's name on the principles of justice the Mahdi will bring."

Maha leaned over, gleeful. "The Qarmatis have come to free us!"

"Did you know about this?" Nasifa asked Maha.

"I hoped, girl. I hoped. You should hope too. He's built a just world."

One woman called out, "It's about time! How long before we all have full bellies and no man owns more than another man? All of us equals before God. Tell us that the Mahdi has come!"

"Abu Said holds the ground for him," the speaker said. "He will come any day. And you must be ready to fight for it. If they are to take Baghdad and relieve Buratha from the hold of this false Imam, you must be the daughters of Karbala."

Three women stood in a group and pledged themselves. "We will fight and we will die! We will goad our men! Kufa, Baghdad, Buratha! All the cities will belong to the Mahdi!"

The girl who had helped the old woman leave spoke. Her voice was thin and high like Layla's, but she challenged him with every bit of herself. "You ask us to die for Abu Said as if he were our beloved Imam Husayn, God bless him and peace. But Abu Said does not carry a drop of blood or guidance from our beloved Prophet!"

One of the three women who had pledged themselves tried to reach the girl, her hands grasping for her, but a sea of arms moving in a wave prevented the woman from reaching the girl. The speaker had wrongly bet that he could move the women of Buratha to abandon their Imam.

Nasifa gasped. "A young Lady Zaynab! What courage!"

The girl shook in her wrap and an elder woman reached up and placed a hand on her back, saying, "Little Nasrin! You speak for us all!"

"Who are you?" The girl demanded. "What authority do you have! Come out from behind that screen and face us!"

The man's voice cracked. "I know! I know what you do not!"

Zaytuna heard something, and it pricked at her. There was resentment in his voice, certainly, but more. She took a breath, trying to settle into herself, to truly listen.

He bellowed, losing control. "I will put all things right!"

Petty confidence in his own knowledge of what was right. Resentment that people would not listen. Desire to control others. All distortions of God's characteristics of knowledge, vengeance, and domination leading to terrible ends. She remembered a similar feeling of danger the day they had lunch with Ammar's family. Walla, it was Aqil ibn Akib. The speaker's voice was unfamiliar, deeper, and emotionally moving. But it had to be him.

Tein and Ammar said Aqil had robbed the agent, along with Utbah and Bishr's men, out of greed. Greed was one thing. But this? Urging these women to abandon the Twelfth Imam and fight in the streets was another. The ghilman would not hold back because they were women. The soldiers would attack, and Buratha's men would come out to defend the women. It would be slaughter. Was he no longer loyal to his own Imam? Did he abandon the Imam out of resentment when his teachers censured him?

None of that mattered. It was Aqil and he could lead them to Utbah!

Other women had come to their feet to stand alongside the girl demanding that the man show himself. Maha, too, had gotten up, but she was moving to join the three women who had gained other allies. All the women were screaming, each word drowned out by the others.

The scholar and the other man were gesturing and yelling behind the screen. Zaytuna stood, grabbing Nasifa by the arm. "We must get Ammar and Tein. The speaker! It's Aqil ibn Akib!"

Nasifa pushed Zaytuna toward the door. The two slowly made their way through the crowd, some of whom were also trying to leave. There were several older women ahead of her in the passageway, and Zaytuna could not get past. She became angry in her fear they would be too late, and tried to remember God's will having put her behind the women, but could not bring herself around to it. Instead, she shuffled forward in frustration until she was out in the courtyard and she burst off in a run toward the tavern.

"Tein!"

But he had already seen her coming. The two stood up from their drunken act and met her halfway, Ammar's hand already on his sword.

"Aqil ibn Akib, he's inside! He's trying to get the women to fight in the streets. He's saying he's Qarmati!"

Tein started for the passageway, but Zaytuna yelled after him. "Stop! There's another door! He came in that way. He'll leave that way."

"Zaytuna." Ammar took her by the arm. "Where's Nasifa?"

She turned around, searching for her. "She was right behind me. I'll go back in and get her. Go find that door!"

Ammar ran back to the tavern owner, demanding to know the location of the other entrance.

As Zaytuna got to the passageway, a crush of women came at her, forcing her out. She yelled at the women pushing her back, "What's happening!"

"The women tore down the screen and attacked the men!"

Out in the street, she stood to the side, hoping to see Nasifa coming through. If Aqil came this way, at least she could stop him. If the women did not kill him first.

There were screams behind her, and she turned around. A troop of ghilman marched into the square, their swords drawn and staffs ready. Men in the tavern, too drunk to move, stumbled against the wall. The green grocer frantically pulled the baskets holding his vegetables out of the square through a door behind him. But the old woman selling dung and bone stood up and walked towards them. Sturdy like Yulduz, her wrap had fallen from her head, and long grey braids fell down her back from under her kerchief. Her hand was up as she walked toward them, demanding they stop. The tavern owner met her, his hands out, too, demanding calm.

She turned away from them to the door. Women were still

streaming out, and seeing the ghilman, scattered in all directions. Zaytuna stood helplessly by, waiting for Nasifa, who never came.

30

Ammar tapped Tein on the back and pointed toward the green grocer. A young man slipped out his shop door just as the grocer pulled the last of his baskets inside and shut the door behind him. The man ran for his life out of the courtyard before either of them could follow.

"It's not Aqil, forget him!" They rushed to the door. Ammar pounded on it. "Baghdad Police! Open up!"

Instead of opening, they heard the sounds of something heavy being pushed against it to block it.

"We're going to have to kick it in." Ammar leaned into the door, trying to push it open.

"Baghdad Police!" Tein yelled. "We're coming through!" Feeling no pain in the heat of the moment, he waved to Ammar to stand aside and gave the door a hard kick, landing his heel against it. One more and the door came partially open, allowing Ammar to wedge in an arm.

The grocer pushed back hard from the other side back, pinning Ammar.

He grunted. "Kick harder!"

Tein kicked again and again. Each time allowed Ammar to wedge himself in further. He reached around behind the door, trying to grasp at the grocer and missing. Tein kicked again. Ammar's fingers touched the grocer's robe. "One more kick on three!"

"One, two, three!" Tein kicked again and Ammar was nearly through. He got a firm hold on the grocer's arm and jerked it down. "Again!" Tein kicked again and this time it was enough. Ammar pushed the door open wide enough to get past.

Once into the dark room, Ammar grabbed the grocer and threw him against the wall, then barrelled forward, tripping over the full baskets, heading for the lamplight coming through the door at the far end. Tein was right behind him.

He came out into the courtyard. The women were in a pile, fighting. Their hair was loose and flying, the women on top pounded on the women beneath. Those under them fought back, trying to get out. He did not see Nasifa and prayed she had escaped and was with Zaytuna.

"Stop!" Tein roared, but nothing would stop them.

They dug into the pile, grabbing the women one by one by the back of their qamises, dragging them aside. One of them returned and jumped on Tein's back. He staggered and tried to shake her off.

Ammar dug back in as several women gave up and rolled out of the pile, revealing Aqil ibn Akib's face smashed against the ground. He was close to being smothered under the women's weight. "Aqil's here!" Taking hold of another woman's arm, Ammar pulled her back harshly to get at him. She fell behind him and scurried back against the wall in fear.

With the woman finally off of him, Tein grabbed hold of another when Zaytuna came running in. She pounced, pulled back one woman and screamed, "Nasifa! The purple qamis!"

"I see her!" Ammar called out. She was underneath the last of the women, on top of Aqil. There was nothing but loose hair and purple cloth. She was not moving. Tein and Zaytuna pulled the woman off of Nasifa while Ammar grasped her, first by one arm and then the other, and lifted her out to him.

Tein took hold of Aqil, dragging him to his feet. The scholar hung against Tein, looking shocked and gasping for breath. He was bleeding from scratches to his face, his robe torn and filthy, his turban and skull cap long gone.

Carrying Nasifa free of the melee of bodies, Ammar sat back hard on the ground, holding her in his arms. He touched her face with the back of his fingers, and her eyes fluttered open. "Thank God, you're alive."

Zaytuna and another woman came and kneeled beside them, checking her legs and arms for breaks. The woman said in low tones, "This one was brave. She was the first to run at him when he tried to escape, knocked him over and sat on him to hold him down. He's a big man. It took all of us lying on him to keep him there." She glanced at the women who had fought the others. "But they tried to save him and we all got to fighting."

"You were all brave," Zaytuna replied.

Ammar whispered to Nasifa, "My love."

Her colour returned with his words. "Ammar," she whispered.

"I have you."

"Aqil?" Her eyes were soft and wet with tears.

"Yes. You caught him."

"Alhamdulillah." She closed her eyes again, turning her face towards his chest and settling in against him. He should have looked away, but did not. The deep opening at the neck of her qamis, which should have been covered by her wrap, revealed soft skin underneath. Her auburn hair spilled out in abundant waves, gleaming in the lamplight. Ammar wanted to pull her hair to his face and drink in her scent. He begged Zaytuna, "Help me."

She understood and took Nasifa into her own arms. But once there, Nasifa came awake, saying this time in a stronger voice, "I can sit."

"Is that safe?" Ammar asked Zaytuna, desperate.

Zaytuna gave him a wry smile. "She's perfectly fine."

The other woman chuckled. "I'll find her wrap."

Ammar got up to find Tein staring at him impatiently, Aqil's huge body locked in his arms. He knew that face. Tein was in pain. Coming back to himself, he stepped around the women, offering to take hold of Aqil. But Tein shook his head, grunting. "I have him. Get some rope from the grocer."

The shock worn off, Aqil torqued his body and turned into dead weight in Tein's arms, trying to break his hold.

Pain shooting across his face, Tein jerked Aqil up, and said in his ear, "I can hold you all night if I have to, so don't bother."

Running back into the grocer's room, Ammar found the man righting his goods in the light of the open door. He stood in a shot.

"Rope!" Ammar demanded.

The grocer rooted around behind him and came up with a length and threw it to him, then retreated to a corner of the room in darkness.

Tein was still holding Aqil. Ammar bound his hands, leaving a lead. Once Ammar had the lead wrapped around his forearm and in his hand, Tein let go and staggered back, breathing and coughing into the pain.

"It's over." Ammar said. "Take us to Utbah ibn Harb."

Aqil did not reply, but sank backwards, dropping his weight to topple Ammar, grab the rope, and run. But Tein was behind him and planted a hard knee into his back, letting him know it would not work.

Ammar got in his face, saying through gritted teeth, "Don't be stupid. If you haven't killed Utbah, you're guilty of nothing but the robbery. It seems like the agents won't report it, so you'll be free to go back to your money and your family."

It only took a moment for Aqil to understand the chance they offered him, and he righted himself. "What guarantee do I have?"

Ammar sorely wanted to punch him, but held back. "Do you think the agents want this before the Police Chief's court or, worse, the High Court? They don't want it exposed. They want it covered up."

His shoulders dropped in defeat. "I thought they had made it public."

Does he want the robbery reported? Ammar gave Tein a questioning glance. He shook his head in reply.

Finally, Aqil said, "I need more than that."

"There is no more and there is no way out."

"You're going to have to leave Buratha and Baghdad after this," Tein said. "It's over for you here. But at least you can go with your life."

"Take us to Utbah and we'll let you go with your family tonight."

Aqil's whole body acquiesced, no longer exploring any angle to escape.

"Good," Ammar said, "Let's go."

With Ammar at the rope, Tein pushed Aqil along from behind. Ammar glanced back at Nasifa, hoping to catch her eye, but she was standing with Zaytuna, her back to him in the near empty courtyard, adjusting a wrap over her body.

Zaytuna noticed them and left Nasifa's side. "What do you need, Ammar?"

"Take her home." But Nasifa had turned and rushed to him. Careful not to touch him, she stood too close all the same. Her wrap covered her now, veiling what he had wrongly seen, and he lowered his eyes when he had not before.

"Uff," Tein said, exasperated at the pause while Zaytuna stepped aside.

Ammar silently begged Nasifa to say something, anything. Instead, she touched his chin so that he would have to look at her. Her gaze said everything he hoped. Consumed, he wanted to hold her, instead of this man on a rope, and have it done with. There was no going back. He said, thick with emotion, "Marry me."

"Yes." She breathed the word, and lowered her face, pulling her wrap across her blushing cheeks.

Aqil pulled sharply at the rope and put all his weight into it. But Tein had hold of him and said to his prisoner, "He's distracted. Not me."

They all turned around as Nasifa's father rushed into the

courtyard, calling her name. She broke away from Ammar and ran to him.

"Maha came to get me." He reached her and held his daughter by the shoulders, looking her up and down. "Are you hurt?"

"No, Father, alhamdulillah. Zaytuna took care of me." She turned back to Ammar for a moment. "Ammar was there. He protected us."

Her father held her close, and she leaned into him just as he saw Aqil bound in ropes. Jerking forward, he yelled, "You!"

"Father, take me home." Nasifa pleaded. "I'm so tired."

He agreed unwillingly as he stared at Aqil, his mouth parting, ready to curse him. Instead, he nodded his thanks to Ammar and led her away.

Tein pressed. "Let's go!"

Aqil walked behind Ammar with Tein at his back. Once out in the streets, they pushed him forward, and he reluctantly led them through the streets toward his home.

"Her father has her. I'm coming with you!" Zaytuna yelled after them. Once caught up with them, she positioned herself next to Aqil. "I heard you in there. Why on earth would you side with the Qarmatis?"

"He what?" Tein said behind her.

"This Imami scholar was urging the women to fight in the streets. Saying the Qarmatis were coming to liberate them." She returned her attention to Aqil. "Why would you betray your own Imam?"

"Betray him?" His voice boomed through the empty street. "I am the only one who is loyal to him! You have no idea what you've done. You think you have solved a crime, but all you have done is destroy the only chance we had of forcing the Imam into the streets to lead the people."

Ammar and Zaytuna looked at each other in shock and understanding.

"You weren't siding with the Qarmatis at all."

"Bishr's friend, Yaqub, told us you thought you were using them," Ammar said. "You intended the robbery to force the Imam out of hiding. When that didn't work, you tried to incite the people to riot. You thought he would come out to protect them."

"Thanks to you, we are lost!" Aqil replied, furious. "The Imamis will never survive now. They had only me. Now they have nothing. Mark my word! And it is all on your heads."

"On your head," Tein called out from behind them. "If they do not survive this, it will be on your head."

"And it will be on the faith of the people, like those women, if the Imamis thrive," Zaytuna said.

Ammar pulled back in shock, examining Aqil and sickeningly seeing himself in him. Aqil's certainty that he knew best. That he was necessary for justice. It was all on him. How was he any different from this self-obsessed man? Believing that there would be no justice for the victims without him solving the crimes? Worse, he justified staying on this job by comparing himself to the Imams, imagining they worked with the caliphate to save their communities in the same way he worked for the police. "My God," he gasped aloud and chose then and there to quit.

Zaytuna was eyeing him. He wanted to tell her everything, but most of all he wanted to have her hand on his back and breathe the name "Allah" in his ear, like she did that day, and help him return to himself, his honour, and his faith.

"And Utbah?" Tein asked Aqil, bringing Ammar around from his thoughts. "What is his role?"

Aqil spat on the ground before him. "He killed Bishr. Bishr was going to reveal that we had robbed the agents."

They all looked at each other. It was something he and Tein had not even considered, thinking it was all about the girl.

Tein followed up. "Why would he do that?"

"You mean Bishr? He had a dream about the Twelfth Imam." Aqil scoffed. "Absurd."

Ammar pulled him to a stop. "Dream?" Zaytuna stared, transfixed, while Tein drew in closer.

"The Twelfth Imam was carrying Abbas in his arms with Lady Fatima beside him and told Bishr never to doubt his existence. The fool took this as evidence that the man existed rather than understanding it was only his guilty conscience taking shape in a dream. Utbah tried to explain that to him, but he could not be dissuaded. So Utbah killed him."

"It *was* the Twelfth Imam in your dream!" Ammar said to Zaytuna, his voice cracking with emotion.

But Zaytuna shook her head, her eyes wide in shock at the two dreams. "In his, not in mine."

He wanted to argue with her. How could she say that when it was obvious they were the same? But Aqil stopped and gestured with his bound hands to a padlocked wood door. Unpainted.

"Here," Aqil said.

The house was just before the Ushnan Bridge. Ammar was angry. They had passed it on their way into Karkh to search for Aqil in Dar as-Silsila. He had not gone into Baghdad to live with the scholars as they suspected. Tein came alongside, looking as angry as he felt.

"No blue door," Tein said.

"With all this going on?" Aqil replied. "There was no time."

"Is your family in there?" Ammar asked.

"No, they've gone. Only Utbah."

"Where's the key to the padlock?" Tein asked.

"In my sleeve pocket." He held his arm out as best he could so Ammar could search it, but the expression on Aqil's face told him it was not there.

"Where is it?"

He shrugged. "I must have lost it in the fight."

Tein said to Ammar, "It's your turn to kick in a door."

"Is this it?" Zaytuna held up a key. "It did get lost in the fight. But I found it."

Aqil thrust his body toward her, snarling. Ammar jerked him back hard.

"Good work, sister." Tein waved her forward.

Zaytuna inserted the key and the padlock fell open, then she stepped aside to let Tein go in. The door creaked open. Ammar followed Tein, pushing Aqil ahead of him, while Zaytuna followed behind.

Utbah sat flat against the courtyard wall, legs pulled in, one hand over his face to protect him from whatever was coming. His other hand lay across his chest, attached to a short chain on an iron stake hammered into the wall. The whole place stank of shit. There was a pile of rags covering a lump and a dried-up, filthy water stain leading away from him.

"What have you done!" Aqil yelled. "Are you incapable of cleaning yourself properly?"

Zaytuna checked each of the rooms. "No one else is here."

Tein approached Utbah.

"Don't hurt me!" He held his arms up again.

Not giving him any assurances, Tein shook the chain on Utbah's arm, and asked Aqil, "I suppose you've lost the key to this manacle, too?"

"Yes. It appears I have."

Tein gave Zaytuna a hopeful look.

Zaytuna said, "I only found the one key."

Ammar untied the rope around Aqil's hands, releasing him. Aqil inspected his abraded, bloody wrists. "Now scholar, you are free, clean up that shit, then get ready to run."

Utbah lowered his arm. "Run? You cannot allow it! He killed Bishr!"

Tein ignored Utbah, saying to Aqil, "Do you have a sledgehammer?"

"Why would I have such a thing?"

Zaytuna went to check the rooms for one, saying over her shoulder, "How did that stake get in the wall if you don't have one?"

"I got it from the neighbour," he said as he hurried into the latrine. Coming out with a scraper and a bucket, he kneeled to clean up the mess. Utbah lunged at him from where he was seated, but Aqil was just out of reach. "Ho!" Aqil said to him. "Watch yourself. These men are here for you, not me."

Tein pushed Utbah back against the wall with his foot. "I need something to break him free."

Ammar was about to go bang on some doors when Utbah said, "Try pulling on it. It is loose, I have been working on it all day."

Tein squatted beside him and pushed the stake from side to side with one hand.

"Can you get it?" Ammar asked.

"Yes, he would have got loose soon."

Pulling back and forth on the stake, Tein asked Utbah casually, "What's this about him killing Bishr?"

"He wanted Aisha for himself!"

"With your bow and arrow?"

Ammar said, "Aqil claims you killed Bishr because he was going to expose the robbery and your plan. Worse, he'd tell everyone he dreamt of the Twelfth Imam."

Voice cracking, Utbah said, "It's not true."

Aqil stood and carried the bucket and scraper back to the latrine and returned, drying his hands on a clean rag, to lean against the wall. "Amru and the rest have come forward. There is a witness to the murder."

Tein kept working at the stake, but Ammar saw his back tense. There were no witnesses, no men coming forward. He wondered if Tein would let on.

Utbah sat up, terrified at the mention of a witness, but still defiant. "Who saw you kill him!"

Walking into another room, Aqil said, "Aisha never left. She found her family and went to the police." He came back out, holding a bag of coins, and shook them for effect. "She was with Bishr the day you met him at Imam Musa al-Kazim's tomb and witnessed everything."

Utbah's chest heaved. His face turned red.

Tein was working on the stake, not seeing the change in him.

"Watch out!" Zaytuna yelled.

Ammar warned, lunged for Utbah.

Tein let go of the stake and turned.

But Utbah was already on his feet, howling like an animal, falling forward as much as thrusting himself wildly towards Aqil. The spike came free and was yanked out of Tein's hands. Utbah found his footing and was across the courtyard and on Aqil before they could stop him.

Before Aqil could drop the bag of coins, Utbah rammed him against the wall. He had the spike in both hands, pushing its length against Aqil's throat. They heard the sickening crunch. Ammar and Tein pulled Utbah back and Aqil slid to the ground, his head to one side, eyes wild, mouth gaping, the bag of coins beside his twitching hand.

Zaytuna screamed, "Allah!"

Tein threw Utbah to the ground, turning him on his side as he squirmed and pinned him fast.

Aqil was still twitching, his fingers grasping wildly. Ammar took his hand, drawing close, and recited softly, over and over, "There is no god but God, and Muhammad is the messenger of God, and Ali is the guardian of God," until Aqil's body quieted and the life was out of his eyes.

"Baghdad Police! Back up!" Neighbours clustered around the still open door. Ammar rose and walked toward them, his face wild with pain and fury, and they scattered. There were no sounds after that, but doors shutting in the empty street and Utbah moaning.

They bound him with the same rope they had used to tether Aqil. Ammar helped him stand while Tein held onto him, making sure he would not run, then draped the chain over his shoulders and handed him the spike to carry. Utbah looked between them, with frantic eyes and spittle running into his beard.

Zaytuna handed the bag of coins to Ammar.

"That probably belongs to the Imam," Tein said.

Without thinking, Ammar asked, "Do we know that for a fact? Maybe this money is from some other source?"

"Utbah's uncle," Tein said, understanding him. "You going to find out where Aqil's family is and get it to them?"

"Yes. But the house probably belongs to the Twelfth Imam. He had to have bought it with the tithe." Ammar said, "I'll tell the imam of the mosque what we think. He can bring the question of the inheritance before the religious court. Maybe get the money back to its rightful place."

Tein explained to Utbah as they walked him to the door, "We're going to take you to a cell in the walls of the Round City. Tomorrow they'll pull you out of that cell and smear you with shit and parade you on the back of a donkey through Karkh and Buratha. Then, they'll execute you publicly for killing Bishr." He glanced back toward Aqil. "Not him. They'll be glad you got rid of him."

"Will you admit to it now?" Ammar asked. "There's no escape."

Moaning, Utbah leaned against them for support. "My hand shot the arrows. But God directed them. The cuts on his arms. How could it be anything other than God's will?" Once in the quiet of the darkened street, he said to Ammar, "God will ruin you all."

Tein and Ammar ignored him, but Zaytuna said, "Another man who thinks he is the hand of God." Then she asked, "What about Aqil's body?"

"We'll keep an eye out for a watchman and ask him to stay with Aqil until a cart can come and get him," Tein answered. "Don't even think of staying there alone."

She held up her hands, acquiescing. Only then did he notice how exhausted she was. They had to get her home.

The four trudged in silence through the moonlit streets towards the Ushnan Bridge, never seeing a watchman. Strangely, there were no ghilman either, as if the order had already come down that the trouble had passed. But Ammar knew it had not. The caliph would have to be satisfied first. And he prayed that Utbah's humiliation would be enough.

Once over the bridge and in Baghdad, they found a donkey cart with the driver asleep in the back, his donkey tethered but asleep beside the cart. Tein woke him. The man got up slowly, but agreed to the ride.

A watchman approached with his torch. Tein said, "I got this," and crossed over to him and said something, pointing to Zaytuna, then the direction of Buratha.

Tein returned. "Zaytuna, he'll walk you home."

She agreed, clearly exhausted and grateful for the watchman. There was no safety in these streets for a woman at night.

"Wait," Ammar said, holding her back. "Tein, can you admit now that Zaytuna's dream was right? That she knew everything. The murder, the political risk, the Twelfth Imam, that the robbery involved people associated with a butter dealer."

Tein held back for a moment, then turned to her. "If you hadn't recognized Aqil's voice, we wouldn't have found Utbah tonight."

Expecting her to snap at him, it surprised him to see her sincerely accept his thanks, saying only, "Alhamdulillah," before leaving with the guard.

The driver pointed at Utbah. "This one goes in the back?"

Ammar nodded and pushed Utbah up into the cart.

Without acknowledging what he had said about Zaytuna's dream, Tein said, "After taking her home, he'll go to the house and watch over the body until the cart comes for him." Tein pushed himself up, wincing in pain, and sat beside Utbah, one hand on him in case he got any ideas.

Ammar took his place beside the cart while the driver harnessed the donkey and they left for the long ride along the Basra High Road to the Round City. With each step, Ammar considered what he would do next. He had committed himself to Nasifa and accepted that he had been betraying his conscience on this job all along. There was no turning back from what he knew was right. What came next, he did not know. But he would not be churning butter. No matter how much it paid. He was relieved when the torches burning outside the Gate House came into view, casting their shadows on the bridge and the guards standing before the closed gates.

Ammar called ahead. "Baghdad Police, we have a prisoner!"

One guard came down a few steps, seeing from his perch Utbah bound in the back of the cart. He waved for them to come. "You can't bring the cart in now. You'll have to walk through."

Ammar paid the driver as Tein got out of the cart. The two pulled Utbah out by his feet until he could sit, then jump down. They walked up the wide bridge to the Gate House, Utbah between them. The guards checked them again to make sure they were who they said. Then they pulled open one of the great gates, just enough for the three to pass through. The Gate House and the bridges spanning the outer and inner city walls were torch-lit, with guards standing at attention.

Utbah slacked now and again in their grasp, his knees weak or trying to stave off the inevitable. It did not matter. They dragged him along all the same. But when they reached Solomon's Gate, he stopped to gape at its grandeur and power in the torchlight. The designs cast into iron by the jinn danced menacingly with the light, and he shook with fear. Ammar too was awed, but by Prophet Solomon's power and wisdom. Although Ammar had decided to leave the police with Tein, the case and all they had done to solve it weighed on him.

Even though they had found the right man in the end, and, if they were lucky, saved the city from bloody chaos, they still served the caliph's ends. He thought then of the Twelfth Imam and wondered if that was why he had withdrawn from his community. But all Ammar knew for certain was that he did not have the wisdom of the Prophets or the Imams.

Past the gates, they turned through the same arch and down the same walkway they had that first day when they found the ghilman in the field below and feared what was to come.

Utbah struggled again. In a near cry, he begged them. "My uncle."

"Your uncle is not coming for you." Ammar said. "He wanted to turn you in to the Banu Furat. We only got to you first."

Utbah's knees gave out, and they had to drag him the rest of the way down. They let him fall at the bottom and let go of his arms. Ammar was certain he would not run. There was nowhere to run.

Tein held out a hand to him. "Stand and face the end like a man."

He stood, and took Tein's hand, asking sorrowfully, as if they were his friends and this might be their final parting, "Will you be there when they parade me and kill me in front of the people?"

Tein did not reply.

"We will." Ammar said. "We won't look away from what we've done."

They walked the last few steps to the iron-barred gate of the jails.

"We have a prisoner!" Ammar called in, but no one came.

Tein struck the bars with the iron spike to wake the guard.

"Enough. I'm here," he complained sleepily as he came around the corner, jamming his turban on his head. A large ring of keys jangled on his belt and he unhooked it to open the jail gate. Awake now, the guard stepped back and took Utbah in as they led him through. "Oh, this one is of money!" he cooed, then cocked his head. "Did he anger the caliph?"

"This is the man who called the ghilman into the streets," Tein replied.

He raised his eyebrows. "You got him! I tell you I was worried. I already sent my girls with their mother out of Baghdad." He chuckled. "If I'd known you were going to catch him, I wouldn't have wasted the money!" Taking hold of Utbah's arm, he asked, "No intake?"

"No," Ammar replied. "We'll get you the paperwork in the morning."

"All right, come you." He patted Utbah on the shoulder. "I'll put you in a cell by yourself. They're going to want you in good shape to kill you."

One last great moan echoed through the cells as Tein pulled the iron-barred gate shut behind them. They walked in silence until they were again on the Basra Road. Tein put a hand on Solomon's Gate, head down, saying nothing but expecting something.

"I'll send word to Ibn Marwan's home. Wake him up with this. But I'll tell him I'm quitting in the morning. I'll suggest those two good watchmen to replace him. Tariq ibn Yusup, and," he thought for a moment, then said, "Ahab ibn Ishaq."

Tein stood up, ready to leave.

"Meet me here in the morning?" Ammar asked. "We'll do the paperwork and then tell Ibn Marwan we quit together."

"You can tell him I quit."

"Don't you want to tell him to his face?" Ammar asked.

"Does he deserve my word?"

He was right. Ammar would tell Ibn Marwan for the both of them.

EPILOGUE

Ziri was in his usual place, holding open the door to Junayd's home as guests streamed in. Mustafa and YingYue's wedding feast was drawing far more than the usual companions on the path. There was a line of people waiting. Tein and Zaytuna, with Layla holding tight onto Zaytuna's hand, fell in behind the last person.

Tein touched his new river green and blue striped turban, bought along with all new clothes for the wedding. All gifts from Saliha who would go without a new wrap and other nice things for a while because of it. He did not want to take them, but Yulduz slapped him lightly on the face, scolding him not to be so proud. In truth, he was grateful for the new clothes. While no one here would have minded him coming to the wedding in the everyday clothes he wore while policing, he wanted to strip himself of the reminder and was glad she understood. He hurt in body and soul from the case and the horror of Utbah's public humiliation and execution that morning. At the same time, he felt as if a weight had been lifted that he would never carry again.

If only Saliha had come with them. Scrubbed clean from the baths, he let her dress him in the clothes she picked out for him. He stood in the matching river green sirwal and qamis, as she helped him into a knee-length green, blue, and red striped robe, and cinched it with his old leather belt. None of it was fine fabric, but he would not be happy in such things, anyway. "We'll get you boots next," she said. He pretended to take his moth-eaten brown wrap with him, but she pulled it away, laughing, shaking her head playfully, and sent him out without her.

"She's testing you," Zaytuna said along the way.

"I don't understand."

"Just be yourself. She'll learn you aren't trying to trick her into something that ends up being a regular marriage."

He did not say he wished for a semblance of it, with easy companionship by day and contracting temporary marriages at night.

"If you bring her to see the aunts and uncles, they'll treat her like your wife. She won't stand for that, not yet. Give her time."

Ziri put his hand over his heart as they passed him, following the other guests through the door. But Tein wondered how much time Saliha would need and, too, what would happen if she became pregnant. They were being careful, but careful was not a sure thing, and it gave him a secret hope that he would never share with her. But a day did not go by that he did not feel the weight of his infant son Husayn laying on his chest and mourn the loss of him. He wished for a child again, and for Saliha to be a mother.

"Tein, keep your eye out for Kamal Ali," Zaytuna said as they walked toward the courtyard.

Layla swung her hand, grinning.

"I am, sister." He pointed across the crowded main room. "Uncle Nuri's wife and son have come." They wove through the crowd, greeting long-lost companions and their families until they found their uncle's widow. Tein took her hand and kissed it, raising it to his forehead, then bowed with his hand over his heart to Uncle Nuri's son and his family.

They faced the courtyard. Young Jibril found them looking nervous. "Your guest is sitting by Mustafa. I thought it best."

As Jibril left to help others to their places, she gripped Tein's hand. "Why would Jibril do that? It's Mustafa's wedding day."

"Jibril doesn't know," Layla said.

"You're right," Tein replied. "He only meant to seat him with me and I'll be right next to Mustafa."

Most of the guests had not yet taken their places. A cluster of men sat around Mustafa on one side of the courtyard and women on the other. Stands were set out, waiting for the great trays of roast lamb, bread, and cucumber-yogurt salad to be placed on them. The oil lanterns were hanging and set into niches in the walls, but would not be lit until after dark, when the remembrance of God began. The centre of the courtyard was open, as always, for those who find themselves taken up by ecstasy to dance when the music and chanting began.

Kamal Ali was sitting on the far wall close to Mustafa, who was himself right beside Uncle Junayd and several other companions and guests. A lively conversation was underway and Kamal Ali seemed to be enjoying himself, but Mustafa looked stunned.

She whispered, "Look at Mustafa."

"It's natural to be overwhelmed on your wedding day." He bumped her with his good shoulder. "You'll know soon."

They stepped into the courtyard, and there was YingYue sitting among the women. She smiled demurely as they clucked and fussed over her in her embroidered red Turkmen headdress with chains of hammered silver hanging around her face like tiny braids. He appreciated her beauty and knew she was right for Mustafa. But Zaytuna was staring at YingYue, and her grip on his hand had gotten even tighter. Prying his fingers loose, he put his arm around her. "I'm here."

She leaned into him and took a deep breath. "God did not intend him for me." She pulled away. "But I can't lie. My heart is broken."

Gesturing across the courtyard where Kamal Ali sat, he assured her, "And someone is waiting to heal it."

Saliha had berated him this morning for encouraging the match, whispering that Zaytuna would be sorry later if she married only because she could not have Mustafa. "It's a terrible risk. She doesn't know what he'll be like in private," she said. "How could you let this happen?" Tein tried to push the thought away. Saliha's last marriage made her worry for every woman, but he met the man and saw how well he treated those in his charge. She did not know what it meant for him to have Zaytuna in the care of a man such as Kamal Ali. It all fell into place in a way he could never have arranged himself, and he was not going to fight it. But he would be nearby, all the same.

"Let's go see him," he said, pulling her along, "and give our congratulations to Mustafa."

Kamal Ali stood at their approach and placed his hand over his heart, offering Zaytuna a deep bow of his head and an even deeper bow to Layla, who giggled in return. Tein glanced at his sister, seeing her smile and her cheeks brighten as she drew the wrap he had given her across her face to hide it. Mustafa, though, seemed stricken at the sight of her shy pleasure and Tein was grateful he was not stuck in love with two different women and could only marry one.

They went to offer their greetings to their Uncle Junayd. On seeing them, the old shaykh stood, holding his arms out to Tein. But Tein stepped back, confused. The proper form was for them to kneel before him. He was not to stand in greeting to them. "Come, come." His uncle gestured with his hands. Although half of Tein's height and breadth, Junayd drew him into a tight embrace that sent a sharp pain through his back. Tein winced, but he did not show it when his uncle pushed him back to face him again. "My son, you have arrived."

"But Uncle," Tein smiled, "I told you last week I would be here for my brother's wedding feast."

"Nevertheless, it's been a long journey."

Zaytuna looked between the two of them, as confused as Tein.

Then, he realized his uncle's response was relief at the case being resolved and Baghdad returned to stability, for now.

They had the news only this morning that the caliph had fallen gravely ill. Changes in power rarely benefitted the people as the viziers and courtiers clamoured for influence to wield over those beneath them. But at least this time, it allowed the Banu Furat to have their way and pull the ghilman out of the streets. The soldiers were marching back to their barracks and would soon be out of Karkh and Buratha.

Early that morning, he and Ammar had walked behind Utbah as the guards paraded him through the streets to his execution. Walking so close, the shoes, shit, and garbage hit them as well and they did not flinch from it. They watched him hang and left him on the gibbet for all to see. He would not be taken down to be washed and buried until tomorrow, and they resolved they would be there for that procession, too.

The imam of the mosque had taken charge of Aqil's body. And Ammar returned to Buratha to leave Aqil's money in trust with the imam for Aqil's widow and children. After the execution, when Tein and Ammar went their separate ways, Ammar asked him if he wanted to know how Ibn Marwan had taken the news of their leaving. Tein shook his head. Truly, he did not want or need to hear it. He was free of it all.

"Baghdad is safe, Uncle Abu al-Qasim, and I've left policing for good."

"Your journey began before you were born," Junayd replied. "You were gifted peace in pre-eternity. God wills some to struggle step by step and others He takes to Him in one breath." He leaned in knowingly. "Whether or not they refuse it."

Tein had never understood most of what his uncle said. He learned long ago not to press for an explanation or the old man would say more to no clearer end. He only smiled at his uncle, saying, "It is a joyous day for my brother, Mustafa."

"Alhamdulillah," Junayd replied, and turned to Zaytuna, holding out his hands. She tried to kiss them, but he tugged them back. "We have heard the good news from your intended, Kamal Ali."

So Mustafa knew, Tein thought. So was not stricken at leaving behind the woman he had loved since childhood for another. It was simply that another man would have her instead of him. Maybe he had thought she would be alone for the rest of her life, and he would always have her that way. As much as he understood, he bridled at it, wanting to say to him, "Leave Zaytuna to be happy and go to your own beautiful, gentle woman."

Zaytuna replied, her eyes welling up and clutching at Tein. "Kamal Ali shouldn't have announced it. Not yet. We haven't agreed on the contract."

"Forgive him," Junayd said. "He is in love." He grasped her hand again, smiling and insistent that she understand. "Your Auntie Hakima has already patted his cheek and called him 'son'. You have our blessing."

Kamal Ali had sat back down, but was watching everything, most especially Zaytuna. She was trembling under Tein's arm. Their uncle was drying her tears with the edge of his wrap and saying, "These are tears it gives me joy to see. My daughter, may your marriage be blessed by God and his Prophet, God bless him and peace."

"And the dream, Uncle, I understand now." She paused and Tein held his breath, worried that she secretly saw herself as some sort of sanctified visionary. "I found out yesterday that the man who was killed had the same dream I had, but for him, it meant something else. And everyone who heard our dreams had their own interpretation and acted on those meanings. The dreams were about the crime and the crisis that followed, but, for me, it was exactly as you said. Everything in the dream, even news of the crime, directed me to let go of my old world and enter the new. Auntie Hakima explained that if I learn to read the signs of my impulses, my dreams, I'll read the signs correctly in the world and know better how to act. And I did." She looked at Tein and smiled. "That's how we caught the killer. Alhamdulillah."

Tein let out a breath of relief.

Junayd replied, "It is impossible to learn by simply accepting teaching without question. You must test it and taste the results for yourself. I'm glad to hear this."

Layla had her arm around Zaytuna's waist and leaned into her.

Junayd addressed her. "And you, little one, come here every day for school. Jibril teaches the children."

"But I have to help Auntie Zaytuna," she objected. There was no mistaking the hope in her voice.

"My daughter, Zaytuna, will make sure you are here. She had the benefit of it, so will you." He turned to scold Zaytuna lightly. "Make sure she has a good night's sleep, though. She seems like she's been up all night praying with you, poor thing."

"No, Uncle," Layla piped up, "Auntie came in late and told all of us everything that happened and how they solved the case."

"Oh?" Junayd said, encouraging her.

"It was bloody!" Her eyes were wide. Tein wondered at Zaytuna, sharing all details of that night in front of her.

Zaytuna cut her off. "No need to discuss that now." She leaned down. "I'll bring you here myself for classes, if I have to."

Layla jumped up and down, still holding onto Zaytuna's waist.

Junayd held out his hands in prayer, and the three of them followed as he said a prayer for her and Kamal Ali's happiness. Tein wanted to ask him for a prayer for him and Saliha, but added their names in his own heart, wondering at himself that he wanted a prayer at all. "Alhamdulillah," he said, as they took their leave, offering their greetings to all the men seated nearby, and then to Mustafa and Kamal Ali. Tein put his arm around Zaytuna, and she moved in close to him for support.

Before Zaytuna could offer her good wishes for their marriage, Mustafa cut her off, audibly choking on the words. "Kamal Ali has shared your good news, my sister. Please accept our prayers for your joy."

She stiffened, unable to speak, so Tein spoke for her. "We are all grateful for your good news and hers." But part of him wanted to haul Mustafa up for saying anything. This was unfair to Zaytuna and YingYue.

Then Mustafa wept. "Zaytuna, my sister."

Kamal Ali smiled, perhaps imagining he was only happy for her and overwhelmed by his own wedding day.

Tein's heart broke. He had been wrong. Only now he understood what it meant for Mustafa to lose her. It was not that another man would have her. It was that he had lost her for good. Letting go of Zaytuna, he crouched before his cousin and lifelong friend, a man as good as a brother, and pulled him into an awkward embrace, letting him weep a moment more. When Mustafa was quiet, Tein stood and put his arm around Zaytuna again, while Kamal Ali leaned in to comfort Mustafa, placing his hand on Mustafa's back.

He expected Zaytuna to weep, too, but her face was still and he could not read her expression.

She only said, "Layla warned me of this," and pulled the girl to her.

Before he could ask her what she meant, she turned away from Mustafa's tear-stained face to Kamal Ali, saying, "Alhamdulillah, you've come to meet my people." Then she leaned over and kissed Tein on the cheek. "You're a good man, my brother. Watch over them both tonight."

"I will," he said.

She left them for the other side of the courtyard to sit with the women.

Returning to the men, he smiled and said to Kamal Ali, "Move over a bit, so I can sit between my old brother and my new brother," and relieved Mustafa from having to be so close to the man who would love and care for the woman he could not marry himself.

COMING IN 2022

The Peace

When a reclusive scholar who is whispered to hold a controversial Qur'an manuscript goes missing, some scholars are only too happy to see him gone, while others are willing to fight to find the only remaining copy of Ibn Masud's infamous codex. The imam of the Sharqiyya Mosque asks Mustafa for help, pulling Tein, Ammar, and Zaytuna into a case that pits them against some of the most powerful men of the empire, including the viziers of the new boy caliph, al-Muqtadir, himself.

CHARACTERS

Arab Naming Conventions

Umm Marwa [Mother of Marwa] Fatima [Personal Name] bint Fahim
[Daughter of Fahim] al-Jarriri [Fahim, the Potter] al-Karkhi [From
Karkh]
1.Parent of Child Name: Abu (Father) or Umm (Mother) of Marwa
2.Personal Name: Fatima
3.Child of Father/Mother's Name (then often a list of ancestry, Parent
Child of Grandparents's Name, and so on): ibn (Son) or bint
(Daughter) of Fahim
4.Nickname or Profession Name: "al-Jarriri," The Potter.
5.Tribe Name or Neighbourhood/City/Region Name. "al-Karkhi,"
from Karkh
Characters are mainly referred to by their parental name or their
personal names in the book. The narrator uses short forms of
nicknames or profession names, Nuri rather than "an-Nuri," or "Ibn
Salah" instead of "Ibn as-Salah." Shortening is an English language
convention of Arab names, but Arabs do it, too, in some regional
dialects.

The pronunciation guide is an approximation for North American English speakers without strong regional accents.

Main Characters

Zaytuna [zay-TOON-ah]: Our heroine, Zaytuna, is a twenty-seven-year-old clothes washer of Nubian and Arab descent. She is the daughter of a female mystic, unnamed in the story, but known as al-Ashiqa al-Sawda, the Black Lover of God.

Tein [TEEN]: Zaytuna's twin, a former frontier fighter, a ghazi. He is an investigator alongside Ammar in the Baghdadi Police's Grave Crimes section.

Mustafa [MOOS-tah-fah]: Zaytuna and Tein's childhood friend, twenty-six years old, sometimes called a cousin or a brother to them. He is a Hanbali hadith scholar of Persian and Arab descent.

Saliha [SAH-lee-hah]: Zaytuna's best friend, neighbour and a corpse washer. She is a twenty-five-year-old Arab who comes from the countryside.

Ammar [ahm-MAAR]: Tein's old friend from his days as a ghazi, the principal investigator for the Grave Crimes Section, and Tein's boss.

Recurring Characters

Zaytuna and Tein's mother, known as *al-Ashiqa as-Sawda* [al-AH-shee-ka as-SOW-duh]: A Nubian woman who is overcome without warning by states of ecstasy in which her ego-self dissolves into the ocean of God's love. Her character is a composite of women from the early period, but most explicitly based on Shawana, a 1st H/7th CE mystic of African descent.

Junayd [joo-NAID]: This character is based on the famous historical Sufi of Baghdad, Abu al-Qasim al-Junayd ibn Muhammad ibn al-Junayd al-Khazzaz al-Qawariri. Junayd is seventy-two years old. He is called "Uncle Abu al-Qasim" in the book, al-Junayd in more formal form, or simply Junayd.

Nuri [NOOR-ee]: This character is also based on a famous historical

Sufi, Ahmad ibn Abu al-Husayn an-Nuri. Nuri is sixty-seven years old. He is a loving father-figure to Zaytuna, Tein, and Mustafa. He is called "Uncle Nuri" in the book, or simply Nuri.

Layla [LAY-luh]: Layla, a ten-year-old Arab servant girl, indentured by her parents at a young age.

Yulduz [YOOL-duhz] and Qambar [KAHM-baar]: Zaytuna and Saliha's neighbours. Yulduz is a bold Turkmen woman, wife to Qambar. Qambar is an Arab Shia who fell madly in love with Yulduz when they were young.

YingYue [ying-yway]: YingYue is an eighteen-year-old Chinese mystic prodigy from Taraz, a city on the edge of the Muslim empire in the East.

Ibn Marwan: Tein and Ammar's sergeant. Fiercely loyal to them, juggles the bureaucracy to keep them independent, except when pressure hits.

Ammar's family: His parents Umm and Abu Ammar, his brother Muhsin, his wife, Tahirah, and their two children (with one on the way). They live on the edge of Buratha on the Kufa Road side. With one exception, they are devout Imamis.

Marta: Marta is Yuduz's best friend. She is a widowed Syriac Christian who brings her children a bit of coin by selling cups of pre-soaked chickpeas, ready to cook, on the roadside, just outside the official vegetable marketplace.

Shahta [Shaah-TAH]: A corpse washer at the Barmakid Hospital and Saliha's boss.

Dr. Judah: We first meet Judah in *The Jealous*. He is a Christian doctor at the Barmakid hospital, attracted to Saliha and bitter once spurned.

Characters in This Book

Bishr [BISHr]: The victim. A Fatihi who helped organize and took part in the robbery of the tithe. A true believer acting for the sake of what he thinks is best for the Shia community at large.

Utbah ibn Harb [UHT-buh ibn harb]: The killer. An irreligious wealthy Sunni who comes from a long line of Shia haters. He is a tall and elegant Arab who enjoys the privilege of his wealth. His family names express reverence for Yazid.

Aqil ibn Akib [AH-keel ibn ah-KEEB]: A young Arab Imami scholar who is tied up in this whole mess. I cannot say more or spoil the fun. He grew up rough, was a wrestler and a brawler, and wishes for wealth and status.

Nasifa [nah-SI-fuh]: The young, poor Arab Imami who takes after Zaynab, Husayn's sister, who spoke truth to power before Yazid after the tragedy of Karbala.

Kamal Ali [kuh-MAL ah-LEE]: A butter dealer who employs Bishr, Amru, and Yacoub, the young men involved in the robbery of the tithe. He originally hails from the city of Fas (now in Morocco), but left as a boy for adventure, eventually finding his way to Buratha, a suburb city of Baghdad.

Ibn Furat: One of the Banu Furat (the brothers Furat) a high ranking Shia vizier in the caliphate.

Abdurrazzaq [ab-dur-raaz-ZAK]: The guard who works for Utbah's uncle.

GLOSSARY

Abbas ibn Ali: Husayn's half-brother who fought at **Karbala.** His story is told in detail in the first chapter of this novel. He remains an example of bravery and self-sacrifice to this day.

Agent: The agents of the Twelfth Imam carried messages back and forth to the Imam in hiding, as well as collecting and delivering the tithe. There was a historical robbery of the tithe from an agent, inspiring this story. See "A Note on History" for more details.

Abbasids: They overthrew much of the Umayyad caliphate in 750 CE. They descended from the Prophet's family line (although not connected to the **Imamate**) and rallied support to their cause on this basis. Although this is the caliphate of the famed Harun ar-Rashid and the so-called "Golden Period," of Islam in which scholarly, medical, and artistic pursuits flourished, they were constantly battling threats to their power from within the caliphate, some of which Ibn Marwan and Ammar list in chapter seven. Within one year of the setting of this novel, 908 CE, they begin losing significant regions within the caliphate to Shia challengers, including Baghdad in 945 CE. The Ismailis and the Buyids ushered in what is called the "Shia Century."

Adhan: The call to ritual prayer. See **Time.**

Agents: See "A Note on History"

Alhamdulillah: "Praise God."

Ali: The cousin and son-in-law of the Prophet Muhammad, husband of Fatima, and father to **Hasan, Husayn, and Zaynab.** He is known as the inheritor of the Prophet's knowledge of God for Sunnis, Shia, and Sufis. He is also famed for his extraordinary bravery and restraint. He refused to kill a man who spit on him in battle lest he harm the man out of petty anger. He is called "The Lion."

Allahu akbar: "God is great." This can be used in times of shock or distress to say, "God is greater than whatever is happening," in times of joy, "God is amazing," and affirming a statement, "You said it," to "Wow."

Assalamu alaykum, wa alaykum assalam: It means literally "peace to you" its reply is "and on you peace" but can basically mean "hi." Arab Muslims and non-Muslims alike use it.

Barbahari: The leader of an extremist Hanbali group who felt it was their job to police the morals of the people. They were disliked. Barbahari and his men would not terrorize Baghdad for ten years after the book is set, but they were useful bad guys for the novels, so here they are.

Bismillah: "In the name of God." Used to start any action.

Buratha: A suburb city of Baghdad, known for its large Shia population, south of Karkh in Baghdad.

Dinar: The largest denomination of money, averaging four grams of gold.

Duha: About twenty minutes after sunrise is completed. Casually, it can refer to the time following as well, broadly early to mid-morning. See **Time.**

Fals: The smallest denomination of money. These and other coins could be chinked, meaning hand-cut into pieces to make smaller denominations.

Fatima: The prophet's daughter, the wife of Ali, and the mother of Hasan and Husayn. Her representation in Shia literature is beautiful and diverse, spanning the naturalistic to the metaphysical. Here I call on her representation as a loving and protective mother.

Fatihi: A group of Shia who differ over the identity of the Twelfth Imam. See "A Note on History for details."

Ghazi: One who fought on the frontier of the empire's expansion. They are held in high respect, unlike the troops who fight internal, civil battles.

Habibi: Masculine form of "my love," or "my dear one." Feminine is "habibti."

Hanbali: Mustafa is a follower of the Hanbali school of law. He is not a legal scholar, but a scholar of hadith. He collects, memorizes, and transmits the reports about Muhammad. But hadith scholars were asked to give legal opinions in the early days.

Hadith: These are individual reports of what Muhammad said, did, accepted, and rejected. There are major compilations of hadith. These compilations may have several similar accounts of the same event or the same saying, or even contradictory accounts. The goal of very early Muslim Sunni scholars was to collect everything, not necessarily to resolve differences.

Husayn: The grandson of the Prophet. See **Karbala**.

Imam: An uppercase "I" refers to the Shia Imams or leaders of their communities. A lowercase "i" refers to the leader of the prayer or the leader of a mosque. The term simply means leader. When used as a title in dialogue, in either case, it is capitalized.

Imamate: The notion that leaders of the Muslim community should be descended from the Prophet's family and marked by a particular intellectual and/or spiritual charisma passed down from the Prophet Muhammad.

Imami: The name for Twelver Shia at the time the novel is set. See "A Note on History" for more details.

Inshallah: "If God wills." It is used to mean "Yes," "No," and "Maybe," and "if God wills," also as a statement of humility in response to praise.

Ismailis: See "A Note on History"

Karbala: After the third caliph, Uthman, was murdered and Ali was ultimately offered the position of caliph, several prominent companions of the Prophet, led by his wife Aisha, challenged Ali's

authority. This challenge ended on the battlefield with Ali soundly
defeating them. Nevertheless, his authority continued to be
contested. After Ali's death, his son Hasan negotiated away his right
to lead, and the caliphate came into the hands of the Umayyads
under the leadership of Muawiyya. After Muawiyya's death, Ali's
other son, Husayn, was encouraged by the people of Kufa to lead a
rebellion against the hereditary designation of Muawiyya's son Yazid
as caliph. Husayn answered the call, but before he could reach Kufa,
he was met on the plain of Karbala by Umayyad forces. The people of
Kufa, under threat from the Umayyads, failed to support Husayn in
battle. Others argue that no rebellion was planned, and the tensions
arose from Husayn's refusal to submit to Yazid at his behest.
Whatever case, Husayn's party, which included many members of the
Prophet's family, were brutally killed, including women and children,
while survivors were marched away and taken into custody. The loss
of the Prophet's family, the loss of the leadership of his family, and
the sorrow of the people of Kufa haunt the Shia religious
imagination, as we see Ammar often experiencing.

Karkh: A large region in Baghdad located to the south of the Round
City, west of the Tigris, and north of Buratha. It was the home of
wealthy merchants, caliphal administrators, and scholars, Shia and
Sunni alike, as well as populations of poor to impoverished
Baghdadis. Tutha is a neighbourhood where Junayd's house is and
most of the Baghdadi Sufis lived, it is not far from the Shuniziyya
cemetery.

Mahdi: See "A Note on History"

Mashallah: "God willed it." It can be used to mean "Well, that's a
done deal," to "wonderful," to "God willed it, so nothing can harm it."

Nabidh: Light or hard cider made from any fruit. It was enjoyed by
all, lightly fermented like kombucha or hard like an alcoholic cider.

Nahariyya: Literally a "daytime" marriage house, meaning a brothel.

Prayer: There are five required ritual prayers daily. They must be
done with specified words and movements. There are many videos
on youtube to look at for examples. There are other supererogatory
prayers performed in the same manner that one can do if one likes.

Zaytuna, like many pious folk at that time, would perform prayers such as these late into the night. There are also distinct ritual prayers for funerals, eclipses, during Ramadan, and other times. Then, there are supplicatory prayers. This is when one calls out to God in one's own words for what one needs or using well-known formulas, some from the Qur'an, others from the Prophet, and still others from respected pious-folk that have become a tradition.

Qamis: A tunic worn by men or women of different lengths over undershirts of lighter or warmer material depending on the season. It was typically covered by a robe or a wrap, or both, in the case of men and women, according to season and depending on wealth.

Qarmatis: A controversial Shia community who threatened the Abbasid caliphate. See "A Note on History" for more details.

Qur'an: For Muslims, the Qur'an is the word of God in the Arabic language, as received by Muhammad through the angel Gabriel over 23 years.

Sama: A Sufi ritual involving music, recitation of prayers remembering God, praise of the Prophet, and meant to induce ecstasy.

Sayyid/Sayyida: Master or Mistress, in the vein of Lord or Lady, typically used to refer to the Prophet and his family by Shia and some Sunni Muslims. Sayyidi means "My Master." Versions of this can also be used as the equivalent of sir or ma'am, as well.

Shaykh: It can refer to any teacher of any sort, with or without credentials, then and now. In these books, I use it to refer *only* to an established Sufi guide. It was not used by Sufis at this time, but since it is the accepted term later and now, I use it.

Shia: Those who would come to be known as Shia were those who believed that the Prophet and God, as articulated in certain verses of the Qur'an, had designated, Ali, his cousin and son-in-law to be his successor rather than Abu Bakr. Although Shia did not use the name at the time of the book, I use it for clarity's sake. Most believe that true leadership is spiritually invested (rather than primarily politically), inhering in those with unique spiritual gifts as Ali was known to have. Ali was passed over three times for the caliphate, and by the time he was offered the position, the young empire was on the brink of civil war. The civil war ended after his death with his adult son, Husayn, and other members of his family and companions, slaughtered at Karbala in Iraq by opposing political forces. Although all Muslims find those events to have been an extraordinary tragedy, the Shia continue to see the world's injustices through the lens of that fateful day. For most Sunnis, it was a terrible wrong, but something best left in the past. For more detail, see **Umayyad** below and "A Note on History."

Sirwal: Loose pants worn under the qamis tunic.

Subhanallah: "God is glorious" can be used as a kind of secular "wow," to a state of spiritual awe and wonder.

Sufi: Up until the late 800's early 900's ascetics, pious folk, and mystics had no agreed upon name they called their practices and inward reflection or seeking ecstasy in God. It would be in Baghdad, in Junayd's community, that these people would begin to use the name Sufi to describe themselves. This name, and practices and attitudes developed there, would spread and integrate with diverse mystical practices, attitudes, and institutions in other regions. By the year 1000, most people on this path would use the name.

Sunna: The "Way" of Muhammad characterized by which Hadith one accepts or rejects. Muslims seek to follow his Sunna in ways small and large, such as drinking water the way he did or being "a man," on his model. While a great deal is accepted and consistent across Muslim cultures and times, Muslims continue to argue, sometimes violently, over other matters. Sexual consent and marriage are important points of dispute.

Sunni: The Muslims who would ultimately call themselves "Sunni," were those who chose to follow Abu Bakr as the first caliph of the Muslim community after Muhammad died. They believe scholars are the inheritors of the Prophet's guidance. There are four main Sunni schools of law and several schools of theology Hanbali, Hanafi, Shafii, and Maliki. See "A Note on History."

Time: Although there were water clocks and sundials, most people kept time by looking at the sun and the stars, but also by the call to prayer (see **Adhan**). There were six calls daily. About an hour before dawn (for a supererogatory prayer). Dawn. Just after zenith. Mid-afternoon. Sundown. After dark.

Twelfth Imam: The final Imam of the Imami community, now known as the Twelvers. He went into hiding for a time until he entered into a period of hiding that last until end times when he would return as the Mahdi and restore justice to the world. See "A Note on History"

Umayyad caliphate: The first hereditary caliphate founded when Muawiyya refused to honour his treaty with Hasan not to designate an heir, but rather to allow the people to choose who would follow him as caliph. Muawiyya chose his son, Yazid, who at Karbala so ruthlessly put down the aspirations of those Muslims who supported the descendants of Prophet's family in spiritual and political leadership. In the period the book is set, the Umayyads were not well-liked, for broader political reasons, as well as their brutal legacy. Some Umayyads are said to have blond hair and blue eyes which were associated at the time with deceit.

Viziers: They serve as chancellors to the caliph in many functions. They often vied for control over the direction of caliphal politics and its financial rewards. At times, they ran the government with the caliph in the background. Several major viziers were Shia, some from the Shia family, the Banu Furat. See "A Note on History"

Walla: "By God," an oath akin to "I swear."

Ya Rabb: "Oh Lord," used as a sincere calling to God to pure sarcasm.

Yazid: The son of Mu`awiyya and the second of the Ummayad caliphs. Husayn and the rest of the Prophet's family were slain at Karbala on his order. To say someone is "no better than Yazid" is to say they are not only unjust, but one who would betray humanity for worldly power.

Printed in the USA
CPSIA information can be obtained
at www.ICGtesting.com
LVHW091408250823
756177LV00004B/889

9 781777 531348